GRIZZLY RIDGE

GRIZZLY RIDGE

Olive Michael Markham

Grizzly Ridge
Copyright © 2013 by Olive Michael Markham
All rights reserved.

Drawndog Press
Cohasset, CA 95973

Cover design by Chris Lombardi
Cover art by Olive Michael Markham

ISBN: 0615824889
ISBN-13: 978-0615824888

For Juhney

ACKNOWLEDGMENTS

Thanks to my wife Diana, whose thoughtful critiques and encouragement made this book possible, and who's loving spirit and maternal ferocity made it easy to write a strong, but tender Mama character.

Thanks to the other folks in my life who lent inspiration to the characters and/or the story: Joan and Rupert Mcdowell, Paula Shapiro, and especially Barry Kemp, whose provincial wisdom and life-prevails made *Mr. Bern* the character he is, and turned a little story into a novel.

Thanks to my parents, Pat and Edna Markham, who instilled in me the importance of family, old westerns and the wild outdoors.

Thanks to Beth Spencer, whose advice, support, and proofreading skills were invaluable in getting me out of the first and second drafts.

Thanks to Chris Lombardi, for his cover design, computer wizardry, and helping get the book finished.

Thanks to my daughter, Juhney. Who, at four years old, planted the seed for this book by asking her papa to make up a story for bedtime. "Once upon a time, there was a beautiful princess who lived in the mountains. One day she met a grizzly bear..."

Special thanks to the canine players, whose names I did not change:

Jack Markham
Phish (Fish) Kemp 1997-2010
&
Little Girl (Chica) Markham 1996-2012
Mother · *Friend* · *Coyote Fighter*

We miss you, Chica and Phish

"*Bruin* has ever been an outlaw and a fugitive with a price on his pelt and no right which any man is bound to respect."
—Allen Kelly

"It's easier to ask forgiveness than to get permission."
—Rear Admiral Grace Murray Hopper

All the old folks on our mountain have a grizzly bear story. I'm not old yet, but this is my story.

Chapter One

Summary, 1909

Mama!" I called, running through tree branches and leaves cloaking the deer trail, my dog Jack leading the way.

"Papa!" I called, leaping over the small creek that separated the wilderness from our homestead. "Papa!" I called again, out of breath and ready to collapse.

They were both standing in front of the house, Mama pointing to where she wanted some fancy accents added to the corners of the porch like she'd seen in San Francisco years back.

"What is it?" they called back.

"A grizzly! I saw a grizzly!"

Papa looked to the woods, "A bear?"

"Not just a bear, *a grizzly bear! I saw a grizzly bear!*"

"A *big* bear? Did Jack..."

"No!" I yelled. "It's a grizzly, a real grizzly bear!"

"How do you know it's a grizzly?" asked Mama.

"It's *huge*," I said, "and it's brown. It's the biggest bear I've ever seen!"

"Is it still there?" asked Papa, finally sounding a little alarmed.

"It's a grizzly bear," I said, "A real *grizzly bear*, Papa!"

"Listen...listen," said Papa. "Just because it was brown doesn't make it a grizzly. Black bears can be brown, you know that. Did Jack chase it away?"

"It *was* a grizzly bear!" I shouted. "You weren't there. You didn't see him!" I didn't mean to scream that, but I guess I did because Papa got that look on his face like I was heading to trouble. I didn't want to be scolded so I started crying. That would usually get me out of trouble with Papa. Not with Mama though.

"Young lady, that's enough raising of your voice. Go in the house now and clean up. Another word and there will be no supper, and no books tonight."

"But Mama..."

"You are through exploring for the day," she said.

I knew they didn't believe me that I saw a grizzly bear, but soon, Papa and Jack headed into the woods and Papa had his big rifle. "It's a *rifle*, Junebug, not a gun," he'd always told me.

My name might be June Allen, but I was born in July. July of 1899, the last year of the old century. Mama and Papa and a lot of other people call me Junebug, Buggy, or just Bug. It's because Papa wanted to name me Junebug when I was born, for some reason, but Mama said she'd seen enough real June bugs to know she was *not* going to have a daughter named after an ugly brown beetle that tended to fly into water troughs and drown itself. So they named me June, but even Mama calls me Bug more often than she calls me June.

We live in the mountains, a place called Grizzly Ridge. Though our ridge is more a settlement than any kind of town, we do have a school, a church, and a small mercantile which mainly sells stuff to the lumber mill, where most of the men work, including Papa. The map at school says we live in the foothills, but everyone here knows we live in the mountains. The Sierra Nevada mountains. Only we don't live in Nevada, we live in California.

It was the middle of the summer, the season I always liked best because there's no school. Even though I liked school, and I was good at school, I liked no school better. I had just turned ten years old, and for my birthday Mama made me a beautiful dress—not too fancy—that I wasn't to wear until school started, and definitely wasn't allowed to wear into the woods. Mama had always made dresses and things and sometimes sold them at the general store in town, which is down in the valley. She could make anything from any kind of cloth. She made all my dresses, some of them beautiful, some of them sensible but still pretty. When I was little, I would tell her I wanted a dress like a princess from one of my books and she made me look just like that princess. Papa never thought being a princess was very practical living in the mountains, because of the dangers and the dirt and all, so he made me a real fine-looking wooden sword that I carried with me everywhere, even dressed as a princess. I had moved beyond needing to dress like a princess, but still carried my sword slipped into an old leather belt that Papa had cut and punched new holes into so it would fit my waist.

I had been wearing my sword that morning, running with Jack through the woods. We were following a newly discovered deer trail that led us farther from the house than we were allowed to go, when I saw the bear. I saw him first which was good because I collared Jack before he could rush him like dogs will do. We always let Jack chase bears away when they're getting too close to the house or to our chickens, but this bear was at least ten times bigger than any of the bears that Jack's chased before. This bear didn't at all look afraid of us, so I don't think Jack really minded me holding him back.

The bear was *huge*. He was in a small thicket of manzanita trees, digging at the dirt. He raised up tall on his back legs and looked at us, huffed a couple of times, then went back to what he was doing. Jack made a little bark and a little growl, then stopped. *No need to make the bear mad*, I'm sure he was thinking. I slowly ducked down next to Jack, and pulling on his collar, got us turned around and quietly sneaked away. It wasn't until we had some space between us and the bear that we started to run. It was on the run home that I got to thinking about that big bear, and what I was thinking was that I had never seen a bear even half its size before. Jack was running so fast, I had to holler at him to wait up, he but he didn't stop. I guess he wanted to be the one to tell Mama and Papa about the bear.

The bear. What was it about that bear? I couldn't wait to tell them how big it was, but there was something else about it, something different. It wasn't until I was in sight of the house that it came to me—*"grizzly bear."*

Papa and Jack didn't come home until after dark, and by that time I had already gotten in trouble again and sent to bed without supper and without my books. Mama and Papa stayed up late whispering so I wouldn't hear them but I could always hear them. Papa said they walked and walked, following Jack for awhile until he thought Jack lost the scent on purpose because he didn't want to find the bear. So Papa started tracking by himself and saw some real big claw markings on a couple of trees and some great big bear scat—that means bear poop—but no bear.

"Could it have been a grizzly?" asked Mama. "It would make sense, there's been a number of attacks on livestock lately. And we do live on *Grizzly Ridge*."

"No," said Papa. "The livestock taking, those are cougars doing that, or poachers. No, there hasn't been a grizzly around here for years. There's hardly a grizzly left in the whole state of California, probably Oregon, too. I'm sure it was just a brown-colored bear she ran into. And yes, it had to be big from what I saw. Jack here wanted no part in finding him."

I couldn't believe what Mama said next. "Remember the bear I saw outside the garden when we first moved onto the mountain? Remember I was sure, just like Bug is, that it was a young grizzly. She knows what a regular bear looks like, we see them all the time. Why couldn't it have been a grizzly bear?"

Mama had a seen a grizzly bear, too? A young one? Maybe it was the same one that I saw. She never told me she had seen a grizzly bear. I wanted to climb down and join the conversation, but I was in enough trouble.

Luckily for me, our house isn't very big. It's a nice house, nice for around here, anyway. We built it ourselves and I helped too. It has an upstairs loft where my room is, which Papa said he was sorry he made because whenever he and Mama wanted to talk at night without me hearing them, they had to go out on the porch. I could still hear them. Our porch goes all around the house which makes the house look much bigger than it really is. Mama wanted a porch outside the front door, so Papa started building it and I guess didn't know when to stop. The porch is bigger than the house. I love our porch, it's one of my favorite reading spots.

Papa worked at the lumber mill so he got a good price on the wood for the house, and he would always come home with wood that Mr. Jonas, the mill's owner, didn't think he could sell. Papa can use any kind of wood for anything. That's how we got our big porch, and Papa promised me he'd have a tree house built before my next birthday.

Our land used to be part of an apple orchard that covered most of our ridge, a long time ago. It was wiped out in a big wildfire that swept through, something that happens every twenty years or so, something we worry about every summer and fall. The story goes, whoever owned the orchard—I forget the family's name—didn't care to start over, planting new apple trees. So the ridge was left to good old pine, cedar and oak trees to come back and give us shade and places to climb, and a place to build our house. But there's still a lot of apple trees up here, from seeds blown by the wind or dropped by birds. We have six trees out by the barn that we tend to, and a few more near the garden that Mama planted herself, so it's like we have our own little orchard. It's great having our own apples, especially for pies. Here and there, throughout the forest, are other apple trees that grew by themselves. Those don't have a lot of apples, because you have to cut the branches back every year to get good apples, but they're there, the wild animals know where they are, and like the apples as much as we do.

Whenever Mama or Papa needed me, they would just holler out toward one of my reading spots. That's where I usually was, with Jack, who's just a little older than me, and who Mama named after Jack London, the writer. Jack's part border collie and part something else. We have another dog beside Jack, a sweet old dog named Chica, which means *Little Girl* in Spanish. Chica is big with soft white hair, velvety ears, and looks like a little polar bear. She's part husky and part something else, but mostly husky. According to Papa, Chica was pretty tough when she was young, got into a lot of fights with coyotes at the house they lived in before I was born. She would still patrol around our place, but mostly liked to lay on the porch. She was retired.

Chica has a Spanish name because Mama can speak Spanish. Mama's Mexican but was born in California, which used to be part of Mexico. She told me she was very proud of her heritage, and I should be too, but she wished she had more people to speak Spanish with. I started to learn with her, thinking it would be fun to speak to each other, and Papa wouldn't know what we were saying. He understands more than he lets on, but can't speak it as well as Mama and me.

The next morning after feeding and watering all the animals, collecting eggs from our chickens, and after Papa left for work, I helped Mama make blueberry pies. We make the best blueberry pies on the mountain, everyone says so.

"Mama," I asked, "why is where we live called Grizzly Ridge?"

"Every place has to have a name," she said. "Maybe someone just liked the way it sounded."

"Was it because there were grizzly bears here?"

"I don't know," she said, not looking up, and I got the feeling, not wanting me to ask her bear questions.

"Mama?...Mama?"

"Yes, Bug."

"Have you ever seen a grizzly bear before?"

"I don't know," she said, but then didn't say anything else, just kept making the pie.

"Mama?"

"Yes, Bug."

"You've never seen a grizzly bear cub? Maybe before I was born?"

"Do I have to tell you not to eavesdrop when your father and I are talking?"

"No ma'am," I said. "Please tell me the story, Mama."

"June..." she started like she was going to scold me more. Instead, she cleaned her hands, poured herself a cup of tea and even poured me a little, and then told me the story as we worked on our pies.

"It wasn't long after your father and I moved up here to the ridge," she said. "We were living in the old cabin, had fixed it just enough so it didn't leak and was clean. It took a lot of cleaning. Papa had started working at the lumber mill, Jack was a little puppy, and I was very pregnant with you. It was summer, very hot like it is now, and I was pulling weeds in the garden, which wasn't easy with a big belly in the way. It was just a little garden that first year, not like we have now. Mostly tomatoes, corn, and some greens. Jack started barking his puppy bark, I looked up and thought I saw a very big dog in the tall grass just outside the garden. I quickly picked up Jack and when I looked again, I saw it wasn't a big dog, but rather a little bear. Not too little, actually, it wasn't a baby, maybe four or five months old I'm guessing. It was brown, kinda scruffy, with paws that looked way too big for him. He stood up on his back legs and we just looked at each other for probably a full minute.

"Were you scared?" I asked.

"No, I wasn't scared. It was the first bear I'd seen up close, but I wasn't scared, didn't grab the shotgun I had nearby. Jack stopped barking. We all just looked at each other. He sniffed the air, turned and walked back into the tall grass. I thought maybe he was welcoming us to the mountain.

"I didn't think at the time it might have been a grizzly cub, and didn't really know why a grizzly would be a big deal, I just thought a bear was a bear. It wasn't until later, after I'd seen a lot of other bears, that I began to notice how the young bear I saw in the garden that day was a little different from the other bears we see. Do you know why they are called grizzlies? Because their coats look, well, *grizzled*. More fuzzy than other bears. And that's what the young bear's fur looked like, grizzled, not slick or shiny like most of the other bears have."

"Did Chica see the bear?"

"She must have seen it. She was laying up by the house, and had to have smelled him and heard Jack yipping. Until she retired, she would always chase bears away. That time she didn't even get up."

"Did Papa think it might have been a grizzly bear when you told him?"

"No, it was just a regular bear cub."

"A black bear that's brown," I said.

She smiled. "Yes, a black bear that's brown. It wasn't until more than a year later when news came of a grizzly bear being killed up by the Oregon border, which is what, two hundred miles away? And everyone around *here* made such a deal about it that I got to thinking about that little brown bear. And wondering... but, it was so long ago."

"What did Papa say?"

"What do you think?" she answered. "He said the same thing then that he's saying now—there's no more grizzly bears. Except he did ask why it's women who always think it's a grizzly bear they saw."

"What's the big deal about saying it was a grizzly bear that you saw, and that I saw? Why would people care about one being killed two hundred miles away?"

"Folks hate grizzly bears, Bug, they're terrified of them. They're much bigger than black bears, more dangerous, and they do kill. That's why there aren't any left, people have gone and killed them all. And now, folks still go crazy whenever there is anyone who says they saw one. Even though it's never a grizzly they've seen. And now all the poachers and hunters and anyone else with a big gun would love to kill a grizzly bear. They could sell just about every part of it for good money, and get their names in the newspaper, too."

"Do you believe me, Mama? That it was a grizzly bear I saw?"

"I believe that you saw a very big bear, and that you believe it was a grizzly," she said. "Maybe it was, and if it was, let's hope he was just passing through and you won't see him again. But, again, it's very unlikely that it was a grizzly bear. Just because we live on Grizzly Ridge doesn't mean we have grizzlies."

Mama could see I was disappointed that she didn't believe it was a grizzly bear I had seen. I thought she would be on my side since she saw one when she was pregnant with me. And Jack saw him too. But now she thinks it was just a regular bear she saw way back then?

After we finished putting together the pies and popping two of them into the oven she looked at me and said, "You know, it was exactly one week after I saw the grizzly cub in the garden that you were born."

I looked up at Mama. "Grizzly cub?"

Chapter Two

When Papa got home from work, even before we sat down for dinner, he asked me to step out onto the porch with him to talk. He spoke so nice to me that I knew I wasn't still in trouble, unless Mama told him I had been listening in on their conversation.

"So tell me more about the bear you saw yesterday," he said.

I told him my story again, this time I was sure to mention that the bear looked very *grizzled*. He listened to me, he really did, and I thought I had surely convinced him.

Papa listened, then told me, "First, Bug, we've told you many times if you see a bear or cougar you're not to run, right? That'll make 'em chase you, sure. Remember?"

"Yes, sir," I mumbled.

"And you know you're not allowed to go wandering past the main road by yourself."

"Yes, sir, I know."

"I know you've grown up in these woods, you know these woods, but these woods aren't just raccoons and rabbits. There's cougars, bobcats, and bears...and wild dogs. And a lot of other things. A lot of dangers for a little girl alone."

"Yes, sir."

"You could have been screaming for help and we wouldn't have heard you, even standing outside like we were. You were too far away."

"Yes, sir," I said again, "I won't do it again."

"I hope not. We don't want to have to rope you to the barn to keep you close."

"No, sir."

"Maybe, we'll just chain a cannon ball to your leg. Would that keep you close?"

"No!" I laughed, hoping that Papa was joking.

"Now, I know you believe that you saw a grizzly...but it couldn't have been one. There are no more grizzlies on our ridge, on our mountain, and probably no more in all of California. There are only black bears now, even though a lot of them aren't black color. We've seen bears around here that are brown, haven't we? You've seen them, Jack's chased and treed them before. They aren't really dangerous unless it's a mama with her cubs, or if you *run* from them. Or if you're a chicken or young goat. They mostly eat berries and...and roots and stuff."

"I know," I said. "You've told me. But the bear I saw..."

"June, I believe that it was a big bear. I believe that it was brown. But Bug, it wasn't a grizzly, okay? And you're very lucky it wasn't. If it was a grizzly, you wouldn't be sitting here with me right now. Understand?"

I didn't say a word.

"Still," said Papa, "I saw some pretty big footprints out there, so let's not wander into the woods for a while, okay? Not until I can find him or be sure he's moved on. And next time... Are you listening?"

"Yes, sir," I said.

"Next time, turn the dog loose."

I was quiet all through dinner, and went up to my room as soon as the dishes were washed. I tried my hardest not to think about bears, any kind of bears. And really, what did it matter what kind of bear I saw? If it *was* a real grizzly bear, I'd probably be eaten already. But I knew what I saw, I knew they didn't believe me, I knew they didn't think I was old enough to know the difference between a black bear that's brown, and a grizzly bear.

"Maybe I could find him again," I said out loud to myself, "and do a really good drawing to bring back and show them. And then me and Papa will go back out with his rifle and...and what? I don't want to kill the bear, even if it really is a grizzly, I just want to... What *do* I want to do with him? Is it even a him? He looked like a him. Should I name him?

"If I find him again then I'll know where he is, and I can take Papa out to see him if he promises not to shoot. Maybe we could trap him and Papa could build a big cage and put it on our wagon and put the bear in the cage and we can go into town and everyone could see a real grizzly bear and we could charge people ten cents to look at him. Mama will need to make big fancy curtains that we'll put on the cage so nobody could see him without paying me first. Then we'll be rich, and we'll be famous, and maybe Jack London will want to come see my bear, too. Maybe he'll write a book about a young princess with a sword who catches grizzly bears! I'd read that book. Is it hard to catch a grizzly bear?" That's what I was thinking.

The next morning when Mama came up to my room to wake me, I hadn't slept a bit all night, my mind repeating, *bears, bears, bears...who cares,* over and over, all night long. She had to push me out the door to do my morning chores. I just threw food at the animals, and didn't remember to clean the water trough. Bears, bears, who cares?

Mama noticed I was in a mood, but instead of getting mad when I stomped through the door without wiping my feet first, she said, "How about all of us go into town today? Papa's taking a wagon load of lumber down and thought we might want to join him."

"I don't want to go to town," I said.

"We can look at fabric for new dresses."

"Do I have to wear a bonnet?" I asked.

"Young ladies do not go to town without their head covered."

"I don't like wearing a bonnet, Mama. Nobody wears bonnets anymore."

"You could have thought of that before using your nice hat to pan for gold."

"I look like a prairie girl. Or a pilgrim. Can't I just wear a scarf?"

"I suppose."

"Can we have dinner at the restaurant?" I asked.

"If you can change your mood," she smiled, "maybe Papa will buy us all sodas at the General."

"With a scoop of ice cream?" I *love* soda floats, but Mr. Shaw,

15

who owns the general store, didn't always have ice cream. When he did, everyone in town knew about it and ate it up before I could get some, but maybe there would be some waiting for me. I figured I could get over my mood for a soda float. Or pretend to get over it.

By the time Papa pulled up to the house in Mr. Jonas' wagon from the lumber mill I was all clean and clothed, helping Mama fold some dresses that she had mended and was taking back down to the general store. I was in a little better mood, but still not happy. I couldn't get that grizzly bear out of my mind.

Mr. Jonas' wagon was much bigger than ours, so there was plenty of room for Mama and me both to ride up front with Papa. Sometimes he had six, or even eight mules hooked up to it when he was hauling a big load of wood. Mama and I didn't ride with him when he hauled a big load. It was too dangerous, especially going *down* the mountain. That day he just had four mules and not much lumber, so it was okay for all of us to ride to town together.

It's a three or four hour ride to town in a wagon. We have our own mule that pulls *our* wagon. His name is London, he's really big, and sweet, and rusty black colored with ears as long as my arm. I named him myself, after Jack London, who's my favorite writer, just like Mama. My teacher said I'm much too young to like Jack London, but Mama said my teacher only said that because I could already read better than my teacher. I wasn't sure about that, I only knew I loved to read. We also have a beautiful horse named Whiskey. He's a chestnut and white Paint, mostly chestnut. I think he looks just like an Indian pony. I didn't name Whiskey. He's been with us since before I was born.

It's nice and cool up on the ridge, even in summer, though I guess it still gets hot, but not as hot as in town, which is in the valley. That's why we don't have many rattlesnakes, because rattlesnakes only like hot, which is great, because I *hate* rattlesnakes! Supposedly, they've been seen all the way up to the top of the mountain, but I've never seen one around the house. The previous summer, when I was little, Papa got bit by a rattlesnake. We were in the valley, almost to town when we saw one sunning itself on a rock. Papa stopped the wagon to show Mama and me how he used to catch rattlesnakes in Texas when he was a boy, was going to show us how to catch it without getting bit. And it bit him. Right on his wrist. His arm swelled up like a watermelon and he was sick for awhile but the doctor said he barely got any poison in him. I heard Mama tell our neighbor that Papa shows me what *not* to do by trying to show me what *to* do. I think I understand what she was saying. Like the time Papa was showing me how to cut down a tree like the lumberjacks do so that it falls right where you want it. Ended up dropping that tree right across the road, landing on the sheriff who happened to be riding by. It didn't kill him, thank goodness. Or the time he couldn't get the wood in the fireplace lit so he showed me how to put just a splash of kerosene on it, and when he struck a match he about blew up the house. Knocked me off my feet and burned off Papa's eyebrows and most of his beard. He did that trick a time again, but only after I ran out of the house first. Mama was not happy. That's why she told Papa she wouldn't let him teach me how to shoot a gun, ever. She said she'd teach me. That made Papa mad as I remember.

Papa dropped us off at Shaw's General Store while he made his delivery of wood. I plopped down on the big bench in front while Mama went inside, happy that I wasn't wearing that silly bonnet.

I have always loved to sit on the big bench at the General and watch the wagons and horses and people go by. I had even seen a few automobiles—driven by rich people up from the big city, scaring all the horses. I've always loved to watch people, but don't always like to talk to them. I'm like Papa that way. So I was just sitting, watching, when who should I see but Papa's friend Mr. Bern walking up. Kinda hobbling up, actually. He had a cane. He used to work with Papa at the mill, that's where they met. Mr. Bern did all the lumber deliveries before that was Papa's job, but got hurt real bad one day when a new guy there unhitched the mules from a wagon plum full of logs without sticking something under the wheels. The brake didn't hold, and the wagon started rolling backward. Mr. Bern saw it and tried to stop the wagon and it rolled right on top of him and then *stopped* on him. Almost did him in. The new guy didn't even try to help, he got scared thinking he had killed Mr. Bern and just skedaddled. Papa and some other men were able to push the wagon just enough to pull Mr. Bern out. He was alive but all broken up. The new guy I bet wished Mr. Bern *wasn't* alive because people say that as soon as Mr. Bern was able to climb onto a horse, he paid a visit to that new guy and the new guy hasn't been seen since.

"Why, hallo...Young Miss June," Mr. Bern said with a smile as he pulled off his big floppy hat to wipe his forehead with a sleeve. Mr. Bern is quite a bit older than Papa, with short, white, wispy hair. He's a very tall, very big man, with a great big deep voice.

He's as a big as a grizzly bear himself, and might look like one too if he didn't keep all his chin whiskers shaved, the only mountain man I knew that did that. "What brings you down the mountain this fine, hot, sunny afternoon?"

"Papa had to bring a load of wood down," I said, "and Mama's in the store with her dresses, and..."

And then I got shy and couldn't think of anything else. He sure was big.

"And?" he said. "And I'll bet there's just enough room on that bench for my broken down ol' body. Would you mind a little comp'ny? You won't be embarrassed to have me sharing a bench with you?"

"No sir," I smiled.

"You're too kind, m'lady. I've got my ol' mare Willa down at the furriers gettin' fit for all new fancy slippers don'cha know, and *whew,* thought I'd come over here for some shade and maybe a cool sodee. Seems a lot farther than it used to be. Did they move this general store on me? Make it farther for me to walk?" Mr. Bern was always funny. "What say, would it be improper to share a couple of sodees with a pretty young lady?"

"I don't think so," I said.

"Your husband's not going to get jealous and come after me, is he? 'Cause I doubt I got the speed to outrun him."

"I'm not married!"

"*You're not?*" he asked in a booming voice the whole street could hear. "Well then, would you do me the honor of accepting these two bits and buying us both a sodee? You pick the flavors, little darlin'. I trust your judgment. Have mine not too fizzy, please.

Fizz makes me sneeze. And here's an extra penny in case old man Shaw done raised the prices agin."

I ran into the store with Mr. Bern's money, quickly trying to decide which flavor he may like, probably sarsaparilla. But maybe I'd surprise him with something really amazing, like a mix of cherry and lemon drop and chocolate! Chocolate's my favorite, with a little strawberry mixed in. And ice cream! I hoped Mr. Shaw had ice cream.

"Bug?" asked Mama, seeing me at the counter ordering up two sodas with coins I was tapping together. "I thought you were waiting for your father. And where did you get...?"

I spoke real fast because I was excited and wanted to explain the whole thing to Mama before she could say no. "Mr Bern has Willa at the furriers and so he came to the General for rest and shade, and we were talking about stuff and he said would I mind to buy a soda for him 'cause he's real thirsty and that I can choose the flavors and that he wants me to have one too, but I said no thank you. But then he gave me his money and insisted, so I didn't think it would hurt. He *insisted*, Mama. I didn't want to be rude. I'll still want one when Papa comes back. Is it okay?"

"You've enough money there for a soda for your Ma, too," said Mr. Shaw, who owns the store.

"Oh, no, it's not our money," said Mama, looking down at me with her eyebrows raised.

Then Mr. Bern bellared through the window, "It's only two bits, Mama, let's all have a sodee!"

Mama and I walked back out to the bench with Mr. Bern. I handed him his soda, hoping he liked his sarsaparilla and lemon drop. I had plum forgot about the ice cream.

"You're too generous, Mr. Simms," said Mama, even before I could thank him. "And here's a quarter for our sodas."

"Oh, nonsense," he replied. "It's my pleasure, it's my two bits. Can't think of anything I'd rather have spent it on."

"Thank you Mr. Simms," I said, or rather I mumbled it. I had forgotten that his name was Bernard Simms and *Mr. Simms* sounded wrong because I'd always called him Mr. Bern. Also I was busy watching him take a sip from his soda to see if he liked it.

"*Whew*," he said. "This sodee's got some zip! I'm not used to drinking anything stronger than watered down coffee, don'cha know." Mama and I looked at each other and laughed. "Please, have a seat you two, do this great honor for an old mountain man." He even stood up for us, though Mama protested and I could see it pained him to stand.

"The day I don't stand for two beautiful ladies is the day I just stop standing altogether. So's the old man makin' a delivery?"

"Yes," said Mama, "it's for the new hotel going up at the end of town."

Mr. Bern said, "What do they need a new hotel for, I ask. More rooms means more people, and there's already too many people here. Wouldn't you agree, Miss Buggie J?"

"I saw a grizzly bear," I said. I don't know why I blurted it out like I did, that wasn't an answer to his question. And yes, I did think there were too many people in town, that's why I loved the mountain. I think the bear was just on my mind so much it was bound to pop out some time. I knew it wasn't what Mr. Bern was expecting in way of a reply. He didn't say anything for a few seconds, which is a long time for Mr. Bern not to say something.

"Ahh, a grizzly bear, you say. Well ain't that somethin'."

"And Mama saw one too."

"June," said Mama, "you don't need to speak up like this about things you're not..."

"Oh, it's okay Missus," said Mr. Bern. "You've got a young'n I know will speak her mind. With your permission, Ma'am... You think you saw ol' Griz? Lately?"

I looked up at Mama, and knew she wasn't happy with my boldness, but Mr. Bern was right, I *do* speak my mind, which sometimes does get me in trouble.

"Yes sir," I said, and told him about the encounter I had with the grizzly bear.

Mr. Bern asked about the bear Mama saw, if she thought it was the same one, only much younger, and she reluctantly told him a little of the story. Mr. Bern listened to every word we said—he's a very good listener—then asked questions about what exactly they both looked like, what time of day we saw them, and of course if Papa had seen them as well.

"No," we had to answer, expecting him to say it's always women who think it's a grizzly bear they've seen. But he didn't, he really thought about it.

Finally he said, "There may yet be a grizzly or two left, wandering around the mountains. They are an amazing breed of animal, those grizzly bears, and ever' time I think I've seen the last of 'em, one more pops up."

"Yep," I agreed, and we both took long drinks from our sodas.

"You know...?" he started to say. "Oh, I'm sure you know."

"Know what?" I asked, and looked to Mama to see if she knew. She shrugged her shoulders.

"Know why our little hamlet is called Grizzly Ridge," he said.

"Our little what?" I asked.

"Our hamlet, our ridge...do you know why it's called that?"

"Because grizzly bears live there," I said.

"*Used* to live there," said Mama.

"Used to, yes ma'am," he said. "Used to be thick as rabbits up there with ol' bruin. By b*ruin* I mean grizzly."

"I know," I said, though I really didn't.

"A little before my time even, but it's been told," he continued, "you wouldn't set yourself on a rock in the shade without givin' it a poke first. Make sure it didn't growl back at ya."

I laughed with Mama, but was picturing how many bears we'd see if they were same in number as rabbits, because we have *lots* of rabbits. And what did he call them? *Broons*? And he called our ridge an *omelet*? Sounded like omelet to me. I'd have to look that one up.

"What's the chance," asked Mama, "one might have wandered onto our ridge?"

"Oh, I know I said they keep poppin' up, but, to be honest, not likely," said Mr. Bern, who saw the disappointment on my face. "But who am I to say, huh?"

I could have spent the whole day talking to Mr. Bern about bears, but Papa walked up after parking the wagon and mules at the livery stable. "Is this old scoundrel botherin' you?" he called.

"Young Miss June here been telling me about the gaggle of grizzlies you got camped out at your place," said Mr. Bern. "Oh,

23

and you owe me two bits."

Papa looked around, hoping no one had heard about the bears. "No, just a child's book-readin' imagination."

I was *not* happy with Papa saying that, Mr. Bern was believing me. That put me back into a mood. And I stayed in my mood all through dinner at the restaurant and all the way home and didn't even want another soda when Papa asked.

I couldn't sleep all night, thinking about the bear I saw, and wondering if it really *was* a grizzly bear. Maybe Mama and Papa were right, maybe I was startled and scared and he looked bigger than he actually was. Maybe he really was just a grizzly bear-looking black bear. And little girls always think it's a grizzly bear they've seen. But Mr. Bern thought that maybe it could be a grizzly bear, "They keep popping up," he said.

Maybe a real grizzly would've eaten me, like Papa said. But the bear I saw looked *grizzled*, like Mama said. There was no way to be sure unless we found him again, and I didn't think Papa would ever let me go with him to look, even though it was me who found him in the first place. I would just have to find him myself. Find him, do a good drawing that no one would doubt was a real grizzly, and that would be that.

The thoughts I had about finding and drawing the bear quickly became a wonderful plan, I thought. I knew it would get me in trouble, but if it worked—which I had little doubt it would— hopefully I wouldn't be in too much trouble. I had to find the bear again, and this time I wouldn't be startled, I'd sneak up on him and hide, and make a really good drawing to show Mama and Papa and then they'd believe me and then we could go about catching him. I didn't give too much thought about how exactly we would catch him, I figured that would be worked out later.

Chapter Three

The list of what I thought I needed for my trip seemed awful long. I would've needed London the mule, and maybe the wagon, to carry all the stuff I had written down. I decided instead to travel light, so the second list was only the stuff I couldn't do without:

- Sword. I wasn't taking Jack, so, in case the grizzly charged me, I might have to stab him, though that would make me sad.
- Papa's folding knife. In case my sword wasn't enough.
- Paper sheets and charcoal. So I could draw him.
- Papa's bedroll. I might be gone for days and days.
- My old short-coat. It might get chilly if I had to go high into the mountains.
- Extra dress, stockings and drawers. 'Cause I needed them.
- Canteen, bread, bacon, and my fishing pole. For food and water.
- A few books. Jack London mostly.
- Lumberman's bag with shoulder strap. To carry everything.

That's traveling light.

I woke up before the sun, and put on what I thought would be my best wilderness dress. It was one I usually didn't like to wear because it was thick, had sleeves that were too long, and wasn't very pretty, but it would be perfect for a long quest into the mountains. I wrote Mama and Papa a brief note informing them of my plans, and to not worry. I apologized for not feeding London and the animals, but I just couldn't spare the time.

I had to sneak out of the house, which wasn't easy. Chica was asleep, blocking the door. I managed to move her out of the way and then Jack was jumping around, excited that I was up.

"What are you doing up so early?" asked Mama from bed.

"Um...Chica has to go outside," I lied, mad at the dogs for waking up Mama, and hoping she or Papa didn't look over. One, because I had my short-coat sleeves tied around my ugly dress, had a stuffed lumberman's bag slung over my shoulder loaded with a knife, drawing stuff and books, my Indian princess doll 'Sarah', and a blueberry pie wrapped in oilcloth. I was holding my shoes in one hand, and was wearing a sword. I looked like I was running away from home to join the Gypsies. And two, because Chica did *not* want to go outside. Old dogs can be so stubborn. I had to all but drag her out the door, then she refused to go farther than the porch, all the while Jack was jumping around, trying to lick my face as I pulled Chica by the scruff. At least Jack went potty. I was wishing we were like most people and not let dogs in the house. I got them both back inside, and leaving my bag on the porch, tip-toed over to peek at Mama and Papa. Chica was starting her gonna-lay-back-down spin in front of the door, so I had to take the chance that Mama had fallen back to sleep. Stopping Chica before she plopped back down, I crept quietly back onto the porch, opening and closing the door ever-so-slowly, because it does creak, something you don't notice unless you're trying to be sneaky.

I hustled to the barn and found the canteen and fishing pole. I also found Papa's compass, which might come in handy, though I wasn't planning on getting lost. I tied a rope to Papa's bedroll so I could wear it over my shoulder. It was much bigger and heavier than I remembered. I thought about leaving it behind, but didn't want to sleep on the dirt, or in grass with the bugs. And it was waterproof, so I could cover myself with it if it rained. Yep, had to take it. I had forgotten about packing bread and bacon, but couldn't go back inside to get it. Chica would have already been blocking the door, and with the glow of the day coming on, Mama and Papa would be up any minute. It was Papa's day off from the mill, but even so, they never *really* sleep in. The blueberry pie would have to do, and there's always more berries in the forest, and lots of fish in the streams. Plus, I didn't have any more room in the bag to stuff in a loaf of bread.

Loaded up with all the gear, I had a hard time thinking I was traveling light, and I hadn't even filled the canteen, which would add even more weight. But if I was going to do it, I needed to just do it. I did, however, return the fishing pole, after taking the line and hook off. I could tie the line to a stick or just hold onto it. I thought that was really smart. I learned that in a book.

A great leap over the clear, gurgling water of our little creek almost landed me right in the middle of it. The gear was so heavy, it was like I was carrying a whole other me on my shoulders. I would get used to it, I told myself. I would get stronger. I looked back at the house one last time, wondering when I would see it again. I knew Mama and Papa would be worried, and maybe even mad at me, but they would understand when they saw the drawings I would bring back. Proof that there was a grizzly bear on Grizzly Ridge.

I turned and stepped into the forest on a real mission. I'd been exploring our woods almost every day since I could walk, but never with such an important goal. I had scouted every little hill and every big rock from the main road down to the edge of the ridge. I'd spent whole days wading through the green fern along our creek, had run along giant fallen cedar trees until the tree was no bigger than a rope. I'd snuck around and through all the different kinds of bushes, quiet like a mountain lion or Indian, and watched a deer or squirrel when they didn't even know I was there. I hoped all my years of experience would help me find that grizzly bear again.

Not long into the mission, instead of sneaking up on anything, I spooked a couple of deer that I should have seen, but I was thinking about the bear and not paying attention. I saw a little bobcat shortly after, and would have been able to sneak up on him, but they don't appreciate getting snuck up on. I made some noise and threw a pine cone at him and he skedaddled. Seeing the bobcat made me think I had better be on the lookout for mountain lions, too. I didn't have Jack to warn or protect me, and with only my wooden sword to defend myself, I might have a problem.

I was much more afraid of mountain lions than bears, even grizzly bears. Folks say when a cougar attacks you, you don't see or hear it before it's too late. They drop out of the trees on you, and then you're gone. I had to stop thinking about that, was just scaring myself silly, and I needed to be brave. I should have brought Jack with me, I always had Jack with me in the woods.

I was watching and searching the trees for mountain lions waiting to pounce, which meant I wasn't watching the trail. I stepped into some bushes and scared up a whole family of quail, panicking me as much as them. "Stupid birds," I said out loud, then laughed a little at being spooked. I stopped laughing, though, when I looked down at what I had thought was a bush. It wasn't. It was a nice little patch of poison oak. That's why you don't walk around in the woods looking at the tops of trees. I backed myself out carefully, but even with my stockings on, I knew I'd be itching later. Danged poison oak, the mountain would be so much better if there wasn't poison oak. I'd prefer mountain lions to poison oak, if I had to choose.

Between scanning the sky for hungry cougars, to studying the ground for poison oak and scittery quail, not to mention rattlesnakes—which I had never seen on our ridge, but still—I got a little turned around. Not lost, of course, just momentarily lacking a direction. The mountain sure looked different without Jack leading the way.

It was a good time to stop and drop my gear for a rest, and the perfect time to use my compass. Well, Papa's compass. I thought I wanted to be heading south, kind of, and to the left, a little. Looking at the dial of the thing, I saw South, but when I got the arrow to point that way, it was aiming in the direction I had just come. I couldn't have been *that* turned around. I really didn't know how to get it to work, to make the arrow point in the direction I wanted to go. Maybe the compass was telling me to go back home. It had been sitting in the barn collecting dust, so was probably broken. And anyway, I couldn't have really been lost, I mean, it was *my* mountain after all, and I hadn't even been walking an hour. Mama and Papa were up and around by then, I was sure. I hoped they weren't too mad. It wasn't like I was skipping school, it was still Summer. I regretted not using the word *mission* in the note I left for them, that would have helped them understand.

I finally got to the main road, the road I wasn't supposed to cross. I knew I wasn't lost. I *was,* however, exhausted and very thirsty. Filling the canteen before leaving would have been a good idea. I dropped the bag and bedroll, stood for a minute, and thought, *if I turn back now, I won't be in trouble.* Papa only told me to go no further than the main road. But if I turned back, that would be like quitting. It would be quitting my mission. Papa had always told me that if I started something, I needed to finish. Mama had always said when I promised something, I needed to follow through. This mission was exactly what they were talking about. They wouldn't want me to quit. Maybe they'd even be upset with me if I quit.

I checked up and down the road, not wanting to cross if I'd be spotted by someone. I don't know why, but I just didn't want to be seen. But I was seen. A family of turkeys walking up the mountain like they had spent the morning in town and were now heading home. The big Tom was in front, I suspected, leading his family of three wives and four children. They all cocked their heads as they passed by me, none of them appearing frightened, maybe because I wasn't pointing a gun at them. It wasn't until I slapped my neck that they got a little spooked and ran. I had felt something crawling on me, it was a tick. I always picked up a tick or two whenever I went into the woods, would even pick them up just walking to the barn, especially after it rained, for some reason. Usually I wouldn't know it was on me until it was *in* me, almost always dug into my scalp, but occasionally they'd dig their tiny heads into other places unpleasant. It was a nightly ritual at our house to check me for ticks, and a constant ritual to pick ticks off Jack and Chica. I had the little bugger between my finger and thumb, and pinched him in half with my fingernails.

I hoisted the bag to my shoulder, almost opening it first to see if a rock or a brick had been added without my knowing it. I thought of going ahead and eating the pie, that would have lightened the bag. But I really wasn't too hungry, and I knew I would be later. I decided to carry the bedroll in my arms, the rope had been working the side of my neck raw. Both sides of my neck, actually, because I had switched sides a few times already.

Now on the road, it wasn't too long before I found the sad little apple tree I was looking for. Unless you knew what an apple tree looked like without any apples on it, like I did, you'd never know it was an apple tree. Just a little taller than me at it's highest-reaching branch, skinny and sprawling all over like a bush, it had never been trimmed, of course. There were some patches of green leaves on the ends of a few branches, but no apple buds. It was still too early in the season for apple buds, but I had the feeling this little tree wouldn't have many anyway. Just one of the random wild apple trees on the ridge. I remembered it to be the entrance to the trail that Jack and I followed when we first found the bear. Good thing I wasn't counting on the compass to help me find the trail, because it was still telling me to turn around and go back home.

Passing the apple tree and plunging into the greater forest, I came to a big clump of blueberry bushes we had stopped at the day we ran into the bear. I was definitely on the right trail. The bushes were full of ripe berries the last time I was there, I had munched on a couple handfuls of them. Now the bushes were almost picked clean, and that was a lot of berries. *Something* had eaten them all. The grizzly? I stood very still, slowly looked all around me, listening for any sound of a bear nearby. There are a lot of sounds in the forest if you really listen. There's the wind through the trees, the singing and twittering of different birds, the knock-knocking of woodpeckers, the chattering and scurrying of squirrels. The more I listened, the louder it got. So loud, in fact, I almost didn't hear the rustling in the blueberry bushes right in front of me. I was startled for a second, but the waist-high bushes weren't big enough to hide a grizzly or a cougar. Maybe a cougar kitten? I'd never seen one, and had been warned since I was a baby never to pick one up, because that would make the mama madder than if you'd stepped on her tail. I looked all around the treetops again, surely I would be able to see an angry mama mountain lion if she was about to pounce me. I wasn't going to pick up the kitten, I just wanted to see it. But if it was lost, or orphaned, I might have to pick it up.

I couldn't see enough through the thin branches and leaves to be sure it was a kitten scratching around. Was probably just a turtle, or a rabbit. If it was a rabbit, that would be cute, too; a little bunny. I could pick a bunny up. I pushed into the bushes a step, gently moved aside the little branches in front of me, and...*Skunk!!*

I don't think I would have been more startled if an African tiger leaped out at me. How I convinced myself it was going to be something cute, I can't say.

Crashing through briars, bushes, branches, and probably more poison oak, I judged myself far enough away from the danged skunk to stop. I thought I had jumped away in time, I only saw him for a second and he didn't even have his rear-end pointed at me. How could he have gotten me? But he got me. Just a little, I judged, having smelled it much, much worse on the dogs, but still. *I'd* never been skunked before.

I was having quite the morning. There wasn't a whole lot else could happen to me, I didn't think. I'd already gotten lost, attacked by quail, been poison oaked, and now skunked. My stockings were torn, my legs and arms were scratched and bleeding, and what else? I was sweaty, thirsty, and my neck was probably scarred forever from that old rope. If I hadn't been on a mission, I might've been lookin' at going home.

I was pretty sure I could find the exact spot where I had seen the grizzly. He probably wouldn't still be there, but it was a good place to start. First, though, I had to find water. Even though I was a little turned around again after being chased off the trail by the skunk, I knew Elk Creek was nearby. Elk Creek was the biggest creek on our ridge—in the spring it was as big as a roaring river from all the melting snow. In the summer, it was shallow, quick, and clear. You could see the fish a mile away swimming over the black and white creek-rocks.

Sure enough, the creek wasn't too far away, it was clear and sparkling and I wanted to throw myself into it and drink my weight in water. I spotted a small clearing on the other side, blanketed with green grass and yellow dandelions. I couldn't have painted a prettier picture than that little clearing. I pulled off my sweaty shoes and torn stockings and waded across to drop the heavy bag and bedroll, untied the coat from my waist, took off my belt and sword, and stepped back to the middle the creek. The rushing water was half way to my knees, splashing up onto my dress, immediately cooling me off. Filling the canteen, I drank down half of it, until my stomach was close to bursting, then drank a little more. A soda float wouldn't have tasted any better than that cold, fresh, stream water.

After refilling the canteen, I tossed it to the grass. I grabbed a handful of wet sand from the creek bank and scrubbed my scratched-up legs, cleaning off dirt and blood and hopefully some of the oak poison. I smelled awful skunky, but water and sand wasn't going to clean that off, and anyway, most of the smell was on my dress. So off came that skunky dress, leaving me in my under-dress. I scrubbed my arms with another handful of sand, then splashed myself clean. As clean as I was gonna get, anyway, without laying down in the stream. That thought crossed my mind, but it wasn't like I was bathing to go to town or to school. I didn't need to be *that* clean, and no matter how clean I could get myself, I would still smell like a skunk.

I had planned on stopping for only a few minutes to rest and fill up my canteen, but I found myself plum-tuckered, and awful hungry to boot. I pulled from my bag the blueberry pie and Papa's knife. My Indian doll Sarah I set beside me—she was probably hungry, too. Carefully opening a corner of the oilcloth, I saw the pie was pretty much a mess. The thin top-crust was no match for all the jostling and crashing around in the jam-packed lumberman's bag. Not needing the knife, I scooped up a bit of broken, sticky crust and stuffed into my mouth. Sarah enjoyed a mouthful, too.

I didn't want to eat all the pie, in case I needed it for later, and since I was at the creek, I decided to catch some fish. I dug into a soft spot on the ground with my sword and immediately found a worm. A pretty big one, actually. So big that he was too big for my hook, so I pinched him in half and slid the hook right into him. Papa always liked that I didn't get icked by icky things.

I found a nice straight stick to tie the fishing line to, and didn't have my hook in the water long when I caught the first trout. He didn't even nibble at the worm, just grabbed it and ran. In no time I had three fine, little trout fish kicking in the grass beside me when I remembered I didn't have anything to cook them with. I had forgotten matches to start a fire!

I found a couple of rocks and hit them together a few times. I knew I needed special rocks to start a fire with, and those weren't those. Everyone knows Indians can start a fire by rubbing sticks together, and Papa and I even tried that once for fun, until we wore ourselves out. We decided it must only work for Indians. Trying the stick thing by myself would be a big waste of time. I was really disappointed in myself for forgetting what should have been the *most* important part of my gear, something to build a fire with. How could I have forgotten to bring matches? Jack London would not have been very impressed with me.

I debated for a while whether I could eat the fishes raw—scales and eyeballs and all—or return them to the stream before they couldn't be put back.

I opened up Papa's folding-knife, and holding one of the flopping fish tight against the ground I put the blade to its throat. I'd seen Mama and Papa clean fish many times, so I wasn't icked about that, and I tried not to think of how it would taste not being cooked. There was no way I could eat eyeballs, but maybe the rest of the fish wouldn't be too bad if I held my nose. Maybe I would even like the taste and insist on eating raw fish even after I returned home. What made me hesitate was thinking that not only did I not have a fire to cook the fish over, I also wouldn't have a fire at night. I'd be completely in the dark, all by myself. Mountain lions come out and hunt in the dark. Bears come out in the dark. Monsters come out in the dark, not to mention mosquitoes.

I had only spent a few nights outside in my whole life, and that was with Mama and Papa and Jack, and we had a fire. I had asked them why we'd never gone camping. "Well," said Papa, "we already live in the woods. Woods is where most folks go to camp." But I wanted to go camping, so Papa set up the big tent he used on hunting trips. Just a stone's throw away from the house, we cooked supper over an open campfire, told stories, and had a great time sleeping in the tent. I loved it so much I made them spend the next three nights out with me.

In the woods by myself, no tent, no Jack, and no fire, may have been too much bravery for even me, and I was already swatting at mosquitoes. Maybe I should have planned my mission a little better. I couldn't believe that after all the trouble I went through to get out there, I might have to go back. *Monsters come out in the dark*, I thought again to myself. I pulled the knife's blade away from the fish's throat.

I didn't want the fishes to die if I wasn't going to eat them, and I wasn't going to eat raw fish after deciding I'd better be back home before dark, so I guess it was their lucky day. I'd have to try another time to find and draw the grizzly bear. That is, if Mama ever let me out of the house again. I picked up all the fish and was about to toss them back into the creek when I heard sticks snapping in the forest close by. And then some bushes rustling, and then I heard a low grumbling sound and a snort and another louder snort and then I saw him, the grizzly bear! My grizzly bear!

Uh oh, I thought, *now what?* He peeked around a big cedar tree looking at me and sniffing the air. He moved out from the tree, stopped, and we just kinda looked at each other. He raised up a little, and looked ten times bigger than before. I slowly backed away but there wasn't much room to back up before being stopped by thick bushes. There was no way this was a black bear with brown fur. His fur was bushy and beautiful, and shook when he walked, bristling in the sun that peeked through the trees.

He slowly lumbered toward me, huffing and snorting. I thought of running away, my plan had been to sneak up on *him*, not to be snuck up on myself, but I did remember what Papa had said, never run from a bear. And a bear that big and that close would catch me in two leaps. Also, I had spent a very unpleasant day in search of the very bear that was now in front of me. I had found him. That's what I wanted, right? Now, if only he wouldn't eat me.

"You...you want the fish?" I said, but was so nervous I doubt he heard me. I was still holding the fish in my hands, so threw them over. A great throw, actually, they all landed right in front of him.

He lightly sniffed at the fish, his big nose twitching back and forth, he didn't appear all that interested in them. He moved to investigate my bedroll and the pile of stuff I had pulled from my bag. He nudged, then stuck his nose into the bag, breathing deeply. He gave a quick sniff to my skunky dress, then found the blueberry pie.

I would have thought he'd eat the pie in one big gulp—wrapping, pan and all, but he didn't. He stuck his nose against the oilcloth and breathed in so deeply, I thought he was going to snort the whole pie up. He gently licked all around the cloth, and finding the fold, used his tongue to pry it open to get at the pie. I was surprised at the careful way he opened and licked at the pie, almost like he had been taught manners as a cub.

It was amazing, to be sure, to be standing not twenty feet away from a grizzly bear dining on a pie I had helped make, but it was also, maybe, a good time to try and sneak away. Not *run*, but sneak. I was pretty well backed-in to whatever type of bush that was behind me, so much so, that I would have had to take a couple of steps toward the bear to be able to slip away. I had really put myself in a bad spot, but instead of trying to escape, as I should have done, I stood and watched him eat. I wasn't afraid.

I thought I heard my name called, right before the big **BOOM** and rumbling echo of a big rifle. Jack came flying out of nowhere, leaped the stream and threw himself at the grizzly bear. I stood watching, unable to move, as Jack and the bear fought. Jack would jump in and bite, and then bounce away quickly before the bear could bite him back. The bear caught Jack with a swipe of his claws and sent him tumbling and yelping across the clearing before turning and disappearing back into the forest. It was over so fast. I didn't even see Papa before he snatched me up and ran us back across the stream. "Jack!" I was crying.

He ran us a little ways before setting me down. He was holding both my shoulders and squeezing real tight which kinda hurt and I could see him talking to me but I don't remember what he was saying, all I could think about was Jack flying through the air, and wanting to know if he was dead. Papa hugged me so hard I couldn't breathe, he only let go when Jack came up behind us, limping and bleeding.

Papa picked me up in one arm and picked Jack up in his other arm and walked us both all the way back home, only stopping a couple of times to rest.

We were quite a site when we finally showed up at the house. I was in my under-dress, riding on Papa's back so he could carry Jack and his rifle. We were, all of us, covered in Jack's blood. Mama had a fit. I was hugged tight, and then scolded like never before.

✳ ✳ ✳ ✳

After a very unpleasant bath with Mama scrubbing me raw and pulling ticks from my scalp, I was sent straight to bed, still smelling like a skunk. Mama wouldn't even let me hold or comfort Jack when she sewed up his wounds. He hurt his leg pretty bad and had a big gash on his neck and another on his back. I couldn't bear to hear him whimpering as she poked him with the needle and thread, so I buried my head under a pillow. I could still hear him. I couldn't, however, hear everything being whispered later on the porch, when they thought I was asleep, but I think I heard most of it.

"So, it *was* a grizzly bear?" asked Mama.

"I can't say, honestly, that I got a good look at him," whispered Papa. "I saw June backing up, and heard him grumbling. I barely saw him through the brush. I shot about the same time Jack rushed him, then saw Jack flying through the air. The bear disappeared into the trees, I grabbed Bug and ran. It happened so fast, all I could think of was getting her out of there."

Mama started to softly cry. I didn't know what to do but knew I should stay up in my room. And Papa still didn't know if it was a grizzly bear? Did that mean I wasn't in as much trouble?

I guess I was probably lucky that I didn't get killed or eaten. But you know, I really wasn't scared of the grizzly bear, and he didn't look like he wanted to kill me. It wasn't until Jack attacked him that he got mean, and then he was just defending himself. I was more scared of Papa shooting and Jack attacking than I was of the bear. I did feel horrible about Jack getting hurt. He was bloodied good, but Papa said it looked worse than it was, that he was very lucky. I promised to make it up to him every day from then on. He thought the bear was going to kill me and almost died protecting me. Papa would have died protecting me. I could have gotten them both killed. What was I thinking?

The next morning when I woke up, Papa was gone, which surprised me because I thought it was his day off. He always makes breakfast for me and Mama on Sunday, he makes real good flapjacks with eggs and bacon. Mama was making the flapjacks that morning.

"Where's Papa?" I asked. She was lost in her thoughts, I had to ask her twice.

"Your father has gone to see Mr. Bern," she finally said, a sad look on her face.

"To pay him back the two bits for our sodas?" I asked. Mama looked at me funny, then her face softened.

"Oh, June...no, not to pay him back for our sodas. Papa is going to see Mr. Bern about the bear. You've really started something this time, young miss."

"What have I started, Mama?"

"After breakfast. We'll talk after breakfast."

Neither one of us was hungry. All I wanted was to hear about what it was that I had started. Mama was just picking at her food, until finally putting down her fork and telling me what was going on.

"Your father has gone to see Mr. Bern about helping him find the bear."

"And then what? After they find him?" I asked.

"You know what the answer to that is."

"I know," I said. And I *did* know, even though I wished it could have been different. Mr. Bern seemed like a strange choice to help Papa, he was always in pain and could barely get around. "Why Mr. Bern?"

"Apparently," explained Mama, "Mr. Bern used to be the Great Bear Hunter around these parts. He's a real mountain man, our Bern, grew up trapping and hunting, then when all the animals had been trapped out, he got into lumberjacking until his age caught up with him and he took a job at the lumber mill."

"Oh. So does Papa think it was a grizzly bear?"

"He's not sure," said Mama. "He didn't get a good look at him."

"Oh," I said again.

"Whether they get the bear or not," said Mama, "you are not to leave our property until after school starts up again. That means no further than our little creek, and no further than the barn."

"Yes, ma'am."

"And I'll be giving you *lots* of extra chores, so you won't get bored. And you will *not* sneak out of this house again to look for a bear, or anything else, is that clear?"

"Yes, ma'am."

"Promise me."

"Yes, ma'am, I promise."

Chapter Four

Not only do we have a horse and a mule, last year Papa brought home a Longhorn cow, got her in a trade for some work he did on a ranch in the valley. He told me not to name her, though, because she was going to be food in a few months once she got fatter. Well she got fatter, all right. Turned out Papa brought home a *pregnant* Longhorn cow. We'd never had a cow before, so it took us a little while to figure it out. I was getting sad too, because I *had* named her, I named her Becky, after Becky in the book *Tom Sawyer*, by Mark Twain, who I'm also supposed to be too young to read, but it's a good book, actually. So Becky was getting fatter and Papa was talking about her being *near ready*. I knew what that meant, and I didn't want to eat her.

It was Mama that noticed she wasn't just fattening up, but was obviously pregnant, at least obvious to her. Papa was still hoping she was just fattening up. Even after Papa agreed she was probably going to have a baby, we weren't quite sure when that was going to happen, until one morning I was out feeding the animals and walked into her stable. Papa had built Becky her her own stable, because she didn't like London or Whiskey and they didn't like her.

I walked in with her hay and noticed her licking something on the ground. I looked closer and saw it was a newborn calf!

So we didn't eat Becky, and she gave us milk which is even better than meat because Papa can always kill a deer for meat, and we trade for pork and bacon. So we had Becky's milk to drink fresh, we also made buttermilk, and we had butter all the time. I told Mama and Papa I had named her Becky, Papa said fine. Then I told him I also named the calf Tom after Tom Sawyer, and told him we couldn't eat him either since he had a name. Papa didn't agree with that. "How about this...we grow him six months and trade him for a new wagon, or three or four hogs next year?" I really wanted to keep him but knew that was probably a good trade for us. And in a year, I was sure I could come up with something that would make Papa want to keep Tom as a member of the family.

Our chickens, I learned when I was young, are best *not* named. Papa warned me not to name them, they're not pets, and the ones we don't get eggs from we eat. And even though we have a good coop to keep out the critters, critters still get them. Every animal on the mountain loves to eat chickens. Raccoons, skunks, foxes, bobcats, mountain lions and bears.

When I was little, even though Papa told me not to, I named a whole litter of chicks that had hatched. There was Rose, Rosebud, Mudbud, Star, Daisy, and Belle. I didn't want any roosters so I named them all girl names. Out of all the baby chicks that were born that spring, it seemed the ones I named were the first to go. Two of them died just by themselves, two others were snatched through the wire by raccoons, and Rose and Daisy were swallowed by a bear that tore into the coop. I cried for every one. We lost other chickens of course, but I only cried at the loss of the ones I had named. I even thought that I had cursed them by naming them. I worried myself a little when I named Becky and Tom, but I figured since they weren't chickens, it'd be okay, and it might save them from Papa putting them on the dinner table one day. But I still worried about them.

* * * *

Papa was gone the whole day visiting Mr. Bern, even through the night. I can remember only a few times when Papa wasn't home at night. Of course a couple of times a year when he goes off hunting, but we've got so much game all around us he's never had to go far. And a couple of times he's had to spend a few days with the lumber crews helping to bring timber down to the mill. But other than that, he's always with us at night. I've always felt safer with him at home, even though Mama's a crack shot with her double barrel shotgun—Papa calls it her *scatter-gun*—and Jack is always ready to go after any critter or trespasser who wanders onto our land. When he's not hurt, that is.

One neat thing about Papa being gone is I got to sleep with Mama in the big bed, which I almost didn't get to do because I still smelled like a skunk. Jack got to sleep with us, too, in the big bed, something that definitely doesn't happen when Papa's home. He gave in to letting the dogs in the house, but sleeping on the bed was out of the question.

Jack was in a lot of pain, and whimpered when he wasn't

sleeping. I kept my hand on him, gently petting and comforting him, and earlier helped Mama clean his wounds and change his bandages. Papa was going to send the vet to the house if he could find him in town, but Mama had already done a good job, it looked to me, of stitching him up. I'd always thought Mr. Howell, the vet, was a little strange anyway. Plus, he had completely missed the fact of Becky being pregnant, which I, and Mama too, thought was something a veterinarian should have noticed. "Even if he *is* a man", said Mama. I think meaning that women know more about babies than men do, even hundred-pound babies.

I loved lying in bed with Mama, we talked about all kinds of things, and listened to the outside critter sounds. Since it was summer, the crickets were singing and the frogs were croaking. We listened to the owls whoo-whoo-ing, and we even heard a mountain lion in the distance. The sound a mountain lion makes is very strange. I've heard them roar, which is scary, but they also make a sound like a woman or a kid screaming or crying, which is even scarier. When a mountain lion is around, all our animals go crazy with fear. Jack heard the cougar and wanted to hide, but yelped when he tried to get off the bed, so we held him with us while he shook. Chica was hiding in a corner, very quietly growling. I think she was afraid the cougar would hear her and know where she was.

I've always thought of mountain lions as *she*, probably because of the sounds they make, and because everyone knows the most dangerous animal on the mountain is a mother cougar protecting her kittens. Which is too bad, because I'd love to see and hold a cougar kitten. I wouldn't hurt it.

Mama and I slept in late the next morning, not knowing when Papa would return. I fed the chickens, Becky and Tom, and spent a lot of time with London. He's still my favorite, even though Tom is cuter. I brushed London good while he was eating, talking to him, telling him all about the big mess I'd started.

"You sure are lucky to be a mule," I told him. "It can be very difficult being a little girl." I must have spent over an hour with London, and it was London who first saw Papa and Mr. Bern riding up. Papa was on Whiskey, Mr. Bern was on Willa, and they were leading two mules wearing heavy packs. Leading them was Mr. Bern's old dog, Fish, who Jack would normally run up and tackle and play with, but Jack was recuperating on the porch from the fight with my grizzly. Fish ran up to the porch trying to get Jack to play, but Jack was still hurtin' pretty bad. I always thought Fish was crazy in the head, he does things like bolting all of a sudden after something that no one else sees. And he did not like me, seemed he was afraid of me for some reason. Mr. Bern told me once that "Fish is just shy around pretty ladies," but he seemed to like Mama okay and she's pretty. I don't know. But Jack liked him, and he never chased our chickens when he visited.

At first I was worried, thinking maybe Papa and Mr. Bern had already gone after the bear and killed him, but I looked and looked, and the closer they came I didn't see a grizzly bear strapped to anything. But he's so big, maybe they couldn't haul him out of the woods, maybe they just left him. I was afraid to go up to them, so I stayed with London, even after they tied up their horses and and mules and went inside the house.

They had been in the house for quite awhile. I had to know what was happening, but also didn't want to know. Then Mama stepped out onto the porch and hollered at me to come inside for lunch. "I'm not hungry!" I shouted back.

"I didn't ask if you were hungry, Bug," said Mama. "I've made a big lunch for everyone, we have a guest in our home and now's not the time for you to be rude."

"We have a guest?" I said under my breath. "It's just Mr Bern for Pete's sake, and I don't want to see *him* today anyway. Everyone in the family has to immediately stop what they're doing and come into the house whenever someone decides to drop by? What if I'm busy with something very important, and on top of that I'm not even hungry, and how about..."

"Now, young lady," called Mama, snapping me out of my building defiance.

"Coming," I called back politely. I could have been stubborn a little longer, probably a lot longer, but like Papa always told me, "Choose your battles wisely," meaning there was no need to get myself in trouble over not coming in for lunch when I knew I'd come in eventually, and I really did need to know what was happening even if I wasn't going to like it, and I'd better save my defiance and getting in trouble for something important. But this was pretty important.

I slowly put away London's grooming kit, slowly opened and closed the stable gate, slloowwlly made my way down to the house. Jack and Fish were lying together in front of the steps. Jack stood up wagging his tail, though he did give a little yelp, and whimpered. Fish barely glanced at me, then up and darted around the corner with his tail between his legs like I'd zinged him with a slingshot. Crazy dog.

I stopped at the door before going in. I could hear Mr. Bern's big voice, like a freight train's horn, retelling the story of the grizzly bear that ate his whole logging crew's campsite one night, with all the men up in trees not able to do anything but watch. So what did that story have to do with killing *my* grizzly bear, I wondered. Did they get him already? They sounded in good spirits, Papa too. I listened, trying to pick out any clues from their conversation. I guess I'd been standing there long enough for Mama to be frustrated with my slowness. She opened the door I was leaning against, spilling me across the floor and landing on Chica, who jumped and ran outside. Chica and her annoying habit of always sleeping by the door.

"Well hallo, there, Miss June Bug," said Mr Bern. "Finished up with all the chores your ma and pa keep piling on ya?"

"No sir," I said, straightening my dress and quickly thinking that if they believed I still had chores to do, I'd have a reason to excuse myself.

"No sir not yet?" said Mr. Bern. "Well, the more chores you got, the less trouble you get, is what my pa believed, or something like that. Me, there weren't enough hours in the day to fill with chores to keep me outta trouble when I was your age. Only by the grace of the mountain and ol' God hisself did I turn out to be such a successful pillar of society."

"Yes, sir," I said.

Mama had a small mountain of salted pork in the middle of the table, and had hard-boiled a whole bunch of eggs. All the bread we'd made over the last couple of days was piled at the end of the table, and after she handed me a plate with a little bit of pork and a biscuit, she walked to the meat cupboard and started pulling out jerky. How hungry could Mr. Bern be? Were there other people coming for lunch?

Mr. Bern had finished his story when I burst through the door, and now everyone was sitting and eating and not talking at all. So what was happening? Not only was I not hungry when I sat down, but now I *really* wasn't hungry. No one was talking about what was going on, if they'd killed my bear or hadn't found my bear, or anything. So finally, I had to ask, "Did you find the bear?"

Papa looked at me, a little surprised, "Oh, no, Bug, we haven't started looking yet. Took most of the day yesterday and up before dawn to get the gear together."

"Haven't had the bear traps out for more'n couple years now," added Mr. Bern, "and wasn't expectin' your pa to roll up with the idea of baggin' your grizzly bear."

Papa and Mr. Bern started talking about where *the griz* may have gone after the last sighting, whether Papa may have wounded him, if he'd be more likely to head to higher ground and such. But did that mean Papa believed me that it *was* a grizzly bear?

"No sir," was all I said when Papa asked me if I may know anything that would help them. I think Papa knew I wouldn't want to help them find my bear, but still included me in the discussion.

It didn't take them long to pack up the food Mama had brought out. They were mostly using Mr. Bern's gear, he had a lot of gear. Papa just added a bedroll, his big rifle, and his rain slicker with some extra clothes tied into a bundle. Papa tied Jack to the steps with a long rope, asking Mama and me not to untie him. He would run and try to catch up, and he was in no shape to run through the woods, and especially not ready to tangle again with a bear. Papa hugged Mama goodbye, then picked me up and hugged me tight.

"You know we have to do this, right?" he asked.

"Yes, sir."

"And you know *why* we have to do it?"

"Yes, sir."

"Alright, kiddo," he said, giving me a kiss on my cheek before setting me down. "You help Mama with everything she needs help with, okay?"

I started to cry, "I will, Papa."

Another round of hugs for all of us, then Papa and Mr. Bern turned onto our little dirt road heading south, heading to kill a grizzly bear. My grizzly bear.

"Be careful, Papa!" I shouted.

He started to shout something back but wasn't loud enough to be heard over Fish barking crazily at nothing, and Mr. Bern whooping, "Don't worry, ladies, I'll have the old man back in time for the next poison oak harvest! Ha haa! Bring him back with a new grizzly bear rug for your parlor! Don't sell the place and move away before we get back, the old man can't cook for hisself! Haa! Hey, I think Fish has found the grizzly's scent already, this is gonna be easy! Ha haaa!"

Mama said to me, "I don't think they'll be sneaking up on any grizzly bears."

"There ain't no rules for the brave! Ain't no mountain we can't tame!... Ha haaaa!"

Chapter Five

Another night alone with Mama. I didn't like Papa being gone, but I could get used to sleeping in the big bed. Jack, too. Although Mama wasn't going to let him at first, she said that last night was special, because he was in a lot of pain. But he had been walking up and down the steps all day, and would've been running around with Fish if we'd have let him.

"Please, Mama, he's still hurt...he's hurt bad."

"Well..." said Mama, and before she could say anything else, Jack leaped onto the bed and plopped down between us, giving us both kisses and whacking us with his tail. "Hurt bad, indeed," said Mama, but she let him stay.

Some varmint did visit in the middle of the night. Jack's hair was standing up on his back and he was growling so loud it woke me up. Mama was already up and standing on the porch with her scatter-gun. The chickens were cackling like they did when they were afraid, but whatever it was, it didn't try to get to them.

"What is it, Mama?" I asked when she came back to bed.

"Nothing, probably just a raccoon or fox sniffing around."

I fell back asleep, but woke up again later for some reason and saw that Mama and Jack were still awake. Maybe it wasn't just a little fox.

The next morning after feeding the animals, and after eating breakfast, who should knock on our door but my best friend K. 'K' like the letter K. His real name is Sterling, which I think is a wonderful name, Sterling Kelvin Hassrick. His parents named him Sterling, but called him Kelvin, both names K hated, even as a little boy. He did like the 'K' when his name was written as Sterling K. Hassrick, and decided that was what he wanted to be called. He even makes his family call him that and won't answer to anything else. K can be a weird kid.

He's a year older than me, his family lives down the road just a ways, and we have a winding trail through the woods that connects our houses. I call him my best friend even though he's a boy. We've grown up together, since we were babies. Mama thought I liked him best because he didn't take any sass from me. I thought I'd like him even *better* if he let me sass him. But I don't think I really sassed him.

I hadn't seen K for more than a month. He got real mad at me a couple of weeks before summer vacation started. We were in the woods, not too far from the house, playing Lawman and Indian. He was Wyatt Earp like he always insisted on, and I was Sacajawea, the Indian princess that led Lewis and Clark across the West all the way to the ocean. She may not have actually been a princess, but I liked to pretend she was, so I could wear one of my princess dresses. So Sacajawea was leading Wyatt Earp through the forest because the Great Wyatt Earp tended to get lost, on the trail of ruthless, desperate outlaws. We were walking along a deer trail on the side of a hill to where the lawbreakers were surely hiding when I heard a *thwank*, followed by "Owff", followed by leaves and underbrush being shaken and broken down the hill. K wasn't paying attention as always and ran *thwank* right into a low branch with his face. He fell backward and down the side of the hill which was really steep if you fell off the trail. I'd never fallen off that trail. Well, he rolled near to the bottom of the slope, about as far as I could throw a rock, which is pretty far. He would have rolled even farther if he hadn't been stopped by a big patch of poison oak. More like a little forest of poison oak. He tumbled about ten feet through little poison oak bushes and crashed into the big poison oak bushes which were the size of trees. He was *in it*. I couldn't even see him .

When he realized he wasn't dead, he realized where he was,and started to panic and scream, something very un-Wyatt Earp, I should think.

"Aaaahhh Aaaahhh! HELPPPP!" he screamed. Plus he was wearing a pack on his back and couldn't move, other than flailing his arms and legs. At least then I could see where he was. Boy, was he in it. He was kind of floundering like a beetle on its back.

"Stand up!" I called.

"*I can't!*" he screamed. "*Help me! It's poison oak! It's poison oak!*"

"I know!" I yelled down. "Try not to touch it!" Good advice, I thought.

Now, the hill really *was* steep. Any steeper and it would have been a cliff. I wasn't afraid of going down there, but I was worried he wanted me to carry him out or something, and I didn't even have on long sleeves. I was in a princess dress, for Pete's sake.

"Roll over!" I called. If he rolled over, he could probably stand up. I started looking around for something for him to grab onto, like some rope, but we hadn't brought any rope. Maybe somebody years ago had fallen into the same patch of poison oak and they had a friend that was a bit more prepared than I was and remembered to bring rope. If they did, I couldn't find it. They probably took it with them. While I was looking around, K managed to roll himself over and take a run at the hill, then I heard an even louder scream. I thought, well...I don't know what I thought, what could be worse than being swallowed up by poison oak? Scorpions? Rattlesnakes? A Skunk?

"Aaaaggghhh, Aaaaggghhh! *Worrmmss!*"

Now, what you should know about K is that for some reason, he has always, *always* been terrified of worms. Any kind of worm. I don't know why. So he had apparently lunged away from the big poison oak trees and fallen again into the smaller poison oak which is worse anyway because it was all shiny leaves almost dripping with poison. Under the poison oak was a half buried rotten log that he split wide open when he put his hand down to stop his fall, and living in the log was a million worms. Not really worms, actually, more like maggoty wiggly things that weren't very happy about having their home destroyed. He made it up the hillside pretty quick after that. I saw the wormy things and they *were* pretty icky, and I've never been icked by worms.

He made it back to the trail, I held out a stick to help him the last few feet which were the steepest. He did a crazy dance, throwing his pack off, and whirling around slapping all the wormy things off, lost his balance and almost went back down the hill. I don't think he would have survived another fall into the maggoty poison oak. He'd of had a heart attack, which I don't think kids normally have.

He was real mad at me for some reason, like it was my fault he fell down the hill. I helped him out of his clothes and picked off the last of the worms, even found a medium-sized tick dug into the middle of his back that I quickly pinched out without telling him. K's afraid of ticks, too.

"I'm all poison oaked!" he said, standing there buck-white naked, then started crying again and wouldn't stop. He put his clothes back on after shaking them like they were on fire just in case there was one more worm hiding. I told him he shouldn't put his clothes on, they were actually shiny from poison oak oil, but he wouldn't listen. He wouldn't talk to me either, just turned back down the trail toward home. Or what he thought was the trail home. I don't think K had ever been poison oaked before. All parents show their kids what the stuff looks like and to never touch it, but being kids on the mountain, and just being kids, at some point we have to find out for ourselves if our parents are telling the truth. K's the only kid that I think listened to his parents and hadn't touched it before.

It was the first day of the last week of school when K showed up with his mama. He was bright red and splotchy and bleeding in spots where he couldn't stop scratching. He had it *bad*, poor thing. The older kids always teased him anyway, for just about any reason, but now they really ganged up on him, like a pack of wolves tormenting the weak runt. Kids can really be vicious. Our teacher, Mrs. Hicks, who always had a hard time controlling us, and who was looking forward to vacation more than even us kids were, told K he didn't have to finish the week, his summer would come a little early that year. I even defended K at school, almost got beat up myself, but he didn't appreciate that, and didn't speak to me all summer. Wouldn't come out of his house when I went to see if he wanted to play. So I was surprised and very happy that K showed up at my house. Maybe he wasn't mad at me anymore.

Mama excused me from washing the dishes. At first I was afraid she wouldn't let me play because I was still in trouble from the bear mission, but she said okay to K's suggestion of us going fishing, which surprised me because if we fished, there would be worms. I think he wanted to prove to me he wasn't a weenie anymore. I ran upstairs to my room and grabbed a burlap bag full of very important stuff. We ran out to the barn to grab the fishing gear, then down the trail to the creek. Jack was barking and crying, beside himself that he couldn't go with us. First Papa left him, now me. Poor Jack.

The creek's just right down from the house, so Mama could still see us from the porch. With the luck I'd been having finding grizzly bears, and hearing the mountain lion at night, maybe I should have at least brought a slingshot. I didn't even have my sword, which I lost when Papa snatched me away from the grizzly last week. I picked up a good oak stick and told K to do the same, we should at least have something to defend ourselves with, something other than fishing poles.

When we got to the creek, K hopped over it to fish from the other side. Which I guess would have been better, there was a nice flat spot under a big pine tree with soft clover under the fallen pine needles, and a big boulder we liked to sit on. It had always been one of my favorite reading spots, but something stopped me.

"I like this side better," I said.

"What?" he asked, "I thought we liked this side. This side has the rock and there aren't a bunch of weeds."

"My mama said I can't go past the creek," I told him.

"Why?"

"I'm not allowed to say." I set my pole down and start digging into a bare spot for worms with the oak stick, quickly finding a couple of fat ones. K sat down on the other side, watching me.

"Can I have a worm?" he bravely asked. I threw one right at him, which made him jump two feet. Weenie.

We glared across the creek at each other. He was mad because I threw the worm at him and I wouldn't go to his side, I was mad because... Why was I mad? It would've been okay with Mama if I sat on the other side of the creek. Maybe I was mad because for the first time in my whole life I was afraid to cross the little creek which would mean I'd be in *The Woods* officially, and there are grizzly bears and mountain lions in *The Woods*. Maybe it wasn't just a fox that had been sniffing around at night, maybe it was something much bigger. This side of the creek is civilization, that side of the creek is dark, dangerous wilderness, or something like that. It didn't help that I could see Mama watching us from the porch, she hadn't done that since I was little.

"Can we just stay on this side of the creek today?" I asked. "I'll put the worm on your hook and everything, okay?" But K wanted to be stubborn for some reason.

"No," he said. "I like it over here. Toss me the sack."

"No." I wouldn't toss him the sack, the burlap sack I kept in my room and brought out only when he would come over. The burlap sack that had his two dolls in it that he kept with me because his mama, and especially his papa thought he was too old for and told him to get rid of, so he secretly kept them at my house. That's probably why he came to visit me after avoiding me all summer, not because he missed me, but because he missed his stupid dolls. One doll was a teddy bear and the other was an Indian Prince doll that he got the same time I got my Indian Princess. We'd played together with them for years and years.

I was the more stubborn like always, so K hopped back over to my side of the creek. I handed him the sack with his dolls to take out while I put worms on our hooks and dropped the lines into the little creek. Maybe I was sad, too, because I didn't have Sarah, *my* Indian doll, having left her at Elk Creek with my sword, shoes, and books. I wasn't going to tell K anything about the bear, and I was hoping he wouldn't ask where my doll was.

While K played with his dolls, I stared into the woods on the other side, watching for movement in the bushes and behind the trees. Other than the usual families of sparrows and blue birds that are everywhere, I only saw a couple of squirrels chasing each other. I wondered where Papa and Mr. Bern were, if they were on the trail of my grizzly, what they were doing that very minute and what stories Mr. Bern had been telling. I hoped they'd be back soon, hoped they hadn't seen my bear, hoped that he just disappeared to the other side of the mountain where no one could find him.

We did catch a few fish that day, little ones. I let them all go.

Chapter Six

Other than chores, which Mama had me doing twice as many of, I couldn't bring myself to do much else, not even read. It didn't help that the poison oak I had run through on my grizzly bear mission was starting to show itself on my legs and arms, and even on my neck. It's hard to concentrate on reading when you're trying not to think about a terrible itch on your body.

Jack was healing quickly, but Mama still wouldn't let him run, so he sat on the porch with me watching the woods and the road. Watching for Papa. He and Mr. Bern had been gone three days. Mama tried to get me interested in other things, but all I could think about was my bear and my papa and Mr. Bern. Whether they got my bear or not, I wanted them to come home.

Mama popped some corn that night and we stayed up reading a few of my favorite stories. I still loved having Mama read to me even though I was ten years old. We finished the popped corn and looked through a stack of old newspapers she wanted to read before the news got *too* old. Mr. Shaw at the General Store saves the newspapers that he hasn't sold to give to Mama when we go to town. I liked the drawings and photographs in the newspapers, but that was about it.

"Hmm," read Mama. "Alice Huyler Ramsey, a 22 year old housewife and mother from New Jersey, became the first woman to drive across the United States in an automobile. From Manhattan, New York, to San Francisco, California."

"How far is that?" I asked.

"Says...three thousand, eight hundred miles."

"How far is that?"

"Well," said Mama, "let me think. To town and back is about twenty five miles, sooo..." She picked up a pencil from her nightstand and scribbled on the newspaper. "It would be like going to town and back one hundred and fifty two times."

"Wow," I said. "Why did she do that?"

"Says she wanted to prove that women can do anything men can do."

"Did her kids go with her?"

"I don't think so."

"I don't like automobiles," I said. "They're loud and smelly, and they scare the horses."

"I don't like them either, Bug, and try not to scratch."

"But it itches."

"It's poison oak, it's supposed to itch, and you never would have gotten it if..."

"I know, I know, Mama. What's that article? *Grizzly Killed Near San Diego*?"

"In the mountains outside of San Diego, California," she read, "a male grizzly bear, weighing approximately eight hundred pounds, was trapped, and then killed by a rancher named Henry Thomason. The bear had been snatching and feasting on his sheep for months, said Thomason. It took four men, all with large caliber rifles to finally bring down the massive beast. It's thought the bear may have come up from Mexico, as it is believed by many experts that no more grizzlies exist in the state of California."

"How do they know there's no more grizzlies?" I asked. "Mr. Bern says they keep popping up."

"I don't know, Bug."

"What about *Monarch* the grizzly?"

"He's in a zoo," said Mama. "That doesn't count."

"I don't like that news. What's something else?"

"Let's see...the city of Santa Rosa is projecting sixty percent of the buildings destroyed in the 1906 earthquake will be rebuilt by the end of the year. And all are expected to have electricity and indoor plumbing."

"Indoor plumbing would be nice," I said. "That means water, right?"

"It does."

"Mama, why don't we have electricity?"

"Why would we need electricity?"

"I don't know," I said. "It says all the houses are going to have it."

"That's only in the cities, I think," said Mama. "What would we do with electricity?"

"I don't know. What does it do?"

"It lights the lamps without needing lamp oil."

"Oh." I tried to imagine how it did that, and wondered why it was such a big deal if that's all it did.

"What about indoor plumbing?" I asked.

"Only in the cities."

"Mama, tell me again how you met Papa."

"It's getting very late, Bug, I think it's time we turn in."

"Pleeaase?"

"Another time. Besides, you know the story as well as I do."

"He met you in San Francisco, right?" I asked.

"Well, outside of San Francisco, but right now, I think it's bedtime."

"And you were living with my tia Annabel, right? And you made dresses and costumes for the dancers and actresses in San Francisco, right? And Papa had a job building a fancy hotel across the street, and he saw you one day but was too shy to talk to you. But then he finally said hi to you?"

"He did. The hotel was finished and he was afraid he'd find a job somewhere else and never see me again."

"And he took you on a picnic?"

"Not for another month," Mama said. "He was very shy, and it wouldn't have been proper for me to go on a picnic right away with a strange young man."

"Did you think he was handsome?"

"I thought he was the most handsome man I had ever seen."

"But Tia didn't like him?"

"Oh, not at first. Somehow she knew that he hadn't been working since the hotel was finished, and so she saw him as an unemployed laborer who wasn't very clean."

"He wasn't clean?"

"Oh, he was clean enough, but your tia thought I should wait for a *gentleman* caller. Someone who owned more than one pair of boots and who didn't have patches on his trousers."

"And Tia finally liked him?"

"Only after he found more work and started visiting me wearing new shirts and trousers."

"That you made for him!" I loved that part of the story. "And tia Annabel never knew it was you that was making him nice clothes?"

"She still doesn't know. Your Papa would have bought new clothes, but he was trying to save up money to one day ask me to marry him. I thought I could help out a little by making him pants."

"And then she liked Papa?"

"Eventually. But she wasn't too happy about me moving away from the city and into the mountains."

"Why doesn't she like the mountains?"

"Because...because mountains aren't the city. Okay, no more talk, it's bedtime."

"Mama, were you ever a dancer?"

"What?...okay, young miss, it's definitely time to go to sleep."

I'd asked her that before, and she'd never answered me. I'd seen Mama when she didn't think anyone was watching slowly turning on her feet and move her arms so gracefully, she just had to have been a ballet dancer. She didn't know that I knew, but I had seen beautiful and fancy costumes in the trunk she kept locked. Costumes like real ballerinas wear. I knew Mama used to make clothes for dancers and actresses when she met Papa, but the outfits in her trunk, I just knew they were hers, that she had worn them. But she wouldn't tell me.

I fell asleep and dreamed of being a ballerina on a big stage. I was dancing, just me, in a command performance for the King of England, who looked like Papa. And Mama was there, too, sitting on an elephant. It was the most beautiful dance the audience had ever seen, but then K walked on stage with his doll and told me he was leaving on a whaling ship in the morning and needed my sword, and then a pack of wild dogs ran into the theater but no one panicked but me, and then I woke up to Jack barking ferociously, and even Chica was barking and growling.

"Mama? Mama, what's happening?"

She was on the porch in her nightgown, holding Jack by the scruff of the neck to keep him from running into the dark.

"June, stay in the bed!" she yelled back to me, but I hopped out and ran to the open door. I could hear all the animals making a ruckus, the chickens were squawking and flying around, London was whinnying, Becky was bellowing. There was a half-moon out, but was still too dark to see the stable. Jack took off when Mama couldn't hold him any longer.

"Jack, *no!*" I screamed.

"Jack!" yelled Mama. "June, you stay here." She stepped off the porch with her scatter-gun to follow Jack. He had gone after something, I didn't know if it was a bear or mountain lion or what it was until it roared.

"Mountain lion," I whispered. Jack must have found her and they blew up into a horrible sounding fight. The cougar was roaring and screaming, Jack barking and snapping, and Mama firing both barrels of her gun. It only lasted a a few seconds. Then there was a terrible silence. Even Chica, hiding in the corner, stopped growling to listen. I stood on the porch and shook, too scared to make any noise. I finally heard Jack running back to the house. He didn't even look at me as he flew up the steps, went inside, and hid under the bed. A couple more booms from Mama's gun really scared me. Mama's gun has a leather sleeve on the shoulder stock that holds four extra shells, I was quickly trying to do the math of how many shots she had left before she couldn't defend herself.

"Mama!"

"It's okay, June," she called. Through the dim light of the moon I saw her walking back to the house.

"Was it the mountain lion?"

"Yes."

"Did it get anyone?" I asked, though I didn't want to know the answer.

Mama walked up the steps and led me back into the house. I could feel her hand shaking, and I could smell the smoke from the four shells she had shot.

"No, I don't think so," she said, "I think it was after the calf."

"Tom? She got Tom?" I asked, ready to panic. I never should have named him!

"No, June, she didn't get him, Jack got there in time."

"Is Jack okay?" I fell to the floor and looked under the bed. Mama lit a lamp and knelt down with me to check on him. He wouldn't come out. I crawled under to see if he'd been bitten or scratched. He had dripped blood on the floor when he ran back in, but from what I could tell, he had only ripped open some of the stitches from before.

Mama was able to pull him out from under the bed, and cleaned his wound. She found only a couple fresh scratches from the cougar. We couldn't believe he didn't have more.

We didn't even try to go back to bed. It was almost morning anyway, and though Mama figured the cougar wouldn't make another try at the animals, we were too tense to sleep. Later in the morning I did fall asleep, and slept hard, without one nightmare.

"Hey, Sleepy, want to help me with the vegetables?" Mama asked, waking me up.

"For what?" I asked.

"Lunch."

"Lunch?" Boy, I had slept a long time, and could have slept the rest of the day and through the night. I didn't really feel like it, but I got up to help Mama cut vegetables. She had the look that said she wasn't going to let me stay in bed, no matter how sleepy I was.

Jack had spent the night under the bed and was still there. Mama said she got him to go outside to pee once and he immediately returned to his hiding spot. Mama had me slide under and push him while she pulled. He was still shaking. Mama put him on top of the bed and we hugged him and pet him and held him some more.

"Why does Jack get so scared with mountain lions, but not with other animals?" I asked.

"I don't know," she said. "Maybe because it's a huge cat. But Jack was very brave last night, chasing the cougar off, even though he was scared. That's bravery, you know, doing something you're afraid of, to protect the ones you love."

"That makes you brave too, Mama."

Chapter Seven

The next morning Mama was up early, walking the property with her scatter-gun and extra shells, hoping the mountain lion had decided better than to come prowling again. I was still a little afraid but wanted to be brave when Mama told me to go with her to feed the animals their breakfast. She made Jack come with us as well, saying Jack and I both needed to be outside and not be afraid.

Jack's leg was pretty stiff, but his wound wasn't bleeding and Mama thought it would do him good to walk around a bit to get the stiffness out. She tied a short rope to his collar so he would follow me. He really didn't want to be outside. I don't think he wanted to fight another mountain lion for a long time.

It had been hard for Jack to stay at the house that whole week and not be able to patrol around the property, so that's what we did first. I tried to get Chica to go with us, but she had already done her rounds that morning. Deciding all was safe, she wasn't about to leave her spot on the porch. I think that she thinks Papa built the whole porch just for her.

It didn't take Jack long to get over his fear of the mountain lion, and then it was hard to keep him from running.

"Don't let him run, yet, his leg's not ready!" called Mama.

He dragged me around to every tree until they were all sniffed and peed on. We sniffed around the chicken coop, then to the barn where he scared off a little raccoon. It was all I could do not to be pulled into the woods on my face when Jack tried to run after it.

We ended up at Becky and Tom's pen. Jack sniffed every spot of ground the mountain lion had touched. I was able to find a few of the cougar's prints in the dirt before Jack's nose erased them. She was *enormous*. *No* wonder Jack didn't want to see her again. Jack had finally tired himself out and spent a long time slurping water from the trough. I was glad he was worn out, because I sure was. I put my arms over the top rail of the pen and laid my head down. Jack's water-lapping was lulling me to sleep when I was jolted back awake by Jack bolting after something that rushed by, almost taking my arm with him.

"Jack, *no!*" I screamed, holding the rope with both hands and looking to see what it was that flew by us. I felt panicked for a second thinking the mountain lion snuck up on us, but then saw Fish the dog. *Fish.* I heard from the other side of the house, Mr. Bern's loud call, "Ahoy on board! Ahoy! Anybody home? Come see the whale we done harpooned!"

"Papa!" I yelled, and ran with Jack down to the house and around the corner. Papa was already dismounted from Whiskey and hugging Mama. I let go of Jack and leaped onto him, he grabbed me and threw me into his arms for a big hug.

"Mama shot a mountain lion! She shot a mountain lion!" I cried.

"What?" asked Papa.

"No," said Mama, "I shot *at* a mountain lion. Everything's fine."

My arms were squeezing Papa's neck tight. He smelled awful, but I didn't care, I was so glad that he was home.

"Were you frightened?" he asked me.

"Uh-huh," I said, "but Mama scared it away. She was very brave. And Jack, too."

"I'll bet you were just as brave," he said.

I looked over Papa's shoulder to Mr. Bern sitting on Willa, and saw only one pack-mule in tow when I know they had left with two. The mule was dragging a big Indian sled made of two long poles, one on each side of the pack-saddle. The tops of the poles were strapped across the mule's shoulders and chest with thick leather belts. The poles supported an old dirty-white canvas tarp tied across them. Lying on the tarp, tied down tight with rope, was a bear. A big—no—a *huge* brown bear. Dead.

My excitement at Papa's return quickly became sadness. I made Papa set me down, and walked slowly over to the sled.

"June," said Papa, "let's go inside, you don't need to see this now."

"Is that my bear?"

"Let's go inside, Sweetie," said Mama, walking up behind me and putting her hand on my shoulder.

"No, Mama, I want to see."

I couldn't believe the lifeless animal in front of me was actually the grizzly bear I had stumbled upon that first day, and then searched out again and watched eat a blueberry pie. I had only seen him those two times, but I had a clear picture of him in my mind—big and round and furry, a huge head with a long snout, his thick dark brown fur tipped with silver.

On his back, cinched tight to the sled, his front paws folded in front, he looked like he was taking a nap in a hammock. His head was turned away from me, so I walked around behind the sled to get a better look. His head was five times the size of my own, his eyes closed like he was dreaming. I looked closely at his face, and tried to remember him when he was alive. I barely knew him, but tears came to my eyes, and I felt terribly sad, like I'd lost a friend.

"So, it *is* a grizzly?" Mama asked, breaking the silence.

"She's a big'n, all right," said Mr. Bern. He may have said something more, but my eyes were on the bear.

"Is he a grizzly?" I asked through sniffles, repeating Mama's question.

"Size of a griz for sure," said Mr. Bern, "and just as mean. We thought she *was* a griz at first, but when we got to take a good look at her...well, looky here." He tried pointing out a few things that made that bear different from a grizzly, like the shape of the head and the size of the claws, but all I could see was a big pile of dusty fur. "But she still managed to kill one of my mules before we could bring her down."

"She?" I just realized he had been calling the bear *she*.

"You bet, the biggest female Black I've ever seen. She sure did give us a fight, too. You were lucky, Miss June, crossing her path. Very lucky indeed."

"She's not a grizzly?" I asked. "She's a black bear?"

"She's what's called a 'Cinnamon Black'," said Papa. "Easily

74

mistaken for a grizzly, especially one her size."

Papa walked up to me and gave me a hug. "Why don't you go with Mama and fix us all something to eat while I tend to the horses."

"Are you sure it's my bear, Papa?"

"It's your bear, June," he told me, sadness in his voice.

I wasn't much help to Mama making lunch, so she let me go up to my room to be alone. I lay on my bed holding tight to my pillow, wishing I had my Indian princess doll, trying not to cry. My poor bear. The girl bear I had thought was a boy, the black bear I thought was a grizzly. I was so sure the bear I saw in the woods was a grizzly bear. The one tied down behind Mr. Bern's mule was big, and brown, but...but he...she...wasn't a grizzly? There couldn't be *two* humongous bears on our little part of the mountain, could there be?

Papa came up to my room after unsaddling Whiskey and getting the mule and horses watered and fed. I rolled over and buried my face into the pillow. I didn't want him to see me crying, and he really did smell bad. I was surprised Mama had let him into the house, but I guess it wasn't an ordinary day.

"Are you okay, Bug?" he asked softly, sitting on the side of my bed. "Sounds like you and Mama had as big an adventure as I had. The mountain lion and all. I'm sorry I wasn't here."

"That's okay, Papa," I sniffled into my pillow.

"Mama says Jack really saved the day."

"M-hmm."

"Jack's a real good dog, huh?"

"M-hmm."

"Uh-huh...a real good dog."

Papa's always been good at comforting me when I would come to him crying with a bloody knee from falling onto a rock, or a black eye from running into a tree, but he was having trouble soothing my broken heart because of a dead bear. I was waiting for him to bring it up, though I wasn't sure I wanted to talk to him about it. Maybe he was afraid I blamed him for killing him...her, and I guess I did for a minute, but only for a minute. I knew he did it to protect Mama and me, even though we do pretty good at protecting ourselves.

After a couple minutes of neither of us saying anything, he started to get up from the bed.

"Is Mr. Bern still here?" I asked.

"Yep," said Papa. "He's taking a bath in the outside tub. Your mother wouldn't even let him on the porch until he bathed."

"But you haven't bathed."

"I snuck in," said Papa. I turned my head and looked up to him smiling. I knew he was joking. Nobody sneaks past Mama.

"Why don't you come down and join us for lunch?"

"I'm not hungry."

Papa sat back down on my bed, and put his hand gently on my back. "Are you upset about the bear?" he asked. I didn't answer. "Was that a dumb question?" I still didn't answer. "Do you want to talk about it?"

"That's not my bear, Papa," I said. Surprising him and myself, too, because I hadn't had much time to think about it, other than not believing my bear could really be dead. And that it was a girl. And that it wasn't a grizzly after all.

"I'm sorry, June," he said. "I really am. But we had to do it. The bear was too big, and too close to the house. He was a danger to you and Mama, and to all the animals."

"She," I corrected him.

"She, that's right," said Papa.

"*My* bear is a he."

"Bug...listen. I know you're sad. I know you didn't want us to kill the bear, but this wasn't some orphaned bear cub that you could play with. This was more like an angry mama bear protecting her cub. What do we always tell you is the most dangerous animal on the mountain?"

"A mama cougar," I said.

"A mama bear, also. The bear we killed was as mean as a mama bear."

"Did she have cubs?" I asked.

"No, she didn't have cubs."

"How can you be sure she's my bear?"

"It *is* your bear, June. I'm sorry. Bern and I tracked her from the very spot where we all had our run-in last week. She wasn't hard to find. Fish picked up her trail and pretty much led us right to her. I know you thought it was a grizzly bear you saw, but this one, she's very big, she's brown, her fur's matted and grizzled gray like a grizzly bear's because of her age. She's probably twenty years old. She may have even been a little *touched*, is why she acted so much like a grizzly. We already had three slugs in her when she charged us and brought down Mr. Bern's mule, who happened to be between us and the bear. It could have been me she attacked.

"I know you felt some kind of kinship with the bear, for whatever reason, but you're also very lucky to be alive right now. Bears are not cute, cuddly little stuffed animals. They are big beasts who can, and do, kill people. They can be just as dangerous as a mountain lion. This bear would have killed you, Bug. And you saw that it's *not* a grizzly we brought in. Just a big brown-colored black bear. We did kill the bear that you saw, the bear that could have attacked and killed you. So no more talk about this being the wrong bear, or that there's still a grizzly out there somewhere, because there's not. Okay?"

I didn't say anything, just buried my face in my pillow again and really started to cry. Papa had said his piece. He kissed the back of my head before climbing back down the stairs, and hopefully into a bath.

I wasn't sure what to think. Papa did make sense. A bear that size had to be the same one I'd come to think of as my grizzly bear. There couldn't be more than one huge brown bear in these woods. We would often see bears in our woods, but they're all much smaller and mostly black. And Fish tracked it from the same spot that I saw him last. Fish is crazy but he's still a dog, and a good tracker according to Mr. Bern. But...the one they killed didn't look exactly the same as before, in the woods. Before, I thought it had silverish tips to his fur. Maybe I was wrong. Maybe I just thought I saw silverish hair cause that's what a grizzly bear looks like and I wanted to say I saw a grizzly bear. Maybe I'm just one of the women who thinks every bear she sees is a grizzly, and every bobcat she sees is a mountain lion. Maybe the bear they killed just looked different because it was dead and strapped tight to a sled.

It was my fault the bear was dead, but like Papa said, it could have killed me, or killed someone else like it killed Mr. Bern's mule. Maybe it was better for all of us that he's dead. Or *she's* dead. Didn't look like a she.

Papa smiled when he came in from bathing to see me in the kitchen with Mama fixing up a big meal.

"What's for lunch?" he asked.

Mr. Bern, who was eating from a bowl of strawberries like they were candy, said, "You done missed lunch, son. Shoulda bathed quicker...like me."

"We're making *supper* now, Papa," I said, as he came up between Mama and me, hugging us both.

We had a great big supper that night; plump chicken and gravy, hot dumplings with butter and molasses, beans with chunks of bacon, strawberries and apple pie for desert. I could have stayed in my room crying all day, maybe even all week, but what I really wanted was for life to be normal again, to have Papa home and hugging me, and all of us sitting down to a big family feast with our favorite guest. The men didn't mention the bear hunt, and we didn't ask them about it. Mama and I told them all about our week, just the women at home, fighting off mountain lions. I was sad for the bear, of course, but was ready for the whole thing to be over.

* * * *

Papa was up early and helped me feed the animals and collect eggs, which he hadn't done for a long time because that had been my job since I was six. He was very impressed with my care-taking of the animals, and the things I did a little different from how he taught me. Like the different sized buckets I used for the different animals so I knew exactly how much feed to give them. I thought of that all by myself.

I showed him where the cougar snuck into the animal pens and where she ran off after tussling with Jack and Mama.

"That's part of life on the mountain," Papa said. "There's dangers up here, sure. But you know what?"

"What?"

"I'd rather deal with bears and mountain lions any time than deal with the dangers in the city," he said.

"Like what?" I was imagining a dark, sooty city with monsters and huge rats behind every corner, and poison arrows shooting out from open windows.

"Oh, just different dangers," he said. "I'll tell you about them when you're older."

"I thought you lived in the city when you met Mama," I said.

"I did. That's why I know about the dangers. Let's go see if Mama needs any help with breakfast."

We all sat down for a big breakfast before Papa left for the lumber mill. I took Jack and a big stack of books with me to the boulder on the other side of our little creek to catch up on my reading and enjoy the short time left before going back to school. I kept a look out for the mountain lion, though I knew Jack would smell her if she came anywhere near.

I had my fishing pole and quickly caught two good-sized brook trout. I kept them cooling in the creek so I could take them home for supper, then stopped fishing for the day because I had too much reading to do and couldn't be bothered by catching any more fish.

Chapter Eight

Over the next couple of weeks Mr. Bern became quite the celebrity. He had taken the bear to town to have it weighed and even photographed. Turned out it *was* the biggest black bear ever taken in the county, and the biggest female taken in all of Northern California, maybe even the whole state, maybe even the whole country! She was a big'n for sure. Papa said she weighed nearly five-hundred pounds, which is unheard of for a female black bear. Even people in town thought it was a grizzly it was so big, or at least half-grizzly.

So Mr. Bern was famous now. "You should be famous too, Papa," I told him at supper.

"Oh, I'm not one for accolades, Bug," he told me, "and it was Mr. Bern's gear we were using, and he did lose a good mule. So any riches that come from this should rightly go to him." After that first day back, Papa hadn't seemed excited at all about the bear they had killed, hadn't wanted to even talk about it. I wasn't happy about my bear being killed, but I had to admit the whole thing was exciting and I was very proud of Papa risking his life and being such a good hunter, which is a big deal on the ridge. More than one neighbor stopped by the house and thanked Papa for killing the bear that had been tormenting their goats and mules and cows. Since the bear was killed, it was only mountain lions folks had to watch out for.

"But there is someone in this family who may be getting a *little* famous from all this bear business," Mama said. "Seems the newspaper wants to talk to a certain little girl that first saw the record breaking bear and... *Escaped with her life*."

"Talk to *me*? Will I be famous too?"

"How about just a little famous," Papa said. "You'll have a great story to tell your class when school starts back up, and a newspaper to prove it. But after that, hopefully, we can put all this bear business behind us. I'm tired of it already."

Me famous? I had to to tell K right away. I'd never been in the newspaper before, I'd never been famous before. I wondered, would they do a drawing of me so everyone who read it would recognize me? Or maybe even do a photograph of me with my sword out like I was fighting off the huge crazy bear like Davy Crockett. That was in one of my books. "May I be excused?" I asked, and put my plate in the sink to wash later, and ran up the ladder to my room to find the story of Davy Crockett fighting bears with just his bare hands and a little knife.

I was more than excited the rest of the day, and couldn't go to sleep that night. I was going to be *famous*. Even a little famous like Papa said would be wonderful. But he still didn't seem excited about it. Why?

Like I said, I couldn't sleep that night, which turned out to be good, because I was still awake when Mama and Papa were on the porch talking into the late night. I think they waited extra long to make sure I was asleep. Mama had been wondering, like I had, what was bothering Papa. He wasn't happy about the bear they had killed, and wanted none of the attention that was being given to Mr. Bern. He wasn't excited about me being in the newspaper, and had been in a bad mood the past few days, even yelling at me a couple of times about the littlest things, which he never did. They were on the porch whispering. I couldn't hear a thing. So I very slowly climbed down my steps, and quietly moved to the open window near where they were sitting. Our house was still pretty new and built real good, but if I wasn't so good at sneaking I'm sure they would have been alerted by at least a few creaking boards.

"Something's been weighing heavy on my mind, Sonia," he whispered. "Maybe it's nothing...I'm sure it's nothing. I'm sure I'm wrong."

"What is it?" asked Mama.

"Well... I'm not convinced that we got the right bear."

My jaw dropped.

"What?" asked Mama.

"I think we got the wrong bear. And more than that, I've been thinking that the bear June saw *was* a grizzly."

"What?" repeated Mama. I think *her* jaw dropped this time. "But it *was* the right bear, you said you tracked it from the spot where you and June had the run-in, and you said it was the same bear you had seen, and there can't be another bear that size around here."

"I know, I know. But something about the bear me and Bern

killed just doesn't look the same. I know I didn't get a good look at the one I shot at before, but I did see it for a second. And it looked different." Papa moved the lantern to the little table between them, then took a folded paper from his vest pocket, slowly unfolded it and straightened it flat on the table top. "This isn't the only thing, but look. I made a rubbing from one of the trees near where I shot at it before, the first time. The bear had made some good scratches on it, the biggest and deepest scratches I've ever seen, just look how big. Now look here, see the punctures in the paper, that's from the bear we killed. I pressed the front paw of the bear onto the paper to trace around it, kind of a souvenir to show how big the bear's paw was, and I couldn't line up the claws with the scratches. Look, it's not even close to being big enough. I pressed the claws through the paper, even spreading them out as far as they would go, farther than what I would guess would be natural for the bear when they scratch a tree. And look at the one here, the third hole. See where the hole is, farther down? The claw was much shorter than the others, probably broke off early in the season and she'd been growing it back. But the scratching doesn't show a smaller claw."

"But..." Mama wasn't sure what to say.

"And that's not all," Papa continued, taking out another folded piece of paper and straightened it. "Look at Bug's drawing of the bear, see here? Look at the hump she drew over the bear's shoulders. Black bears don't have that hump. Only brown bears have that hump. Grizzly bears."

"But that's just a drawing from a little girl, you can't go by that."

"Wait here," whispered Papa. He stood up, and lucky for me it was dark in the house because he walked right through the open door, tripping over Chica who was laying in the doorway. "Chica! Dang dog!" he breathed through his teeth. I saw him look up at my loft to see if the noise had woke me, then tiptoed over to my little table in the corner where I keep my drawings and writings. He looked up at my loft again to make sure I was asleep, then picked up some of my drawings, and tiptoed back out, passing right by me again in the dark.

"Look, Sonia," he said, and went through some of the drawings, picking out a few to show Mama. "These are her older drawings of bears. I know they are just children's drawings, but look, she draws a smooth back, flat shoulders, and no claws on the feet. Only with the grizzly bear does she draw the hump and long claws."

"But still," Mama said, "you got the bear. There hasn't been any livestock taken since then, we haven't seen any signs of another big bear, *any* bear, much less a grizzly. Why hasn't there been more livestock taken if it's not the right bear? It *has* to be the bear."

Papa was quiet for a minute. "I'm sure you're right," he finally said.

"Have you mentioned any of this to Bern? What does he think?"

"He was there when I put the bear's paw onto the paper. He saw the difference, but just brushed it aside because he was so happy about the kill. He was just as happy that it wasn't *a* grizzly we shot. He knew the female would be *some* sort of record. And I was caught up in the moment as well, thought I must have done the rubbings wrong or something. I didn't have a doubt at the time it was the right bear. Wasn't until after we got back did I start

86

thinking about it."

Wow. I could not believe what I just heard. I could have stood there all night listening, but Papa seemed to be done talking and blew out the lantern.

"Let's not mention any of this to June, agreed?" he said. "Or anyone else for that matter. As far as anyone else is concerned, we got the right bear."

I made it quickly, quietly back up the ladder to my room just as Mama and Papa walked back into the house. They got undressed and went right to bed. There was no sleeping for me that night, and I didn't hear Papa snore even once, so I think he was awake all night too.

I think I had slept only two minutes all night when Mama was getting me up for chores. I knew the animals had to eat, but couldn't they sleep late once in awhile? I didn't want to be too much of a grump or Mama would have suspected I had been up late listening to them again. And boy, last night, what I heard...I still couldn't believe it. My bear was still alive! I should have been more happy than I was, but I had accepted that he was dead and that it was the best for everyone. Now he's not dead? But the livestock hadn't been picked on, and no one else had seen him. Maybe my bear moved on to another part of the mountain, maybe Papa did shoot him that day and he went off wounded to die. Maybe the big brown-colored black bear Papa and Mr. Bern killed was the one that was taking people's goats in the middle of the night. Maybe me and now Papa were both wrong, and the bear I thought was a grizzly really wasn't, and was in fact the same bear that they killed. Lots and lots of maybes.

Mama didn't let on, or say anything to me about what Papa had told her the night before. She looked pretty sleepy herself. I guess none of us slept much.

I was pretty sure I needed to go out into the woods and try to see my bear again, if he was still alive. I say pretty sure, because I promised I wouldn't go looking for him again, and I would be in *huge* trouble if they found out. But as far as anyone really knew, the bear Papa and Mr. Bern killed *was* my bear. They hadn't told me otherwise.

Whether my bear was dead or not, it was clear Mama wasn't letting me go into the woods for any reason. She had me busy with lots of added chores, had me help her cut cloth for dresses, so many dresses we couldn't sell or wear them in a year's time. She had all my time filled up, and it was just a few more days until school started again. We hadn't talked about the bear, any bear, which would have been very strange had I not overheard everything Papa told Mama that night.

She finally let me go to K's house, only after begging and pleading with her to let me go, and promising not to leave the path, go straight there and straight back. By that time I was crazy with wondering about my grizzly, if he was okay, if he was still around, and if he even existed. But I promised to stay on the path to K's, and I was just happy to be out of the house. Jack seemed to enjoy it too, because the whole time I was confined to the property, so was Jack. His leg was all healed, and he ran and ran, disappearing into bushes on my right, then shooting across the path to vanish into trees to my left. Dogs sure know how to have fun in the woods. It wasn't long before he spooked a couple of rabbits from their home in the brush. They bounded onto the trail, heading right toward me. Stopping suddenly when they saw me standing there, they turned and hopped together back up the trail. Jack came out of the bushes beside me, excited and happy, and sat down to watch the rabbits disappearing over a small rise.

"What kind of rabbit-dog are you?" I said. "Let's get 'em!" And off he went, with me trying to keep up. It's pretty fun chasing rabbits. He gave up the chase after another sprint, giving me a chance to catch up with him, but then smelled something else and lit into the woods, again followed by me. I think Jack wanted to find every critter on Grizzly Ridge and give them all a little chase.

It wasn't too long before we burst from the forest onto the main road. Not exactly burst, I guess. Jack was waiting for me, his long tongue panting, as I pulled my tired 'ol legs along. It had been awhile for both of us since we last scampered so hard. I was surprised we had made it to the road so fast, and alarmed that we had made it to the road at all. We were supposed to be on our way to K's house. "*No detours,*" Mama had growled. I didn't mean to take a detour, but "Jack took off into the woods and I had to follow him. I didn't want him to get lost." Mama would never buy that.

"C'mon, Jack, let's get to K's. *No more detours,*" I growled like Mama.

I started walking down the main road, which I knew would hit the little road that would take us to K's. Jack fell in beside me and I noticed he was limping.

"Oh, Jack. I told you not to chase the rabbits, you're leg's not ready."

I squatted down, checked where he had his stitches, and rubbed his leg. He was okay, just needed a little rest. We both did. I remembered the last time I was on the main road by myself, the day of my mission to find the grizzly bear. It seemed so long ago. Now here I was again, not far from where I found him. I listened as hard as I could and studied the woods all around us. I even sniffed the air like Jack was doing. If my grizzly was alive and close by, I couldn't smell him.

By that time I didn't know if I even wanted to visit K. We would always end up in an argument over what to play, and if I didn't let him have his way, he would pout. He was a year older than me, for Pete's sake, and he'd still pout. But he was my best friend, and we were already half-way there. "C'mon, Jack," I said, and we headed down the road to K's. We would have made it there, too, if I hadn't noticed something beside the road. The sad little apple tree by the trail leading to Elk Creek. I had thought the trail to be much farther in the other direction, maybe I didn't know the ridge as well as I had bragged. The little tree had tiny apple buds growing on a few of it's skinny branches. Still looked pitiful, but it was trying. Of course, my mind wasn't on the little tree, but on the trail. I hadn't planned on finding the trail again, honestly. I also hadn't planned on doing what I was about to do— check out that little clearing by the creek.

The stream was even lower than the last time, and very quiet. I held on tight to Jack's neck as we snuck up to the stream. I knew it was very unlikely that my bear would be there, he may not even be alive anymore. At the least, he had been scared away to another part of the mountain. But I was still a little disappointed. I turned loose of Jack and we splashed across Elk Creek to the familiar little clearing.

When Papa was with Mr. Bern tracking the black bear, he had retrieved his bedroll and lumberman's bag I had left behind on my mission, but didn't bring back my sword, or my Indian princess doll. I hadn't wanted to ask about them. Maybe he forgot them, or didn't think I deserved having them. I found Sarah, my doll, under a bush, dirty and damp with a hole torn into her tummy where it looked like a mouse or squirrel pulled out her wool stuffing. My sword was leaning against a tree. It looked to be the tree with claw scratches that Papa made his rubbing from. I put my hand up to the ripped up bark, trying to spread my fingers as wide as the markings. Big, big bear. Where are you?

I sure missed my sword, but thought it best to leave it. Maybe I *didn't* deserve it. Plus, if Mama or Papa saw it back at the house, they would know I was out where I wasn't supposed to be, again. I would have to leave the sword, but I was taking Sarah home with me. We never did make it to K's.

Chapter Nine

Summer was over, the vacation part anyway. The couple months kids get off to help their families with harvesting, hunting, sawing down trees and splitting firewood, setting traps and making moonshine. Although the kids who make moonshine don't go to school, usually. My school on the ridge was pretty new, only a few years old. Before that, Mrs Hicks, the teacher, taught school at the church. Only a few kids ever went to school anyway, but Mrs. Hicks thought that a real school building would bring more kids in to learn. It did a little, but only after Mr. Hicks agreed to drive a wagon around and pick up a lot of the kids, then return them home after school. We live close enough to school that we could walk to it, or rather Mama walked with me and K. But now, K and I were going to be old enough to walk by ourselves.

I loved my teacher, Mrs. Hicks, more than I loved school, actually, though she never believed the books I was reading, that I was really reading and understanding them. Some of them, of course, I had a hard time understanding everything, but I skipped over the hard parts to the parts that I liked. My favorite book was *The Call of the Wild*, by Jack London, even though I got scared when I got to the dog-fighting parts. For a starting-school present, Mama and Papa gave me *White Fang*, also by Jack London. They special ordered it all the way from San Francisco. I had just started reading it, and although I didn't like the beginning when the wolves attack the sled dogs, it could be my new favorite book. Jack London's from San Francisco, you know.

K and I were the youngest at my school, of about twelve kids, even with Mr. Hicks's coach service. Sometimes more, sometimes less. Once a brother and sister a little older than me came for one day. We had never seen them before, and never saw them again. I guess their family was just passing through, which was sad, because the girl seemed nice and she smiled at me. Often I wished I had a friend my own age that was a girl, that I could play dress-up with and play dolls with. K's my best friend, but he wasn't going to want to play dolls forever. Even though he tended to drive me crazy, he did make me laugh, he was fun to play with most of the time, he did let me boss him some, and he could make designs in the dirt when he peed, which he was very proud of.

The first week of school was pretty boring, and there wasn't even one new kid. Just the same old ones, and I was the only one who actually read anything away from school. The first week Mrs. Hicks spent most of our days reteaching basic stuff and trying to get the older kids to pay attention. The only interesting thing was K getting punched. That happened about twice a week the previous year, so I guessed the new year would be the same. K had always gotten picked on by the older boys, and they didn't even know about his dolls. But they remembered him getting poison oaked at the end of last year, so of course they chased him with twigs of the stuff. It didn't even have to be real poison oak to scare K, they could just say it was poison oak. The older kids didn't want to touch it either.

I mostly sat by myself and read. I finished *White Fang*, and it was officially my new favorite book except for the beginning, and I also brought *Huckleberry Finn,* by Mark Twain to read in school, which Mrs. Hicks rolled her eyes at. No kid in my school could read that. It was very hard to read, the words were small and the characters talked funny, but I was reading it anyway, as best I could.

Now that I think about it, I probably learned more when I wasn't in school. Mama and Papa both love to read, books on all kinds of different subjects. Mama loves poetry and plays and reads to me from William Shakespeare, and we've even acted out whole scenes for Papa. And Papa loves big, long novels and books on science and history. They both teach me things I've never heard Mrs. Hicks teaching even the oldest kids. Now that I think about it, the only thing I liked about school was Mrs. Hicks being so nice to me, and I got to wear pretty dresses.

At the end of the week, on Papa's day off from the mill, we all went to town for a treat and so Mama could take to the general store all the dresses I had helped her make.

"Let's not mention to anyone in town about still thinking there's a grizzly bear loose, okay, Bug?" Papa told me. "Because there's not."

"Okay, I won't," I said. I really *did* start something the last time I blurted out about the grizzly. Now, I didn't want anyone knowing about him. He was my secret, and, until I found him again, I couldn't be sure myself that he was even alive.

It was at the General that we saw Mr. Bern again. For someone who says he hates towns, he sure seemed to spend a lot of time there. He was basking in the glow of his bear-hunter fame, and showed us a fancy paper that made it official that his was the biggest female black bear ever killed in the state of California. That *was* pretty amazing, and it was official. But was it my bear? I still didn't believe it, but I wasn't sure. Mr. Bern sure was happy, though. He had just gotten a shave at the barber, and smelled of expensive after-shave stuff.

"And looky here, Miss June Bug, a fine lady such as yourself will appreciate this." Mr. Bern held out one of his big feet, his old boot shined and polished. "A twenty cent shine for a two cent pair of boots. Think me a gentleman now? Before you answer, I must confess these boots to be older than you are."

"Yes sir," I smiled.

Mr. Bern had something for me, too. He went to his saddlebag on Willa, stepping carefully so not to shuffle too much dirt and dust on his shiny boots, and came back with a necklace made of beads and three claws from the bear he and Papa killed. His wife Patty—I've never known if she's really his wife but people call her that—made it special for me. It was beautiful, a thin leather string with red and yellow and blue wooden beads and three bear claws wrapped tight at the top with red cotton twine coated with a thin layer of wax.

We spent the morning in town and had a good lunch at the cafe near the new hotel. I never mentioned my grizzly bear once to anyone, though a lot of people saw my bear-claw necklace and asked me about the big bear Papa and Mr. Bern took down. A man from the newspaper, who introduced himself as John Phillips, even stopped by during our lunch and asked me about the bear. I told him the story, and finished by saying I was very proud of my papa and was glad there's no more big bears on the mountain to kill people's goats and cows. I was a whole lot less excited about being in the newspaper than I was before.

I was very good about keeping my grizzly bear a secret, but apparently Papa found it difficult. I found out later that he and Mr. Bern had a long conversation about Papa's concerns that there's still a grizzly on the mountain. But since we hadn't seen him—if he even existed—they figured he would have moved on up the mountain or someplace else. I think the last bear hunt took a lot out of poor Mr. Bern, so he wasn't too enthusiastic about another hunt for a while, and he still believed they had killed the right bear anyway.

Apparently Mr. Bern had a hard time keeping it a secret, too, because *apparently*, over the next couple weeks or so, he got to telling people, and laughing about, how the little girl that first saw the bear was convinced they got the wrong one, and that she thought there was still a grizzly on the mountain. Most people just laughed along with him, and didn't think much of it, but most people also couldn't keep anything to themselves, so the little chuckle about the little girl who sees big grizzly bears got passed around and finally made it to a man who *did* think something of it. Of course I didn't know that yet.

After seeing Mr. Bern, and talking with the newspaper man, and especially because of what I'd overheard Papa saying, I knew I had to keep looking for my bear, my grizzly bear. Just to see him again. I knew I had to be realistic, though. Meaning I probably would *never* see him again. Also, he was probably a she and she'd been killed already. But being a kid, how realistic could I be? Should I be? Not very.

* * * *

The following day I didn't have school, so I asked to go to K's house with Jack. Mama sent me with one blackberry and one apple pie to give to K's mama, wrapped tight in oilcloth, then wrapped in twine with a knotted loop so I could carry them, and they'd stay in one piece hopefully if I didn't drop them too many times. I grabbed my copy of *Tom Sawyer* and hit the trail. I told Mama that K had trouble reading a book so advanced, but that Tom could teach him a thing or two about mischief. K was a boy, he needed to be more mischievous. I was going to read it to him.

I didn't quite make it to K's house. I can't say that I had no intention of going there, it was just that Jack saw another rabbit on the trail and we somehow ended up at Elk Creek. It wouldn't be long until the Fall rains filled the creek to it's banks, but that late Summer day the water was down to a narrow ribbon winding through the wide, rocky creek-bed. I hopped across it, no splashes, to the familiar little clearing on the other side.

Even though the encounter with the bear at that spot had been scary, with Papa shooting and Jack fighting, I found it peaceful, and wanted to have good memories of the place. I untied and unwrapped the blackberry pie. Sharing it with Jack while I read from a randomly selected page of my book, we ate close to half of the pie, washing it down with water from the creek. I had plenty of time to still visit with K, and still a pie and a half to give to his mama. I did the best I could to re-tie the bundle, and thought I had it good enough to carry, but not two steps to the creek, the apple pie slipped out of the knot and dropped onto it's side. "Dang it," I cursed, seeing a bulge under the oilcloth, knowing the one uneaten pie was ruined. At least too ruined to present to K's mama as a gift.

I was pressing the bulge back into the pan when I heard a low grumble from Jack. He was shaking, and the hair on his back, from behind his ears to his tail, was standing near straight up. I quickly grabbed his collar. Before looking up, I knew I was right, that the bear Papa killed wasn't my grizzly. *My* grizzly was standing up on his back legs at the opposite side of the clearing. No doubt about it, he was a grizzly. His head was *huge*, pretty much everything about him was huge, and he looked to be over ten feet tall. He was the biggest *anything* I'd ever seen before. His fur was fluffy with the ends of his hair a light silver. I couldn't really see if he had a hump over his shoulder, but imagine he did. I say he, but I still didn't know if he was a he or not. Looked like a he.

I picked up the half-eaten, cloth-wrapped, blackberry pie and flung it to him. I remembered him liking blueberry pie, so, as long as he wasn't particular about his pies, he'd be happy with blackberry, and wouldn't eat me or Jack, hopefully. It was a pretty good throw, not landing too far from him. The pie had burst from the oilcloth when it hit the ground, blobbing onto the grass at the grizzly's feet. He sniffed loudly at the crust and filling as I backed us up a few steps, ready to run, which I was told never to do, but I was gonna do it anyway.

He gently licked at it a couple of times, but didn't seem interested. He stepped over the broken pie toward us, grumbling and lolling his head back and forth. Jack finally started barking. I finally got scared. Still holding Jack and intending to flee, I took a quick step toward the coming bear, picked up the apple pie, threw it at him, turned Jack and ran us right into the thickest bush I had ever come across on our ridge. I then remembered it to be the same bush I backed myself into the last time I had seen the bear. Papa had saved me then. Jack stopped barking, but with my fingers tight on his collar, I could feel him shaking. I slowly turned my head, fully expecting the last thing I would see in the world would be the bear's enormous teeth.

He wasn't right behind us, however, he had opened the oilcloth and was lapping up the apple pie filling with a tongue as long as our mule's.

My grizzly bear loved apple pie! Or at least preferred it to blackberry pie.

We stood and watched the bear finish. It was exactly like the last time I was with him at the clearing—standing, watching the monster-beast eating a pie, when I should be tiptoeing away to safety. I looked to the other side of the creek, half expecting Papa to again appear with his rifle. I've always tended to repeat my mistakes, but for some reason, they seemed to work out better the second time.

He ate the pie a lot slower than I thought a grizzly bear would. Jack would never eat it that slow, and he's just a dog. He then lay down and started rolling in the grass. I laughed out loud, forgetting he still could get up and come after us. I also forgot about keeping hold of Jack, and suddenly Jack leaped at the bear. "Jack!" I yelled, terrified the bear would kill him. But Jack stopped short and watched for a second, then crouched down and hopped back up. Jack wanted to play with the grizzly! But he startled the bear, who maybe remembered Jack from the last awful encounter, and the bear rolled back up, his ears laid back, popped his jaw together a couple times, and looked like he might charge. But he didn't, he just gave a grunt, turned and disappeared into the bushes. Wow. I picked up my book, collected the pie pans, and walked to K's house.

So my bear was alive. And he didn't kill and eat us. He didn't seem mean. But I couldn't tell anyone, or Mr. Bern and Papa would go after him again and Papa was already thinking my bear was still alive. I squatted down on the trail, looked Jack right in the eyes, and said, "This is our secret, okay? We can't tell anyone about the bear, okay? Not Mama or Papa, K, or your friend Fish especially." Jack promised not to tell, and we made it K's without incident, and returned home before supper. I hoped my mama wouldn't ask K's mama how she liked the pies.

* * * *

The weeks went by, and it was a wonderful fall. School was

school, everyone thought I should like school more than I did, but most days were just Mrs. Hicks breaking up fights and trying to teach the older kids how to read the simplest words. She always had a hard time keeping everyone's attention. Papa said when he was a boy in school, the teacher was a man, and any kid that spoke without being spoken to first would get the palms of their hands smacked with a thick ruler, or their backsides blistered with a hickory stick that the teacher had made special just for that purpose. Every kid was terrified of the teacher, so they all paid attention. No one was terrified of Mrs. Hicks. I thought of bringing her a hickory stick. K would've still gotten punched.

I spent a lot of time outside reading. I had a new Jack London book called *The Sea-Wolf*, which I had been pestering Mama and Papa for because I thought it was about a wolf that lived by the sea. It was actually a story about a seal-hunting ship with a bunch of rude men that cursed a lot. I tried to read it but wasn't relating too well to the characters. I didn't know why it couldn't have been about a wolf that lived by the sea. I planned on writing that book myself.

The best part of the fall, however, just happened to be my grizzly bear. I would hike out into the woods with Jack about once or twice a week and most times would find him. I couldn't always swipe an apple pie so sometimes I'd just bring apples, which we had a lot of from our tiny orchard. He wasn't always along Elk Creek, sometimes we'd hear him grumbling behind a tree along the trail. Sometimes he would find us—I'd hear teeth clicking, Jack would start tail wagging, I'd turn around and there he'd be. I would toss him an apple, and we'd sit down and read. I did the reading, of course, Jack and the grizzly did the listening. He never stayed long with us, and I never tried to touch him or pet him. I knew he wasn't a pet. It was enough just to be near him, knowing I was probably the only girl in the world who could stand that close to a grizzly bear without screaming or being eaten. And knowing there were hardly any grizzlies left anymore, maybe none in all of California, I thought he was probably lonely and liked our company. I sure *hoped* he liked our company and wouldn't decide he'd rather have a little girl for a snack than half of an apple pie.

I so loved my hikes in the woods with Jack. I was always very careful because there were still a lot of dangers for a young girl alone, but visiting my bear made me feel happy and wonderful. It's what I looked forward to every week and I wanted to see him as many times as I could before the winter snow came.

Then Alan Kelly showed up at the house and everything changed.

Chapter Ten

I was returning home with Jack after *taking pies to K's mama*, which meant I had just visited my bear. He was getting real good at finding me on the trail, and even surprised me that time because he was so close to our house. I still never tried to pet him, and didn't know what he'd do if I did, but he let Jack come up to him and he would playfully swat and knock Jack around, with Jack growling and play-biting him.

I was in a wonderful mood skipping down the trail to the house when I saw them. I didn't know what to make of all the horses and men out by the barn. Mama hadn't said anything about company, and anyway, I didn't recognize any of them. They had what looked to be a big wagon with a cage on top, and a whole pack of a dozen or so hound dogs barking and jumping around, so of course Jack took off before I could grab him. The dogs were all tied to their wagon with leather rope and chains which is the only reason they didn't attack and kill Jack, because they sure wanted to. One of the men jumped into the middle of the angry barking pack and began cursing and hitting the dogs with a big black stick to get them to settle down. They wouldn't settle down for nothing, mostly because Jack was barking to beat all and was jumping at them and taunting them, getting them worked up into a frenzy. It probably didn't help that he smelled like a grizzly bear.

I was screaming and running as fast as I could go, knowing those dogs could break loose and kill Jack at any moment. The man stepped between the hound dogs and Jack and yelled at me to *get my dog out of there or he'd shoot him himself.*

I frantically tried to grab Jack but couldn't get hold of him because he didn't want to be gotten ahold of. I was screaming and crying and was terrified of the dogs barking and the men yelling and afraid they'd shoot Jack if I didn't collar him. I didn't even hear Mama and the fury she was giving them all as she grabbed me and Jack both and ran us into the house, past Chica who had decided to stay on the porch to bark.

"*Are you okay*?" she asked me a couple of times, finally calming me down from my sobbing which couldn't have been easy because I saw in her eyes a fire that would have scared me more than any pack of dogs if the fire had been meant for me. But it wasn't, it was meant for those men. She turned from me and flew out of the door, closing it tight behind her. I saw her through the window having strong words with a man on the porch, before she continued down the steps and out of sight. That man, I recognized, was John Phillips, the newspaper man who had asked me questions. And standing next to Mr. Phillips was a man I hadn't seen before, a tall man dressed very sharply. Oh, and Mama had her scatter-gun.

I was trembling-scared, holding tight to Jack's neck, waiting for the sound of Mama's gun, wondering if she was going to shoot the hound dogs, or the mean man, or all of the men and their horses too. I sat listening for what seemed forever. Mama was yelling and the men were yelling back and I couldn't make out what they were saying, but it sounded awful, and then I remembered seeing guns with the men. They all had guns! There was going to be a big gunfight and Mama was going to be killed! I jumped up screaming, flew crying out the door expecting to see the absolute worst scene imaginable and hoping to somehow stop it. Before the tears completely overwhelmed my eyes, I saw she had her gun pointed at the crowd of men, some of them hollering "Calm down," waving their arms and pointing at her. I ran straight to Mama and right smack into her, slamming my face hard on her backside, knocking me flat on my back, and near knocking me out cold. That stopped my crying, pretty much stopped everything. Through my tears I tried to see what it was I ran into. Couldn't have been Mama, I thought, she's soft. I wiped and fluttered my eyes, looked up to a circle of giant men standing above me, silent and staring down with shocked looks on their faces. Where was Mama?

"Oh, June." Mama knelt down and picked me up, still holding the scatter-gun, "I told you to stay inside." I looked over at my audience, all quiet and big-eyed and slack-jawed. I held tight to Mama's neck as she scolded the men some more, this time much more quiet and a little more controlled. I didn't hear the men say anything back. I looked up to see the strange well-dressed man closing in on us and I screamed.

Mama spun around with her scatter-gun pointed at the fancy man, who was holding up a handkerchief and nervously saying, "Ma'am, ma'am... your daughter's nose."

My nose was bleeding down my face and dripping all over the back of Mama's blouse. Mama accepted the handkerchief—it was too fancy to call it a 'hanky'—and wiped my face, telling me to hold it tight under my nose.

Mama cleaned me up inside the house. Luckily, I had slammed the door on Jack when I ran screaming to Mama, keeping him inside, or the fight that was ending would have surely started up again. I still had the man's fancy handkerchief under my nose, was watching Mama watching the men outside leaving. Finally, I asked her, "Mama, are those men really going after my bear?" Even though I had been panicked nearly the whole time they were there, I did manage to hear some of what Mama and them were yelling at each other about.

"That's what they said," she told me.

"Why were they here?"

"They wanted to know where it was you had seen the bear, and where your father and Mr. Bern had shot the female."

"But Papa killed the bear that I saw. The bear's dead."

Mama turned from the window and stared me in the eyes, "That's what I told them, that the bear you saw is dead and that it wasn't a grizzly." She kept staring at me, she was acting kinda strange. "That was the truth, wasn't it?"

"Uh-huh."

"That the bear you saw is dead and that it wasn't a grizzly bear. That the bear you saw is the same bear that Papa killed." Mama's voice was rising. "That there never was a grizzly bear on our mountain, that you were wrong about seeing a grizzly bear and just have too much of an imagination from reading too many books!"

Mama was crying and sat down in the chair across from me. "That every bear a little girl sees is a...she thinks is a...grizzly bear." She was sobbing. I knew I was in big trouble, but all I was thinking was that Mama had finally sat down after saving me and Jack and standing up to a bunch of big mean men with vicious dogs and guns. My mama is little but she was amazing that day. Someone should write a book about her.

"Mama?" I asked quietly when her crying slowed. I'd be crying too if my face didn't hurt so much.

"Where have all my pies been going, June?" She asked.

"What?"

"I know they haven't been going to K's mother, and I doubt you've been eating them all. Tell me. What have you been doing with them?"

I didn't know what to say, so I said what all kids say when confronted with a tough question, "I don't know."

"Did you think I wouldn't notice?"

I didn't want to say, "I don't know" again, so I didn't say anything.

"June, what have you been doing with the pies? Have you been trying to find your bear again?"

I tried to start crying even though Mama's not the one that ever works on, then looked at the fancy handkerchief hoping my nose had started bleeding again, anything to get her to stop asking me questions.

"*Have* you found your bear again?" she asked.

How could I tell her? I *couldn't* tell her. How did she know? Did she know? I could've eaten all those pies myself. I felt my tummy real quick to see if I could make it big enough for her to believe I had. Mama would never buy that. But I couldn't tell her because she'd tell Papa, and he'd be furious at me. He would go back out with Mr. Bern and kill the real bear this time. My bear.

"Mama, why do all those men want to kill one bear?"

"They don't, June. They want to capture it alive."

After all the excitement, Mama and I took a long nap together, and slept the rest of the afternoon until Papa got home. The anger Mama felt at that man yelling at me was brewing up in Papa as we told him what happened, even though Mama said everything was okay until Jack ran up to the dogs, and that the newspaper man and his friend were very apologetic and sorry for the situation they caused by showing up.

Papa was outraged at the men coming onto our property and threatening his family. It takes a lot to get Papa riled, but when he does it can be frightening. The angriest I've ever seen him was a couple of summers earlier when we were in town and some strange men were being rude to Mama while Papa was at the livery stable. They were saying awful things in Spanish and laughing, only a little bit of it I understood. Mama tried to ignore them, I think because I was with her. Then one of them stepped closer and grabbed her arm. She turned just as Papa's fist slammed to the side of the man's head from behind, knocking him down and out cold. Papa gave him a horrible sounding kick before turning to the other man who should have been running away, but stood there maybe to apologize. Papa slammed him one, too. He was still awake when he hit the ground and Papa went to kicking him hard and stomping on him. Mama yelled at him to stop, I was screaming-crying. Papa would have killed the man if a couple of our friends hadn't been there and pulled him away. Papa even tried to punch our friends until Mama calmed him down. I'd never seen violence like that before, and didn't think Papa capable of it. But anyone messing with Mama or me is asking for big trouble.

Mama talked quietly for a bit, then Papa—still pretty angry—told us the same group of men showed up at the mill and asked him the same questions.

Turned out, the newspaper man from town was friends with a man named Alan Kelly, the fancy-dressed man who had given me the fancy hanky. Turned out Alan Kelly used to be a reporter for a San Francisco newspaper. He also happened to be a bear hunter. He had been sent out to capture a live California grizzly twenty years back by William Randolph Hearst, the richest man in California, who also owned the newspaper. Even back then folks weren't sure there were any more grizzlies left in California, so Mr. Hearst thought if he could not only find one but also capture it, he would give it to the city as a gift and more people would buy his newspapers.

It took Alan Kelly with a bunch of men more than six months to find and capture one, down south somewhere. They named the bear *Monarch*, and he still lived in San Francisco in his own cage. *Everybody's* heard of Monarch, and he was supposed to be the last grizzly in all of California.

Alan Kelly became pretty famous after capturing Monarch. After hearing about another grizzly bear, *my* grizzly bear, Alan

Kelly got another rich man interested in hiring him to capture the bear. My bear.

"What did you tell them? asked Mama.

"Well, I told him where I first saw the bear, and where me and Bern ended up getting her, and some other places where we'd seen other signs of bears," he said.

"You told them where to find him?" I asked, alarmed.

"I told them where we killed..."

"They'll know we lied to them, Papa!"

Papa looked at me a little confused, "What did you lie to them about?"

"Mama told them she didn't know where we saw the bear, and I wouldn't tell them anything, and...but now..."

"What could you have told them?" Papa asked.

"They'll find him!"

Papa squatted down so he could look me right in the eyes. "Who will they find?" he asked. "June?"

"What?" I replied, realizing I might have said too much.

"Who will they find? Your bear?" asked Papa.

"June," said Mama gently, "Is there something you want to tell us?"

It was hard, but I knew I had to tell them the truth. I told them everything. I told them I overheard Papa say he thought they killed the wrong bear, and even though it took me awhile, I had found my bear again. I told them how I would take pies and apples into the woods when I was supposed to be going to K's house. How Jack and I would almost always find him, but rarely in the same spot.

When we did find him, I would lay the pie on the ground and step back a ways because he still wouldn't come too close to me. I told them Jack and my bear were friends and would play, that I would sit and watch them, and sometimes I would read to him until it was time to go home. I told them I had read to him that very morning before we walked into the posse at the house. I told them my bear had never once tried to hurt me or Jack and that he just liked our company. And apple pie.

When I had finished telling them, surprisingly, they didn't look all that mad. Papa looked more baffled than anything else.

"This can't be true," Papa finally said. "Are you making this up? Because if you are, it's not..."

"It's true," I said.

"So..." said Papa, "you think it's really a grizzly bear?"

"He *is*, Papa. He's bigger than the one you and Mr. Bern killed, he's got grizzled fur and a big head, and...and he's got a big hump on his back. That's a grizzly bear, right?"

Papa stared at the ground for what had to have been more than a minute. "So you've seen the bear today. This morning?"

"Uh-huh...yessir," I said. "I took him a pie, I read him a story, and Jack even wrestled with him. Which is why, I think, the mean dogs wanted to attack Jack. Because he smelled like a grizzly bear."

"Took him a pie and read to him," said Papa, still looking at the ground.

"June," said Mama, not sounding much more convinced than Papa, "how many times have you...visited with him?"

"I don't know," I said. "Maybe twenty times?"

"*Twenty* times?" exclaimed Papa, not looking at the ground

111

anymore.

"Ten times," I quickly said. "Just ten times, I think."

"Did you know about this?" he asked Mama.

"I...I suspected something," said Mama, a bewildered look on her face. "But not...no, I didn't know. *Twenty* times, June?"

"Ten times," I repeated, regretting I had ever said twenty, which was way more times than I could have possibly visited him, but 'twenty' just popped out. I quickly tried to count the number of times in my head, and was about to say "only five times," which wasn't true either, but sounded better.

"Ten times, twenty times," said Papa. *Now* he was looking mad. "There's no way you've been playing with a grizzly bear, June. Or *any* bear."

"Jack played with him, I only took him pies. And read him stories."

"Read him stories... June, stop lying to us."

"But I'm not lying, Papa, I promise! Mama knows about the pies."

"I don't *know* anything, June," said Mama. "You told me you were taking them to K's mother."

"Show me," said Papa.

"Huh?"

"Let's go. Show me the bear. The grizzly bear."

"I don't know where he is," I said, realizing how bad that must have sounded to Papa, after I had just told them how I had visited with him *twenty* times in the past month.

I didn't really want to, but I lead Papa into the woods. But first I had a screaming fit when Papa went into the house for his rifle, and only agreed to take him after he put it back. Mama could not be talked out of bringing up the rear with her scatter-gun, but she promised not to shoot unless my bear attacked Papa. "Can you please shoot *before* he attacks me?" I heard Papa whisper to her. It was our first family hike in a long time, but instead of looking for a place to set up a picnic, we were looking for a grizzly bear.

With Jack leading the way, I was sure we would find him. It was just that morning that Jack and I had last visited with him, I figured he'd be in the same place, or not far from it. I *did* want to find him, mostly to prove to Mama and Papa that I was telling the truth. I was hoping they would see that he wasn't dangerous, and so wouldn't want to kill him.

"Please be there," I whispered as we approached the spot. "And please don't attack Papa."

He wasn't there. Or anywhere near, as far as we could see. Jack couldn't even find him. I wondered if he had heard the shouting at our house with the bear posse, or had even seen the vicious hound dogs and big cage. I wondered if he knew that was for him. In any case, he was gone. There were enough paw prints in the soft dirt where he and Jack had wrestled that Mama and Papa did believe me. Papa squatted down a long time over the clearest print, putting his hand over it to see how big my bear was. Much bigger than Papa, for sure, and bigger than the record-breaking black bear he and Mr. Bern had killed. Papa fanned the dirt with his hand, erasing the paw print. Standing up, he said to Mama and I both, "Not a word of this to anyone, okay? Agreed?"

"Do you believe me, Papa?"

"When we get home," he said, "we'll talk."

It was a very quiet walk home, and nearly dark when we stepped onto the porch. Papa hadn't spoken a word, Mama either, which probably meant they were thinking hard about how to punish me. I was thinking hard, too, about how to avoid getting punished. I didn't come up with anything good.

"I'll heat up something," said Mama as she stepped into the house, closing the door behind her, almost hitting me in the nose as I tried to follow her.

"June," said Papa from behind.

"I'm sorry I lied," I said, still facing the closed door. I actually wasn't sure I had lied, I just hadn't told them things. I knew I promised not to go into the woods, but that was before they had killed the big black bear, and Mama had let me go to K's house again. I just hadn't told her I was also visiting my bear. I didn't tell anyone the pies meant for K's mama were going to my bear, but no one asked. Maybe K's mama didn't want the pies, she never asked about them, either.

"What were you thinking?" asked Papa.

"I don't know."

"You lied to us, June. You could have been killed, you know that don't you?"

"Yes, sir. But...but, no sir."

"I really don't know what to think about the story of your reading to a bear. But I do believe you frequented the bear in some way, despite promising us that you wouldn't."

"But Papa..."

"I do, June, believe he is a grizzly. I've believed that for awhile, actually. Now, learning that you've found him in the woods on a

114

number of occasions, I...I still can't believe..."

"Papa?" I turned from the door, and wanted to ask him to please not hunt my bear down. That for some reason, he had never tried to hurt me or Jack. But Papa wasn't in the listening mood.

"You will not so much as leave this porch, unless it's to feed the animals—*our* animals. I'm not going to ask you to promise you'll stay out of the woods, because you've already broken that promise. But young lady, you *will not* go into the woods again. It's going to be a long time before we can trust you, June."

"What about school?" I asked.

"Your mother will take you to and from school. And you will not leave her side."

"Yes, sir."

"You could have told us, June. You could have told us the truth," he said, reaching past me to open the door. "Now, inside. Wash up."

Disappointing Papa, and Mama too, was not something I had planned on. It wasn't something I was used to doing, either. I'd always been a pretty good kid, hardly ever getting in too much trouble. It just seemed lately that trouble was on the lookout for me.

* * * *

At school, all the kids had heard about, and were talking about, the Fancy Posse. Everyone knew about them visiting our house and getting in a fight with Mama. Everyone knew it was because I had supposedly seen a grizzly bear. Some of the kids were saying

115

they had seen the grizzly bear, too, and that their papas were getting a posse together themselves and were going to catch him first. I didn't believe them for a second, and I didn't say anything to them about my bear, other than the bear I had seen was shot and killed by Papa and Mr. Bern, and it wasn't a grizzly. I didn't tell K anything different. I may have wanted to, but I couldn't imagine K keeping a secret as big as a grizzly bear.

At the mill, Papa stuck to his story that he and Mr. Bern had already killed the bear. It wasn't a grizzly, he didn't remember where they had killed it, and the Fancy Posse was wasting its time. At the house, Mama had her scatter-gun with her always, ready to shoo off anyone that came to ask about the bear. All of us had had enough of folks wanting to know where the bear was, or might be.

And all this time I couldn't see my bear. Mama wouldn't let me out of her sight, even escorting K and I to school and back every day like when we were little. She was worried about strangers on the road, of course, but I think she was also afraid of me taking off into the woods to find my bear again, and maybe running into some crazy hunters. And there were some crazy hunters for sure. A lot of them already lived on the mountain and were men and whole families we tried to avoid, but now it seemed they were coming from everywhere. We'd see a lot of old mountain men with necklaces of bear claws, their mules loaded down with bear traps, but also some well dressed men with brand-new rifles out for adventure. Mama was right when she told me that a grizzly bear on the mountain makes people crazy. There hadn't been a grizzly on our ridge for years and years, so just the possibility of there being one was really big news. Nobody but me even knew for sure there was grizzly bear, but the rumor had taken off like a mountain wildfire, and with the arrival of the Fancy Posse, pretty much everyone believed it for a fact. They figured a posse wouldn't have come all the way from San Francisco with all those men and equipment if there really wasn't a grizzly bear.

Our mountain was getting strange and dangerous. I was so worried, with all the hunters and dogs traipsing through the woods, somebody was bound to run into my bear. And maybe giving him pies and apples and being nice to him had made him think all people were nice like me. He might not even run away if he saw hunters coming, and by that time the hunter's dogs would smell him out and he'd be done for. I knew he was very smart, he had to be smart to stay hidden without being seen or shot by *someone,* but now there were just too many rifles on the mountain, all aiming at him. *And* the Fancy Posse that wanted to capture him alive and put him in a zoo somewhere.

Chapter Eleven

With all the crazies with all their guns and rifles and dogs running around, Mama was especially alert with her scatter-gun when Papa wasn't at home. So it was pretty lucky for Mr. Howell, our veterinarian, that Mama didn't shoot him when she noticed a strange horse tied to our corral and someone inside the shelter with London.

Mama was still mad at him after she realized who it was. He should have come to the house first. Mr. Howell was still nervous, almost shaking, even after he sat on the porch with us and Mama assured him she wasn't going to shoot. I don't think Mr. Howell liked guns, and especially didn't like them pointed at him.

Papa told me Mr. Howell was an Easterner, started out as a people-doctor in the Army, in the Cavalry, and found he enjoyed fixing up horses more than fixing up the soldiers. He got out of the Army just before the Spanish-American War broke out, moved to California and became a veterinarian. I guess he had enough of the Army and getting shot at even though he was just a doctor and couldn't have been shot at too often, I would think.

I had a hard time picturing Mr. Howell in the Army. He was

short and round , wore tiny round glasses and had thick, curly hair he tried to hide—it seemed—under a bowler hat that was more than a size too big.

He always seemed nervous and jumpy. People gossiped about him that he was a veterinarian so he could order powders meant for the horses and take them himself. I assumed they meant powder medicine. I never saw him with powders, but always saw him drinking bottles of medicine whenever he visited our animals. He must have really been sick. He was drinking so much medicine after Mama scared him he even had to go to his saddle bags and get another bottle. He seemed more relaxed after Papa came home and they walked back out to the corral. I went with them to watch Mr. Howell, make sure he was gentle with London and the Longhorns.

I don't know why Mr. Howell even came to see our animals, he barely looked at London's sore leg, didn't even look at Tom or Becky or Whiskey. Spent near the whole time with Papa talking about the Fancy Posse. He sure was talking a lot more after his second bottle of medicine, or maybe he was just happy to be away from Mama and her two-barrels. He was bragging about Alan Kelly personally asking him to look over the mules they had brought for the *expedition*, as he called it. It had been a week since they set off. He asked if Papa had heard any news of them capturing a grizzly.

"No, not a word," Papa told him. And of course Mr. Howell tried getting Papa to talk about the bear he and Mr. Bern killed, and if Papa thought there might really be a grizzly out there, and if his daughter had really seen one like the town was saying.

"Naw," said Papa. "Bern and I killed the bear that June saw. Wasn't a grizzly. There's no grizzlies on our mountain."

They talked about this and that for a while longer, when Papa surprised me by asking Mr. Howell questions about Alan Kelly and the posse. Questions like how much money they were getting for the bear. Who was it that wanted a live grizzly bear anyway? Also, if the bounty was for anyone who brought down a grizzly, not just Alan Kelly. Why would Papa ask that?

"That, I don't know," said Mr. Howell. "Mr. Kelly was petitioned for the task, but if someone other than Kelly brings in a grizzly, I should think they would be compensated."

"Who's doing the petitioning?" asked Papa.

"Well," said Mr. Howell, "I don't know if I should say. Mr. Kelly himself wouldn't give that information when I asked. However, I did become friendly with some of his men, sold them a whole case of Elixir. They mentioned the name William Selig."

"Who?" asked Papa.

"William Selig," said Mr. Howell. "He apparently makes motion pictures."

"Really," said Papa. "And why would he want a live grizzly bear?"

"That…" thought Mr. Howell, "you'd have to ask him yourself."

"Did they tell you how they plan on capturing one?" asked Papa. "Sonia said they had a big cage on wheels. How would they get it into the cage? I mean, if there *were* a grizzly on the mountain."

"Which there isn't?" asked Mr. Howell.

"That's right."

"Well, they didn't tell me outright how they were going to do it, but they did have a large assortment of rope and chains, had a lot of everything, to be honest. And they also had a couple of Indians in the group. Indians know wild animals, know how to track them. I expect they'll rig some sort of trap, either that the bear would fall down into, or a big snare that would hold him. I suggested to Mr. Kelly a sedative for the bear, to put the bear to sleep, but for some reason he wasn't interested. Maybe since he caught one bear twenty years ago, he thinks he's an expert. I think he's putting too much faith in the Indians, if you ask me." That made Papa curious.

"What do you mean by *sedative*? Like for surgeries and such?"

"Something like that, yes," said Mr. Howell.

"So, you'd catch the bear in a trap and then make him breathe in the liquid?"

"That could be one way, yes, though I suggested to Mr. Kelly to use a needle to inject it into the beast."

"A needle?"

"It's called a *syringe*," explained Mr. Howell. "Like a sewing needle that's hollow inside, with a chamber attached that holds the drug. You stick the needle into the beast's muscle and then push the sedative into its flesh. Should put him right to sleep if you do it correctly. This is brand new medicine, very cutting edge if you will."

"You've done this?"

"Oh, yes," said Mr. Howell. "It's just a matter of getting the solution right, considering the breed of animal, the animal's weight, it's disposition and such."

"Not on bears, I'm sure," asked Papa, "but you have used it successfully on other animals to put them to sleep?"

"Uh-huh, yes," said Mr. Howell, though not very convincingly.

"You wouldn't just use chloroform?" asked Papa

"Oh, I wouldn't. Chloroform is good for cleaning infested wounds, and I know it's replacing ether as the preferred anesthesia for dentists and some doctors, but you still have to have the patient breathe it in. I don't know how easy that would be when your patient is a big bear."

"So you just stick a needle into the bear and he would go to sleep," said Papa. "But you'd have to get close enough to stick the bear."

"Well, I wouldn't," laughed Mr. Howell. "A horse is one thing, but I'm not getting anywhere near a wild grizzly bear. But someone wanting to do that, yes, would have to get up close and stick the bear with a needle."

"Interesting," said Papa.

"But," said Mr. Howell, "as you said, there's no grizzlies on the mountain. So all of this is academic, correct?"

They talked a while longer until Papa finally got Mr. Howell to leave. I think he would have asked to spend the night with us were it not for Mama in the house with her scatter-gun.

Papa was quiet the whole evening after Mr. Howell left. He had a book in his lap but I didn't see him reading it, and if Mama or I asked him something, we'd have to ask him two or three times before he heard us.

* * * *

"Your mother and I would like to talk to you about something," said Papa. I was pretty sure I wasn't in trouble, they hadn't left me alone long enough to do anything troublesome. "We'd like to talk to you about your bear."

"I haven't gone to see him, I promise."

"Oh, I know," said Papa. "Thank you for keeping your word. No, what we'd like to talk to you about is...uh...well, we can all be pretty sure your bear is still out there. Even with all the hunters on the mountain now, no one has been able to get him. If they had, we would've heard about it. That is one smart grizzly bear. For whatever reason, you're the only one that I know of who has been able to find him, and have done so on numerous occasions from what you've told me, and I believe you. Now look, somebody's eventually going to find him, even if he's moved out of the area, somebody, somewhere is going to get him. There's just too many people looking for him now to stay hidden forever. If it's not the bear posse that finds him it'll be some hunter, or just someone with a gun. A dead grizzly is very valuable."

"You want to kill my bear?"

"I'm not talking about killing him, June, and I wouldn't have even thought about trying to capture him alive before, but talking to Mr. Howell the other day really got me thinking. If what he says is true, that there is a medicine he can make up that'll put the bear to sleep, then it may be possible for just a small group of us to capture him, catch him without hurting him. Or him hurting us."

"No." I shook my head.

"Now listen, Bug, there's only one group out there wanting to bring your bear in alive, everyone else just wants to kill him. I know you don't want to hear that, but it's true. And I imagine you're very sad over the thought of the bear even being captured and taken off the mountain, but, the best you can hope for is for him to be captured. Now, Alan Kelly and his men will probably do that. Kelly's the man that brought in *Monarch*, you know. They're experienced, they've got good equipment, good hound dogs, and they've even got Indians with them, for Pete's sake. But maybe it could be us that captures him. There's a lot of money that would go to the ones that brought in a live grizzly."

"How much?" I asked.

"That, I'm not sure, but it must be a lot. The money could really help us out, June. I've told you about the rumors every year that the lumber mill may not be around much longer, the big companies keep buying up all the timber and eventually will put us out of business. The mill doesn't pay great wages anyway, but we've managed all right. But if it closes, I'd have to find work in town or somewhere else. I'd rather not move us, we all love the mountain and the home we've built here. I've thought about starting up a business, building houses and barns up here on the ridge, but we would need money to get that started.

"And this rich man, William Selig, I hear he makes moving pictures, and already has a lot of animals for the pictures he makes. But he doesn't have a grizzly bear, and he wants one from California."

"Why?" I asked.

"Why does he want a grizzly?"

"Why does he want one from California?"

"Oh, maybe because there's not supposed to be any left, I really don't know. Maybe he wants to make a movie with the bear.

Maybe he wants to take one of the last ones out of the wild so the bear doesn't get killed by hunters. Maybe he wants to breed the bear like they've done with Monarch.

"So, if my bear has a bunch of bear cubs, will they live in the woods?"

"Honestly, I doubt it," said Papa. "Not many people want grizzly bears in the woods anymore. But this Selig, he wants to build a zoo, with a big area for the grizzly. And think, if your bear lived at the new zoo, he wouldn't have to always be trying to find food, he wouldn't have hunters trying to shoot him all the time. He'd be happy. And you could visit him."

"We could visit him?"

"Sure we could," said Papa.

"Where's the zoo?"

"Well I hear it's not built yet, but I think it's going to be near Los Angeles, the city. You've heard of Los Angeles, right?"

"Where is it?" I asked.

"Oh, I don't think too far. Close to San Francisco."

Mama, who still hadn't said a word, looked over at Papa with raised eyebrows. She didn't want me to see her do it, but I saw.

"And we can visit him? And I can take him pies?"

"We can visit him, yes," said Papa. "But what I'm asking is if you would help me find him, tell me if there's a good place to look. I've searched the areas where you've seen him, but all I find is old signs of him. Maybe he's moved on up the mountain, what do you think?"

"I don't know."

"Well, how have you found him before?"

"I don't know."

"So you don't know where a good place to look for him might be?"

"I don't know."

What I did know was that Papa was getting frustrated with me, not being able to tell him where to find my bear. I know he thought I just wasn't *willing* to help, and maybe I wasn't willing. The truth was, I wasn't sure myself how I found him. I just did.

If I was the only one who could ever find him, then maybe all the hunters and posses and everyone else would never discover him, and they'd get tired of looking. I could go back to bringing him pies, and sit and read while he slowly licked the pan.

"I've already talked to Bern about looking for the grizzly," said Papa. "Tomorrow, I'm going into town to talk with Mr. Howell about this medicine he told us about. Maybe Howell would come too, since he'd have to prepare the stuff. If the sleeping stuff really works, I think we can bring the bear down with three men. I think we should try."

Mama, who hadn't said anything the whole time, finally added her thoughts, "Like your father said, June, somebody will eventually find him. I'm sorry, but that's the reality of it. I'm very sad, too. He might be the same bear that I saw right before you were born. I've often thought that young bear visited me that day to give his blessing to my little baby. Maybe that's why he's let you find him in the woods all those times and has never tried to hurt you. You *do* have some connection to him, something no one else has ever had with a wild animal, much less a grizzly bear, that I know of. I know you think you'll be betraying him, but you'll really be helping him. June, can you see that?"

"Yes, ma'am," I told her, though I didn't agree with her, or Papa. I *would* be betraying him, and I would miss him terribly if he were gone, even if I got to visit him. But when would I be able to visit him? We'd never been to Los...where was it? Well, we had never been there. Not once.

"We can find him on our own," added Papa. "You know Mr. Bern's a good tracker. But with your help, I bet we find him much faster. Hopefully before someone else does."

"I'll think about it," I told him.

Chapter Twelve

I hadn't seen my bear in weeks. Mama never let me out of her sight except when I was locked inside the schoolhouse. We hadn't heard of anyone capturing or killing him, which would have been big news. Mr. Phillips, the local newspaper man, had been traveling with, and writing stories about, the Fancy Posse's search for my bear. According to his stories, all the men were skilled mountaineers, noble and honorable and clean. Though they hadn't captured the *Great Beast* yet, they *had* managed to kill four black bears, two mountain lions, a rare wolverine, numerous coyotes, and other rabid varmints that were just waiting to pounce and kill any civilized town folk foolhardy enough to visit the mountain. He didn't mention anything about the men almost getting shot to pieces by a little Mexican woman, and scaring her daughter half to death. I might have believed Mr. Phillips's grand stories if I hadn't met the mean, smelly, rude lot of them. They were, however, searching right where I thought my bear would run to if he knew he was being chased by a posse.

Our mountain that fall had become a very bad place for bears. We had already heard of more than a dozen black bears being

killed, not counting the Fancy Posse's number. Some were
brownish in color that the hunters tried to pass off as grizzlies, but
no one bought it. The weather was getting colder which meant the
bears were loading up on food, getting fat for winter, and often
coming closer to where people live, so they were easy to find and
shoot. I was worried that my grizzly would get careless, or go to
unfamiliar places in search for food and be seen. Did he know how
many men with guns were looking for him?

One day, a group of hunters came to the house, already drunk
and nasty and it was just past breakfast. Luckily Papa was home
that day and walked out to speak to them. I recognized one of the
men as a local moonshiner and poacher who had a big family with
a passel of kids that never went to school. He had one of his boys
with him who was a bit older than me and who looked glassy-eyed.
I hoped he hadn't been drinking as well. I thought I remembered
his name to be Toby. They had a dog, but he was fat and mangy
looking. Probably laid around all day guarding the moonshine.
Jack didn't like him and they stared at each other and growled the
whole time.

Papa, with his rifle in hand, spoke calmly to them for a few
minutes. Mama and I watched closely through the window, and
were very relieved when they rode off. Papa wouldn't tell them
anything helpful, but I did hear them say they were going to start
looking along Elk Creek and work their way east up the mountain.
That was the area I thought my bear might be hiding. I didn't say
anything about that to Mama or Papa, but it did trouble me that
they could stumble onto him.

For the next few days, I was beside myself with worry. I didn't feel good about breaking my promise again, and knew if I got caught it would mean the biggest trouble I'd ever been in, but... I finally decided I just had to see my bear again, just for a few minutes. I had to see if he was okay and warn him to stay away from Elk Creek. How would I warn a bear? And how would I sneak away to find him? Mama was walking K and me to and from school every day, and I was still confined to the house except for feeding the animals. I wasn't even allowed to go as far as our little creek anymore.

I thought about it and thought about it. I had to sneak away and get back before anyone knew I was gone. I almost decided against looking for him, the consequences if I got caught would be huge, but the plan I came up with was just too good. It was flawless, a really marvelous plan. And it would happen at school on Friday.

Uneasy as Mama was about all the crazies with guns wandering around taking shots at anything even resembling a bear, I was surprised she let me go to school at all. I was also surprised she didn't bring her scatter-gun with her. "I'm not Annie Oakley," was what she said when I asked her about it. What she didn't tell me was that Papa had bought her a little pistol that she carried loaded in her purse whenever she left the house.

Shortly after Mama left us at school that morning, Mrs. Hicks was already frazzled. She was yelling at a couple of the older boys to untie their sister from a tree. They'd done it before without getting yelled at, but this time they had a rope cinched tight around her head and she was screaming like they were killing her. She's usually even meaner than that to her brothers, so maybe they *were* trying to kill her. Her name was Penelope. I've always been glad I wasn't born into that family.

As lunch time approached, I told Mrs. Hicks I was leaving.

"Leaving? Where to?" she asked.

"My mama told you, didn't she?" I said. "I'm supposed to meet her for lunch at the lumber mill, 'cause Papa's getting off early today and we're all going to town for the weekend."

"What are you going to do in town for the whole weekend?"

"My Aunt Annabelle is visiting from San Francisco. She's afraid to come up to the mountains with all the bears and hunters running around, so we're spending the weekend with her down at the new hotel. She's a *lady*." I spent two days thinking that up.

"The new hotel is finished?" she asked. "I didn't think it was finished yet."

"Umm...the old hotel. We would have stayed at the new one if it was finished."

"Maybe I'll go with you." she said.

"What?"

Mrs. Hicks laughed a tired laugh and told me to enjoy myself.

So far so good. My plan was to trek into the woods to just two spots I thought my bear might be hiding, and be back before school was over and meet Mama down the road and tell her school got out a little early. Instead of school books I had packed eight apples in my pack. I always had good luck finding my bear when I brought apples. I was leaving school when K ran up and asked me where I was going. I had forgotten about K and him blabbing to Mama about me leaving school. Part of my plan was to meet Mama down the road, but what about K? He was supposed to walk home with us. He would have to leave school early too if my plan was to work. Oh, boy.

I told K he needed to fake getting sick about a half hour before school ended and wait for me behind the big oak tree by the main road.

"Why?" he asked. "Where are you going?"

"Just do it, please. I can't tell you where I'm going, but it's really, really important."

"What about Mrs. Hicks? She'll know you've gone somewhere."

"I told her I was meeting Mama early and that we were going to town for the weekend, so that's where I'm going."

"You're spending the night in town? Why? Who's going to walk me home?"

"I'm not *really* spending the weekend in town, that's just what I told Mrs. Hicks. I just have to do something, it'll only take a couple of hours. I'll meet you at the corner a half hour before school's over, then we meet my mama as she's walking up the road. And we tell her school got out early and we don't tell her anything else. Okay? So just tell Mrs. Hicks you don't feel good. A *half hour* before school's over. Will you do that? Please?"

K thought for a minute. "We shouldn't lie to the teacher, June."

"It's not lying if you really don't feel good. You're always complaining about not feeling good."

"Yeah, but...I feel okay today."

K only agreed to the plan after I threatened to bring his stupid dolls to school and show all the older kids what he played with at my house. He could really be a pain sometimes. I would never have included him in my plan if I could have avoided it, but if he could just do that simple thing I asked him to, the plan would still work perfectly.

I hopped off the road onto a tiny trail only me and the critters knew about. It was the shortest way to Elk Creek. Dealing with K cut into the time I needed to find my bear, warn him about the mean hunters, and get back to school to meet Mama, so now I really had to hustle. I knew right where I wanted to look. A little ways from the creek were a few mini-canyons and ravines that were thick with oak trees and blackberry vines, a great place for a smart bear to hide. But also close to where those poachers were going to be looking.

With the shortcut I was taking, I had to creep down a really steep part, holding on to every little bush and rock I could reach so I wouldn't slide all the way to the bottom. It was harder than I thought it would be, and I got real dirty. How would I explain the dirt to Mama? I reached the first area before too long, but had hoped to get there sooner and wasn't sure I could get back up the way I came down. I'd have to follow the big trail all the way around, which would take much longer. I didn't have any time to spare.

My bear wasn't hiding in the first couple ravines I checked out. All the blackberries were gone from the bushes, so something had eaten them but it looked like they'd been eaten long ago. I quickly ran around, looking all over the ground for bear poop, but the only sign that a bear might have been there recently was some diggings like he was after roots or maybe even snakes, if bears ate snakes. I did find an old rope half buried under the leaves, something K would have appreciated last spring to get him out of the poison oak. The rope was pretty mossy and wet so I left it, but now I knew where a rope in the woods would be the next time I needed one.

I held out apples in both my hands and made clicking sounds with my mouth like my bear does when he sees me. I walked a little farther, made my way down to the creek to where there was a deep pool I thought he might visit to catch fish, but, no bear.

I wasn't sure what time it was, but had already been searching longer than planned. I knew I should be heading back before Mama showed up at school. This whole search was probably a huge waste of time, I thought. Not to mention that I was filthy, sweaty, and all scratched up from leaving the trail. I would just have to find him another time, if he was still around. I hoped he was okay.

With a big sigh, I tossed my apples into the surrounding bushes, one at a time. I turned and started back, thinking of the story I'd be telling Mama, because it had to be really, really good. "K better keep his big mouth shut about me leaving school," I said out loud.

I stopped where I thought the deer trail should be that would take me back toward school, but was having trouble finding it under the fallen leaves and little bushes when I heard something behind me. Something moving. I turned, but didn't see anything. *My bear?* I thought. *Mountain lion?* I stepped lightly as I could, slowly walking back to where I had tossed the apples. I hid behind a big tree and listened. Whatever it was, it was definitely eating the apples, I heard crunching and slurping. Mountain lions didn't eat apples, bears do. My bear does. Excited, I slowly, nervously peeked around the tree, ready to duck back in case I was wrong, but I wasn't wrong. My bear! He was chomping down on one of the apples!

He looked awful, actually. Was much skinnier than I remembered him to be, and there was a sadness and dullness in his eyes. I didn't go any closer. He looked at me, shook all the dirt from his fur, making a big dust-cloud, and clicked his teeth like he always did when he was glad to see me. Papa told me grizzly bears will click their teeth when they're about to attack you, but I didn't think my bear knew that. I smiled and clicked my teeth to him, and tossed him the rest of the apples from my bag.

Poor thing, he was so hungry. And so skinny at a time when all the bears were supposed to be fattening up for winter. He obviously had a rough time with all the hunters and dogs tracking him. But it was him and he was alive! It had been a month since I'd seen him. Everyone thought he would have moved to higher elevation by now, but for some reason I thought he might still be close, and I was right.

I had tears in my eyes as I watched him eating. They were only apples, but it was probably the best meal he'd had in awhile. He swallowed the last of the apples and looked at me for more.

"Sorry", I said, but then checked my bag, and hiding on the bottom was one more apple. I pulled it out and almost tossed it to him when I had an idea. I held the apple out to him and took a gentle step forward, then another step. He raised his head and took in deep breaths, smelling the last little apple. He started shifting his weight back and forth in a kind of playful dance. I moved back and forth with him, clicking my teeth and hoping I was doing the bear dance correctly. He took little steps toward me, moved into a crouch and almost crawled the last few feet, the whole time staring at the apple and breathing in its smell. The last few inches were the hardest for him, he was practically on his belly and reaching up with his snout from below. I moved my grip on the apple from the sides to hold it from the stem. My hand was shaking so much I don't know how the stem stayed connected but it did, and he reached his tongue out like a hand and took the apple.

Even though he wasn't quite the size of the first time I saw him, standing this close to him after not seeing him for so long was overwhelming. Like it was the first time all over again. I'd never felt so small in my life.

The last apple was swallowed quickly and he looked to me for more. I pulled my bag inside out to show him there wasn't any left. For a second I was afraid he might decide that I looked good enough to eat. If he was as hungry as he looked, he might forget that we were friends. For another second I thought that us humans had put him through so much—chasing him and shooting at him and trying to trap him—that he was probably owed at least one little girl to eat. But he didn't eat me. I sat down and we just stared at each other. Boy, was he big. I then noticed that a piece of his left ear looked to be missing.

"Did somebody shoot your ear?" I looked closer, and yep, there was what looked to be a jagged bullet hole that had taken off the top of his ear. Someone came awful close to getting *The Griz*, huh? Putting a bullet that close to his head, wow. His ear was dirty and caked with dried blood and bits of leaves. I wondered if he would let me touch it...I could clean it for him. I had thought about trying to touch him before, to pet him, after he had seemed comfortable with me bringing him pies, but whenever I tried to move close to him, he seemed to get nervous. His ears would go back flat against his head and would look at me like "that's close enough." I had thought if maybe I gave him a name he liked, he would let me pet him, but then realized that was thinking silly. Plus, I was afraid it would put a curse on him like I'd cursed the baby chicks I had named.

It was different this time. This time he was injured. I moved my hand toward him slowly, trying to look as non-threatening and comforting as I possibly could. I tried my best not to be afraid, you always hear that animals sense fear and then they pounce on you. His ears didn't go flat, he seemed like he was going to let me touch him. He didn't look frightened, or have a "touch me and I'll bite your hand off" look. Maybe I was being foolish, or just being a young girl, but I thought I could heal him. I'd fix his ear and give him a big hug and he'd let me ride him out of the woods and we'd show up at the house together and he'd live with us.

"Can I keep him?" I'd ask, and Papa would say, "Okay, but he's your responsibility. Don't expect your mother or I to feed him or pick up his poop."

"Yeah, you can stay!" and he'd be clicking his jaws in excitement at finding a real home. I thought all that and more in only a half a second. My hand hadn't moved any closer, and he still seemed calm, so okay, I was going to touch him.

"Do you want to smell my hand, first?" That's what you're supposed to do with strange dogs, let them sniff your hand and hope they don't bite it. But dogs aren't big enough to swallow you whole, either.

"If I'm really going to help you, help keep you hidden, you're going to have to really trust me, okay?" He laid his humongous head down on his front paws, just like Jack does.

"Well, here goes." I took a deep breath, and knowing I might never ever get another chance like this, I reached out and lightly touched the top of his snout.

Ka-powww... a rifle shot, very close by. My bear was up in a split second, leaping over me. It must have been one of his big paws that hit me on the forehead, knocking me flat onto my back. I lay still, looking up at the ceiling of branches and leaves that blocked the sky, a loud ringing in my ears, not knowing exactly what had happened. Did someone shoot at us? I wondered. Did I get shot? I felt stunned but very calm. "Mama and Papa are going to miss me."

It seemed like I was lying there an awful long time, but was probably just a few seconds. I heard through the ringing in my head a crashing of underbrush and sounds of men shouting. "I got him! This way!" Somebody was coming through the bushes toward me. Someone with a rifle.

"Get up, June," I said out loud. "Get up." I turned to look if my bear had been shot, but didn't see him. I jumped to my feet and started to run as someone burst through the brush behind me. I quickly ducked behind a tree to hide, shook my head to get my wits back, and heard men's voices off in the trees a little way. But whoever had just come running out of the bushes was now stopped on the other side of the tree. I could hear breathing.

I stood as still and quiet as I could, but my heart was pounding in my chest and my breathing was so loud I thought there was no way I wouldn't be heard. I put my hand over my mouth and tried to quiet myself. I wished more than anything to be back in school where I should be, plus, by then, I was definitely going to be late meeting Mama.

I listened for every little sound of whoever was on the other side of the tree. I heard every breath he made, but he didn't seem to be sneaking around toward me. Maybe he didn't see me jump behind the tree, I really *was* quick about it. Then I heard the voices in the distance again. "Which way? Don't lose him!"

Who did they lose? My bear? Did they lose the guy on the other side of the tree? I could hear his breathing getting faster and louder. Then strange sounds like a little kid moaning really scared me. I squatted low in the bushes and slowly peeked around the tree, not knowing who I'd see there, hoping the kid sounds weren't really a little kid that they shot, or worse, a trick to get me to show myself. I peered around very carefully and...I didn't see anyone standing there. I raised up a little, looked farther around and saw...

It was a deer, lying on the ground right where my bear and I were only a minute ago. It was too big to be a yearling, and it didn't have antlers, so it had to be a doe. She was having an awful time breathing. I stood up, looking around for anything else to come leaping out of the bushes, and quietly stepped toward her. She'd been shot in the side, just behind her shoulder. From the deer and elk that Papa brought back from hunting, I knew she had been hit close to her heart. It was a good shot that should have killed her already, but she was still alive. I stepped closer and squatted down on one knee. Her blood, thick and dark, was pumping out in rhythm to her beating heart. She had a confused look in her eye, she didn't know what was happening.

"Poor deer." I put my hand on her neck to calm her. "I know it's not fair...I know. You'll feel better if you can just let go. Just let go."

I hoped she was comforted at least a little bit by me talking to her. She took a couple more troubled breaths, then stopped. Nothing that big had ever died right in front of me before.

I sat a few moments more with her, forgetting that there was someone close by with a gun, and they might not be finished shooting it. I felt something running down my forehead and between my eyes. I touched it, blood. My bear really knocked me good when he heard the gun shot. He didn't mean to, and it didn't even hurt. I looked at the blood on my fingers, very red like it's supposed to be, but not as dark as the blood coming from the deer.

The voices were growing louder, they must have figured out which way the deer had gone. I heard a dog barking, too, so knew I should probably skedaddle, even though it wasn't me they were hunting. It would look strange to find a little girl out there all alone, and they might recognize me as the girl who supposedly saw a grizzly bear, and figure my bear was close by.

I started back up the little deer trail. If I didn't find the *big* trail right away, I planned to just keep hiking in that direction until I came to the road. There was no way I was going to make it back to school in time to meet Mama like I had planned. Even though I wasn't sure exactly what time it was, I knew I had spent way more time in the woods than I had wanted to. For all I knew, school was already over and K had told Mama that I had run off. If only I had a watch, I would have known for sure. A watch was going to be at the top of my Christmas list.

Even if I had somehow found my way back to school in time, as filthy as I was, I knew I was already in trouble. I thought I might as well just make my way home. Maybe I would run into Mama on the road before she was too mad. At least I had found my bear, and maybe saved him from those hunters. I glanced around for him, one last time, but he had long disappeared. He was much better at hiding from hunters than I probably was, though I always won at hide-and-seek. But that was usually just with K and he was easy to hide from.

I didn't get very far when I heard the men break into the clearing. I couldn't run any farther down the trail without them seeing me, so I climbed the closest tree. It was a good sized oak, normally a fun tree to climb, but I wasn't thinking about fun then. They stepped out of the bushes and walked over to the deer. It was the same group of dirty poachers that stopped by our house a couple of days ago. I was right about them getting close to my bear.

Their fat, mangy dog was the last to come through the bushes. He didn't seem like he was enjoying the hunt. Didn't even look at the deer, just plopped down like he was going to die himself. But then he got up and wobbled over to my bag that I had left behind. He snorted over it briefly, then waddled around in a circle, sniffing the air.

They would definitely see me if I stepped back onto the trail, the only way to sneak out of there would be through the trees and bushes. I quietly slid down the trunk of the oak tree, the bark scratching my legs and arms. I put one foot on the ground, and *crunch* went the leaves. I froze in place, maybe it just sounded loud because I was trying to be so quiet. I listened for a reaction from the men, and didn't think anyone had heard me. I peeked around the tree to take a final look before making my escape and saw the old dog, he was waddling right toward me! I quickly shimmied back up the trunk to a low branch. I pulled myself up until I could stand on the limb and looked again, the dog was still coming. But he didn't look like he had seen me. I thought about making a break for it, I was sure that dog couldn't catch me, and the men who took half the day to find a wounded deer would never find me. I was about to slide back down the tree when I heard one of them yell.

"Hey Dog! Get back here! Where you going?"

"That's some great huntin' dog you got there, Whitey," another one said. "Couldn't even track a gushin' deer."

"Oh, leave him alone," said the man who I guess was Whitey. "He's tracked more deer than you've ever even seen."

As I listened to them argue about the dog, and then argue about lord knows what else, I knew it was my last chance to get away. I wasn't going to slide down the trunk again, I was going to jump. I had to get out of there. I turned on the branch to make my great leap, and looked down to see where I would land. Standing on the trail, at the foot of my tree, was the old, fat dog. His nose was pointed up at me, snuffling and sniffing. It wasn't until I turned back to hug the tree that his old, blind eyes found me. He stopped smelling the air long enough to pant a few times before taking in a deep breath, lifted his head and wheezed at me, what must have been the best bark he could muster.

"Go away," I wheezed back. I didn't have anything heavy with me, so grabbed a handful of oak leaves, and threw them at the dog. They floated gently down around him, didn't scare him a bit. I tried moving a little around the tree and pulled up to the next branch, but the dog could still see me, or at least still knew where I was. He wheezed again, coughed a bit, and wheezed at me some more, he just wasn't going to stop.

"Pleeaasse go away," I begged him. I was getting real scared now. It's one thing to be seen in the woods by strangers, but to be found hiding in a tree is quite another. I started to whimper. Why wouldn't that dumb old dog just leave me alone?

"Please, please, please...go away." He had stopped his snorting, I looked down and he was finally gone. I peeked around the tree and saw him toddling back to his people. I wondered again what time it was getting to be, Mama was going to be really mad if I didn't get back soon. I didn't even want to think how mad Papa would be. I was going to be in *so* much trouble.

The hunters were a big problem. They could be there into the night if they decided to clean the deer where she lay. But that might occupy them enough for me to slip away, I just hoped I could get away before dark. Boy was I going to be in trouble.

I poked my head around the tree again, pushing aside some thin branches to see what the hunters were doing, and what they were all doing was looking toward me! I didn't know if they'd seen me yet, but Toby, the boy, had just picked up my bag, and they must have remembered the old dog being real excited about something down the path. I froze. The biggest, meanest, dirtiest hunter of the bunch snatched the bag from Toby and started walking toward my tree. The dumb old dog perked up and lumped ahead of him, happy that someone finally believed him.

"Well, look what we got here!" said the big man. I was afraid to look down. Maybe he was looking at a different tree. Maybe there was a raccoon or a possum in the tree next to me.

"Please don't see me, please don't see me."

A hand touched my foot. I kicked hard and tried to skooch farther up the tree, but that was the highest I could go. He grabbed at my foot again, I kicked him again and screamed. He was laughing.

"Git down here girl! Git down, let's have a look at ya."

"NO!" I cried.

"Say, Toby, come here, boy. Come here. You know her? Ain't this the Grizzly Girl? Come down, gal, we ain't gonna hurt ya." Then his friend, who wasn't as big, but was even more dirty and smelly, snuck up and jumped, his hand locking around my ankle. I screamed and pulled, but he had too good of a hold. I heard Toby yell, "Leave her alone!" I don't know if Toby pushed him or something, but the man jerked, taking my shoe with him and I heard scuffling below like Toby was catching heck, and heard Toby's pa yell at one of them and then they were all fighting. I was hoping they'd all pull out guns and shoot each other and I could climb down, find my shoe and walk home. I just wanted to go home.

I could see Toby walking back toward the dead deer, he turned around and yelled at them once more to leave me alone. He had blood coming out of his nose.

"You git down here now!" A hand grabbed my leg too tight for me to wiggle out of. I fought him, kicked, yelled and screamed but he was pulling me down with his weight. I somehow slid free one more time and pulled my legs up under me. I knew I couldn't hold myself up like that very long. What did they want with me? I looked down at the smelly one grabbing a branch to pull himself up after me. The big one saw me looking down and smiled a horrible black smile and raised his rifle. I started to cry.

"Girly, don't make us shoot you down," said Big One.

"Don't shoot at her you fool, you might hit me!" growled Smelly.

"Oh I'll shoot her if I have to... *Git down*, not going to say it again!"

"Don't shoot her I told you, I'm gonna git her."

BOOM! The sound echoed and echoed through the forest.

"You men, don't you move!"

"Papa?... Papa! I'm here!" It was Papa's voice! It was Papa's gun that shot!

"June, stay there!" yelled Papa.

Ka-Powww! went the rifle right below me, then **BOOM BOOM** from Papa. It all happened so fast, and it was so loud, I wasn't sure what had just happened. The ringing in my head from getting hit by my bear, was replaced by ringing from the guns going off right below me. Had Big One just shot me? I've heard stories that you might not even know if you've been shot. Did he shoot

Papa?

"YOU MEN DON'T MOVE!" yelled Papa, "YOU DO NOT MOVE!"

"Papa!" I screamed.

"June!" yelled Papa, "Stay there!"

I wanted so much to jump down and run over to him, but I was too afraid to let go of the tree. Afraid of falling, but also afraid to see what had happened below me. I heard painful sounds, groaning and cussing from below. I looked down at the men and was shocked to see Big One lying on his back, holding his stomach, bright red blood seeping out through his fingers. He also had a hole in his pants leg, the fabric smoking from where the hot bullet hit.

Papa had fired a warning shot when he saw Big One pointing his rifle and threatening to shoot me. Big One then leveled his rifle and shot at Papa, luckily missing him. Papa quickly returned two shots, hitting Big One in the leg, and then in the stomach.

Big One was staring up at me with a puzzled look and made gurgling, gasping sounds just like the deer had made not long ago. "You...shot me!" he growled, looking right at me. Curiously, he looked even bigger than before, sprawled out on the ground, moving his legs like he was walking. I closed my eyes real tight and held on to my tree, wishing this was all a bad dream and I'd be waking up in my bed any second.

Smelly One and Toby's pa stood together over Big One, too afraid to move. The old, fat dog huffed a couple times, then hobbled behind the men and lay down. Toby stood motionless by the deer as Papa walked into the clearing, rifle at his shoulder, aimed at the older men.

"Get over there with your pa," Papa told Toby.

Toby walked on very wobbly legs. "Sir, I tried to stop them," he was trying to tell Papa, but his voice wasn't working so well. Big One was thrashing around, groaning and cursing.

Smelly One started to squat down to his friend. "You really want to help him?" Papa coldly asked, his rifle pointed right at Smelly One's face. Smelly slowly stood back up, looking at Papa with the most hateful face I had ever seen. A face that would be in my nightmares for years to come.

"Whitey..." said Big One, "help...me."

"C'mon, Mister!" yelled Whitey, the Smelly One, "Let us help him!"

Papa had Toby pick up Big One's rifle and a couple of pistols and knives the other men had before letting them attend their partner. Unless they were doctors, I didn't know what they could do to help. Smelly tore open Big One's shirt. I glimpsed down just for a second and it looked like a lot of blood. I heard Smelly saying the bullet passed through—I've read that was better than if the bullet was still inside, but...

"We need mud to pack this wound," Smelly told Papa, "I'm goin' to the creek."

Papa held the rifle dead steady, pointing right at Smelly. "You'll wait," he said.

Papa had Toby collect every gun and rifle in their party, unload them all, throw the pistols far out into the woods and smash all the rifles against a tree. It seemed to take a long time, but no one moved, and the only one speaking was Big One, cursing at Papa. I held tight to my tree.

"I tried to stop them, Mr. Allen," Toby said. After getting rid of all the guns, he took a place next to his pa. He had been crying as he busted their rifles in half, but now had stopped. He still looked real scared. I was scared, too.

I couldn't stand it any longer and slid down the tree, hopping over Big One's twitching leg. I ran crying to Papa.

"Don't shoot, don't shoot, Papa!" I threw myself against him and squeezed as tight as I could. He rested his hand on my shoulder, gave me a squeeze of his own and pushed me around to the back of him.

"Please, Papa. No more shooting, please," I whimpered into Papa's back, ready for another gun blast to explode any second. No one spoke, it was so quiet except for Big One's horrible groans and curses. We all just stood, it seemed like for hours but was probably less than a minute.

Finally Toby's pa spoke. "Don't kill us, Allen. We weren't going to hurt your girl. It was that idiot, and we weren't going to let him... he wouldn't have. My boy...my boy here...all my kids at home, they need their father."

"If I see any one of you near my family ever again," Papa told them, "I'll put you down like the no good skunks you are. If I hear of any of you approaching, or even looking at my family, I won't warn you." With that, Papa picked me up, backed us up slowly until we were out of sight of the men, turned and hustled us away.

"I'll get you for this!" yelled the Smelly One as Papa carried me away, "We know who you are!"

I was shaking and crying, and I think in shock. "Is that man dead?" I cried, "Papa, is he going to die?"

Papa didn't say anything. He kept me under his arm, walking steady through the brush and finally onto a trail I recognized. I thought he would put me down, but kept holding me tight, and it was starting to hurt.

"Papa," I said. "I want down now, I can walk...please, I want to walk." But he didn't hear me, just kept walking and holding me even tighter. "Papa, let me down, it's hurting... Papa, *you're hurting me*."

Papa dropped me flat onto the trail. "What were you thinking, June? Huh?... and do not tell me 'I don't know'. You lied to us, you lied to your teacher, you disappeared from school. Mama comes to get you and no one knows where you are. She finally got K to tell her which direction you went, but even he didn't know where you were going or what you were doing. Your mother searched and called for you, finally she ran all the way to the mill to get me. She was in *hysterics* when she got to the mill, do you know that? Do you know how lucky you are that I even found you?"

"Where's Mama?" I was crying as I sat up.

"Mr. Jonas and his wife took her home in their wagon. They're all waiting at home right now for word if you're alive or not... What were you doing?"

I really didn't want to mention my bear or that I went looking for him again, but there wasn't any story I could come up that would be any better. "I found him," I whispered.

"What?"

"I found him again. I fed him apples."

"No you didn't."

"Yes, I did, I fed him apples, and then those men shot a deer and..."

Papa grabbed my arm and yanked me up. "Papa that hurts!"

He looked into my eyes, and said through gritted teeth, "This ends now." He let go of my arm after a little way down the trail. Whiskey was waiting for us, tied to a little oak tree. Papa mounted up first then pulled me up behind him. We didn't talk the whole way home. Papa would occasionally turn Whiskey around so he could look behind us, but we weren't followed.

Mama was on the porch with Mr. and Mrs. Jonas, worried and waiting. I thought I would be in big trouble with her, too, and I probably was, but she pulled me off Whiskey and we just held each other and cried.

Chapter Thirteen

Papa wasn't saying anything to me, would barely look at me. He stayed home from work, would stay home for more than a week. Shooting Big One had stirred up a hornets nest among the Johnson clan, the big poaching-moonshining-ragpicking family. We heard Big One was still alive but was in a lot of pain and was madder than a stepped-on rattlesnake. His name was Clem Johnson and he was, other than Old Man Johnson, the family leader. He and Whitey Johnson were threatening to get back at Papa, and maybe me, too. So Papa stayed at home, wouldn't go to work, had all his guns loaded and close to the doors. Mama kept her pistol and scatter-gun close when Papa walked out with Jack in a loop around our woods. Mama even wore her pistol in a holster on her hip. I knew it was a very serious time and nobody was happy about any of it, but I thought Mama *did* look just like Annie Oakley. She looked so beautiful and tough and from then on I wanted to wear the guns when K and I played. Let him be Sacajawea.

"Is Papa ever going to talk to me again?" I asked Mama.

"Of course he will, June. He's got an awful lot on his mind right now, I'm *sure* you understand. Just give him his space, let the dust settle a bit, and then we'll be able to move on. But things aren't going to be like before, young lady. You've used up all your liberties for a *long* time. Think about that. You'll have to really show that we can trust you. You don't want to be in a family where we can't trust what you tell us, do you?"

"No ma'am. Is the Sheriff going to arrest Papa?"

"No, June. Papa's not going to be arrested."

"Is he going to arrest the Big One? He shot first."

"I don't know," said Mama. "Mr. Bern has gone and spoken to the sheriff about what happened. Your father will probably meet with him when he thinks it's safe to go to town."

"When will it be safe?" I asked.

"I don't know, June."

I was kept home from school. I was kept home from everything, I couldn't even go outside by myself. Mama had me by her side morning to night. Cooking, cleaning, reading quietly. Papa stayed on the porch mostly, and even when he came in, he didn't have anything to say to me. I had finally done something so awful that even Papa didn't want me. I cried a lot when no one was looking, what else could I do? I was too ashamed to approach Papa to say I was sorry, again.

It was a very quiet time. I read when Mama wasn't making me clean something that I had just cleaned the day before. Mostly reread Jack London, but also old newspapers Mama had already read and were in the fire-starting pile next to the cookstove.

"The Wright Brothers," I read aloud to myself, "sell the world's first military airplane to the United States Army." I'd never even seen a real airplane, and to be honest, until the day I might see one with my own eyes, I wasn't going to believe they could really fly. It just didn't seem possible. And why would the army want one?

"Mama?" I asked, so bored I couldn't read anymore. "Mama, can I sew some beads on your holster?"

"No, June."

"What about..."

"No, June, I don't want you making it pretty, or even looking at it. I don't like wearing this thing at all."

When Papa wasn't on the porch cleaning his guns for the hundredth time, he was out walking the property and woods. Mr. Jonas had given him two weeks to be home until things hopefully worked themselves out, but not much had happened, and the two weeks were about up. Mama said he was worried about having to leave us during the day when he returned to the mill.

Mr. and Mrs. Hicks came by to drop off school assignments. She wasn't happy with me either. Barely looked at, or spoke to me. Mr. Hicks at least asked how I was doing.

"Mama, does Mrs. Hicks hate me?"

"She doesn't hate you, June. But think, if Papa hadn't found you when he did, and something awful had happened, how do you think Mrs. Hicks would have felt? She feels betrayed by you for lying to her, and she feels responsible for letting you leave school. I don't blame her at all for being upset with you."

I had let a lot of people down.

* * * *

"The ol' lady finally come to her senses?" hollered Papa from the porch. It was the most, and definitely the loudest I'd heard him speak in two weeks. I ran from the kitchen to see who he was talking to.

"And what..." yelled back Mr. Bern, "kicked me out? Is that what yer sayin', Allen? She obviously ain't got a lick o' sense to her, or she'd never of let me hang my hat with her in the first place, ha haa."

We had all hoped that after more than a week had passed since the shooting, without an incident, the Johnsons would have cooled down. I guess they hadn't, since Mr. Bern had one of his mules in tow loaded down with stuff, and planned on staying with us awhile so Papa could return to the mill without worrying about us during the day. He set himself up a living area in a corner of the barn with a bed made up of straw bales, had two cedar stumps for a seat and table. After feeding animals with Mama, she let me walk over to the barn and say hello.

"Hellooo," I called. Fish shot out the door past me with his tail tucked under. Crazy dog.

"Why hello, there, young'n, pull up a stump."

Mr. Bern was sitting on one of the big cedar rounds, sharpening the biggest of four knives laid out. It was as big as a sword. He was wearing old overalls and nothing else that I could see. He had one traveling bag for clothes and little items, but against the wall I counted three rifles, a shotgun twice the size of Mama's, and an antique-looking musket. I guess that meant he was ready for business.

He saw me looking at the guns, imagining the battle that must be coming. "I do come prepared, you say? Naw, mostly just like havin' them around, plus, don't want nobody stealin' them if they see I ain't at home. Don't expect I'll get the chance to use 'em any time soon, but you never know. I don't like to get myself in trouble for lack of shooting back, don'cha know."

"They're going to shoot at us?" I asked.

"Oh no, no," he said, noticing my wide eyes. "That's not what I was saying at all, or not exactly. I just meant that...ahh, well, I think it was just a poor choice of words. That happens with me from time to time."

"Yes, sir."

Mr. Bern picked up the next knife to sharpen. "Interestin' times we're living in, Miss June. Nine years into the *twentieth century*. Say, do you know why they call it the twentieth century even though it's the nineteen hundreds?"

"No, sir. Why?"

"Oh, I don't know," he said. "I was hopin' you could tell me. Don't make much sense, does it? But yeahhh, interestin' times. The outlaw west is s'posedly dead and buried, *the rule of law* and such now, yet here we are in the middle of an old fashioned feud, what do'ya say?"

Papa wasn't speaking to me, Mama wouldn't discuss our recent troubles with me, so having Mr. Bern in conversation about the Johnsons brought up something inside of me, and I started to cry.

"It's all my fault! Everybody blames me!"

"Miss June," said Mr. Bern, who in no way seemed comfortable talking in a serious manner to crying little girls, "I know this is all a shock to you. You're young, you're...ahh...young. You know? I'd like to tell you this is nothin', but I can't. You're young, but you're old enough to be told the truth. I know your ma and pa aren't ones to...ahh...gloss over what's happenin', and I won't insult you, being a young woman and all, by tellin' you all's milk and molasses. 'Cause it ain't right now. Understand?"

"I think so."

"Yeah, I know you understand. I mean, you're just a little thang, but I'll be derned if I haven't been amazed by you since the day you started talkin'. Now, if you was a little chipmunk with a tiny brain and still believed that babies were dropped by a stork, and that the Tooth Fairy was real then I'd be speakin' to you different."

"The Tooth Fairy's not real?"

"Oh, ahh...sure he's real," said Mr. Bern.

"She."

"Huh?"

"The Tooth Fairy's a she."

"Oh, yes, of course. Now what I was sayin'..."

"Is the Easter Bunny real?"

"Ahh...of course he's real... He?"

I nodded.

"But gettin' back to what I was sayin'..."

"Is Santa Claus real?" I was afraid to ask that one, but did.

"Ahh...now what I'm telling you, is things in the grownup world can be complicated. And ahh...ahh...so, so why don't you tell me what you know, what your ma and pa have told to you."

"Not much, really. I know I shouldn't have lied."

"Okay."

"I know I caused a lot of problems."

"Okay, well…"

"I know Papa shot that man because of me, and now they want to shoot us."

"Uhhh…well… the man getting shot was…ahhh…I would say that the man would probably *not* have gotten shot if'n you weren't, you know, ahh…*there*. As far as them shootin' at you, don't you worry about that, not gonna happen. And forget my little joke before about shooting back or whatever it was that I said, okay?"

"Okay."

"So, Miss June, what exactly were you doing there? If you don't mind my askin'. Your pa's told me about gettin' into it with Clem and Whitey, but wouldn't really say much about why you were out there in the first place."

I wasn't sure I wanted to tell Mr. Bern everything, or what I should tell him. He was a bear-hunter, for Pete's sake. But he *was* there to help protect us, and him wanting to go after my bear again didn't seem as important as keeping us safe.

So I told him. "I snuck away to find my bear and I found him and fed him apples but then the bad men shot a deer and I hid in a tree but then their dumb old dog found me and then they found me and they weren't nice and then Papa showed up and Big One shot at him so Papa shot Big One and I thought he was going to shoot them all but he didn't, then he carried me all the way home and now the Johnsons want to kill us and…I'm sorry for the whole thing."

"Yeah, well…whoo. That's a lot to happen to someone so young, huh? And I know you're sorry and all…but do you know about sorry? Sorry is in the past. Things happen, and now here we are, now. You understand? Now, best I see it, we get through 'til the dust settles, we don't harp on our mistakes, but we remember 'em, and do our best to not do 'em again. Understand?"

"Yes sir, I understand. Will Papa ever speak to me again?"

"Of course he will, Junebug."

"Does he still love me?"

"Of course he does," said Mr. Bern. Then he got a look like he was thinking real hard. "Listen here. I've known a lot of men in my days. A lot of good men, and a lot of bad men. And none of them, good, bad or in between, has ever loved his family more than your pa loves you and your ma. Now, most men I've known ain't ones to be tellin' their family how much they love them, or tell them anything at all. Men are that way. *I'm* that way. But your pa tells you, right?"

"Yes, sir."

"Yes, that's right. And your pa is one of the best men I've ever known, he's tough as leather in the sun, a man you want standin' next to you in a fight. But I've not seen a man be so tender with his wife, and so loving to his little girl. He don't treat you like a little china doll either, does he? He teaches you things, he spends his time with you. He wants you to know the world around you so you ain't beholden to no one in your life. I know you're young, and all this mess is a shock. But don't be thinking your pa don't love you. Don't you ever think that. He's got an awful big responsibility right now keeping you safe. When all this passes, you and him I bet will be even better together than you were before. Now, what were you sayin' about feeding a grizzly bear apples?"

I told him I had been visiting my bear all summer, taking him apples and apple pies, and though I'm not sure if he believed everything, he listened, and seemed like he believed me.

"Hmm. Is that all true?" he asked. "Please don't take offense at my askin', it's just I've come across plenty of grizzly bears in my younger days and I can't remember a one that would let someone near them, much less feed them by hand without bitin' that hand off and then the arm too."

"It's all true! I promise!"

"Okay, now," said Mr. Bern, "I'm amazed that he's still alive for one thing, with the mountain crawling with hunters an' trappers. And it sounds like he's had a rough go of it by your description. He's gonna have a heck of a time this winter if he don't start fattenin' up. Bears around here don't really go into a full winter hibernation usually, unless it's a very cold and long winter, but they do hunker down. He needs to be fat for when it snows and he slows down. If he don't, he'll have to stick to the valley where it's warmer. He'll be seen, sure, lookin' for food around folks' barns, snappin' up their little poodle dogs 'cause the berries have passed season. Naw, he'll have a heck of a time, sure."

"Have you killed a lot of grizzly bears?" I asked.

"A long time ago. I've done my share of killing grizzlies, yep. Wolves too. It's just what we all did. Now, I wish we *hadn't* killed 'em all. Wolves, grizzlies, wolverines, made the mountain interestin'. Indians, too. Made the mountain a *real* mountain. But some trains you can't stop. Indians, and all the wild things with big teeth were in trouble the day some ya-hoo found a gold nugget shinin' back up from their mornin' bath in the creek. Nope, civilization don't stand for nothing wild, nothing it can't control.

It's a shame."

"Yep...sir."

"Yep," agreed Mr. Bern. "I actually miss livin' in a grizzly range. Added a little fun and excitement to the mountain, don'cha know."

"Yep."

"I don't know that I'd miss skunks much, though," smiled Mr. Bern. "Would you? Why can't they be gone?"

I laughed, "I wouldn't miss mosquitoes either!"

"Ain't that the truth, Miss J."

＊ ＊ ＊ ＊

Papa and Mr. Bern stayed vigilant in protecting the house. When Papa returned to work, Mr. Bern took his place on the porch, guns and rifles at the ready. When Papa came home in the evenings, Mr. Bern usually rode off on Willa for an hour or so, or sometimes went to his house for the night. Everyone knew about the shooting by then, and Mr. Bern learned Clem Johnson was still awful mad about getting shot, and still swearing he'd get even. The Johnsons had been telling the story that Papa shot Big One in an argument over the killed deer. That Papa was out hunting and thought *he* was the one that killed the deer. Mr. Bern was able to at least tell folks that Clem was threatening me, and shot at Papa first, that it had nothing to do with a deer. He swore to me that he'd never mentioned my grizzly bear to anyone. Mr. Bern was also paying more visits to Sheriff Pettigrew on our behalf. I was still worried Papa would be arrested.

Papa seemed a lot more at ease since returning to work, and

since nothing bad had happened as far as the Johnsons were concerned. He even started talking to me again, not much, but some. I was still confined to the house, and his conversations with me were short and boring. Like how school was that day, and reminding me to help Mama. But he did tuck me into bed and read me stories, and that's probably what I missed most when he had his back turned to me. I promised myself I'd try real hard to make him and Mama trust me again, and next time I wouldn't mess it up.

The Johnson's threat of revenge was looking more and more hollow. Nothing had happened. Papa was more relaxed, and Mama hadn't put on her gun belt in days. Mr. Bern was still with us, his wife Patty had taken the train to Sacramento to visit family and he asked if he could stay in the barn a while longer. "I tend to git myself in trouble," he told us at supper, "if'n there ain't a woman around, or *two*, to keep me in line."

"You can stay as long as you'd like, Mr. Simms," said Mama. "We enjoy having you, and can't thank you enough for your concern and help."

"Ohh," said Mr. Bern, "no thanks are necessary, ma'am. I was kinda hopin' ol' Clem *would* show up causin' trouble so *I'd* have a reason to shoot him. Do you know he stole a whole wagon load of pelts from me? Half a season's trappins'. Was twenty years ago, but he and Whitey stole 'em. Never could prove it, but I know it was them."

"I didn't know that," said Mama.

"Yeahhh," continued Mr. Bern, "Whitey was just a teenager then, but both of 'em and their whole dern family's been nothin' but trouble for years and years."

"You know what *I* heard," said Papa. "I heard the bad blood between you and Clem started way back when you both were wantin' to marry the same girl. And she picked him."

"Nonsense," said Mr. Bern. "Don't believe a word, Miss June. Me and Clem Johnson don't like each other 'cause of stolen *pelts*, no other reason."

"I believe you, Mr. Bern," I said.

"But you know," said Mr. Bern. "You know...I mean...how could a woman that good lookin' and sweet as plum jam and jelly all mixed together, how could a woman like that marry such a no-good, dirt-eatin' drunkard as Clem Johnson, I ask you."

"I don't know," I said, though I don't think it was me that he was asking it to.

"Anyway," said Mr. Bern. "Everything always works out for the best, don't it? I'm much more happy with my Patty than I ever would have been with ol' What's-her-name."

I loved having Mr. Bern as a guest at our home, and would run to the barn to visit him every day after school. We'd talk about things until Mama called to me to pick greens for supper, and Mr. Bern would grab his cane and walk with me to the garden. Fish still didn't like me and would run off to find Jack, or hide whenever I was around, but that just meant I had Mr. Bern all to myself.

As quiet as it was, with no trouble at all from the Johnsons, we were all glad to have Mr. Bern staying with us one night in particular. It was pouring down rain, thundering, and very dark between huge flashes of lightning. Mama and I were baking bread,

Papa and Mr. Bern were out on the porch with Fish, talking and watching the lightning show. Jack was hiding under the bed, terrified of the thunder. I don't think old, deaf Chica even knew there was a storm, and was napping in her usual spot blocking the door.

Fish heard it first. Animal calls, like wolves, from a couple different places in the near woods. Papa and Mr. Bern walked out into the rain to investigate, and was obvious it wasn't wolves. One, because there weren't any more wolves on our mountain, and two, they began laughing and yelling curses. Mama and I stayed in the house. I was horrible-scared and grabbed hold of Mama after she strapped her gun on. She turned down the lights in the house, so no one could see in, then told me to go upstairs, but there was no way I was going to let go of her.

Gunshots came from the woods. Papa later said he heard the barn getting hit, and was afraid they were shooting at the animals. He and Mr. Bern fired back, then no more shooting. We could hear the wolf calls and laughing and whooping in between booms of thunder. They seemed to be retreating into the woods. I was scared, but knew I was safe with the grownups I had around me.

"Was it Johnsons?" I asked when Papa and Mr. Bern came inside to dry off.

"If it was," said Papa, "probably just Johnson kids, shooting at the barn. Nothing to worry about."

Well, *I* was worried. How could I not be worried when people were shooting at us from the dark woods? Maybe they weren't just shooting at our barn, like Papa said, maybe they were shooting at Papa and missed because of the rain and thunder. Mama seemed worried too. She was especially troubled a couple of days later, when walking K and me to school, a group of Johnson boys were riding slowly on their horses right toward us. There were four of them. They didn't stop or say anything rude, they didn't say anything at all. Not even "hello," or tip their hats to Mama which is what men and boys are *supposed* to do. Then, when they had passed by us a ways, we heard a couple of them howl quietly like wolves. I knew it was them that were in the woods that night, just like Papa said. Mama told me to keep walking. K had no idea about anything. I never told him about our barn getting shot.

"Where's Mr. Bern?" I asked when Mama and I got home from school and noticed Willa missing from the barn.

"He left earlier," said Mama. "Miss Patty's back, so it was time for him to go home".

"Is he gone for good?" I sadly asked.

"I'm sure we'll see him again soon."

We saw Mr. Bern the next afternoon, actually, riding in with Papa. He had met Papa at the mill with some pretty big news.

"Whitey Johnson's dead," Papa told us when we had all finished most of our supper.

"The one you..." asked Mama.

"No," said Papa, "the other one."

"Smelly One," I said. "What happened, Papa?"

"He wasn't in our woods that night?" asked Mama. "We didn't shoot him then?"

"No, no," said Papa.

"Don't know the details quite yet," said Mr. Bern, "other than he showed up dead yesterday. Along with a number of his kin."

"Wow," I said. Even though I hated him for grabbing me that day, it was hard to picture him dead. I don't think I'd ever met anyone who died before.

"What does that mean for us?" asked Mama.

"Nothin' really," said Papa "Other than we got a few less Johnsons mad at us now."

"Sheriff'll be makin' a visit soon," said Mr. Bern. "I've spoke at him a couple times now about the Johnsons, in roundabout ways, about them bein' in a lather. He'd already heard ol' Clem took a few bullets, and had heard the lies being put out by them, too. He just wants to talk to the mister here, clear the whole thing up."

"Will you be arrested, Papa?"

"No, June," said Papa, "I won't be arrested. The sheriff just wants to ask a few questions. I should have gone to him right away, but I didn't. I asked Bern to go in my stead with a promise that I would talk to him when I felt it safe to ride to town. He said to sit tight and he'd visit me at the house. It'll all be fine."

First Clem Johnson getting shot by Papa, now Whitey and even more Johnsons getting killed. I've always been glad I wasn't a Johnson.

Chapter Fourteen

Sheriff Pettigrew rode up to the house, led by his two Labrador Retriever dogs. Jack scrambled up the road to meet them, they turned and raced around the house together. Mama and I were in the garden pulling up carrots and beets for the root cellar when the dogs flew by us. The sheriff was greeted by Papa out front of the house and they walked inside. Mama told me to go check on the animals or play with the dogs so they could speak with the sheriff alone.

That was something I just couldn't miss! I walked toward the stable until Mama went inside with the vegetables, then snuck back to the house. I started to crawl under, because I knew I could hear real good under the house and they'd never know I was listening. But with the thunder storm and all the rain, it was pretty muddy under there. I pulled my dress up and tied it around my waist, then decided that wouldn't do. Mama would know I was under the house listening if she saw mud on me. "Why did I have to wear a white dress today?" I whispered angrily to myself, then pulled my dress completely off and laid it down folded, on a clean patch of grass. I'd still get my under-dress dirty, but I could hide that until

I cleaned myself up, and maybe I wouldn't even get too dirty if I was careful. So, I dropped down and scootched under, crawling on my hands and feet until I was right below the kitchen, where Mama was heating coffee for the men. I could hear perfectly, just like I was in the room with them. *Sometimes*, I thought to myself, *I'm so smart it's scary.*

"Now first off," I could hear the sheriff saying, "don't tell me anything about anything, all right? I'm not here, and we're not talking."

Next I heard Papa, "Understood. Can I ask what happened to Whitey Johnson? We heard he turned up dead."

"Well," said the sheriff, "appears that Whitey, one of his cousins, his sister, and her husband made a two-wagon delivery of liquor over to Helltown. They stayed a bit, playing cards, probably all drunk by that time, and drunk ain't always the best condition to be in when gambling at someone else's table. Seems they must have lost most or all of the money they were paid for the liquor, so of course they accused the Massey boys of cheating, which they probably were. Guns came out, and all the Johnsons but for the sister were shot dead. She reported to the family they were stiffed on the payment, then all shot. All killed. Now the Johnsons are out for blood against the Masseys. So whatever disagreement they may have had with you before is probably, if not forgotten, then at least put way on the back burner."

I wondered how the sister got away with so much shooting going on? Did any of the Masseys get shot? I could hear the Sheriff and my folks walk back out to the porch. I started crawling that way so I wouldn't miss a word, when Jack, who was still being chased by the sheriff's dogs, dashed under the house followed by his pursuers. They were pretty excited to see me under there and knocked me over into the wet dirt, kissing and licking me, and putting muddy paw prints all over my under-dress. So much for being careful. I shoved Jack off of me and pushed the labs away. Thinking I had gotten rid of the dogs, I started scooting toward the porch, when I looked back one more time to see Jack and one of the labs playing tug-of-war with my dress!

"*Jack!*" I whisper-yelled, not wanting the grownups to hear me under their feet, then scrambled as fast as I could toward the dogs. Before I could get there, the dang dogs took off! With my dress!

"And why this isn't an official meeting with you," continued the sheriff, "is that I really don't know what, if anything happened to Clem Johnson. I heard he'd been shot, then I heard he died, then I heard he'd never been shot after all. He never visited with the doctor, and none of the family will talk to me. It's all been just hearsay and rumor so far, like always, and the rumors get bigger and bigger, you know. Your name's been mentioned as a shooter, and nearly all the rumors are playing out that if you did in fact do some shootin', that you were in the right. That was backed up by a couple talks I had with Bern Simms. Simms is usually a pain in my side, but I do consider him an honest man. Now, you don't have to, but it may be a good idea for you to come down to the jail and let me take down a statement from you. If what I've heard is anywhere true, you've got nothing to fear from the law. But if someone does come forward that's involved, I'll have to officially open an investigation. I have to. So I'm saying it's definitely to your benefit to talk to me first. All I'm going to say for now.

Anyway, I'll take my leave. Thank you, Mrs. Allen, for the coffee."

"Thank you, Sheriff," said Mama.

"Say," said the sheriff, "is that your daughter?"

"Oh, my word," said Mama, stepping off the porch to me racing after the dogs in my underwear, filthy as if I'd been wrestling in a pig's wallow. Jack had won my dress from one of the labs and was doing his best to keep his prize. I still hadn't hollered at them, afraid the grownups would hear me. I was so furious at them stealing my dress I didn't even notice I was running right in front of the porch. I must have been quite a sight.

So, the sheriff wanted Papa to go down to the jailhouse? Would Papa be arrested? They weren't too eager to fill me in on what I'd missed while chasing the dogs around the property with no clothes on. Mama made me bathe in freezing cold water in the outside tub, and was none too pleased with my eavesdropping or ruining my dress.

"It was the dogs that ruined it, Mama, not me," I argued, but Mama wouldn't listen. I didn't even try to make up a story that time, how I ended up filthy and out of my clothes. What story could I have come up with that wouldn't have gotten me in more trouble than the truth?

Chapter Fifteen

Mr. Bern pulled up to the house in an old, creaky wagon pulled by two big mules, his horse Willa in tow. The wagon was much larger than ours, with a longer bed and extra tall wheels. Looked like it had rolled off a cliff before Mr. Bern found it and nailed it all back together. It was loaded with rifles, traps, ropes, chains, axes, saws, and stuff I didn't know what the heck it was. He parked it by the barn, unhooked, set up Willa and his two mules with a couple armfuls of hay, then set up his own straw bed before unloading some of his things from the wagon. Was he moving in with us?

"C'mon over here, Miss Buggy J!" Mr. Bern called to me after seeing I'd finished feeding our animals. "What d'ya think of my wheels?"

"Nice," I lied.

"Have had this ol' wagon for years and years. The fella that give it to me had it for years and years, but she's a tough'n, for sure."

"Kinda like you," I said.

"Ha Haaa!" Mr. Bern laughed, and laughed some more. I hadn't thought what I said was as funny as that.

"Yes, ma'am," he said when he finally stopped laughing, "I can see her similarities to me—big, old, broken and ugly, but still rollin' along, hey? Me an' my wagon, we're two of a kind."

"Yes, sir," I laughed, though I didn't think Mr. Bern was *ugly*, just extra rugged-looking.

"Oh, but what I was going to show you...just look at these wheels, would you? Notice how big they are?"

"Yes, sir."

"Got these off an old freight wagon years back, a wagon that took *ten* mules to pull it, it was loaded down with so much. But up here in the mountains, don'cha know, with a couple of good mules tuggin' it along, you can roll over just about anything. Great for pullin' through snow, too."

"That's good," I said, still wondering why he had all his stuff with him.

"Now looky here, do you know what these are?" He was standing next to a pile of huge animal traps at the back of the wagon.

"Traps," I said quietly. I had hoped, since Papa hadn't said anything to me in awhile, that they had forgotten about the idea of going after my grizzly bear again.

"Yeah, traps," said Mr. Bern. "But do you know what, ahh...these are bear traps. And not just bear traps, but *grizzly* bear traps. Much, much bigger'n regular bear traps."

My heart sunk when he said 'grizzly bear traps'.

"And looky here," he continued, "I've spent the past two days sawin' the teeth off 'em, see how they don't have teeth? And looky this...do you know what this is?" He held up a black hoop. "This here is a rubber thing that goes onto the wheels of a BI-cycle, a *tires* is what the fella told me it's called. And see, I cut 'em up, and we'll fit them over the trap-jaws, and when your bear steps into the trap, the jaws snap shut but there's no teeth and the rubber's attached to it. So *one*, it won't hurt him, and *two*, feel this, kinda sticky when you move your hand over it, huh? So *three*, it'll hold him sure."

"You're sure it'll hold him?" I asked, hoping it wouldn't.

"Well, I'm sure hopin'," he said, then looked at me close. "What you thinkin', young'n? You're lookin' downright scowly today."

"So you're going after my bear?" I asked.

Mr. Bern looked surprised. "Your pa didn't tell you?"

"Well," I said, "I guess he did a long time ago, before the business with the Johnsons. But he hasn't said anything lately. I thought he had forgotten about it."

"Huh. Maybe I should have waited to show you all this. Your pa and me got a good plan thought up on how to catch the griz alive and take him down the mountain. He's got the vet comin' up with some magic potion to put him to sleep and all...I'm sure he'll be talkin' with you about it."

"June, will you walk with me?" asked Papa. We walked around the property like we used to do when I was little, when we would venture into the woods and he'd point out all different things. The different trees and wild flowers, the birds and the bugs, and any little critters we'd be lucky enough to sneak up on.

"I'm riding into town tomorrow to finalize things with Mr. Howell, the vet," he told me. "He's going to help me and Bern try to capture the grizzly."

"Yes sir. I heard."

"I know we haven't spoken about the bear in a while," said Papa. "Haven't spoken about much at all in a while, have we?"

"No, sir. I know you're still mad at me."

"No, June, I'm not still mad...well...*mad* is not the right word. I'm...ahh...I don't know the word. I still think about how close you came to getting yourself into something you couldn't get out of, even after promising us you wouldn't go into the woods. I'm still disappointed that you lied to us, *twice*. The second time nearly got you killed."

"Yes, sir."

"Anyway," Papa continued, "Bern's been baiting the areas where we've seen the bear, and that's where we'll be setting the traps."

"Baiting?"

"Yes, baiting," said Papa. "You know, uh...putting things around the area that the bear might like to eat, so he'll keep coming back. Like old deer meat, and Bern even threw apples all around. We know he likes apples, right?"

"He likes apple pie even better."

"Yeah, I do too," Papa chuckled. "I hope you're okay with this...if the Doc's medicine works, we should be able to catch him, take him down alive. I'd rather it be us than Alan Kelly and his men. It would also be a lot better than some hunter shooting him, don't you think?"

"I guess."

"A grizzly can't stay hidden forever. Somebody's going to find him."

"What if the stuff doesn't work?" I asked. "The sleeping stuff?"

"Well, we're hoping it will."

Papa spent the rest of the evening with Mr. Bern, doing some thing or other to his old wagon. They worked right through supper. After Mama and I finished eating, she stacked two plates of food and told me to take them out to the men. I didn't want to know what they were doing and didn't want to take plates out to them. Mama made me.

Night time was coming sooner every evening, and the temperature was definitely getting cooler. It was the first night that we had a fire in the fireplace. I put on my coat and walked out to the barn where Papa was lighting a couple of lamps so they could work into the night. I looked up to see our nightly family of bats zooming around catching all the tiny bugs. It wasn't winter yet if the bats were still flying.

"You see?" said Mr. Bern, "I told you if we stayed out here long enough, the food would come to us."

"Thank you, Bug," said Papa.

"What are you doing?" I asked. I guess I was a little curious.

"Here, I'll show you," said Papa. He set his plate down and hopped into the bed of the wagon. "You know what this is, right?" Behind the wagon's seat was a big spool of thick rope, with a crank handle on the side.

"A winch," I said. I knew what it was because they use them at the mill to move logs around, only ones a lot bigger.

"Very good," said Papa, "We've been building up the wagon to hold the winch. The winch is up front here to pull the grizzly into the wagon once he's asleep and tied down to Bern's drag-sled. You know, the *Indian sled* we used to bring out the big black female we ahh...killed. And here, this floor slides out the back and makes a ramp up to the wagon, so he should slide right in."

Papa sure was pleased by what they had done. And I guess it was kinda neat, or would have been if it wasn't made to catch my bear. There was a lot of heavy rope and chains hung on the sides, I guess to hold him down once he was in the wagon. "If he's asleep, why do you need all the chains?"

"He might wake up," said Mr. Bern.

"It's just in case," said Papa, "Can't be too safe handling a grizzly bear."

"It won't hurt him?" I asked.

"No, Bug," said Papa, "It won't hurt him. He won't even know he's in a wagon."

"And you're sure it'll work?" I asked.

"Sure hope so," said Papa.

"Ha!" cackled Mr. Bern, "I told her the same thing—'Sure hope it works'."

"We just have to get him into town," said Papa, ignoring Mr. Bern's outburst. "Sheriff Pettigrew said we could use the old jail building in town to hold him until we can move him to the zoo."

"The rich man's going to buy him?" I asked. "In Los..."

"Los Angeles," said Papa. "We've got letters sent to him, and to his company. He hasn't responded yet, but I'm sure he will."

"What if he doesn't?" I asked.

"He will."

When I left with Mama for school the next morning, Papa and Mr. Bern had the wagon all loaded up and were waiting for Mr. Howell to join them. They planned to set up the traps at Elk Creek, at the place where I had first given my bear a pie, and where Papa had shot at him and snatched me away to safety. That seemed like such a long time ago, and so much had happened since. I gave Papa a hug, of course, but it was a quick goodbye. I wasn't ready for them to come riding up to the house with my bear in the back of the wagon, and what if the vet's sleeping stuff didn't work? Would they kill him?

All day at school, I couldn't stop thinking about my bear. Thinking that Papa and Mr. Bern, and Mr. Howell, too, were really, finally, out in the woods with traps and guns trying to capture him.

I was more than a little surprised after we were dismissed for the day to see Papa waiting for me outside the schoolhouse. He was supposed to be out in the woods. They didn't already get my bear, did they? Papa smiled, but it wasn't a big smile. I stopped, afraid to go any closer. Papa came up to me and picked me up in his arms.

"Why aren't you in the woods?" I asked him. "Where's Mama?"

"Well," he said, "things have changed a little, and I have the afternoon off, so thought there's nothing I'd rather do than walk you and K home from school."

"Where's Mama?" I asked again.

"She's at home. I just thought it would be nice if I picked you up today. Is that all right?"

I hugged his neck tight and whispered in his ear, "Did you get him already?"

"No," Papa whispered back. "We'll talk about it when we get home, okay?"

"Were you hunting June's bear?" asked K.

"What do you know about it?" I snapped. "You're not supposed to know anything."

"Hey, Bug..." said Papa. "He just asked a question. And the answer, K, is no, I wasn't hunting June's bear."

"You weren't?" I asked.

"I'll tell you all about it when we get home."

"All right," I said.

"I just asked a question, June," said K. "You didn't have to bite my head off."

"So, you two," said Papa, "how was school?"

* * * *

"*My bear's dead?*"

"I'm sorry, Bug, that's what the town's saying," said Papa.

Mama was making food when Papa sat me down at the dinner table. I knew something was wrong from the way they were acting. Mama had given me a long hug like she hadn't seen me in a week.

"How, Papa? How do you know?" I asked as Mama stepped behind me and softly rubbed my back with her hand. "Are you sure?"

"We'll find out for sure as soon as we can," he said.

"Who told you?"

"Mr. Howell, when he finally showed up this morning, came

with the news. He said Alan Kelly, the Fancy Posse...they got the bear."

"But they were going to capture him, Papa, not kill him."

"Seems they had a problem, Bug, and ended up having to kill him," said Papa. "According to Howell, the whole town's talking about it."

"But what about the big cage, and the dogs, and the *Indians*?" I started to cry.

"I know," said Papa. "Howell said they tracked him all the way to Ponderosa Ridge. He said the bear fell into a big pit they had dug. They had ropes and chains on him, and were pulling him into the cage when he broke free. They had to shoot him."

"Why did they have to shoot him, Papa?"

"June," said Mama, "the bear killed two men. They had to shoot him."

"Good! I'm glad he killed them! I wish he killed all of them!" I ran up to my room to cry alone.

I wept until my pillow was as wet as if it were left outside in the rain, then I cried a little more. I surprised myself by suddenly stopping. I think I ran out of tears. I felt terribly hungry, and without another whimper stepped down the ladder and climbed into Mama's lap.

"Papa?"

"Yes, sweetie," he said from the other side of the table, his dinner plate barely touched.

"Do you know it's my bear? Could it be another grizzly bear?"

"I don't know, June," he said. "I doubt there would be another grizzly nearby. Mr. Howell said they were going to bring him to town in the next day or so, we'll know for sure then."

"Could it be another black bear that's brown?"

"I've told you all I know," he said. "Mr. Howell just said the whole town's in a tizzy about it, they're all waiting to see the bear for themselves. We'll know...soon."

He told me that after hearing the news from Mr. Howell, he and Mr. Bern still took the wagon to Elk Creek. He said Mr. Bern wasn't going to believe the posse killed our grizzly until he saw it for himself. They looked the area over, but there hadn't been any sign of my bear in a long time. And with the news about Alan Kelly killing him, Papa said he felt demoralized, and didn't think they should waste their time setting up traps until they found out for sure. *Demoralized* sounded like an important word and I was sure to write it down after I found out what it meant.

Mr. Bern wasn't happy either, mostly because he had spent so much time cutting the teeth off his traps. He was a little surprised the bear was so far away, but the bear obviously had moved on, not having seen a sign of him anywhere.

Papa settled back into his old routine of working at the mill all day, coming home to tell us the newest rumor of when the mill might close. I walked around in a funk. I was demoralized.

I couldn't get out of my head a scenario of my bear falling into a big hole dug by the Fancy Posse. Surprised, frightened, then terrified when the barking dogs and men with rifles jumped out of the bushes. "We got you!" My bear thrashing and fighting off the dogs, getting more and more tangled in the trap, men throwing lasso after lasso around his neck. Then finally, with one last lunge of his body, he snapped all the chains and ropes and made a desperate run to the safety of a huge blackberry patch with huge thorns that would have torn up anyone trying to follow. But before he could get to the thorny vines, Alan Kelly stepped in front of him, blocking his path. My bear stopped. Raising a shiny silver pistol as big as my leg, and with an evil smirk on his face, Alan Kelly shot my bear dead.

Mr. Howell was right about one thing, the whole town and the whole mountain was talking about the grizzly bear getting killed. But as the days went by, the stories were different about where the bear was killed, and even who it was that killed him. And as the days went by, not Alan Kelly or anyone else brought the dead bear to town.

Then one weekend afternoon, as we were sitting down for a lunch of ham and vegetable stew, Mr. Bern surprised us all when he rode up to the house on Willa. Fish of course was yapping and leading the way.

"Ahoy!" he excitedly called. "Ahoy in there!"

"You're too late," Papa called back, stepping onto the porch, "lunch is over."

"What did I tell you, son?"

"I don't know," said Papa, "what did you tell me?"

"The bear, *our* bear. He's still out there somewheres."

"What?" asked Papa.

"What?" asked me and Mama, jumping up from the table to join Papa on the porch.

"Yeah, boy," said Mr. Bern. "Don't know who started the rumor of his demise, but y'know, once a whiskey barrel gets rollin', it ain't easy to stop, even with all the drunkards a chasin' it."

"Huh?" I looked up at Mama.

"Those fools didn't kill no grizzly bear," explained Mr. Bern, climbing down from Willa.

"Are you sure?" asked Papa.

"Come inside, Mr. Simms," said Mama. "June, will you fill a bowl for Mr. Simms, please?"

Mr. Bern joined us at the lunch table. Though all our bowls were full, he was the only one eating, also the only one talking. We all wanted to hear his news. Mama didn't even say anything about his table manners.

"I knew somethin' was up," he said with a mouthful of stew. "Anybody gets a grizzly bear, they're gonna be in town the very next day collectin' back-slaps and accolades, and getting their portraits done as the Great Western Hunter, don'cha know." He took another big spoonful of stew, half of it dribbling down his chin as he spoke. "When I rode into town this mornin', had ten men and two ladies run up to me askin' if I'd heard the news. I said, 'What news is that?' They said, 'The news that Alan Kelly didn't CAP-ture no grizzly bear, didn't *kill* no grizzly bear, and didn't have none of his men get killed by no grizzly bear, either.'"

"Who'd they hear that from?" asked Papa.

"Was told to everybody by the newspaper man Phillips. Seems he got his fill of travelin' with Kelly's yahoos, and came back to town. He was more surprised than anyone hearin' the news the outfit he was with was supposed to have killed a griz. Said it wasn't true. Said they'd seen some signs, but never got near a grizzly on our mountain. Said Alan Kelly was going to move his men down to the Yosemite area to check out another supposed grizzly wanderin' around. Said to watch the newspaper for his story."

"Wow..." I said.

"Wow's right, young'n," Mr. Bern chuckled. "Is why I said I'd believe a killed griz when I see a killed griz."

"But..." said Mama, "you haven't seen any signs of him in a long time, correct?"

"Not near by, that's true," said Mr. Bern, "but I have seen signs of him moving up the mountain. Fish even tracked him a coupla times, but lost his scent. That's one smart bear. Don't know how you kept findin' him all summer, Miss J. You should be the one trackin' him for us."

"So, what are you thinking?" asked Papa. "Should we try again?"

"*I* think so," said Mr. Bern. "Done ruined all my bear traps. Be a shame to never see if they'd work or not. 'Course it still depends on Doc's *Miracle Medicine* workin', which...you know. And it'd mean movin' up the mountain a little. Could be gone awhile."

Mr. Bern left us that day with a whole lot to think about.

Chapter Sixteen

Mama and Papa waited until late at night, when I was sure to be asleep before allowing a word to be said about my bear. They couldn't have really believed I would let myself fall sleep and not listen in, could they?

"What do you think, Sonia?" Papa asked, as Mama joined him on the porch.

"I don't know what to think," said Mama. "Whether or not that Kelly fellow got the bear, it's not...I mean...Bern's been tracking and trying to find the bear for weeks now, and hasn't come any closer than finding an old footprint and a couple of dried out bear piles, correct?"

"That's only around the places that June's run into him," said Papa. "Bern's seen other indications of the bear, suggesting he's movin' up the mountain. It's been too dangerous for him around here with all the hunters and shootin' going on. June herself noticed him shot in the ear. Someone's going to get him."

Mama and Papa sat, quiet, thinking. Papa spoke, "Why not us get him? If we can get him, get him alive, that Selig fellow pays for him, that could save us, Sonia. You know the rumors about the mill getting shut down, it's going to happen, I may not have a job come spring."

"How much would he pay for a bear?" asked Mama, "What if he won't pay you anything? He hired Alan Kelly to find the bear, he may not pay anything for one that you brought in. It may not be worth the trouble, or risk."

"I'm sure he'd want our bear," said Papa. "Why not our bear? And why not us? I mean, we're the only ones to have actually seen the bear."

"*June's* the only one who has seen him," said Mama, starting to get upset. "You saw something dark moving in the bushes. Why is it that with all the hunters, trappers, and trackers looking for him, our daughter is the only one who has ever found him?"

"I don't know," said Papa. "It would be nice if she'd help us find him, we may be able to find him if she'd help."

"Help how?" asked Mama. "Tell you to go to Elk Creek? You've been there. You know the places where she's found him. You've gone there, and still haven't seen him. And now, you and Bern are going on a long trip to trap him? You'll be just another hunting party following old footprints up the mountain."

"What do you suggest we do? Not try?" asked Papa, getting a little upset himself.

"How long do you think you'll be gone?" asked Mama. "You've already taken time off from the mill. And what about me and Bug? It hasn't been that long since someone's taken shots at the house. Being alone during the day is one thing, but..."

"I know, I know," said Papa. "I was thinking you and June could go stay with the McDougals until I get back."

I couldn't stay quiet any longer. "I don't want to go to the McDougals!" I shouted.

"June, you're supposed to be asleep!" called Mama as I was climbing down the ladder.

"I don't want to stay at the McDougals," I said again, stepping over Chica to join them on the porch.

"June," said Papa, "you need to be asleep. Your mother and I are talking."

"But you're talking about *me*. Why can't I talk, too?"

Mama and Papa looked at each other, not saying anything. Then Papa spoke, "Okay, do you know where the bear is?"

"No."

"Do you know where he *might* be?"

"Maybe."

"Where?" Papa asked.

"Why can't me and Mama go with you? Why do we have to stay here?"

"Because," said Papa.

"But I might could help if I was with you," I said. "Even Mr. Bern said I should be the one tracking him."

"That's not a good idea," said Papa. "Bern wasn't serious. If you could just tell me where..."

"I don't know where," I said, "I don't know how I find him. I just do."

"You'll help find him if Papa lets you go?" Mama asked me.

"Hold on," said Papa, "there's no way..."

"I'll help," I said.

Mama got up from her chair, held my shoulders and looked me

in the eyes. "You'll help Papa and Mr. Bern find your bear?" she asked. "Help them *trap* your bear?"

"Uh-huh," I said, "I'll try."

"Wait a minute..." said Papa.

"We're going with you," Mama told him. "If you're going, we're going, too."

And that was that.

* * * *

It was a few days later when Mr. Bern showed up at the house in his rickety old wagon, a canvas tarp covering the grizzly traps and chains and gear, pulled by his two big mules. His horse Willa was tethered and bringing up the rear. We had been alerted to his arrival by Fish, of course, the yappingest bear-dog on the mountain.

I was already regretting my decision to help them find my bear. Although I knew it would be better if it was us that found him and not some hunters, I couldn't help feeling that I was double-crossing him. I imagined myself in the woods at one of our favorite spots, where I'd have a huge, fresh-baked apple pie for him. He'd poke his head out from behind a tree and smile a big toothy smile, so happy to see me again. He'd make a big leap over some bushes and land right in the middle of a dozen bear traps. I shuddered whenever I thought of that.

I think I said I would help them just because I didn't want to get left behind. Also, I never would have thought Mama would say what she said, that we were going too. I never would have thought

Papa would let us. They got into another argument about it, mostly about me and where I would be if they did catch my bear. It was decided that I would stay at Mama's side from the moment we left our house to the moment we returned.

The plan was for me to help find a good spot where my bear might be. Papa and Mr. Bern would set the toothless traps, bait the area with apples and then wait. I was to be a good distance away, with Mama, by the wagons and mules and would stay there no matter what.

Mr. Bern wanted to bring some of our chickens as bear bait, but I wouldn't let him. He still had part of a deer that was salted and wrapped so not to smell too bad, but it did smell pretty bad. "I know your bear's partial to apples," said Mr. Bern, "but I haven't met a bear yet that could pass on rotting venison. Yum yumm, huh?"

"That won't attract mountain lions, too?" I asked.

"Oh, no, Miss J, lions only eat what they themselves kill. Don't you worry."

"What about buzzards?" I asked.

"Buzzards, sure," said Mr. Bern, "but with the salt wrap it'll take 'em awhile to find it."

If and when my bear steps into a trap, Mr. Howell will poke him with the medicine that makes him fall asleep. Then they'll roll him onto Mr. Bern's Indian sled, carefully haul him back to the wagon, winch him onto it and strap him down. And then get him to town before he wakes up real mad. That's how it was supposed to go, anyway.

Though I had mixed feelings about agreeing to help capture my bear and ship him off to a far-away zoo, it was fun sitting with the grownups, having a big feast of a dinner, and listening to old stories of hunting and adventures. Mr. Bern told a story of his younger days as a trapper, getting mixed up in a little war with the lumber company he eventually went to work for. Papa told us a story of getting robbed and getting his horse stolen when he still lived in Texas, but then getting his horse back and a few more besides, from the men who had robbed him. He said he hadn't planned on coming to California, but that was the direction the men were chasing him. "If I hadn't had my horse stolen, I never would have met Mama." I'd never heard that story before.

Papa started to tell us about meeting Mama when she was a dancer but she quickly shushed him. So Mama *was* a dancer!

"Don't let us old folks use all the story time, young'n," said Mr. Bern. "Tell us a story of your'n."

"I'm too young to have a story," I said.

"Oh, come on," said Mr. Bern. "You're only a part of the biggest story this county has had in a mule's age. You're the Grizzly Girl, haa!"

I didn't feel like telling any more grizzly stories, and sure didn't want to talk about the mean men grabbing me and Papa shooting Big One. I didn't even like thinking about that story.

"Okay, well, have I ever told you about my friend K getting poison-oaked?"

"Naw, Miss J," said Mr. Bern, "don't believe I ever heard you tell that one."

Mama and Papa were both smiling, trying not to laugh as I told

Mr. Bern. By the time I was finished, he had almost fallen out of his chair he was laughing so hard.

"And that's a true story," said Mama.

"Well, I think that story's got us all beat, what d'you think?" Mr. Bern said. "And being the best storyteller of the night wins the Grand Prize!"

"Grand Prize?" I laughed.

"Hey, shouldn't there be a vote first?" asked Papa.

"Well, I vote for the young Miss June Bug, and unless Missus wants to finish the story of her dancing days..."

"Mr. Simms, please," said Mama.

"And since I'm holding *half* the grand prize here in my lucky overalls, I say the winner is the young June Allen."

He pulled out of his bib pocket something wrapped in soft cloth and handed it to me. It felt like a metal pipe through the cloth. I unwrapped it and... "What is it?"

"It's a monocular," explained Mr. Bern. "You know, a pocket glass. You see, hold it tight on this end...now pull hard on that end there."

"A telescope?" I pulled on the brass end piece, and out it came. My own telescope! "Oh, thank you, Mr. Bern," I said. "Look, Mama, look, Papa...now we can see things a long way away. Right?"

"Oh, yes," said Mr. Bern. "Can see lots of good stuff, maybe even spot our grizzly bear, what'cha think?"

"Yes, sir, and maybe I can climb that big oak tree by the canyon and look down on all the people in town. Can I do that?"

"Oh, I don't know if it's *that* powerful, it's just a pocket glass," said Mr. Bern. "But it is from the Big War, won it off'n an old, old Yankee colonel in a card game years back. Said he had been a Yankee colonel, may have just been an old man. Anyway, it's just been sittin' on my shelf all those years waiting for a reason to spy on somethin' again."

"Wow, a Yankee colonel! Papa, isn't this the best?"

"Well, hold on there," said Papa, walking up with a bundle of his own. I hadn't even noticed him leave the table. I moved my telescope to him coming closer, but it was too blurry to see anything.

"If you're going to take that with you on our upcoming adventure, you're going to need something to carry it in." The bundle he had was a leather belt with things attached to it.

"Wow, thank you, Papa," I said, and took the belt he had made and laid it out on the table, right on top of my dinner plate. The belt was a beautiful shiny brown, with a couple of flowers carved near the buckle and my name 'June' cut into the back. It had a holster of sorts, also with designs.

"That's for the monocular," said Papa. "The telescope,"

There was a big pouch with a cover, I looked up at Papa.

"That's just a pouch for anything you want to put in it," he said.

"What's this?" I asked, it was a wide piece of black leather looped around to form a sleeve and riveted to the belt. It had lots of blue and white beads sewn on around the edges.

"Do you know what a *scabbard* is?" Papa asked. "Well, that's not really a scabbard, but it's close enough to hold your..." Papa pulled from behind and slashed the air with...

"A new sword!" I yelled, "Papa, thank you!"

"No, ma'am," said Papa, holding it out to me. "It's *your* sword, look...I found it in the woods one day when I went back to check for bear sign. Cleaned it up a little."

Not just cleaned it up, but fixed it up beautiful. The wooden blade was so smooth and shiny, and had leather wrapped tight on the handle, with a beaded loop of leather to put my hand through so I wouldn't drop and lose it again. I had tears in my eyes as I held it, *my sword*. "Thank you, Papa, thank you so much."

"Not just me, Mama did all the bead work on the sword and the scabbard."

"Thank you, Mama, I love it. Thank you Mr. Bern, too, for the mono...scope."

"You're quite welcome, young'n."

"So, you think yourself properly outfitted now?" asked Papa.

"Yes, sir! Now we just have to fancy up Mama's holster."

Chapter Seventeen

Mr. Bern left that night to come back with Mr. Howell in the morning. I think Mr. Bern was afraid our vet would chicken out or change his mind. Well, morning came and no Mr. Howell, or Mr. Bern. Around lunchtime Mr. Howell rode up, but no Mr. Bern.

Mr. Howell explained, "He said for me to leave without him, that he was going to pick up someone else."

"Who? Who's he picking up?" asked Papa, not happy that we weren't already on the trail. During the time we waited for Mr. Bern to show, Mr. Howell took out the sleeping medicine and big needle they were going to use on my bear. Papa attached it to the end of a long stick, almost as tall as he was. He had designed for it a clamp of sorts to hold the needle, and they practiced sticking it into bales of hay. The needle fell off a few times, but Papa finally got it fixed so the needle would stay on, and after stabbing the hay a bunch of times, Papa looked pleased like it was really going to work. "I think the trick is to use it like a sword and not a spear," he said.

Even though it looked like we weren't leaving that day and it was pretty cold outside, I was dressed and ready to go in a new winter coat Mama had made from an old quilt, a new pair of wool lined boots to keep my feet warm, and my new sword belt. I was sitting on the wagon watching Papa and Mr. Howell through my new telescope and thumbing through some old *Weekly Readers* Mama had given to me for our expedition. If nothing else, this expedition was getting me lots of stuff. I got to looking at a story about the Donner Party, a group of folks coming to California through the mountains who got stuck in an early snow and ended up having to eat each other. I was only ten, but even I had heard of the Donner Party, though I had forgotten until just then. I wished I hadn't forgotten because there we were, going into the same mountains and it looked like an early winter storm might come. The days were definitely getting cold and there had been morning frost on the ground in the morning all week. I was getting up to insist to Papa we postpone the expedition until next spring or at the very least pack more food just in case we got stuck in snow, when I saw someone coming out of the woods, walking right toward the house.

"Who is this stranger?" I said out loud, though I'm sure I was the only one who heard myself. There wasn't enough time to run to the house and grab Mama's scatter-gun, and Papa was too busy with the vet to hear my calls. This one I would have to deal with on my own. Before pulling my sword, I figured I should have a closer look at the stranger. He looked quite plump and was wearing a strange outfit and appeared to have something in his hands. Telescoping my new telescope, I nervously peered through the lens, getting a closer look at the trespassing stranger. A trespassing stranger with a...a gun! I knew it!

I pulled my sword, he presented his gun. This was going to be ugly.

"Hey, June, look at the new air rifle my pa gave me. Is that your old sword you lost?"

It was K, of course, but he was dressed like an Indian, or mountain man of some kind, a big leather shirt with fringes on his sleeves buttoned over his fat winter coat, a red bandana around his neck, and a wide-brimmed, floppy hat on his head.

"Did the outfit come with the gun?" I asked.

"First off, it's a rifle, not a gun. And second, it's a *uniform*, not an outfit. And third, Miss Know-Nothing, it's a real Sons of Daniel Boone outfit. I'm in the Sons of Daniel Boone now. Is that a real telescope?"

"What's a Son of Daniel Boone?" I asked as I handed him my telescope and he handed me his rifle. "Is this real? Is it loaded?"

"Of course it's real, and it wouldn't do much good if it wasn't loaded." He looked again at the rifle, then said, "No, it isn't loaded... This scope it neat! Where'd you get it?"

"So, how do you load it? Is it a real gun?" I asked him again, taking perfect aim at the daytime moon.

"Sure it's real, it shoots a little bullet, called a *bb*. You put in the bb's here to load it. Then you cock it, and when you cock it, it loads up with air, and now it's ready to shoot."

"Do you have any bb's?" I asked.

"Pa said I have to practice without the bb's first...'cause they're just like bullets."

I took aim again at the moon. K looked through my telescope at the moon. I squeezed the trigger. *Pchew!* I shot a little burst of air.

"Hey, I think you hit it!" said K.

"Not bad for a girl, huh?" I said. "So, can girls be in the Daniel Boone thing?"

"Don't be silly. Of course they can't."

"Why not?"

"Girls can't do stuff like...like boys can," he said. He was looking up at Mr. Bern's overloaded wagon by the house. "Are you moving or something?"

"What? No...I'm leading a dangerous expedition into the woods to capture a giant grizzly bear. That's my gear."

It took K a second to hear what I had just told him. "No you're not."

"Don't believe me. Why do you think I have a telescope and my sword, then, and a wagon loaded down with bear traps and chains and guns and...and stuff? We're leaving as soon as Mr. Bern gets back with some more guns. Bigger guns. And I'm in charge. So what's the Daniel Boone thing?"

"Huh?" he asked, looking over the gear, and probably thinking about the guns.

"What do Daniel Boone kids do?" I asked again.

"Umm, the Sons of Daniel Boone. We ahh, you know, go camping and stuff. I don't really know. I just got my outfit today. I know we shoot guns, though."

"Without bullets?"

"No, I'm pretty sure with bullets."

"You want to see the bear traps?" I asked.

"Okay. So they're letting you go with them to get your bear?"

"Yeah," I said sadly. "Papa talked me into it."

"And you're going to kill him?"

"Oh, no, we're going to capture him alive, or try to," I said, "so he can live in a zoo, instead of being hunted on the mountain."

"Why do you need bigger guns if you're not going to shoot him?"

"We're expecting to run into outlaws."

Papa came over to the wagon with us and made a big deal out of K's new rifle, but he'd never heard of the Sons of Daniel Boone, either. As we were looking over the bear traps and the other gear, Jack came flying out from under the house and joined the crazy dog Fish in making laps around the property like we'd be betting on the winner. Mr. Bern came riding in on Willa. He had someone else with him, a young man riding a mule, who was dressed almost exactly like Mr. Bern. Brown and black plaid lumberman coat over old overalls, big old brown boots and an old brown felt hat. He could have been a young Mr. Bern before Mr. Bern got loud.

"Evenin', evenin' all!" Mr. Bern trumpeted. Did he know he was wearing the same clothes as that other fella?

"Sure sorry about losin' the day like this," said Mr. Bern. "I got to thinkin' that it would be to our benefit if we had a strong back with us to get that bear into the wagon. I'm no good to lift anything, and Doc, well, he ain't goin' to lift much either. He was already shaking and downing his bottles at the thought of having to even get *near* a bear. Oh hey, Doc, there you are. You're the only able body among us, Allen."

"Don't let Sonia hear you say that," said Papa.

"And me too!" I shouted.

"I stand ever corrected" said Mr. Bern. "Now my nephew Elam here, come here boy, introduce yourself. Elam here is strong as a bear hisself. Kinda dumb, but we just need his back, you know."

"All right, good. We paying him?" asked Papa.

"Payin' him? Ain't payin' him nothin'. His ma still owes me for an old woodstove I got for her last year."

"Must have been a nice stove," said Papa.

"No, not really. But she can start a fire in it, so it works jest fine," laughed Mr. Bern.

"Never be holdin' to your family, huh?" said Papa.

Mr. Bern laughed, "Naw, or your eldest might be CON-scripted to rassle grizzly bears, haa!"

"Welcome to our little adventure, Elam," Papa said, shaking his hand.

"Hey there, Miss J, did we go and hire on a cavalry scout to lead us?" asked Mr. Bern. "Shoot, I didn't have to bring Elam along after all. This young fella looks downright *dangerous*, wha'cha say?"

K looked pretty terrified that Mr. Bern had noticed him.

"He's a real Sons of Daniel Boone, and they shoot guns and everything," I said, trying to build up my friend. "He's got a new rifle and he's going shooting with his pa later today."

"Is that so?" said Mr. Bern, very impressed. He walked Willa up to the side of the wagon and held out his hand. "Name's Bernard Simms. Pleased to know you, sir."

K was nervous, but seemed happy that a man as big as Mr. Bern had just called him 'sir'.

"They call me K, sir," he said proudly and shook Mr. Bern's hand.

"*Kay*, you say?" Mr. Bern asked, then seemed to remember something. "Oh, my, poison oak! You're the poison oak boy, right? When Miss J here told me that story, I about rolled out the door I laughed so hard!"

I was glad K's gun wasn't loaded, the way he looked over at me. A look even Mr. Bern noticed.

"I'm sorry there, Mr. Kay, don't mean to laugh," said Mr. Bern. "I myself could tell you poison oak stories that would curdle your turtles."

"A right of passage for these parts," said Papa.

"That's the truth," continued Mr. Bern. "We've all been there. We've *all* been poison oaked. Shoot, I *still* get poison oaked and I'm supposed to be retired, haa! Just wait, Mr. Kay, 'til your pa makes you clear a whole acre of poison oak and you stir up a town of ground hornets. You didn't stir up hornets, did you?"

K shook his head. "No, sir," not feeling as embarrassed.

"He stirred up worms, though," I said. "K's terrified of worms."

Chapter Eighteen
Part II The Expedition

I didn't get any sleep the night before we headed out. First, I was thinking and thinking about the expedition, if we would find my bear and if the traps and the sleeping medicine were going to work. I thought about the nice zoo he would end up in and if it really would be nice, and if he would think I betrayed him. Then I was thinking about the Donner Party and hoping it wouldn't snow on us, but wondering who would be the first one in *our* party we'd have to eat. If it came to that, which I hoped it wouldn't. I decided on Elam, because he was so big and I didn't know him. I thought I could probably eat someone I didn't know. If I had to.

When I finally fell asleep, I had a nightmare with the Mean Men climbing up the tree I was hiding in. Papa kept shooting at them but missed every time and couldn't stop them climbing to get me. I woke up screaming. It was still the middle of the night, but Mama came to my bed and after holding me for a while, said we should just get up and start the stove for a good breakfast for everyone. We tiptoed quietly to the kitchen, stepping over and around the sleeping, snoring men in the middle of the floor.

Everyone was soon up and working to get the mules and horses fed and load up anything that wasn't already loaded. It was the coldest morning yet, and still a couple of hours away from dawn. Papa had Mr. Howell hold a lantern so they could see what they were loading where. Mr. Howell didn't look like he knew how to help, other than hold the lantern. His time to help would come. I watched them through the window in the kitchen as Mama pulled out a hot batch of biscuits for breakfast. I helped her put sticks of bacon into each one so we could all have a quick meal and even eat while we rode.

It was exciting watching the men walking in and out of the lantern light, their breaths misting heavy like smoke in the cold air. It seemed such a grand adventure that I was a part of. I even forgot what it was we were loading up to do.

By the time the sun was starting to light up the mountain, we were all ready to go. I was bundled like an Eskimo, had so many layers on I had trouble buckling my new sword belt around me. And I was still cold, even with my new winter boots, and a wool scarf wrapped around most of my face under my floppy cowgirl hat. I was having a time trying to climb up onto the big wagon to join Mama, when Papa surprised me by lifting me up onto Whiskey to ride with him.

"I thought I wasn't allowed to leave Mama's side," I told him.

"Well, that's true," he said as he climbed onto the saddle and pulled me onto his lap. "But since you're leading this adventure, Mama told me it was okay if you rode with me the first day. That okay with you?"

"Yes, sir." So, I was really going to lead the expedition! Mr. Bern had called it a *hunt* earlier, but promised to call it an *expedition* from then on after I got mad because we weren't supposed to be hunting my bear. Papa and I were followed by Mr. Bern on Willa, Mr. Howell on his horse named Russell, then Mama driving the big, old wagon. Mr. Bern's nephew Elam brought up the rear on his mule. I didn't know his mule's name. Elam was so big I'd been afraid to ask. I asked Mr. Bern and he said to ask Elam, he don't bite. I decided to just call his mule 'Mule'.

Fish was already yapping and chasing the air, and we hadn't even moved. Poor Jack was tied to the porch because Papa wanted Chica and him both at the house to watch over the place while we were gone, though I don't know how protected the house would be with Jack tied up and Chica old and deaf. I guess any outlaws breaking into the house would trip over Chica lying in front of the door, and then Jack would bite them if his rope reached. Our neighbors the McDougals were going to check on them and the other animals and keep everyone fed while we were gone. Jack was barking and jerking at the rope like he'd never see us again, and it worried me, what if he knew something we didn't? What if he was trying to warn us? I read where animals can sense things that people can't. All the dogs in San Francisco, a few years before, knew an earthquake was coming and tried to warn the people but no one listened, just like we weren't listening to Jack. I didn't want to leave him behind. I thought we should take Jack and leave Fish, but no one was listening to me, either.

Mama and I had packed and prepared enough food for everyone for about a week. I brought up the story of the Donner Party and thought we should have twice as much food but Mama said we didn't have that much food, and that Papa could shoot a deer if we ran out. I said the Donner Party had guns, too, but they still starved. Mama said, "Well we're not the Donner Party."

"We ready?" called Papa when we were all lined up to go. "Everybody ready? Are you excited?" he asked me.

"I guess so, yes." Leading an expedition was exciting, the trip into the mountains with a wagon full of guns and gear was exciting. Missing school was exciting. But I felt sad about my bear. Maybe we wouldn't even see him.

"Hey Doc!" said Mr. Bern. "You were with the Seventh Cavalry, right? What did Custer say when it was time to get the troops movin'?"

"Well," replied Mr. Howell, "I joined the Seventh some years *after* Custer's unfortunate, ahh, passing. But the officers would usually say *Hi-oh*, or something to that effect, to get things rolling."

"Naw," said Mr. Bern. "He'd say, 'Last one's still got his scalp gotta buy the whiskey,' ha haa!"

"Oh, yes," said an unamused Mr. Howell, "that's funny."

Mr. Bern looked to me, "Can you believe I just now thought that up, Miss J?"

"Mr. Simms..." scolded Mama, though she was smiling.

"What?" he asked. "That wasn't funny? I thought that was funny... HI-OHHH!"

With that, our Great Grizzly Bear Expedition began.

* * * *

Close to where we last saw my bear, when Papa saved me from the Big and Smelly Ones, we stopped. Papa and Mr. Bern rode down the creek trail while the rest of us stayed with the wagon. I was secretly glad Papa wouldn't let me go with him. I still had nightmares about Big One and never wanted to see that part of the creek again. That was one of the spots Mr. Bern had baited with a bunch of buried apples, hoping my bear would find them and stay close. A few apples were dug up, but obviously by hungry raccoons.

"Nope," Papa said when they returned about an hour later. "Not a sign of a bear. Was hoping we'd get lucky with signs of him here, but nothing."

Mr. Bern looked to me, "Which way, Miss Buggy J?" and smiled big, proud of his rhyme.

"Umm," I thought, "I think he'll follow Elk Creek farther up the mountain, but not too far."

"Sounds good," said Papa.

The sun had been shining all morning and it felt like we were just on a nice ride out on the mountain. We rode by my school, I was hoping the kids would be out playing, so they could see me, but they were all inside.

"Do you wish you were in there with your friends?" Papa asked.

"No, sir," I said, shaking my head.

I loved riding with Papa on Whiskey. I had my new telescope out and saw a couple of deer that no one else was able to see. I was hoping we could get closer to them so I could see them even more up-close, but with Fish yapping like he was, they slipped away before we were anywhere near.

"He smells somethin'..." said Mr. Bern, surprising me when he pulled his rifle from its scabbard. Mama stopped the wagon and picked up her scatter-gun. "Smells something, sure." I couldn't tell the difference between Fish's barking now and his barking almost continuously since we left the house, but I guess Mr. Bern could. Papa walked Whiskey between where Fish was barking and the wagon. He lifted me off Whiskey and handed me to Mama. She passed me to the wagon bed right behind her so she could shoot if needed. I started to pull out my telescope to spot what might be coming, but instead leaned right up against the back of Mama and hid my face in her hair. I didn't even think to pull my sword.

Fish leaped into the brush as Papa pulled out his pistol. I covered my ears and closed my eyes tight. He was gone for just a short time, then came bursting back out, followed by Jack!

"Jack!" I yelled. He came scrambling out of the bushes with his tongue out and his tail wagging so fast I don't know how it stayed on. The mules got a little spooked as he darted around, not knowing who to visit first, frustrated that we were all up in the air on horses or the wagon. "Jack! C'mere, boy... Hop up!" I called. After one try where he fell back down, he made a great leap to the top of the wagon wheel then into Mama's lap, licking her face and my face too.

"You dog, I tied you good!" said Papa.

"Can he stay, Papa?" I asked.

"Well...we're not turning back now. Guess Chica'll have to

watch the place by herself."

"You can stay, boy!" I said.

"The McDougals will think they lost our dog," said Mama.

"Yeah," said Papa, "but we can't lose a day taking him back. How'd you get away?" he asked Jack.

I think Papa was as happy as I was that Jack had escaped. We continued on, Jack sitting between me and Mama, and Fish barking even more, jealous of Jack getting to ride.

Coming upon some trails that would lead back down to Elk Creek, Mr. Bern asked if I agreed this would be a good place to scout out a spot to set the traps. This was where I advised we go, but now I wished I hadn't suggested it. Even though I couldn't feel my bear close by, it would be a perfect spot for him to be. The mountain was so beautiful, and though it was really cold, it was my bear's home. He would never want to leave it. I never should have agreed to help.

My bear might not have wanted to leave the mountain, but Elam sure did. It was only half a day since we left the house, but Elam was already complaining. About his saddle being old and uncomfortable, about his feet being cold, and how it was much colder up there than the valley and he didn't have any gloves.

"Boy," said Mr. Bern, "your complainin' ain't gonna make your fingers or your little toes warmer. Maybe you forgot when winter comes, it might get cold."

If anyone should be complaining already, it should be Mama. Mr. Bern's old wagon had horrible seat springs, and we had moved off the main road a good ways back. The little road we were on was rutted and rocky and strewn with fallen limbs. Riding with Mama felt like having someone hitting the bottom of the seat with a big hammer, even though we were going pretty slow. We had to go slow, or we'd both be bounced right onto the ground, Jack too. Also, there was no horse under us to at least warm up our bottoms and it was really, really cold. Mama had me pull out a couple of blankets for us to sit on and wrap around our legs, and we had Jack between us so it wasn't too bad, but it would get colder. Mama never complained, and I wasn't going to complain either, I promised myself.

I got to go with the grown-ups when we stopped to scout an area to place the traps. I rode with Mama on Whiskey, and Papa rode down on Mr. Howell's horse. Mr. Bern came on Willa, Elam and Mr. Howell stayed with the wagon and held on to the dogs who didn't like being left behind at all.

I had my telescope out as we traveled down the trail to a big wide spot on the creek. I climbed down with Mama and looked around. I closed my eyes to see if I got a feeling of my bear being close. I couldn't tell. I didn't know if I ever really got a feeling before, either. And now, if I happened to get a feeling of some kind, I didn't know if I wanted to tell anyone. I had everyone looking at me for some reaction. I led them away from the horses, Mama holding tight to my hand. I looked for underbrush where he could hide, and a big open area by the creek where he could roll around. But this place was too easy for folks to get to, and he'd be hiding from people.

"I think he's been here, but he'd be in a place where there' s not an easy trail," I whispered.

"Sound reasoning, young'n, I would agree," said Mr. Bern. We were all whispering, and listening.

"The trail looks to get smaller up-creek," Papa quietly said. "How about we go a little farther than the trail?"

"Okay," I said.

"So which direction are we heading?" Mama quizzed me. "North, South, or West?"

I had to think only a moment, "It's umm...Elk Creek comes down from the East, so we're heading East."

"Very good," said Mama. "So which direction is the creek flowing toward?"

"Umm. It's flowing *that* way."

"HA!" bellowed Mr. Bern. "Great answer, Miss J! You are definitely born of the woods."

I smiled at what I thought was a compliment, but were we not whispering anymore?

We rode up-creek for a spell. Almost a mile, I'd say, but I'm not good at figuring miles yet. Papa said we'd gone about a mile, and I agreed with him. The trail shrank down to a path, and then to no path, and we were squeezing between oak trees and pine trees, and then shoving through manzanitas and big bushes whose names I didn't know, but which all had thorns or stickers, grabbing and scratching us. "How do animals live in this stuff?" I asked, not wanting to complain, but *ouch*. The horses weren't too happy, either, and neither was Mama. I was supposed to be the poison oak spotter, too, but had a hard time even looking for it with all the thorns scratching me. The trail finally opened to a small clearing, free of thorns, and we all got down.

Papa and Mr. Bern stood off by themselves, whispering. "What do you think?" Papa asked him.

"I think this looks like a perfect place. Good cover, huckleberries mostly eaten, appearance of a bear trail yonder, and looky there, bear's been diggin' after grubs." Mr. Bern walked over and slowly lowered himself to a hole dug into the wet ground. "I'd swear to it these claw marks are too big for a black bear. Anyone see scat?"

I found one pile of bear poop, but Mr. Bern was sure it was too small for a grizzly bear to have made. "The bigger the heap, the bigger the sheep," he told me. "In this case, the bigger the bear...but that don't mean this ain't a good place for him."

I closed my eyes and still didn't feel my bear near. I opened them to Papa, Mr. Bern and Mama all staring expectantly at me. I didn't want to tell them I didn't feel anything, and Mr. Bern seemed to think my grizzly had been digging there and he knew more about grizzlies than I did, so I told them, "I think this is a good place."

We made our way back through the thorny bushes, and up to the wagon to get the gear. Papa and Mr. Bern were anxious to set up the traps they'd done so much work on, removing the teeth and all. Papa told Mama and me, "Even if this isn't the right place, it'll be good to get 'em set up, see what happens."

I was relieved when Mama told me we'd be making camp by the wagon and making supper while the men set things up. I really didn't want to go down through those thorns again. Papa and Mr.

Bern were talking about where best to set the traps. It occurred to me that we were really going to try and capture my grizzly. A wave of sadness hit me hard and I wished I'd never agreed to help catch him.

"Are you okay?" Mama asked me. "You're so quiet."

"Just tired."

Mama and I were still a ways from the road when I heard Mr. Bern yelling up ahead. Mama hupped Whiskey and we made it to the wagon.

"How much food have you eaten?" Mr. Bern was hollering.

"Not much," said Elam. "I was hungry. We didn't know when you were coming back."

"Uh, I didn't eat anything...maybe one little bite," stammered Mr. Howell.

"You ate a whole morning's biscuits!" yelled Mr. Bern.

"I like biscuits!" Elam yelled back.

"And a whole apple pie?" Mama noticed.

"That was for my bear!" I added.

"Not the whole thing," said Elam.

"I only had a bite," said Mr. Howell.

Mr Bern and Elam got into an awful row, mostly Mr. Bern yelling, but Elam was yelling back. I had just met Elam that morning, but the only words I had ever heard him say had been either complaining or yelling. I didn't like Elam. Yep, he'd definitely be the first one we eat. If we had to. Plus, it'd be only fair, since he was eating everyone else's food.

"Mr. Simms, please," said Mama. "We still have plenty of food, and we've got a big bag of flour to make fresh biscuits. But Elam, we brought just enough food for all of us. So, please, next time wait for meal time when we can all eat."

"Yes, ma'am, sorry."

The way Mr. Bern lit into Elam, you'd have thought he had eaten all the food. And now it was about the time to make supper, but it would also be dark soon and Papa wanted to set the traps down by the creek.

We all got busy making camp. There was a little clearing for the wagon and fire pit, and the ground around the big pine and oak trees was free of bushes. I helped Mama unload skillets and plates and food to cook while Papa got a fire started. It was suggested to Mr. Howell that he unload all the tents, and Mr. Bern glared at Elam.

"Unhook the mule team, Dingus," Mr. Bern told him, "and get the big one loaded with traps and chains. I hope you enjoyed your biscuits, boy, 'cause that's all you'll be eatin' tonight."

Elam either knew very little, or cared very little about horses and mules. Or maybe he was just really mad at his uncle Bern. Whatever the reason, he kept walking right behind the mules with clanking chains and traps and throwing them on the ground beside the big one, even bumping into their backsides once or twice. I knew not to do that.

"Boy, you're gonna get your head kicked in, you spook one of them mules by clanking around behind them," said Mr. Bern.

"I'm sure you'll miss me."

"Well, your mother might...maybe."

Elam had so far only loaded one trap on the big mule's pack saddle which I could see was making Mr. Bern mad. So Mr. Bern hobbled over and grabbed two traps out of the wagon with his hand that didn't hold his cane and was loading them himself. They were talking ugly to one another again, but quiet enough I couldn't hear, other than Mr. Bern telling him, "Your elderly ma would've been more help on this trip."

"Why don't they like each other, Mama?" I asked.

"This is just between us, okay?" Mama whispered to me. "Mr. Simms told me his sister wanted him to take Elam the next time he had a hunting trip. I guess he's never been one for providing for the family. Doesn't like work all that much, either."

"Why?"

"Some people are like that. And I don't think Elam's mama brought him up where he was expected to help out."

"Why? He's so big."

"I don't know, June."

Before long, the pack mule was loaded. "All right," hollered Mr. Bern, "let's get these things set before we can't see not to step in 'em ourselves."

The men were going together to set the traps, even Elam. Papa wanted everyone to know where they were if we caught something and all had to rush down. Except for Mama and me—we were supposed to stay with the wagon if my bear was trapped. As the men were mounting up, we heard some rifle shots echoing through the mountains. I looked up at Mama.

"Just hunters," she calmly told me. "It *is* deer season, remember."

"Maybe ya'll should come down too," said Papa.

"We'll be fine, Patrick," Mama said. "When *don't* we hear rifles during deer season. Just don't you forget to bring in a couple of bucks for the smokehouse when our expedition is over."

"Will do," smiled Papa.

While the men were setting the traps, Mama and I set up the tents and cooked supper. We had smoked venison with eggs and beans. Venison is, of course, deer meat, and I tried not to think of Mr. Bern bringing a rotten deer leg to try to bait my bear, and made extra sure we didn't get the good meat mixed up with the bad meat. But I'm pretty sure we cooked the good stuff. We had a lot of venison jerky, too, but most of that was for Fish and Jack.

It was neat cooking food for an expedition party. I wasn't too sure how the tents were supposed to go, so Mama mostly did that while I cooked the food. I was nervous at first, cooking by myself—beans are easy, but it was the first time I'd cooked them in a pot hanging over a campfire. I did it all by myself, even the coffee. I waited until the men came back to start the eggs so they'd be good and hot, and Papa was very impressed with my cooking. Mr. Bern said I could get a job as cook in a lumber camp, but probably not until I was older.

Chapter Nineteen

P apa? What if a raccoon steps in a trap?"

He laughed, then said, "Mr. Raccoon would be awful surprised, wouldn't he? Actually, these traps are just for big animals, you need a lot of weight to set them off. You need to be a bear...or a cougar."

"Or a vetra-narian," added Mr. Bern. Mr. Howell didn't think that was funny.

"What if a *black* bear steps into a trap?" I asked. "Or a mountain lion?"

"That's a good question," said Papa. "We did see a lot of bear sign that was probably from a black. Hey, Bern, what are your thoughts if we snare a black? Been so focused on Griz, I hadn't given much thought to catchin' anything else."

"Ahh, well, we'd shoot it," said Mr. Bern. "No getting the trap off any other way I would think. And bear meat's delicious, wouldn't be a bad thing to trap one."

"Shoot it?" I asked.

"Well, Bug," Papa said, "a bear's not going to sit still to let us... Hey Doc, how much of your potion have you got? If we accidentally snagged a different bear, could we stick it? See if the stuff really works?"

"Uhh, yes, yes. I made up quite a bit, there's enough," said Mr. Howell.

"If it even works," said Mr. Bern quietly. Then not so quietly said, "Okay then! If it's a black that gets trapped, we send in Doc to get in some practice sticking a bear without getting his arm bit off, ha!"

"And if we snare a cougar?" asked Papa.

Mr. Bern thought about it a second. "We send Elam."

We all chuckled about that, except for Elam. I got up to collect the plates for cleaning, was walking over to Mama and the wash tub when I overheard Mr. Bern talking quietly to Papa. "So when we trap the *right* bear, our grizzly bear," said Mr. Bern, "and Doc there sticks 'em, and he *don't* fall asleep, then what's your plan? I mean, the chance of our bumbling vetra-narian inventing something like that seems..."

"I know," said Papa, "I know. He swears it'll work, but if it doesn't, which, yes, is a possibility."

"A good possibility, if you ask me."

"Well," said Papa, "then I guess we'd have to shoot him. Hate to do it. Can't just leave the trap stuck on him. No getting him down the mountain if he's awake and angry."

"Whoo, your young'n ain't gonna like that a'tol."

"No," said Papa, "no, she won't. We'll just have to see what happens.

"Still," said Mr. Bern, "wouldn't be a bad trip, goin' back with a grizzly bear rug."

"Hmmm," sighed Papa. "June would hate us the rest of our days."

* * * *

I knew Elam was told he couldn't eat supper with us, and he was off by himself in the dark, but nobody told me not to give him anything. And I *was* the cook, and there *were* a couple extra eggs and a strip of meat, so I took him over a plate. He wasn't far off, just on the other side of the wagon which was good because it was dark and I wouldn't have taken his plate too far. He was standing close to the wagon looking strange, and I first thought he was stealing food again. I would have run back to others and told them he was stealing food if he hadn't seen me. So I walked up to him and held out the plate.

"Here," I said. Elam reached out to take it and had apples in his hands. I knew it! He was stealing apples!

"I'm not eating the apples," he said.

"Okay," I said, and turned to go back and tell everyone that Elam was eating the apples.

"No, really," he said. "Look." He set the food in the wagon and then started tossing apples into the air and catching them. He was juggling them and doing a good job. A *great* job considering how dark it was.

"Okay," I said again and walked back to the others.

They were all sitting on blankets around the fire, Mama saying how she would be sure to pack chairs on the next expedition. Mr.

Bern was tending to one of the bear traps, wrapping a leather strip around the rubber so it would stay on. I'd been around those traps a lot lately, but I could never get over just how big they were, and even with the teeth sawed off, they still looked mean.

"Have you used these traps a lot? I mean with the teeth still on?" I asked Mr. Bern..

"Yes ma'am, caught many a bear with 'em. Many a bruin."

"Have you ever accidentally stepped on one?" I asked.

"No, I haven't," he said. "A good trapper always knows where his traps are set. Or should know. And I've always marked 'em real good, too."

"I bet it would hurt to step in one," I said, thinking if I were to step in one, also thinking about my bear stepping in one.

"Wouldn't be pleasant," Mr. Bern chuckled. "Let me think...there *was* a fella once, I'm rememberin'...but you don't want to hear that story."

"Yes I do," I said, "I'd love to hear that story. Please, Mr. Bern?" I think he would have told us the story even if we had all asked him *not* to tell it, he just liked being asked.

"Oh...all right," he smiled. "Now, what story was I gonna tell?"

"Some fella stepped in a bear trap," I said. "Did he die?"

"Don't get ahead of me, young'n," he said, "Oh, what was his name, the fella what stepped into a grizzly bear trap. What was his name. Anyway, I think I've told you the story of the big griz eatin' our timber camp years ago."

"I love that story," I said.

"Well, after that griz ate the whole dern camp, ate one of our mules, scared us all half to death, well, after that, our crew of

216

lumberjacks wasn't good for nothin'. Everyone was too scared to work, afraid ol' Griz would jump out any second from the scrub and eat one or all of us. We had a number of men sneak off they was so scared. So, the foreman, he goes down the mountain to get more men and more guns, don'cha know. Also picked up about a dozen bear traps which were set around the camp. Well, one night...naw, I don't think it was even dark yet, but this fella who's name I can't remember, he walks out into the woods to do his business I imagine, and steps *WHAP*, right into one of the traps."

"Did he die?" I asked, snuggling close to Mama.

"Naw, but he let out a scream the likes of which I'd not heard since the day I was born."

"Mr. Simms, please," Mama quickly scolded, though I wasn't sure why.

"Oh, pardons, Missus," said Mr. Bern, "and young Missus...I only meant I was such a big baby, you see."

"We get it, Bern," said Papa, trying not to laugh. "So the man stepped in to a trap..."

"Right," continued Mr. Bern. "This feller lets out a scream the likes I'd never heard before. I had just got back to camp with some of the other men when we heard the screeching. Well, we thought the bear was back and had grabbed someone. So everyone picked up an axe if they couldn't find a rifle, or whatever else they could get their hands on, and ran into the trees to save the man from getting' *et* by the bear. I mean *everyone* ran, right into the woods. Now, a friend of mine running beside me, his name was, ahh, Samuels, well *he* steps into a trap, *SNAP*, not ten feet in front of me. So now he was screaming, too, you know. I saw him with the trap on his leg, but the other men who didn't see, thought that *Samuels*, now, was being attacked by a bear, too. Well, everyone just stopped, they were terrified. Maybe there was *two* bears this time, or more. I was yellin' for help, others were yellin', two men screaming, nobody knew what the heck was happening. It was, you know, *chaos*, that's the perfect word, chaos. And now the men who had grabbed guns, now, they thought we were being attacked by an *army* of grizzly bears, and what do they do? The dumbskies, they start popping off those guns and rifles and pistols in just every direction."

"Oh, my," I said, my eyes big.

Mr. Bern started laughing, "Oh my is right. I laid flat on the dirt, trying not to get shot while I helped Samuels get the trap off his leg. And now I thought, too, maybe there *was* an army of bears attacking us, why else would there be all the shootin'? Oh, lord, lookin' back, it does make you laugh."

I hadn't even thought of laughing until he said that. "So, what happened?"

"Oh, guys started figuring out what had happened, got help to the two who stepped in the traps. Turned out, the traps were set by just a couple of men who barely marked where the traps were, just a chalk marker on the tree nearest the trap. Well, most of the trees in that forest were marked, the ones we were to cut down, so nobody, even if they saw the mark, would probably think much of it. So, nobody but those two knuckleheads even knew where the traps were. Which is why I've always since marked my bear traps with a flag of red canvas on a stick, so you know there's a trap there."

"That's smart," said Mama.

"Well, yes and no. I've had more traps stolen than bears caught because of it. Other trappers see the flags and just take the traps for themselves. Traps ain't cheap, you know. Used to be, trappers and hunters were honest to the end, but no more."

"So did you lose all your traps?" I asked.

Mr. Bern laughed, "Well, I'd lose some, then just go look for someone else's traps to ahh, borrow. And you know the thing was, some of the traps I'd steal were the very traps got stolen from me! Ha haa! You see, no honesty anymore. And ahh...if we could keep that just between us."

I had to laugh at the thought of Mr. Bern sneaking around the woods stealing his own traps back.

"Sure hope we get your griz," said Mr. Bern, "and some kind of reward money, since I've probably ruined most of my bear traps by cutting the teeth off. Whoo boy, these things ain't cheap. How'd you talk me into all this, young'n?"

Chapter Twenty

The night was really cold, but we were toasty warm in the tent. I was snuggled between Mama and Papa, and had Jack laying across my feet. The men took turns during the night staying up with the fire, listening for traps getting snapped and guarding against all dangers. It was a quiet night, nothing exciting happened. Although I was exhausted from the long day, I had trouble getting to sleep. Mr. Bern's story of grizzly bears attacking his camp maybe wasn't the best to hear on our first night out in the dark woods. I wasn't afraid of *my* bear attacking us, but what if there were others?

I opened my eyes to a beautiful yellow glow as the morning sun hit our tent. Mama was lacing her boots up and humming a little song. Her boots weren't as warm as mine, but she never once complained about her toes being cold. I stayed in bed a little while longer, was really enjoying lying in a tent, under a big pile of blankets, in the woods, on a mountain. I'd never been camping before on the mountain. Setting up a tent just a stick's throw from our house hardly seemed like camping compared to this. I thought about those nights in the tent on our property, how exciting it was. When Mama and Papa got tired of sleeping in the tent with me, they said I could invite K over to spend the night, all by ourselves. Well, all by ourselves with Mama. She had a big fire going for us, we roasted corn and told scary stories until it was time to turn in. K had never been camping before, not like I had, and the first sound of an owl had him shaking and wanting to be taken home. We ended up with our bedrolls on the porch, Mama too, and in school on Monday he bragged to everyone how he had gone camping.

I knew we were on an expedition to catch my grizzly bear, but was it also camping?

"Yes, it's camping," said Mama, when I asked her the question. "We've finally brought you camping, June."

Everyone was sitting around the fire warming up and enjoying the breakfast Papa had made. Even Elam was there. I was a little mad at myself for being the last one up.

"Nothing better'n a good breakfast, cooked hot out under the cold trees, is there, Miss J?" asked Mr. Bern.

"No, sir, I guess not."

"And even your pa can't mess up bacon too bad," he laughed. "But he does tend, I've noticed, to make the coffee *way* too strong for my delicate palate."

"Papa makes *great* breakfast," I said. "You should try his flapjacks."

"Thank you, June," said Papa.

We heard a loud rifle shot echo through the trees.

"Somebody got his buck," said Mr. Bern. Then there was a few more shots, close together. "Whup, somebody *missed* his buck," and everyone laughed.

Papa and Mr. Bern rode down to check the traps. We all would have heard if a bear or anything else had been caught during the night, but they wanted to check them anyway, replace apples that may have been taken by little critters and check for any sign of my bear sniffing around. A raccoon had a wonderful find in the apples, but other than that, nothing was disturbed.

"Are you getting bored?" asked Mama, seeing me laying across the wagon seat, staring up at the clouds.

"Kind of," I said. If I had known what she had in mind, I would have replied with an enthusiastic *no*, but I didn't.

"Then it's the perfect time to work on your studies."

"My what?"

"You didn't think we'd take you out of school without bringing along your school books, did you?"

"Well, no," I mumbled, though honestly, I was thinking *yes*. "Mama, what if my bear steps into a trap, and I have to help? I can't be distracted by school work."

"We'll start with grammar. Scoot over," she said, climbing onto the wagon seat next to me.

After studying for awhile, I was saved by Papa, who walked up to the wagon, his little twenty-two caliber rifle in one hand, and my sword belt and telescope in the other.

"If it's okay with your mother, how about joining me for a little *mountain study*. There's something I want to show you."

With only a half-scolding look from Mama, she let me go. I excitedly strapped on my sword, ready for an adventure. What Papa wanted to show me was a group of huge black vultures up in the trees. Papa told me to look through my scope at the ground, below the trees they were perched in. I scanned the woods, and sure enough, saw a whole other bunch of them on the ground. We snuck up quietly through bushes and around trees and watched what appeared to be a big meeting of vultures. Like they were standing around discussing something very important. Some of the ones in the trees turned their little bald red heads and looked at us, and one of them spread his wings like he was going to hop from his branch and swoop down. I got scared, but Papa said it would be okay if we stayed put and didn't move any closer. He asked to borrow my telescope.

"There it is," he said, "a big ol' buck they found."

He handed the scope back to me, I looked again and finally saw a big rack of antlers poking out of a wall of black wings and red leathery heads. "Is it the one we heard someone shoot at yesterday?" I asked.

"Could be...yeah, I bet it is. Too bad...it's as big as any blacktail I've brought home."

We slowly backed away and returned to camp so I could tell everyone what we saw.

"We should keep an eye on that carcass," Papa told me. "Might be awful tempting to a hungry grizzly bear."

Back at the camp, Mr. Bern and Elam were at each others throats again, so I didn't tell anyone about the buzzards. Mama suggested they stay at opposite ends of the camp, just like little kids. Mr. Bern took Fish and went off scouting by himself for awhile, and Elam moved his tent into the trees a ways, to be off by himself. I thought that was a little foolish since we were in bear and mountain lion country but I didn't say anything. I hadn't really said anything at all to him the whole trip. I still didn't think I liked him, but I was fascinated by his juggling. He was juggling with pine cones now because Mr. Bern yelled at him about the apples being for the bear and for those of us who worked around the camp, not for loafers practicing to be circus clowns.

"Does Elam want to be a clown?" I asked Mama while we were out gathering firewood.

"I have no idea, June," said Mama. "Why don't you ask him?" I think Mama was tired of Elam's loafing and juggling, too. We needed to get supper started and there we were, collecting wood, which Elam could have been doing. He stayed off by himself at suppertime, too, so Mama told me to take him a plate, much to Mr. Bern's surprise.

"If you'll pardon me, Missus," said Mr. Bern. "Maybe if you let him go hungry, he'll be inspired to do a little more work around here without me havin' to yell at him."

"I know he could help out more," said Mama, "but I'm not going to let him go hungry. And we need him strong for when you men catch the grizzly."

"Here, I'll take him his dern plate," offered Mr. Bern.

"Oh, no," said Mama, "June can take it to him."

Elam was juggling when I got to his tent. "Do you really want to be in the circus?" I asked him when I handed him his supper.

"No, Uncle was just saying that to be mean."

"I think it would be neat to be in the circus," I said.

"Well...yeah. I think so, too, but don't tell anyone. That's how I got the idea to learn juggling. I guess it would be a good life, being around animals and traveling. Want me to teach you?"

"Sure," I said, thinking it strange what he had just told me. The short time I had known him, he seemed like he didn't like animals very much and hated traveling.

"See," he showed me, "you toss the first cone up in the air. When it gets up about this high, you toss the other one up, and then the other. I packed 'em with dirt so they'd have a little weight. The apples were perfect for juggling, but, the cones work okay." He did it himself for a few minutes, keeping four pine cones going for a long time. He handed me two, and showed me how to start. Throwing them up was easy, catching them without looking seemed to be the tricky part.

Mr. Bern back at the camp saw us juggling together. "Oh, Lord, are we a huntin' party or a travelin' carnival?"

"Perhaps your grizzly has a dream to join the circus as well," said Mr. Howell.

"Huh?" asked Mr. Bern, surprised at hearing the vet speak up.

"I meant perhaps, if we all juggled, such as when we travel the road, he'll think we are a circus troupe and will simply fall in line with us. You know, to join us."

"Well, that don't make any sense a'tol," said Mr. Bern, who no doubt knew Mr. Howell was trying to make a joke. "Why would a grizzly want to join a circus? Everyone knows it's only *camels* that want to join the circus."

"I see," said Mr. Howell, not planning on making any more jokes.

"I figgered you'd of known that, being an animal doctor and all."

"You're quite right, I should have known."

Juggling was much harder than it looked, but I was able to keep two pine cones in the air for a couple throws before they fell to the ground. I wasn't ready for three, yet. Mama finally called me to come back to the camp.

"Coming!" I called back. Then said to Elam, "You know, if you'd just help out around camp some, people would like you. Maybe even your uncle."

I turned to walk back to the fire when Fish jumped up barking.

"It's just me, dumb dog!" I snapped, then saw Papa stand up real serious looking. For a second I thought he was going to scold me for saying 'dumb dog', but I can usually say 'dumb' without getting scolded. They just don't like me saying 'stupid', which I used to say about everything when I first learned the word. But then Jack started barking and growling as well.

It wasn't me the dogs were barking at. Coming slowly down the mountain road was a group of five men on horses. They were older boys, actually, and one of them I recognized. It was Toby, the boy who had been with his pa and the Johnson men, one of which Papa shot. Toby looked to be the youngest of this group, too. When he saw me by the fire and then saw Papa stand up, he halted his horse like they were about to step off into a canyon, falling behind the others as they moved closer to our camp.

A few of the boys had rifles, I noticed, as Mama quietly called me to her side. Papa and Mr. Bern walked out to greet them. Papa was wearing his pistol at least. I never would have been alarmed by seeing men or boys with guns before all that mess with the Johnsons. And might not have been too alarmed this time if that boy Toby wasn't with them. Were these Johnsons too? Were they still out to get us for shooting Big One?

I carefully watched the boys talking to Papa. They were talking friendly, pointing to the woods behind us, and then pointed up the road from where they came. Elam walked over and seemed to know at least a couple of them. Toby stayed back, he was the only one who looked nervous. One of the other boys trotted back to him and apparently told him it was okay, that Papa wasn't going to shoot him. Or something like that, because he slowly came up with the rest of the group.

They chatted for a little while, then the riders moved past. They may have been talking friendly to Papa and Mr. Bern, but I saw their faces when they rode by, a couple of them tipping their hats to Mama and me. There was something mean about them, something ugly. Something like I saw in the eyes of Big One and Smelly One. Toby rode past without looking over.

"Well," said Papa when he got back to us. "We know who shot that buck the buzzards were feasting on."

"They shot the deer?" I asked. "Then lost him?"

"Yep," said Papa. "Remember those shots we heard yesterday?"

"What a waste," said Mr. Bern, his eyes closely following the riders as they lazily rode down the road. "Grow up on the mountain and can't even track a buck after shootin' it."

"Who were they?" asked Mama.

"Johnson kin," said Papa.

"*Johnson* kin?" asked Mama.

"A few of 'em anyway," said Papa. "Don't know if you recognized him, but the one boy on the tan horse was with the Johnsons that day we had our run-in."

"I remember him," said Mama.

"Them two holdin' the rifles," said Mr. Bern," are actual Johnsons, if I ain't mistakin'. Idn't that right, boy?"

"Yeah," said Elam. "The oldest is Morgan, and his younger brother's named Joe. I knowed 'em since I was young, at least knowed *of* them. The young one, Toby, I've seen around. Other two I don't know. But I think they're all right."

"What do you know if they're all right," snarled Mr. Bern. "You don't know if they're all right."

Papa asked, "Whose boys are they? Which Johnson family?"

"Ahh, I believe," thought Mr. Bern, "Albert Johnson was their daddy. Is that right?"

"I think so," said Elam.

"Yeah. Old Albert," said Mr. Bern. "He run off years ago, right after a daughter was born, if I remember. Don't know where to, don't know why for. They were raised partially by Whitey, though."

"Whitey?" I asked, "The Smelly One?"

"What did you tell them about us being here?" asked Mama, sounding almost as worried as I was.

"Deer huntin'," said Papa.

"Did they recognize you?" Mama asked.

"Well, the boy Toby sure knows who I am," said Papa. "The rest of 'em know now, too."

"So," asked Mama, "they're heading back down the mountain?"

"Said they were goin' to fetch some of their dogs," said Papa, "so they don't lose any more deer."

That made me *more* worried. "They're coming back?" I asked. If they came back with dogs, and my bear was near, they might find him before we did. And they wouldn't try to catch him alive. And maybe they were lying, maybe they did want to get back at me and Papa for shooting Big One. Maybe they would be coming back with more guns and meaner men.

"It's okay, everybody," said Papa. "They were just up here hunting. They've got no reason to bother us."

"And," added Mr. Bern, "they know we're a group o' shooters. They know we'll protect ourselves."

Papa said everything was okay, but I don't think he really believed it. Of course they had a reason to bother us. Papa shot their uncle—or however Clem Johnson was related to them—and it might do good for their standing in that screwed-up family if they were lucky enough to get back at the ones that shot him. That's a reason. Another reason might be that they were dumb, stupid, moonshine-drinking, mean boys who just liked bothering folks. I knew their kind.

It didn't surprise me at all when they started shooting their rifles a few minutes after leaving. "Just showing off," said Papa.

Even though we weren't supposed to be worried about the young deer hunters, it was getting dark, so the men worked to bring the horses and mules in closer, hobbling their legs so they couldn't get stolen or spooked and run off. They brought in a lot of wood and kept the fire big. It was decided that two men would stay on watch together instead of just one. Mama kept her shotgun close and wouldn't let me farther than an arm's length from her the rest of the evening, except when she put me to bed and returned to the fire to talk to Papa.

We were all kept awake by occasional rifle shots through the night, and wolf howls not made by wolves. I was scared at first, then mad that they couldn't just leave us alone. Mama tried to reassure me and get me to sleep, but she wasn't sleeping either. I was surprised I wasn't more scared, having had such a horrible experience before with the Johnson dirtbags, but I had my sword with me, and Mama and Papa and Mr. Bern. I figured together we were more than those boys could handle.

Papa was asleep with us in the tent early the next morning when we were awakened by a bunch of gunshots, sounding awful close. It was no doubt the dirtbag kin, but Papa found out it was Mr. Bern, too, when he stepped out to check on things.

Mr. Howell was by the fire, holding tightly to an old pistol Mr. Bern had handed him. He told Papa that Mr. Bern had quietly saddled up Willa and taken Fish to go talk to the troublemakers. Mr. Howell looked more frightened than I was, as I followed Mama out to the fire.

"He said he was going to talk to them," said Mr. Howell. "I tried to dissuade him, but you know he would never listen to me."

"Why didn't you wake me up?" asked Papa angrily.

"I, I...don't know," stammered Mr. Howell.

"Well, they've stopped firing," said Papa, who then grabbed his saddle and was going to follow on Whiskey. "I'll check it out."

"No, Patrick," said Mama. "You're not going to leave us."

"Don't leave us, Papa!" I cried.

"Elam," said Mama. "Would you go check on your uncle? You said you know those boys."

"Yes, ma'am, I'll go look," said Elam, who probably wouldn't have agreed to go if it wasn't Mama asking.

Elam hopped up onto his mule without putting on the saddle first, was given the old pistol from a shaking Mr. Howell, and was ready to leave when Fish came running into camp, followed by a strolling Willa and Mr. Bern.

"Boy," called Mr. Bern, "I'd figured you'd know to check when a pistol's loaded or not, before riding off into battle." Elam looked at the pistol, and no, it wasn't loaded.

"It wasn't loaded?" asked Mr. Howell.

"What happened?" asked Papa.

"Oh, not much. You know," said Mr. Bern.

Mr. Howell, who had been shaking since Mr. Bern had first left, said, "Well, I didn't sign on to fight in gun battles with mountain delinquents. No matter how much you pay me, it's not enough."

"You're paying him?" asked Elam.

"Calm down, Howell," said Mr. Bern. "Not going to be any more gun play from those knuckleheads."

"Are you sure?" asked Mama.

"What happened?" asked Papa again.

"Oh, got tired of them makin' noise all the night," said Mr. Bern, climbing down from Willa. "Rode up to politely ask 'em to keep the noise down, cuz there's folks trying' to sleep over here, and they must have thought I was a deer and pointed a rifle at me."

"They shot at you?" asked Mama.

"Well, you know, I wasn't in much danger," said Mr. Bern.

"They can't hit nothin.' I fired into the air a couple of times and they ran like little bunnies. They won't be back."

"Well this is where I must make my leave, I'm sorry to say," said Mr. Howell.

"You're not going anywhere," said Mr. Bern. "They's just kids trying to create a story to tell when they get home. Show 'em you're not afraid, and they git gone. You're not afraid, are you Doc?"

Mr. Howell, not very happy at all, but with all of us looking at him, said, "No. No, I'm not afraid."

"Good!" said Mr. Bern. "Guess I could've left the bullets in that pistol after all. Was afraid you'd shoot yourself in the leg, you were shakin' so."

"Just nerves in the morning," said Mr. Howell.

"So they're gone?" asked Mama.

"Yes, ma'am," said Mr. Bern, "they're gone. I can almost guarantee they won't make another peep."

There was a pretty long discussion, sometimes heated, among the adults about whether those boys would cause any problems, and if there were any new signs of my bear. I stayed out of it, because I was sternly told to stay out of it. Papa did apologize later and asked what my opinion was.

"I think we should stay," I told him, "and bring my bear down so nobody can hurt him." I think that was my opinion.

It *was* decided we weren't going to be intimidated by a small group of teenagers. Just to be safe, though, Mama and I were not to be left alone in camp, and they would keep the two-man watch at night at least until we were sure the boys had left for good.

Chapter Twenty-one

After the morning's excitement, I helped Papa make flapjacks for everyones' breakfast. And whether it was me telling him he would be liked if he helped out, or whether being included in the adult discussion made him feel important, Elam took it upon himself to collect the morning firewood without being asked.

"Just flapjacks this morning, Bug," Papa told me when I brought out the bacon. "Should probably conserve a little on the meat, just in case we're out a few days longer than planned. We'll see about getting a buck of our own this afternoon. That'll give us more meat."

"No sign of my bear yet?" I asked.

"Nope. Bern said Fish is acting like there's something big around, but haven't seen a sign yet of your bear.

The Misters—Bern and Howell—loaded up with apples and the rotten leg of venison, and were heading down to check the traps. This time Elam asked to go with them to help. Mr. Bern looked like he was about to say no, thought there should be another man in camp besides Papa, and Papa thought so too, but Mama assured him we'd all be fine. To make her point, she strapped on her pistol and picked up her scatter-gun. I ran to get my sword belt I had left in the tent. When I returned, the men were already down the trail. It was Mama, Papa, Jack, and me, as if we had come to the mountains for a week of camping, just the family.

I spent the morning practicing juggling with the pine cones. Jack stood by me and tried to grab them when they fell. Papa stood listening and watching the woods around us but would look over and nod when I juggled good. I wanted to explore the forest around our little clearing, but instead stayed near Mama and looked through my telescope at the birds and squirrels. I scanned the woods for any sign of those dumb boys, and also looked for my bear. It seemed forever since I saw him last. I told Papa I could probably find him myself if I could go out with an apple pie, and then have him follow me to where the traps were. Papa told me to just stay close.

After awhile I realized I hadn't so much as opened a book since we left home, other than school books. I lay down in the tent and started rereading *White Fang*, but being alone in the forest made the vicious wolves in the story a little too scary. I knew there wasn't supposed to be any more wolves on our mountain, but there wasn't supposed to be a grizzly bear either. So instead I took out the story on the Donner Party, remembering what Papa said that morning about conserving food. We had enough food for about a week, but what if we had to be out there longer? It was even colder than the day before, and the sky was dark with big clouds and it looked and smelled like it would rain or snow. And if it snowed, what if we got trapped? I should have brought different books.

Sure enough, a little before the men got back to camp, the sky grew black, the clouds started thundering, and down came cold rain. Small drops at first, then all of a sudden a downpour. Mama and I scrambled into the tent while Papa threw on his big rain slicker and made sure all the supplies were covered with the wagon's tarp.

"Mama, is it going to snow? Are we going to get stuck up here?" I nervously asked.

"I never should have given you that reader on the Donner Party," she said. "We're not going to get stuck, Bug. It's not snowing, it's raining."

The way it was pouring down, I became less worried about getting stuck in the snow and more worried about getting washed off the mountain.

"Papa!" I yelled. "Get out of the rain!"

"In a minute!" he yelled back. The rain was coming down so hard, I could barely hear him, and then the thunder really started booming. Jack, who was supposed to be out helping Papa, came crashing into the tent. He got halfway through the flap before Mama tackled him. I don't know if she realized it was Jack and not a wolf or something when she stopped him, because I didn't, and I screamed.

"Jack, you're soaking wet!" she yelled, and tried to cover him with an old blanket we were using as a towel, but just then a huge explosion of thunder shook the tent and the ground underneath us, and nothing could have held Jack back. He shot under the blankets to hide, Mama trying to pull him back out. She flung all the covers off and tried to push him out of the tent, but he was not budging and slipped out of her grasp to bury himself under the covers again. I would have helped her, but the thunder had me scared, too, and I was in more of a mind to join Jack under the covers than to get him out. Mama lifted the blankets, quickly piled them at the back of the tent, then laid right on top of Jack with the old blanket and dried him best she could. Both wet and dirty with muddy paw prints, Mama and I looked at each other and laughed. Jack wagged his tail a little, still frightened of the storm, but if Mama was laughing that probably meant she would let him stay. The whole tent, including Mama and me, smelled like a wet dog, but at least we were safe from the rain. I didn't care much for the thunder, though. Thunder above a tent is quite different than thunder above a house.

"Whoo," said Papa, opening the tent flap to check on us. "Nice little clap of thunder, huh? Ya'll okay? Not scared?"

"Come in the tent, Papa," I told him, trying not to sound frightened.

"I'll wait 'til it stops. I'd get the inside as wet as the outside if I climbed in there right now."

"Aren't you afraid of the thunder?" I asked.

"I'm not afraid of anything, Bug. Hey, have you guys seen Jack?...Jack! Get out here, you danged dog."

"He's scared, Papa."

"He's getting all the blankets wet," scolded Papa. "Don't let him under the blankets for Pete's sake...Jack, out here, *now*."

"Just let him stay, until the thunder stops," said Mama. "He's already got us as wet as we're going to get."

"Let him stay, Papa. He doesn't want to get wet again."

"What about me? I'm getting wet."

"We asked if you wanted to come in and you said no," I told him. "Jack said yes."

"Uh, huh. So you stayin' dry in there Bugglet?"

"Yes, Papa."

"Well, kick the dog out soon's the rain lets up."

"We will."

"Hey, I think the boys are back," said Papa before he stepped back into the storm.

"The boys?" I jumped to the flap, thinking he meant those Johnson boys had returned, maybe using the rain as a cover to shoot us. But Papa meant the Misters and Elam were returning to camp. *Those* boys. Peeking through the flap, I saw Mr. Bern, who had a good long coat like Papa to stay dry, or at least drier than Mr. Howell and Elam, who both had thin ponchos and looked more than a little miserable. It was obvious they hadn't found my bear in one of the traps, but I still wanted to listen to what they had seen, if anything. The rain was just too loud, getting louder, and it was still thundering. I couldn't hear a thing they were saying.

"Mama!" I yelled over the roar of the rain pouring onto the tent. "Mama, I'm scared!"

"It's okay, June!" She yelled back. "It's just rain!" But it wasn't just rain, it was thunder, and soon it was wind, too, roaring through the trees and blowing our little tent one way and then the other. The tent flap, even though it was tied in two places, did little to keep out the storm.

Papa worked quickly to hammer the tent stakes deeper into the ground, then started shoveling a trench to direct the water around

237

the tent, but it was still getting in. Mama had a couple of cooking pots turned upside down, atop of which she piled all our blankets and pillows to try to keep dry. We had a tarp set on the ground, or would have been standing in mud. Instead, we were standing in cold water on top of the tarp.

The wind, the thunder, then the rain, finally, mercifully, weakened. It had been so loud, it was like standing next to a freight train. A train that was spraying a million gallons of water and shooting off canons. Then as quickly as it had overtaken us, it had stopped.

Mama and I stepped out of the tent, rain slickers over our cold, wet, muddy clothes. I held my doll Sarah in the crook of my arm, Mama dragged Jack by the collar. I gasped at the sight of our camp. *Drenched* wasn't close to describing the scene outside our tent-flap—it looked like a huge tidal wave had washed over the top of the mountain, leaving mud, tree limbs, branches, pine needles and leaves everywhere. Ours and Mr. Bern's tent were standing, but Mr. Howell's tent had collapsed into a heap, and Elam's tent was completely missing. Most of the animals seemed to be missing, too. Papa was standing next to Whiskey, calming him, and Elam, who was squatting under the wagon, had hold of his mule's reins. I spotted Mr. Bern's mule team off in the trees, but no Mr. Bern, or Mr. Howell, nor their horses. Maybe it *was* a tidal wave that came through, or the very least a hurricane.

"How fun was that?" asked Papa, smiling, and leading Whiskey by his bridle over to us.

"Papa, where's..."

ke...ke ke POWWW oww oww... exploded a come-from-nowhere, punching thunder-boom right above our heads, bursting my ears and dropping me to the wet ground. Papa held tight to Whiskey, but Mama couldn't hold Jack, who shot past me, returning to what he thought was the safety of our flimsy tent.

"Are you okay, Bug?" asked Mama, lifting me from the mud, and barely keeping her own composure while the sky continued to rumble. "That was close, huh?"

"I don't like thunder," I said shakily, but I didn't cry.

Elam's mule loped past us, heading for home. He was quickly stopped by Mr. Bern, who was coming up from the road, leading Mr. Howell's Russell, who had tried to make a break for it as well.

"Whoo-boy!" called Mr. Bern. "That last one shore tickled my nubbins, how 'bout you?"

Chapter Twenty-two

The storm seemed to be moving farther up the mountain, leaving us with cold drizzle. The horses were secured and given an early supper, with half an apple each as a treat. Mr. Bern retrieved his mules, Elam found his tent, but where was Mr. Howell? I followed Mama and Papa to the pile of canvas that had been the veterinarian's tent. It was moving, slightly, and mumbling. Mr. Howell emerged, with the help of Papa, soaked, disheveled, and thoroughly unhappy. I offered him an apple.

Mama led me away from Mr. Howell's cursings, or what I assumed were cursings. With Mr. Howell, I was finding it hard to tell, unlike Mr. Bern. The ground was covered with all the leaves that had been knocked from the trees in the storm. Soggy, soft and squishy under our shoes, it was like walking on a big, cold, wet sponge. We tidied up the tent as best we could, set aside the wettest blankets to dry by the fire if ever the rain and drizzle stopped. At least the thunder had moved on, and there never was any lightning to be worried about.

The wagon was wheeled close to the fire, and I helped Papa string up a couple of clotheslines—two ends tied to the wagon, the other ends tied to trees. I was surprised when Mama came out with the blankets to dry, because it was still raining.

"That's just water dropping from the trees," she said. So, it's *rain* if the water falls from the clouds, but not if it falls from the trees. Wherever it was coming from, it was still getting us wet, especially when a gust of wind blew through the branches.

Sitting on whatever we could find to keep our bottoms off the wet ground, we all huddled around the fire, which had been drenched as well, but had been brought back to life with a lot of hat-fanning and blowing on a few smoking embers. With blankets and clothes hung up, it was almost like we had built a cabin with no roof, a cabin that wasn't all that cozy.

I helped to heat up a pot of beans and make coffee. I didn't know if anyone else was all that hungry, I wasn't, but it gave us women something to do while a couple of the men bickered, I won't say which ones. It was hard to be friendly, apparently, being wet and cold. And poor Mr. Howell must have gotten real sick in the rain, because he was drinking from his medicine bottle until it was empty, then started on another.

The fire was beginning to dry us, the hot food helped to warm our insides. If anyone had the right to be in a bad mood, it was me. I discovered my books underneath the pile of wet blankets, thoroughly soaked with most of the pages stuck together. The reader of the Donner Party was completely ruined, having been no more than a thin-papered magazine. I hung *White Fang* on it's own little clothesline, hoping to save it. I wouldn't consider it ruined if I could still read it, but it made me upset. My school books, of course, were not even touched by the water. By the time we turned in for the night, *White Fang* was pretty much dried, though puffed up like it had five-hundred pages. I put it under my fire-warmed pillow to flatten out while I slept. That would always be a very special book to me, the crinkly-dried pages would forever have the scent of camp smoke, reminding me—for good or bad—of our expedition.

"Allen...Allen, get up. We may have caught him." I thought I heard the voice in a dream, urging me out of my sleep. I woke with a start as Jack trampled over the top of me to join Fish who was barking madly outside. It was the middle of night.

"Mama? What's going on?"

"I'm not sure," she said, having been startled awake as well.

"Got something trapped," said Papa, throwing on his boots.

"My bear?"

"I'll find out," and Papa scrambled out of the tent. Mama and I grabbed coats and boots and quickly dressed. I had trouble connecting the buckle on my sword belt in the dark, but finally got it, grabbed Sarah, and joined Mama in front of the tent, staying out of the way as the men prepared the horses.

I watched Mr. Bern in the waving light of the campfire, buckling Willa's saddle cinch, and barking orders. "Boy! Get the big mule ready with the pack harness and lead! Strap the drag sled to him and then get your's saddled!... Doc! Get your potion ready! Doc, get out here!"

Elam was running around frantically with the mule's gear, Papa was throwing his own saddle on Whiskey, but Mr. Howell was missing. He was still in his tent, crawling out only when he heard

Mr. Bern's anxious footsteps heading his way. The elixir he had been drinking around the campfire must not have had time to help his sickness, because he was awful slow and sluggish, and looked a little confused.

"C'mon Doc," said Mr. Bern, a little quieter than before. "Get your kit ready, let's see if you can put a grizzly bear to sleep."

"Huh? In the dark?"

With the dogs barking and all the other carrying-on by the men, I hadn't heard a thing from the creek, but then the dogs stopped for a moment to listen themselves. All was quiet for a minute but for a breeze slipping along the tops of the trees, and then we all heard a faint, terrible sound—a deep bellowing from out in the dark—and the sound of a chain being jostled. That was all I heard before the dogs exploded again, but it was enough to knot my stomach. "It's happening," I whispered. "It's really happening." I hugged Sarah as tight as Mama was hugging me. We all strained to listen.

"Doc!" yelled Mr. Bern. "Let's go!"

Mr. Howell was backing himself out of the tent holding his medicine bag, the long poker-thing that he was going to stick my bear with, and a lantern.

"Ready, ready," he said. "Just need to fill...ahh, my lantern's low on oil."

"You don't use a dern lantern on horseback, didn't we go over all this?" said an increasingly frustrated Mr. Bern. "Grab a torch from the wagon. Don't light it 'til you're mounted, and try not to set the forest ablaze."

Mr. Bern was mounted and itching to go. He had his big rifle in a scabbard on one side of Willa's saddle, and his cane tied to the other side. In his right hand he held one of his homemade torches, which was a stick about four feet long and wound thick and tight on one end with fabric and burlap that he had earlier told me had been soaked in a recipe of coal dust, pine tar, and kerosene. Elam had a hold of the big mule's lead rope, the mule that had the Indian sled, ropes, extra torches and chains all strapped to his pack.

"This may be it, folks," said Mr. Bern, as he dipped the tip of his torch to the campfire. *Whoosh*, it flamed. "Me and Elam will take the dogs and gear down, make sure griz don't slip out of the trap and get away. Allen, you'll bring the vet?"

"Right behind you," said Papa.

"Ladies," said Mr. Bern, tipping his hat, but not really looking at us, then led Elam out of the camp.

Papa guided Whiskey over to us, handing Mama her scatter-gun. "You'll be okay here?" he asked.

"We'll be fine," said Mama. "Promise me you'll be careful."

"I promise...if anyone comes poking around here who shouldn't be poking around here, don't hesitate to use the shotgun."

"Don't be thinking about us," said Mama, "be thinking about the bear in front of you."

"Are you sure it's him, Papa?" I asked.

"We'll find out shortly," he said. "If it is him, Elam will ride back to get the wagon ready, okay?" He gave us both a big hug before climbing onto Whiskey. "Ready, Doc?"

Mr. Howell was having a little trouble. He had replaced his lantern with a torch—as Mr. Bern had suggested—and was holding onto the medicine stick and the torch in a way that was jabbing Russel in the side of the face as he was trying to pull himself onto

244

the saddle. It was a good thing he hadn't lit the torch yet, but still, the horse was spinning around trying to get away from that thing with Mr. Howell hopping along with him, one foot in the stirrup. I wanted to go over there myself and give him a boost, but Papa was already in the saddle and heading over. Slowing Russell down so Mr. Howell could mount, Papa then touched the end of his torch to the campfire before walking Whiskey back over to us for parting words. With the dark shadows on his face from the bright torch, he looked a little scary, but in a handsome way, like a pirate.

I looked over at Mr. Howell. Leaning way over to light the torch like Papa had done, he was pulling Russell to the left, toward the fire. The torch flared up with a *whoosh*, right under the horse's chin. Russell spooked, reared up, and off tumbled Mr. Howell. Luckily not into the fire, but he was slow getting up all-the-same, and no longer looked eager to ride down to the creek, not that he looked all that eager to begin with.

"We need to get down there," Papa sternly told him, after asking if he was okay. I didn't hear Mr. Howell say that he *was* okay, but he pulled himself back onto Russell's saddle to follow Papa. I ran and picked up the flaming torch that he had dropped and handed it back to him. If it *was* my bear in the trap, Mr. Howell had to be there with his medicine. He was needed.

✳ ✳ ✳ ✳

Mama and I stood close to the fire to keep warm, and anxiously waited for the men. With her scatter-gun still in hand, she threw on a couple branches before sitting us down on a stump. It had been hard to hear anything but Fish's yapping, but soon I was able to make out Mr. Bern's voice, though I couldn't tell what he was saying.

"Do you think it's him, Mama? My bear?"

"I don't know, June. If it is your bear, then that's a good thing. Mr. Howell's medicine is going to put him to sleep, and we'll take him to town in the wagon, and he'll be safe from hunters, and...and that's what we came up here to do."

"I know," I said, trying to convince myself that it was a *good thing*, that it was all going as planned, and it would all work out for the best. I was too nervous to sit, so got up and walked quiet circles around the campfire. "Mama...do you think Papa's there, yet?"

"I don't know," she whispered, listening to the darkness as carefully as I was.

I was listening so hard, I had a picture in my head of my ears perked up like Jack's. I thought it was working, listening like a dog. Though all the sounds were pretty faint, I was able to pick out my bear's roars between dog barks. It didn't really sound like a roar, maybe because it was coming from a distance, maybe because of the mountain echo, but it sounded more like a very big sheep. But instead of *bah ah ah ah* like a sheep, it was more like *wraaaaaaa*. I was probably hoping it was a sheep they had trapped. There finally came a long pause in the barking, I stopped my loop around the fire-pit and what I heard was definitely the roar from a bear. Mama heard it, too. I returned to pacing the fire-pit when I thought I heard Papa's voice calling "Doc!"

If Papa was calling for Mr. Howell, did that mean it *was* my grizzly and they were ready to stick him and put him into a sleep? Or, would they do that to the wrong bear also, so Mr. Howell could practice not getting his arm bit off?

"Mama...is it my bear?"

"I don't know, June. But, I think we should assume that it is. It's a good thing, remember?"

The dogs were barking more than before, and I was able to make out the yells of Mr. Bern, but couldn't tell what he was yelling. I couldn't stand not knowing exactly what was going on, and figured there had to be an extra torch for Mama and me. We could follow the trail down, we knew the way.

"Come help me," said Mama, resting her scatter-gun against a wagon wheel. "Let's clean out the wagon."

"We're going down there?"

"No, of course not. But we can get the wagon ready." I stood motionless, listening to the dark. "June?" she asked.

When I didn't respond, Mama walked over to me. I looked at her, but she was staring at my feet. "What are you standing on?" she asked.

"Huh?"

"What are you standing on?"

I looked down, I had both feet on a stick. I had been rolling over it with my shoes, from toe to heel, without even thinking. Just a stick? I looked to the end of it, to where Mama was staring, and saw the medicine-injector-thing attached.

"Oh, no, Mama, it's Mr. Howell's stick!" I jumped off of it like it had been a rattlesnake, then bent down and picked it up. I don't know how it could have gone unnoticed until then, other than our

247

minds being occupied so. The stick was longer than I was, wet, with mud stuck to it from me pressing it into the ground. The metal tube-with-a-needle-thing had a wine cork stuck onto the end, and it all seemed undamaged. I held it to the light from the campfire and could see the medicine through a strip of glass on the side. "What do we do?"

Mama took it from my hand, and we both stared off to the black forest, listening.

"Mama," I said, alarm beginning to take hold of me, "if they don't have the stick, they'll shoot him. They're going to shoot him, Mama!"

"Here," she said, "hold the stick. Let's..." She went to the wagon, digging around, and came out with a fresh torch.

"Let's go, Mama. Let's hurry," I said, already starting into the darkness.

"June, wait! We can't just go running down the trail. Your father is expecting us to stay at the camp."

"But Mama, they're going to shoot my bear!"

"They'll send Elam back for the stick when they notice it's missing."

"Mama, we can't let them..."

"All right, June. Here's what we can do. Let's go to the head of the trail and try calling to them, okay? They might be able to hear us."

"Okay, but let's hurry, Mama, please."

I had the medicine stick in one hand, my doll Sarah in the other. Mama snatched up her scatter-gun and stepped to the campfire to light the torch. *Whoosh.*

"Please hurry, Mama," I said again, starting down the road to the trail. We hadn't a moment to lose.

"Wait for me, June." She caught up to me halfway to the trail. "We'll call to them, but if they don't hear us, then that's it. It's a mile to the traps, the trail is muddy, and we are *not* going on foot. Do you understand?"

"Okay."

"I mean it, Bug."

"Yes Mama, but hurry!"

We made it to the trail-head and stopped. Mama held the torch high, lighting up a good portion of the forest in front of us. The floor of the trail was indeed muddy, and mucky, and choppy with hoof-prints from the horses and mules. We strained to listen for voices, or of the sound of a rider returning for the forgotten stick. A strong wind was blowing up from the creek, hitting us right in our faces, and carrying the sounds of dogs barking and my bear, bellowing frightfully. I didn't want to think of the horror he must be going through— trapped, with vicious dogs and strange men with burning torches and rifles surrounding him.

"Papaaa!"

"Paatriiick!"

Our voices didn't go far, didn't echo, just seemed to die in the wind. Still, we listened for a reply, but heard only the sounds of my bear. I thought the dogs must have heard us, because they stopped barking for a few seconds.

"Let's try again, together," said Mama.

"Paappaaa!" we yelled as loud as we could. Surely they heard that! We tried it one more time, again no response. I thought I could hear Mr. Bern, but very faintly.

"It's the wind," said Mama. "They can't hear us because of the wind."

"We have to go down," I pleaded.

"No, June."

"They need the stick. They're going to kill him!"

"They'll send someone back for the stick, June."

"No, Mama, they're going to kill him! Mr. Bern said they'd have to kill him!" I made a move down the trail, Mama quickly grabbed the back of my coat.

"Papaaaaaa!" I screamed with all I had in me. I paused only a moment to listen for a response before taking a quivering, deep breath to scream again, when the boom of a single rifle shot pierced the silence and echoed through the mountain. My legs gave out, and I dropped to my bottom as if the bullet had weaved it's way through the trees and found my own heart. In a way, it had. "Noooo!"

Chapter Twenty-three

It was late in the morning when I finally rose from the blankets, buttoned up my big coat, buckled on my sword belt, and climbed out of the tent. My breath rose into the air, and if it were any other morning, I might have wondered if my breath was helping to make new clouds high above me. The sun was out, and though it was still cold, it could be called a nice day. That is, if it were any other day. Mama, who was by the campfire, saw me standing in a daze, and walked over with two steaming cups of tea.

"Good morning," she said.

"What are they doing?" I asked, noticing Papa, Mr. Bern and Elam off in the trees behind the wagon, with blood on their clothes.

"Here, have some hot tea," said Mama. "It'll do you good."

I took the warm tin cup in my hands. The tea wasn't too hot, I sipped without having to blow on it. I stood with Mama, sipping my cup, looking over at the men, and thinking back to what had happened during the night.

After the rifle shot from the creek, I had to be physically dragged back to camp by Mama. It was all she could do to keep me from running-screaming down the muddy trail. In the tent, I buried myself under as many blankets as I could and cried until my eyes ran dry. I couldn't believe Mr. Bern had shot my bear. Or was it Papa that had done it? Why couldn't they have taken a few minutes and come back for the medicine stick? I had wanted to take it to them, but Mama wouldn't let me go. We could have made it down the trail in time.

"June?...June?" It was Papa's voice in the dark. "June, wake up." He was in the tent, kneeling over me, his hand on my shoulder. He thought I was asleep, but I was just pretending. I had heard him and Mr. Howell ride back into camp, heard them whispering with Mama.

I quickly sat upright, wrapping my arms around his neck. I didn't want to see his face, but I desperately needed to hug him. "I could have brought the stick down, but Mama wouldn't let me go." I started to cry.

"Hey, hey," he said to comfort me. "It's okay. "It wasn't your bear."

"Why didn't you come back for the stick, Papa? You needed the stick!"

"June, did you hear me? It wasn't the right bear. It was not your bear."

"What?"

"It was a black bear in the trap."

"Are you sure?" I squeezed his neck even harder and continued to cry. "But...but you had to shoot it?" I asked between sobs.

"We had to, yes."

"Because you didn't have the sleeping medicine?"

"Right. And the bear was struggling so much that...how 'bout I tell you more about it in the morning if you'd like, okay?"

"Tell me now. Please?"

"In the morning. Mama told me how upset you were, I just wanted to let you know that it wasn't your bear. Okay? Now, go back to sleep. Try to sleep."

I guess I was relieved that it wasn't my bear that they killed, but it could have been. It could have been my grizzly that stepped into the trap, and the sleeping medicine Mr. Howell promised would work would have been a mile away. It could have easily been my grizzly that they would have had to shoot. It took me awhile to get back to sleep.

"June's up," I heard Papa say loudly from the trees. Mama was standing in front of me with her cup of tea, blocking my view. I had to lean around her to see what the men were so interested in behind the wagon. I figured it to be the bear they had killed during the night, but I didn't figure on glimpsing the bear on the ground, already removed of fur. Mama didn't want me to see it, either, which was why she kept moving in front of me.

"I've seen dead animals before," I told her grumpily.

"I know," she said, "we just thought you may not want to see this one."

"Why? I know it's not *my* bear."

"Okay," she said. "I'll let you decide."

I had never had a problem with seeing the deer and elk Papa brought home from hunting. I even enjoyed sitting out with him as he cleaned them. It was kind of gross, but I had always been fascinated with what was inside their bodies, especially after Papa told me that we had the same stuff inside us, more or less. And as long as it wasn't one that I had named, I had no problem helping Mama pluck and clean chickens for supper.

I had seen many animals skinned and plucked, but I had never seen a skinned bear before. It's skin—what was underneath the pelt—was...well...it looked just like a person's skin. And not only the skin, but the bear's body looked strangely like a person's, like a human. I wasn't expecting that at all, and stopped short, with Mama stopping with me.

"That's a bear?" I asked.

Papa had never hunted bears that I knew of, had never even killed one that was trying to steal chickens. He'd sick Jack on them to chase them off, or at the most, would fire his rifle into the air to scare them. I hadn't thought about that before, why Papa never shot bears. Everyone else did when a bear was spotted on their property, even if the bear was just passing through. I would have to ask him about that, I thought, but later. I walked with Mama back to the campfire to warm up and have a late breakfast.

"Mama," I said, staring down at my plate of beans and a biscuit, but picturing the black bear in my mind. "I don't think I can eat a bear."

"You know what?" Mama replied. "I'm not sure I can either."

* * * *

Papa, after cleaning himself up and changing clothes, poured himself a cup of coffee and sat on the ground next to me. He told me about Mr. Howell getting lost on the trail the previous night. "I thought he was right behind me," he said, "and then, he wasn't."

"How did he get lost?" I asked.

"He, ahh, lost his torch for starters. It got knocked out of his hand by a tree branch. I guess when it hit the branch, it sort of...*threw* bits of fire all around, and his horse, as you saw in camp, had already had flames in his face once last night. He bolted straight ahead when he should have turned with the trail. When Doc got control of him, he was in the dark with little idea where the trail was. I finally found him and we made it to the traps."

"Would you have tried to use the needle-stick on the bear?" I asked.

"Howell figured he lost it in the woods, so we never thought about coming back to camp for it. But yeah, we would have tried it. Maybe it's best not to mention anything about it to Mr. Howell, okay? He feels pretty awful about last night, took plenty of chaffing from Bern already."

"I won't say anything... Where *is* Mr. Howell?"

"He's, I think, hiding in his tent."

"Would have been nice to know if his sleeping stuff works, huh?" I asked.

"Would have been nice," he agreed. "The trap held the bear, so at least we know those work."

"There wasn't a way to get it off him?" I asked.

"No, Bug, I'm sorry. And I'm sorry that you thought we killed your grizzly."

"It's okay."

"We really, all of us, want things to work as planned. We all want to bring your bear down alive. We don't want to kill him."

"I know, Papa."

"We'll probably be moving the traps tomorrow, if no luck tonight," he said. "There's an area a bit farther up, still by the creek, we're thinking of trying it out there."

"And if no luck there?" asked Mama, who moved between us, wrapping us in a big hug.

"Then we go home," said Papa. "We can try setting traps closer to the house, or, forget about it until spring. We're not going to spend the whole dang winter up here."

"It's only been a few days, Patrick," said Mama. "You trapped one bear, it just wasn't the right one."

"You're right," he said.

I could tell Papa was frustrated. I think he had hoped we wouldn't have much trouble finding my bear. After all, I had never had any trouble finding him. Running into those Johnson boys I think worried him, and the big storm we just went through worried him as well. The weather could easily worsen, at any time.

"Any suggestions, June?" he asked me.

"No, not really."

"We'll give it a few more days, okay?"

"Okay."

I hadn't thought it would, but seeing the black bear—killed, and skinned—really affected me. I felt sorry for him, but mostly it made me terribly worried for my own bear. I knew my bear was very smart, and good at hiding and keeping away from hunters and dogs and trappers, but he wouldn't be able to stay hidden forever. He would eventually be found, and most likely killed, and end up just like the poor black bear. Like both of the black bears Mr. Bern and Papa had killed.

I couldn't shake from my mind how much the bear, without his fur, looked like a person. The size of him was so close to that of a man. Why would bears and people look so much alike without their fur or clothes?

No way was I going to eat bear meat. And neither was Mama, to the disappointment of Mr. Bern, who excitedly took over cooking duties, to fix a big bear-steak supper.

"Ah, c'mon, ladies," said Mr. Bern. "This here is a delicacy, and a recipe learned to me years ago by a crazy mountain man that spent his younger years as a chef at a fancy, expensive restaurant in Saint Louis, Missoura."

"What recipe is that?" asked Papa, with a smile. "Salt and pepper and grease?"

"That, yes. I also ground up a few acorns, rubbed the meat with pine needles, and now, I'm sprinkling a touch of *paprika*. That's what I'm callin' *the secret*... don't tell nobody."

"What's paprika?" I asked, only a little curious. Mostly I was feeling depressed, and guilty, because the bear meat spattering in the skillet smelled pretty good.

"Paprika, little darlin', is this powder-stuff right here. I guess it comes from a paprika root somewhere, but I purchased this. Always have a bag with me. You sure, Miss J, you don't want a little taste?"

"No thank you."

"Missus?" he asked Mama.

"I'm sorry, Mr. Simms. I'll pack the bear meat in what salt we can spare, but, I think I'm with Bug on this one."

"Don't know what yer missin', but I guess I understand. We got plenty, you know, if you change your mind. Doc!" he yelled over at the tent. "You alive in there? Eat now or don't eat at all! And try not to get lost between your tent and the campfire."

Mr. Howell had been in his tent all day, still sick, I figured. I hadn't seen him since he rode from the camp with his torch the night before. When he climbed out, I was surprised to see him clean and shaved, and apparently over his sickness, whatever it was he had.

Mama handed me a plate of beans and a biscuit, then skewered a thick strip of venison to cook over the fire next to the skillet of frying bear.

"Mama...may I be excused? I'm not hungry."

"Bug, you've barely eaten all day," she said. "You need to eat something."

"I'll eat later. I promise."

"Not too much later, okay?"

"Thank you, Mama," I said, and excused myself from the dinner-circle. I tried to call Jack with me to walk around, but he was planted between Papa and Elam, itching for a chance at a dropped sliver of meat.

I took Sarah and we walked over to the horses and mules. I picked an apple out of the basket and tried to sneak it to Whiskey. But the other animals saw, and Willa especially gave me an angry nickering. To make up for it, I gave them all good scratches on their big snouts. The sun had been out for most of the afternoon, and though the air was still cold, the horses were warmed and comfortable. I stayed with Whiskey, patting him and laying my face against his side in a kind-of hug, feeling the warmth on my cheek, and listening to his big heart beat.

"You want a brushing, boy?" Whiskey loved getting brushed, and it would take my mind off the sad thoughts I couldn't stop thinking. I turned to the wagon to look for his brush when I thought I saw something move out in the woods. I stopped, and tried to focus between the trees, but couldn't see anything. I stood motionless, my eyes searching the trees and brush. Did those Johnson boys come back? Was probably just a deer. I couldn't be sure, but I thought I could see puffs of smoke, or steam from behind one of those trees. So, it could be a Johnson. But, on the other side of the tree I thought I could make out...something brown. But the whole forest that time of year was some shade of brown. Deer are brown. It was probably just a deer.

I slowly pulled my telescope from it's leather pouch, keeping my eyes glued to the tree. I slid it open and put it to my eye... *Which tree?* By the time I was sure I had located the right one, whatever was trying to hide had either hidden itself better, or run off. I was startled by Jack stepping up beside me, and for a second I was going to scold him for making me lose the tree again. He was looking into the woods as well, his nostrils opened wide and twitching, trying to breathe in whatever scent he could from the still, mountain air. His ears were up, and he tail was wagging.

"Jack?" I asked, looking back to the forest. "Was that him?" Jack must not have thought so. He scampered back to where the food was. I stood searching, listening, and sniffing the air. I started to walk into the trees for a better look when I heard Mama call me. A ceiling of clouds had quickly moved over us, carried by a cold wind. Our sunny day was coming to an end, soon to be replaced by a steady, gentle rain that would last into the night.

Chapter Twenty-four

Are we sure this is a road?" I asked Mama after the latest thump on my rear-end as the wagon tossed and pitched.

We were on our way higher up the mountain. The men had retrieved the traps early that morning while Mama, Papa and I loaded up tents and hooked up mules. I was a little surprised we were moving to a new spot, the attitude of everyone last evening was pretty low. Mr. Howell was ready to head home, Mama told me he was embarrassed about getting lost in the woods, and I heard him complaining about missing his bed. Elam hadn't wanted to go on the expedition in the first place, even though the black bear trapping was more excitement than he'd ever experienced before. I was ready to go home, too, even though I knew if we didn't capture my bear ourselves, he would most likely suffer the same fate as the black bear.

I guess what we were traveling on was considered a road, but it was terribly rutted, muddy, and strewn with leaves, pine needles, and tree limbs. There were water-filled holes we didn't know how deep they were until we pulled right into them.

"The wagon will float, right?" I asked Mama, having read about

Conestoga wagons that the settlers had used. They floated. "Are we sure this is a road?" Mama wasn't answering. She was concentrating on the mules, trying to keep us moving forward.

It wasn't a road. A trail maybe, but even calling it that was a stretch. It was so muddy in spots that of course the wagon got stuck. Mr. Bern and Papa tied ropes between their horses and the two mules, and pulled us out of the muck. We were using half the day to go nowhere.

"Is this really a road?" I hollered to Papa. I wanted *someone* to tell me it was a road.

"The only one up here," he hollered back. "Wasn't too bad a few seasons ago when we were bringing logs down. The crew had this road as smooth as Main Street."

I wanted to believe Papa, but smooth as Main Street?

"There's a clearing not too much farther," hollered back Mr. Bern. "We can stop and rest."

"Did you hear that, Mama?" I said. "We're stopping!"

"Thank goodness."

Mr. Bern tried to volunteer Elam to drive the wagon and give Mama and me a break from the bouncing, which of course Elam didn't want to do. "We're fine in the wagon, Mr. Simms," said Mama.

"We are?" I asked. We weren't sitting on blankets anymore, because even when it wasn't raining—which it still was—water coming off the trees dripped on us continuously. *Tree rain*, I was starting to call it. The blankets were just soaking up water, so we tossed them in the back, and had to sit on the hard, wooden, cold seat. Which was wet.

I tried looking around as we were getting bounced, having the idea that the puff of smoke I saw for an instant the previous day was in fact my bear, and that if it *was* him, maybe he was following us. Following *me*, anyway, because he missed me. I didn't see one sign of him. As much as we were getting thrown around, he could have been sitting right beside the trail waving at me with a flag, and I still might have missed him.

We crept and bounced along through the mud, over fallen limbs and even a whole tree that had to be moved out of the way. We had to cross what looked like little rivers of muddy water, a couple of them not so small. There was nothing to do but go right through them and hope we didn't raft away. Elam looked over at me once and said, "So where's this stupid bear of yours? You don't know where the bear is, and we're doing this for nothing." That hurt my feelings, and even though I liked Elam teaching me to juggle, I didn't like Elam. We hadn't even traveled far up the mountain. It was farther than I'd ever been before, but there was a lot more mountain up there before we reached the top, which, hopefully we wouldn't be going *that* far. Elam and Mr. Howell acted like we had been traveling a month. Elam's poncho, I guess, wasn't terribly waterproof so he was wet and cold, was shivering and his lips were blue. But still, even I knew that complaining wouldn't make you warmer, and Mr. Bern had told him that a few times already. I might have felt sorry for him if I wasn't wet and cold also, if we weren't *all* wet and cold. And if he hadn't been rude to me.

The only ones who were enjoying themselves were Jack and Fish, who chased every rabbit they could find, and they found a lot of them. I just knew one of those times they'd go after what they thought was a rabbit and it would turn out to be a skunk. Mr. Bern shot a couple of the rabbits for supper that night. Rabbit sure tastes good, but I had to not think about how cute they were before they became supper. I guess it's that way with deer, and squirrels, too. Just about everything that's cute. And bears that look like people.

* * * *

Nighttime was coming earlier every day, and by the time we crept along to the clearing where we were supposed to have a rest, it was already close to dark and time to make camp. That was fine with me, the day had been wet, cold, bouncy and miserable. And we'd traveled only a short distance.

We set up our camp on a raised area at the edge of the big clearing Mr. Bern told us about. We had to think about whether running water could get to the tents or wagon and wash us away in the night. Mr. Bern started telling a story of just that, before Mama told him to stop. I was more concerned about being snowbound than getting washed down the mountain. For some reason I pictured getting washed down the mountain would be like a ride at the county fair, and we'd end up washing right into town where I could get some candy at the general store. But if we became snowbound, why couldn't we make sleds, or turn the wagon into a sleigh and go back down the mountain that way? Why didn't the Donner party just sled back down the mountain? Maybe they didn't think about that.

The clearing was a big meadow ringed with trees. There were a few oak trees, and pine, but lots of big cedar and fir trees. It looked to me like someone had wanted to build a little town there, then decided not to for some reason, or maybe the town got washed away in a storm like we'd been suffering through. Papa said it had been logged about six years back. Was once an oak grove, he told us, they stopped cutting when they ran out of the biggest oak trees.

"I helped move the logs down from this spot, actually," Papa told me after we all climbed down from our wagon and horses. "You probably don't remember, but I was up here for a month driving a mule team, moving the big logs one or two at a time. There's a big cliff not far into the trees, *Mayor's Leap*, I think they call it. The mountain just drops off into a deep, narrow canyon, just a little ol' creek at the bottom. I'll show you tomorrow if you'd like."

"Why's it called Mayor's Leap?" I asked.

"Story was told to me," said Papa, "there was a tiny little settlement up here years back—just a few little shacks, really— some families lookin' for gold. When you get any number of people together, there's always someone who thinks they're the one's got to be in charge. So this one fella, he's the one wants to be in charge. He comes up with the idea that they are a real town, and a real town of course needs a mayor. No one else thinks that, but he does."

"Did they name the town?" I asked.

"If they did, I don't know what they named it," continued Papa. "So, this one man who wants to be in charge, he spends all his time and effort into writing up papers and organizing a vote, even talks a couple of the other men to put their names on the paper too, though no one else cares anything about being a mayor. The big day comes when the hat gets passed around, all the papers are counted, and what do you think happened?"

"I don't know," I said.

"The votes are counted, and the people all voted for one of the *other* men. The fella that thought the whole thing up, spent all his time writing papers when he should have been pannin' and diggin' for gold, got two votes out of a dozen." Papa laughed, "And the funny part, I thought, was that the man had a wife and a near-grown son that voted, so if the man voted for himself, that means that only one of his own family voted for him! Anyway, the man was so angry and depressed about not getting to be mayor after the whole thing was his idea, that he went to the cliff and threw himself over the edge. That part's not as funny, I guess."

"Who became the mayor?" I asked.

"Well, nobody had wanted a mayor in the first place, and the man that ended up with the most votes declared he didn't want to be mayor. So they didn't have a mayor. Just continued on with their business. But that's how that stretch of canyon wall came to be called *Mayor's Leap*.

"So there *was* a little town on this spot that got washed away," I said.

"I don't know if it was right here," said Papa, "but close. Maybe we can go scout if we have some time, try to find those old shacks. Good idea?"

"Yes sir!" I said. "Maybe they left behind gold, too!"

"Maybe," said Papa.

Mr. Bern, who had been listening to Papa's telling of the story, spoke up, "Y'know, I never did believe that story of the gold-camp mayor jumping off the cliff."

"Is that right?" asked Papa.

"Naw," said Mr. Bern. "I heard it was Mayor Fiskens from town that got all the lumbermen angry as ants when he wanted to outlaw whiskey on not only Sundays, but Saturdays, too. They run him up into the mountains and told him he could either jump, or become a lumberjack for life, ha haa. Let's just say he didn't become no lumberjack. And it's Mayor's *Jump*, not Mayor's Leap."

"You see, Bug," Papa told me, "Mr. Bern here doesn't believe any story if he's not the one a'tellin' it."

"Nonsense!" hollered Mr. Bern, then laughed.

The clearing was sure big enough for a town. They must have taken a thousand trees from there. It was wide open with a lot of little tree saplings no taller than my waist sprouting up. There were piles of old limbs and stumps that the loggers couldn't use, and Papa said they make those piles to burn and also leave some of 'em so rabbits will have a nice place to make a home. Jack heard Papa say "rabbit," and took off looking for one, sure enough scaring a couple out of their brush-pile home.

There was what looked to be a nice little pond not too far from us. I thought it would be great to catch some fish for supper, to go with the rabbits that Mr. Bern had taken. I thought if we were able to get other meats for food, we wouldn't need to cook bear meat again.

"We can check," said Papa, "but I think it may just be where they burned out a couple of big stumps, just filled up because of the rain."

"But there could still be fish, right?" I asked, figuring every pond, no matter how it got filled up, had to have fish in it.

"Let's go look," he said, and took my hand. We got to the pond, and Papa was right. It was smaller than what I first thought, was pretty shallow and no fish.

"Was a good idea," said Papa. "It's always good to check. But I do think we can fill up our water jugs here."

"Hey, you guys find a bath tub?" asked Mr. Bern, who had followed us.

"A bath tub?" I laughed. I knelt down and splashed the water. "It's freezing!"

"Oh, Miss J," said Mr. Bern, "You've gotten spoilt by heated-up water. And here I thought you was a real mountain gal. Unless you two want to go first, I think I'll go find my clean socks and somethin' to dry myself off with. Been awhile since I've had a real mountain bath. A bath of any kind come to think of it, haa! Not countin' getting rained on."

"Mama!" I yelled as I raced back to camp, "Mr. Bern's gonna take a bath in the pond, and the water's freezing!"

"With the fish?"

"No, there's no fish, but Mr. Bern's gonna take a bath and the water's freezing."

"That sounds like a good idea for all of us," she said.

"But the water's freezing..."

"How 'bout I get a fire going and you can heat up some water?" offered Papa.

"That would be wonderful," said Mama.

"June," asked Papa, "want to help me fill up some jugs before Bern sits in our drinkin' water?"

Papa gathered up our two big water containers, and I collected canteens from everyone. We hustled back to the pond to fill them before Mr. Bern had a chance to bathe. He had found an old burlap sack he was going to use as a towel. He was pretty excited about his bath.

"Don't know what you're missin', Miss J," he said. "You're next, Stinky!" he hollered to Elam. "And wouldn't hurt to sit yourself in here too, Doc!"

I passed the canteens around, even to Elam who I didn't want to talk to, while Papa and Mr. Howell gathered wood for the campfire.

I had a few minutes before helping out with supper, and tried to get in a little juggling with my pine cones to warm myself up while Papa got a fire started. I still liked juggling, even though I didn't like Elam anymore. I moved behind the wagon so Elam wouldn't see me.

K-BOOMMM!!

I dropped the pine cones and whirled around in time to see a big ball of flame above the campfire, saw Elam and Mr. Howell face down on the ground, the horses and mules were kicking and whinnying. Papa was standing in front of the fire pit next to a little can of kerosene, swatting his hair.

"Patrick!" yelled Mama, "What are you doing?"

"The wood's too wet," said Papa. "I was just helpin' it. Guess I used a little too much."

269

"Are you okay, Papa?" I asked as I ran up to him.

"Of course, Bug," he said, his hair still smoking.

"Didn't we bring paper? Or dry kindling?" asked Mama.

"Got wet," said Papa.

"At least the ker-o-SENE didn't get wet, huh?" said Mr. Bern, coming back from his bath. "Just don't use all of it, Allen, you know how I like to put a splash into my mornin' coffee."

"Won't need to use any more tonight," said Papa. "The fire's going...it's, well...maybe just a little bit more."

Papa reached for the can of kerosene and I ran and hid behind the wagon, joined by everyone else this time. Mr. Howell was filthy with mud, having thrown himself into a puddle when the kaboom happened. "I bet he takes a bath now," I whispered to myself.

"Mr. Simms," asked Mama, "can you get a fire going without using kerosene?"

"Oh, sure. Done it countless times, wood wetter'n this," said Mr. Bern. "But the boy needs to learn, you know. I mean, he's what, only forty years old now?"

"Thirty two!" Papa yelled back. "And you just stay over there."

BOOM went the fire, again scaring the horses and mules, but this time the wet wood stayed lit and we all came out from behind the wagon and continued with our evening.

We had the food cooked and eaten in no time, the rabbits Mr. Bern shot tasted delicious. Then Mama and I bathed with heated water. Real mountain gals can heat their bath water if they want. Papa washed up with what was left, and we joined the others around a big campfire. Everyone except Elam, who was off by himself as usual, and I didn't think Mr. Bern had even yelled at him since calling him Stinky. Maybe that hurt his feelings, but he really did stink. I guess we all did until we bathed. Mr. Howell was all cleaned up and smelled good, Mama asked him if he had bathed in the pond. I was impressed that Mr. Howell washed in that freezing cold water, I didn't think of him as a mountain man at all.

"No, no," he told us, "I'm much too used to warm baths, I'm afraid."

I think he saw me smelling him. He said, "Wait right here," and returned a few moments later with his doctor bag, and pulled out a little cloth sack that smelled *really* good. He opened it and picked out four tiny bottles, holding them in his hand.

"I'm sorry I didn't think of these before," he said. "I happen to have with me a sampler bag of colognes, and it just so happens to include a few vials of lady perfumes."

I looked at Mama and she nodded, so I picked up the bottles and smelled each one. Mama showed me how to carefully open one and if I liked the smell, to use the cap to dab a little onto my wrist.

"Thank you, Mr. Howell," Mama said to him, but looking at me.

"Thank you, Mr. Howell," I said, and really meant it.

"So now," asked Papa, "do we call you Mountain *Ladies?*"

"You better," joked Mama, and picked out a perfume for herself.

"Now what *I* want to know is..." started Mr. Bern.

Mr. Howell cut him off, "Mr. Simms, I am occasionally called to perform necropsies on fallen animals." He looked to me, "That means I have to sometimes cut open dead animals to see why they died. Very important work. You can imagine the smell... I simply dab some cologne onto a cloth mask so I don't smell the animal. As much. You know in eighteenth-century England, during their great plague, people were terrified to bathe, convinced the bathwater carried disease, and so..."

Mr. Bern cut *him* off, "Plan on doing many nicro-popsies on our expedition?"

"No, but I always keep a small sample of cologne in my medical bag, just in case."

"In case," said Mr. Bern, "you have to perform an emergency nickle-poopsie?"

I burst out laughing at hearing 'poopsie', then looked to Mr. Howell, afraid he would be mad, but even he thought it was funny. "Ne-CROP-sy, Mr. Simms," he laughed, "and I don't mind admitting to using cologne on a daily basis. Don't want to offend, you know."

"Let me see a bottle if you don't mind," said Mr. Bern. "I've been known to offend. This may just help my social acceptability, what say."

Mama picked out a cologne she liked for Papa, he let her put it on without too much protest, and I tried out *every* perfume on my wrists. Soon we all smelled good. Except for Elam, of course, who still wouldn't come over. We had a great time laughing and trying perfumes and Mama got me up with her to stand in front of the fire and make shadows on the surrounding trees. We tried to dance like real ladies do, but with all the clothes we had on to keep warm, the shadows looked more like pillows with stubby arms than belles at a ball. Papa jumped up and played like he was a bear. Mama and I pretended we were terrified of being eaten, but then the bear made friends with us, like my bear made friends with me.

I had no trouble getting to sleep that night. I was clean, and even though the tent and all the covers still smelled like a wet dog, I smelled good. Mr. Howell made a gift of the perfume bottles to Mama and me, and even gave Mr. Bern the little bottle of cologne he favored. I wasn't thinking about the coldness, wetness or trying to trap my bear. I was thinking, "I like camping."

* * * *

The next morning Mr. Bern was in a boil. Elam had left at some point in the night, and no one knew where he was. I first thought maybe the Johnson boys had been following us and kidnapped him, but his mule and saddle and what little stuff he had were gone, too. Mama suggested he might have gone out hunting, and was sure he'd return soon. I was afraid he'd wandered into the dark and off of Mayor's Leap. Mr. Bern rode off with Fish to look for him, returning a couple hours later, said Elam looked to be making a bee-line down the mountain and he wasn't going to chase him that far. We were all mad at Elam, Mr. Bern the maddest, of course. Mama thanked Mr. Bern for minding his language when I was in earshot, but I was still able to hear some words and phrases that were new to me. I'd never repeat bad words, of course, but I would have to tell K a few of them. He was a boy, he needed to know words like that.

Even I was surprised Elam had left. Though I knew he hated being out there, I didn't think him capable of sneaking off in the middle of the night, leaving us one man short. Mr. Howell was concerned we'd need Elam if ever we found my bear. Mr Howell wanted to go back, too, had been complaining as much as Elam

273

lately, and was down to just a case, plus a few of bottles, of Elixir medicine. I saw him counting them.

"We can't go on without Elam," said Mr. Howell.

"We'll be okay," said Papa.

"We're better off without him, Doc," fumed Mr. Bern. "I know you'll miss your complainin' buddy, I just ask you don't try to pick up his slack in that department."

"I don't think I've been complaining Mr. Simms, I do have experience with difficult travel. Lest you forget, I was with the Seventh Cav...."

"The Seventh Cavalry, yeah, yeah," Mr. Bern cut in. "You've mentioned that at least forty times since we left. Tell me, were all the brave Seventh Cavalrymen as big ol' whiners as you? Or..."

Papa broke in, "Bern, c'mon."

"It's only been a couple days for Lincoln's sake!" said Mr. Bern.

"I thought you knew right where our quarry would be," persisted Mr. Howell, "that the young lady would lead us right to him. I didn't know we'd be this far up in the mountains with winter coming on and no sign of him for more than a week."

"Five days," said Mr. Bern.

"More than a week, Mr. Simms," said Mr. Howell, an edge to his voice.

"Are we sure," asked Mama, "without Elam, that even if our bear is trapped, and Mr. Howell's medicine works, that we'd be able to get him into the wagon?"

"Sure, we're sure," said Mr. Bern. "Pardon my abruptness, but we wouldn't've got all dressed up in our mountain clothes and come up here unless we thought we could do it. We would've had a good practice at it, too, if it weren't for *someone* screwing up."

"I thought we were counting on Elam's strength," said Mr. Howell, ignoring the *screwing up* remark.

"You're givin' that idjit way too much stock, there, Doc," said Mr. Bern. "What I said about us being better off without him, I meant it. It's much better to have old mules you can count on to pull a wagon than to add an unpredictable young ox to the team. Now, it's my own fault I didn't know all this before. I was tryin' to do the boy and his ma a favor by takin' him out on the trail. But we had planned this excursion without him, so in my mind, we're no worse off. We're *better* off, actually. And I just realized I may have called the missus an old mule, for which I am *most* sorry."

"Quite all right, Mr. Simms," smiled Mama. "I understand the analogy."

"Look," said Papa, "we know how to bring large animals down the mountain. Just me and Bern brought down a near five-hundred-pound bear not long ago. The only difference now is that we'd be bringing down a bear that's still alive."

"*If* that potion of yours works, Doc," said Mr. Bern.

"How long do we intend to search with no success?" asked Mr. Howell. "I've got a practice in town. I can't, I'm sorry, stay out here all winter. What if we get snowed in?"

"We'll stay out here as long as it takes," said Mr. Bern, who was now red with anger. "And you will too unless you want to walk back."

Papa tried to keep calm, "Give it a couple more days. I'm sure with us following his tracks, we'll find him soon. We're close."

"This potion of yours better work," said Mr. Bern.

"Well, I'm not positive that it will," said Mr. Howell. "I've never tried it, to be honest."

"I knew it," scowled Mr. Bern. "Maybe we should try it out on *you*."

"I believe it might work, it *should* work," said Mr. Howell, "but... also, I've gone over the application with Allen. You don't really even need me...it'll work fine without me."

"Just a couple more days, Doc. Okay?" said Papa.

It was decided we'd stay camped where we were, the road was terribly muddy and would only be worse farther up the mountain. Mr. Bern made Mr. Howell go with him and Fish to scout and set up the traps. Not wanting to leave Mama and me alone in camp, Papa stayed behind. Jack, too.

I asked if I could go with Mr. Bern to scout the new trap site, but the weather was looking awful unpredictable and they might not get back before dark. I don't know why I wanted to go, maybe I was just real bored. Maybe I wanted to see if there was a sign my bear had visited where they were setting the traps. I had been looking around the clearing with my telescope every now and then, hoping to spot him. A couple of times I thought I saw something, but it turned out to be my mind playing tricks. But maybe not...I just wasn't sure. Ever since the black bear had been trapped, I had a feeling that he was nearby. Fish was supposed to be a good bear-tracker, so we were probably hot on his trail. I just wished I could see him. When the Misters rode off to set the traps, I gave one more look through the telescope, and decided to try to forget about my bear for awhile. I grabbed a couple blankets from the tent, and made a real comfy reading-spot in the back of the wagon, sort of a hidden fort, and spent the afternoon reading the crinkly and smoke-smelling pages of *White Fang*. White Fang was scared of men, just like my bear.

Chapter Twenty-five

B ug, get your sword," said Papa, finding me in the wagon. "Let's go exploring."

"Where are we going?" I asked. "To look for gold?"

"I thought I'd show you Mayor's Leap, maybe shoot a few squirrels. I doubt we'll find any gold, but you never know."

I ran to the tent and got my sword belt, then walked with Papa and Jack across the clearing and into the woods. It was quite a walk to get to the other side, Jack had plenty of time to run to every limb-pile to scare out rabbits. We stepped into the woods and soon saw a squirrel sitting on a pine tree limb, picking apart a little pine cone.

"There's one," I whispered, and pointed.

Papa quietly lifted the little rifle to his shoulder and clicked off the safety. He had saved, and bought brand new, a Winchester pump-action twenty-two caliber at the beginning of summer, telling Mama and me about all the squirrels he'd be bringing home. He hadn't had much opportunity to even shoot it, because of all the trouble I had stirred up. I pressed my hands over my ears and watched the squirrel. The rifle *pop*-ed, not loud at all, I didn't even need to cover my ears. The squirrel dropped from the tree. Jack ran over to it and wagged his tail, telling us where the squirrel had landed. Jack knew not to pick up a squirrel, having done it a couple of years ago and getting his nose nearly bit off, because the squirrel was still alive. I walked over with Papa, the squirrel was dead. Poor squirrel. "Good shot, Papa."

"It's a good little rifle, huh? Finally get a chance to use it." He picked the squirrel up, cradling it's limp body in his hand, and held it out to me. I looked at it, then looked at Papa.

"Here," he said.

"Do I have to?"

"No, but if you want to eat it, you can carry it."

I took hold of the soft, warm tail. The light, wispy fur poked through my fingers. It was much heavier than I expected. It was a pretty big squirrel, fattening up for winter, I imagined. Papa smiled, and though I wasn't thrilled about holding it, I felt good being out on a real hunt with Papa. He shot one more squirrel, just as fat as the first. I walked behind him, carrying our supper by their tails, glad I wouldn't be eating bear.

"Let's go check out the cliff," said Papa.

"Okay," I said. I had forgotten about the cliff.

We walked up a little rise through the trees. Papa stopped and asked, "You see it?"

I looked, but didn't see anything. I looked closer, and finally noticed where the trees appeared kind of fuzzy, and smaller than they should be. They had to be on the other side of the canyon.

"There?" I pointed. "Behind those three pine trees?"

"That's right, good. Now, don't get in front of me, okay? We'll walk up slow, then crawl to the edge." When we got nearer, I could see the trees on the other side, the ones that had looked out of focus before. The ground below us became rocky, and I finally saw where the land dropped off. We stepped onto a humongous, flat rock that was the lip of the canyon. "That's far enough," said Papa. He got down on his knees, set aside the rifle, and made Jack sit. I set the squirrels down and crawled with him the last few feet before laying on our stomachs at the cliff's edge.

"Wow," was all I could say. It felt like we were five miles up in the air. There was a strong wind blowing through the canyon like it was water, and the canyon's edge was it's river bank. Papa grabbed the back of my sword belt. I looked over at him.

"Mama might get mad at me if I let you fall," he smiled.

The canyon on the opposite side was thickly treed with every type of green tree on the mountain—pine, cedar, juniper, fir—all the way to the edge of the creek that ran through. Our side of the canyon, where I was looking over, was a wall of rock that went straight down to the boulders and river rocks.

"What creek is down there?" I asked.

"That's Possum Creek. You know, the one that runs into the Sacramento River, west of town?"

"Possum's a big creek, huh?"

"Yep, bigger'n the Elk, and mostly boulders and waterfalls. Fast, dangerous water when the snow melts. Hey, look over there." He nodded to our left, I looked down and saw two Bald Eagles, their white heads almost shining against the dark greens and browns of the canyon. They were gliding, wings out, one behind the other. They flew silently below us and on down the canyon.

"Ever seen birds flying below you?" he asked.

"We're higher than the eagles!" I had never thought about it before, but I'd never seen the top of a bird, not when it was flying. That sight was amazing to me. We watched as they became smaller and smaller, then turned with the canyon to the south, and disappeared.

"That was incredible," I said, then looked to see a black raven following the same path through the air. "I never knew we had a canyon like this on our mountain."

"Yep, it's here. It's actually not that big of a canyon. It's big here, where we're at, but after it turns south, it gets smaller and smaller."

"And this is where the mayor leaped?"

"That's the story. Never did find him."

"Wow. How far down is that?"

"Oh, I'd say two hundred feet, maybe two-fifty."

"Is that more than a mile?"

"No," chuckled Papa, "not even close. It's an awful big drop, though."

"I guess," I said, somewhat disappointed it wasn't a mile.

I peered over the edge as far as I dared, could feel Papa's hand tightening on my belt, and looked straight down to the thin ribbon of green and white, snaking through huge boulders and under old, fallen trees. I tried picturing what it would look like when the snow melted and made it into a raging river.

"Here," said Papa, putting a little rock in my hand, the size of a chicken's egg. "Toss it over." I dangled my arms over the canyon's lip, and lobbed the rock out a ways, following it down until it disappeared. I couldn't tell if I had hit the water.

* * * *

I raced with Jack ahead of Papa back to camp, holding up the two squirrels, and excitedly reporting to everyone about Mayor's Leap and the eagles, and remembering to tell Mama that Papa held me so I wouldn't fall.

Us Allens had a delicious, roasted squirrel supper with biscuits, while Mr. Bern cooked up more of the bear meat for himself and Mr. Howell. Our supply of venison was just about gone, but if Papa could get more squirrels or even a deer, we'd be fine. I still didn't want to eat the bear. I could just eat beans and biscuits every meal if I had to.

"Mr. Bern," I asked when we were nearing the end of our meal, "why did the black bear, after you skinned him...why did...I mean...his body looked just like a...a man. I thought. With a bear's head and paws."

"Well," said Mr. Bern, "I s'pose there's a resemblance. You know, the Indians up north, up there, they believe they can change themselves into bears, and bears can change into humans."

"Is that true? Can they do that?" I asked.

"Well...Indians have lots of stories like that. As far as if it's true or not, I can't say. I'm not an Indian. But you know, bears can stand up and walk, and they got elbows and knees just like us folks do." He had both arms out to his side, swinging at the elbows like a broken scarecrow.

"Could it have really been an Indian that you trapped?" I asked.

"No," Papa quickly said. "It was just a bear."

Mr. Howell said, "Most, if not all cultures have creation stories involving animals." It was unexpected whenever he spoke about something that wasn't a complaint, so I and everyone else looked to him. "In the Bible, for instance, the snake in the Garden of Eden. Jonah and the Whale. Then there's Romulus and Remus, the founders of Rome, raised by a she-wolf. *Canis Lupis*...that's Latin for wolf. I'm not sure the Latin for *she-wolf*, however.

"That's not what she's askin'," said Mr. Bern. "We're talkin' about Indians and bears. *Bruin*, that's Latin for bear. You doctory types love your Latin."

"The Latin word for *bear*, Mr. Simms, happens to be Ursa, or Ursus," said Mr. Howell.

"What's *grizzly bear*?" I asked.

"That would be, I believe, *Ursus Horribilus*."

"Wow, like horrible bear..."

"Yes," said Mr. Howell, "that's exactly what it means."

"Hmph," grunted Mr. Bern, though he was still looking at Mr. Howell, waiting to hear what he would say next. We were all looking at Mr. Howell, waiting.

"Well, ahh," he started, like he had forgotten what he was talking about, but then remembered. "Oh! What I was going to say about *Ursa* is...you may have heard the term, *Ursa Major*? Do you know what that refers to?" he asked, looking at me. "I know you've seen it, many times."

"I don't know," I said. I hoped he didn't think since I figured out *horrible bear*, that I knew Latin.

"I know," said Mama, in a teasing way toward the men. "It's the

283

Big Dipper...right?"

"Very good," said Mr. Howell, sounding like a teacher. "The Big Dipper, *Ursa Major*. It means *Great Bear*."

"Don't look nothin' like a bear, Doc," said Mr. Bern, looking up at the clouds. "Looks like a dipper, a *big* dipper. Is why we call it the Big Dipper. Don't suppose the Little Dipper means *Little Bear*?"

"As a matter of fact," said Mr. Howell, "*Ursa Minor*."

"Nonsense."

"Why is it the Great Bear?" I asked, thinking Mr. Bern was right, the stars looked much more like a dipper than a bear.

Mr. Howell explained, "It's from the Greeks."

"Figures," said Mr. Bern.

"In Greek mythology...well, have you heard of *Zeus*?" Mr. Howell asked me.

"Yes," I said, but I didn't know who he was.

"Zeus was the greatest of the Greek gods, and he had a...a friend, let's say, named Callisto. And Callisto became...ahh...she was to be with child, you see. Zeus's child."

"Were they married?" I asked.

"And there was a goddess," continued Mr. Howell, ignoring my question. "A goddess named Artemis, the great Goddess of the Hunt. She found out that Callisto was with child, and she became furious..."

"Why?" I asked.

"Why?"

"Why was Artemis furious?"

"Oh. Well, that part's very complicated. Suffice it to say, she was not happy with Callisto, and she, being a goddess with all manner of powers, turned the young nymph Callisto into a bear."

"Was it because they weren't married?"

"So, Callisto, who was now a bear, when the time came, she produced a son. A human son, Areus. Years later when Areus was a young man, on his way to becoming a great hunter, he one day had his sights lined up, with his bow and arrow, on a *bear*."

"His mama?" I asked.

"Yes, his mama. Only he didn't know that, of course, it was just another bear to him. Zeus saw what was about to happen, and he decided to rescue Callisto. He used his immense power to snatch her away just as the arrow flew from Areus's bow, and he freed her into the sky where she would be safe, and could watch her son grow into a great man. Without the fear, of course, of her son trying to kill her again."

"Wow."

"So, when you see in the night sky, the Big Dipper, now you know it's really Callisto, the great mother bear, *Ursa Major*, keeping a watchful eye on her son, Areus."

"Wow, I never knew that," I said. "Did you know that, Mama?"

"No," she said. "I knew it was called Ursa Major, but I never knew why."

"Did you know, Papa?"

"No, I didn't. Very fascinating."

"Did you, Mr. Bern?"

"Of course I did, young'n. Just never did believe that story. You can't believe a thing that comes out of a Greek, I've learned. Learned that the hard way."

"Is that right?" Papa asked. Then to me, rolled his eyes. I giggled.

"You betcha," replied Mr. Bern. "You see, there was this old mountain man, name of Flanders, and he was a Greek..."

"A Greek named *Flanders*?" Papa asked.

"Well, I'm sure when he goes back to Greece, they call him Flandopolis, or some such, I don't know."

"*Flandopolis*?"

"Are you gonna let me tell my story? Doc here's been borin' us with his story without interruption."

"Sorry. Please continue."

"You see, this Greek, Flanders, you couldn't believe a thing the man said. Why, I remember this one time..."

We had a great evening, together, the men telling stories, each one bigger than the last. I listened, and loved every one. Unfortunately, with the clouds blocking the sky, there wasn't a chance to see one of the Dippers, one of the Bears. I would never look at the stars the same way, I told myself, and when I got back, I would look for a book on Greek stories. Greeks couldn't be all that bad, if they wrote about bears.

Chapter Twenty-six

I was up early with Papa, making the coffee and breakfast. It had been our biggest and best campfire yet. No one wanted it to go out and have Papa blow up the camp again trying to restart it. After breakfast Mr. Howell took over cleaning the pans and plates and packing away the cooking stuff, but only after getting yelled at by Mr. Bern to pull his weight.

"I spent all afternoon yesterday setting up traps with you," argued Mr. Howell.

"Yeah," said Mr. Bern, "and I'd of gotten 'em set up faster if you'd stayed in camp. *Dishes*, Little Dipper."

Since Mr. Howell was doing the cleaning, Mama and I took a little walk with Jack. I had three apples, wanting to show Mama how good I was juggling while we walked the edge of the clearing. I could just about keep three apples going for a few seconds, but having mittens on made it difficult. I couldn't take them off, though, without my fingers freezing. Mama said she was very impressed with my juggling, having only learned a few days ago.

"I'm sorry I haven't found my bear yet," I told her.

"It's not your fault, Bug. I think some of the men were

disappointed we didn't find him the first couple of days, only because you had been running into him so often. And so close to our house. I think they thought it would be easy."

"Did you think it would be easy?" I asked.

"No, but I guess I didn't think we'd be climbing the mountain like we are."

"*I* thought it would be easy," I said. "To find him anyway. I've always been able to find him, or he found me."

Or he found me, I thought to myself. That's right. Half, or even most of the time I had come across him, it was *him* that found *me*. Since we'd been on the expedition, I had sort of felt him close a few times, and had thought I glimpsed him in my telescope. The night before, I had a strange feeling he was very close by, but thought it was because we were supposedly on his trail and we were deep in bear country, what used to be *grizzly bear* country. But now I really felt him. Close. I stopped and looked around. Had he been tracking us, instead of us tracking him? Why hadn't Fish found him? He's supposed to be such a great bear-dog.

"June? Have you been listening?"

"Uh huh."

I didn't know what it was, but I knew my bear was close. I looked down at Jack, he was staring at the trees with his ears perked, but I guess he couldn't smell him. The wind was blowing at our backs into the trees so neither Jack nor Fish could smell him even if he was right inside the treeline. I just knew my bear was near, he must have been following *me* the whole time. He must have really missed me, and wondered why I wasn't going into the woods to see him and bring him pies.

Could I really let him be captured and put him in a zoo? It's just like jail. I thought of the black bear that we had killed, had never stopped thinking about him. How he was trapped, looking for food because he was hungry. How he looked with his fur gone. How he's now food for the men and the dogs. I couldn't bear the thought of my grizzly ending up like that.

A big, freezing cold gust of wind blew through Mama and me. The coldest air I'd felt yet. Winter had arrived. Was it still winter if there wasn't snow? My bear may not make it through the winter, and there's still a lot of guns on the mountain pointed at him.

"Come on, June," said Mama, "let's go back, we'll freeze."

Would I rather have him dead on the mountain, or alive in a zoo?

"June, now. It's too cold."

Mr. Howell's sleeping stuff *better* work. "He's here, Mama."

"What? Come on, Papa's waiting for us."

"He's here," I said again.

"Who?"

"My bear. He's here."

"Here?" she asked, looking to the forest. "I thought you said he'd be by the creek."

"He's been following us...following me. I can feel him." I looked down at Jack, he must have finally smelled something. His tail was wagging and he was trying to see the bear in the thick trees. Mama tensed up, searching the trees and bushes and listening for any sign of him.

"I don't see him," said Mama. "Do you see him?"

"No, I mean, I might have seen him a couple days ago, it's...I just know he's out there. Over there, somewhere."

"You're sure."

"Yes, ma'am. I'm sure."

I threw the apples into the trees, hoping he'd poke his head out to pick up one. He didn't.

"I know he's there, Mama."

We walked back to the men. The cold wind was blowing hard against us, I had to cover my cheeks with my mittens so my face wouldn't freeze.

Mr. Howell had finished the dishes and was mounting up with Mr. Bern to check the traps down by the creek.

"I knew an old trapper-man long ago, name of Howell," Mr. Bern was telling him. "We called him 'Howie' for short. Mind if I call you Howie?"

"I'd rather you not."

"Anybody call you Howie before?"

"No. Doc is fine."

"But you ain't a real doctor, are ye?"

"Yes, Mr. Simms, I am a doctor of veterinary medicine. A real doctor."

"That ain't a real doctor."

Papa had just dumped a big armful of wood next to the campfire when we walked up.

"Your daughter has something to tell you," said Mama.

I hesitated, knowing this might really be it. I hoped I was doing the right thing.

"My bear is here," I said. "Over there, in the trees."

"You think he's over there in the trees?" asked Papa.

"She says he's been following us the whole time," Mama told him.

"Did you see him?" he asked Mama.

"No, I didn't see him."

"But *you* saw him?" he asked me.

"No, but I know he's there. He's watching us."

Mr. Bern, who had walked up with Willa said, "Well, let's go have a look," and pulled his big rifle out.

"No!" I yelled. "You said you wouldn't hurt him!"

"Oh, no, I won't shoot him, young'n." Then to Papa, "We should have a look first. At the least."

"You'll scare him away," I said. "That's why we haven't found him, 'cause he's scared of you. You'll scare him away and then he'll freeze to death or get killed by hunters!"

Mr. Bern gave Papa a questioning look like, 'Are we really going to believe her?'

"June," said Papa, "we *should* have a look first. All the traps are down by the creek, we're not going to bring them all up before checking it out. We figured him to be near the creek. You've always seen him near a creek."

Mama spoke up, "Maybe he's always seen by a creek because that's where June always explores."

They dragged me all the way out there to find my bear, and now that I knew where he was, they didn't believe me. I turned and hugged Mama.

Papa spoke to Mr. Bern, "Well, we've banked the trip on June being able to find him. *We* haven't found him ourselves. We've probably been leading June on this trip more'n she's been leading us... She looks awful certain."

Mr. Bern looked to the tree line. "Yeahhh, well...can't say as I've been encouraged by the luck we've been havin'. Grub's only gonna last a few more days anyhow, if we don't get buried in snow first. It's up to you, Allen. Whatever you want to do."

"You really think your bear's just outside the clearing?" Papa asked me.

"Uh-huh. Yes, sir."

"Okay," said Papa and looked at Mr. Bern.

"What do you think, Fish?" said Mr. Bern, looking down. Fish wagged his tail. "Well, all right! What're we standing around for? Doc! Let's go bring them traps back!"

Chapter Twenty-seven

While the Misters retrieved the traps from the creek, Papa, Mama and I moved the whole camp to the side of the big clearing farthest from where the traps would be set. It was only a couple hundred feet, according to Papa, but would put us behind a little clump of trees. We wouldn't be hidden, but we wouldn't be out in open.

We were getting pretty good at setting up camp. In no time, we had the wagon moved, the animals tethered, and the tents staked. We needed a new campfire, but Mama didn't want Papa to start one if he had to use kerosene. So after making a new circle of rocks, Papa grabbed a flaming log and raced over to the new spot, tossing the log in the middle of the rock circle before burning himself. It became a fun game, cheering on Papa to 'run!' as he was chased by Jack. I even grabbed a couple little sticks from the fire and ran with them. Before long, we had a big new campfire roaring and Papa didn't have to blow anything up. He found a couple of big logs near the new camp and dragged them over to the fire-pit, made like he was dusting off the tops of them, and said, "This camp deserves some seats!"

Even as I was laughing and having fun moving our camp, I kept
my eyes and ears on the clearing, wanting to see my bear, but also
hoping I wouldn't see him. Hoping I was wrong about him being
so near, and that he had moved on to another, safer part of the
mountain.

While I helped Mama with supper, Papa and the Misters set up
the traps way over on the other side of the clearing, not too far
from where the mountain dropped off into Mayor's Leap. Mr. Bern
said he had planned on leaving half the traps down by the creek,
but they were having so much trouble getting back to the road with
all the muck on the trail that it would have been impossible to get a
bear out of there, anyway. So they set up all six traps, two inside
the treeline, with the rest leading out of the trees to the basket of
apples. Papa anchored most of them to trees with big chains. The
two closest to the basket he hammered long steel stakes into the
ground. Then they carefully opened the jaws of the bear traps and
covered them with leaves and pine needles. It was Mr. Howell's
job to hammer in a stick with a piece of canvas tied to it just to the
left of every trap so we'd all know where the traps were.

"Bears don't know flags," said Mr. Bern when I asked him
wouldn't my bear know where the traps were.

The traps were all set and covered just before dark. Papa took
an armful of apples and tossed them into the woods, and all around
the traps, leading to the basket which was about half full. Mr. Bern
had left his leg of venison down by the creek. By that time it was
really rotting and growing things and Mr. Howell refused to travel
anywhere near it.

"That should do it," said Papa, and he joined Mama and me in the tent to play checkers by lamplight until it was time to sleep. Of course I didn't get much sleep that night. I hadn't had much sleep the whole trip. I was thinking about my bear, and listening carefully for any sound of him outside. The wind had picked up and was whistling loudly around the tent, so I probably wouldn't have been able to hear anything anyway. I was still awake when Papa was awakened for his turn at night watch. The men had decided it was okay to have just one of them on watch again.

* * * *

I woke up to our fourth day at the big clearing, tired and damp. The moment I scootched out from the pile of blankets I was cold, too. Mama and Papa had been up a long time, but I didn't feel bad about sleeping in. Listening for the snap of a trap all night had me so tired I would have stayed in the tent all day if I didn't have to *visit the outside*. I planned on quickly doing my thing and returning to bed, but was called over to the fire for a breakfast plate that had been saved for me.

Tiny flakes of snow filled the air. They were so small, it didn't even look like they were falling, but kind of dancing weightless around through the air, like dandelion wings in the spring. The ones I was able to follow to the ground, disappeared onto the wet ground. It felt and smelled like winter.

"It's snowing," I said. "Is it really winter, now?"

"Oh, it's been officially winter for a while, now," said Papa, " but looks like we may be having the first snow, huh?" No one seemed

295

excited about the snow. I wasn't all that excited about it, either. It's one thing to look out the window of a warm house at the falling snow, quite another to step out of a cold tent into it, with the chance of being stranded.

It was a small breakfast, just a biscuit and a piece of bacon. I sat on a log with the plate on my lap and watched the trees and the dancing little flakes. I wondered if my bear was thinking about the snow, if he thought he had better find a place to hibernate. Everyone was quiet and worn-out looking. Even Mr. Bern, who I figured no matter how tuckered, would have a hard time staying quiet. I imagined him talking and talking about how tuckered he was. As I was thinking that, Mr. Bern limped over with his cup of coffee and eased himself down next to me.

"Whoo, young'n," he said, "I shore am tired this mornin', how 'bout you? One thing about winter, makes my old bones not want to get up out of bed. Why, if it weren't for havin' to visit the outside I think I would just stay under the covers 'til spring."

"Yes, sir. Me, too." I had the same thought that very morning, but I couldn't tell Mr. Bern *that*.

"How I do envy the bears," he continued, "sleepin' all winter. Wish I could do that. How do you think it is, they can *hold* it that long?"

I laughed. "I don't know."

"These days, seems I can't hold it for even one whole night, much less..."

"Pie, anyone?" interrupted Mama, walking up with one of the apple pies we'd been saving for my bear.

"Pie? For breakfast?" I asked.

"We're celebrating this morning," she told us as she cut out warmed pieces for Mr. Bern and me. "It's the first snow of the winter, and even if it weren't, I think we could all use a little celebration."

"Thankee, Ma'am," said Mr. Bern. "I was just tellin' the young'n here how when one get's old, it's not as easy to..."

"Yes, Mr. Simms, I heard. Anyway, I thought we all deserved a little something special for working so hard this past week. And even if we go back empty-handed, I think this trip will be a good memory for all of us...hopefully. Eventually."

"Here, here," chimed in Papa, and raised his cup of coffee.

"Let's toast!" I said, and looked for my cup. Mama found it and poured some water into it, but Papa stopped her.

"Here, let me see that," he said, and poured the water out, replacing it with coffee from the steaming pot. "I have been very impressed, young lady," he told me, holding my cup up, "very impressed indeed with all your hard work and your help. You're growing up, June, growing into a wonderful young lady who has no trouble taking care of herself. You're growing up, so here's a grown-up drink."

"Thank you, Papa," I said as I took the steaming cup.

"Maybe we should add some water," said Mama.

"No, it's okay," I said. I had always loved the smell of coffee, but for some reason had never tried it.

"Nothin' better'n a good cup of mountain coffee to go with pie," said Mr. Bern, holding his cup out to Papa. "Freshen my cup please, sir."

We all raised our cups with Papa and he began his toast, "Here's

297

to..."

"Wait!" I said. "Where's Mr. Howell? We can't toast without him."

"Yes, we can," whispered Mr. Bern.

"Doc took his plate back to his tent," said Papa. "He'll be here for the next toast. So, here's to our little expedition, on the first snow of the season. May we return home successful, but if not, may we all return home safe. Cheers."

"Cheers," we all said back, me the loudest, then clinked our cups together. I took a tiny sip from the steaming hot cup of coffee and...

"May I have a little water in my coffee, please?" I asked, and all the grown-ups laughed. Mama poured out half the coffee and added water, then put in a bunch of sugar. It really wasn't too bad after that, almost tasted like hot chocolate. And Mr. Bern was right, the pie tasted wonderful with a little coffee to wash it down.

* * * *

Every day of our expedition had brought something new. That morning something happened that I never thought would happen. Not the coffee, but right after that. Jack had been laying over by our tent, sulking, because Papa had yelled at him not to beg while we were having breakfast. Papa left the fire to put away the horse's feed bags, so Jack of course snuck right back in and sat down in front of me, staring at the half piece of bacon and the biscuit on my plate.

"Jack..." I scolded him in a low, deep voice, "no begging." He turned his head, but his eyes slowly sneaked back to fix on the food. "No begging," I told him again, and he got up and went back to the tent to sulk some more. Then Fish, who was lying on top of Mr. Bern's feet, came and sat next to me. "Fish," I said in my growly voice, "no begging." Instead of turning away, he laid his head on my lap next to where the plate was. I was about to tell him 'no begging' again, but then realized this was the closest I'd ever been to Fish, and he'd certainly never laid his head on my lap before. I looked at Mr. Bern, not knowing what Fish was doing.

"Oh, he's not beggin', Miss June," said Mr. Bern. "He wants you to scratch his head. Don't think he's ever begged in his life, come to think of it. Rarely see the dog eat, much less beg."

"Oh." I rubbed the top of his head lightly, then gave him some good scratches. "So, does Fish like me now?"

"Sure looks like it, don't it? Maybe with you growin' up, huntin' squirrels and grizzly bears, and now drinkin' coffee, he figures he'd better get on your good side, what d'ya think?"

"I guess so," I said. "Yeah, you're a good boy, aren't you, Fish? Good boy." Jack ran back, jealous that Fish wasn't sent away. He scootched right up beside Fish, knocking my plate to the ground. "Jack!" He grabbed the biscuit from the dirt and took off, followed by Fish. I was mad for a second, then laughed, watching the dogs running around the clearing. Jack the absolute happiest a dog could be, having stolen a whole biscuit and gotten away with it. And Fish just as happy, having someone to chase.

* * * *

I spent most of the day in the tent, trying to stay warm. It continued to snow little flakes, turning the ground white with the thinnest of layers. I tried reading and playing checkers with Mama, but just couldn't concentrate. I was too concerned with listening for the sound of a trap snapping shut. Papa and Mr. Bern spent their time unloading everything from the wagon, checking and cleaning the winch and chains, and cleaning their rifles. I walked over to Papa and we took turns throwing sticks for the dogs and searching the tree line with my telescope through the falling snow. Neither Jack nor Fish were retrievers, and not once did they bring a stick back to us. We'd throw it, they'd tear off after it like the one that got to it first would win a hundred dollars. Soon as they got to the stick, they'd both break off and run in a big circle back to us, leaving big designs in the thin snowfall. So, maybe Fish really did like me now. He'd never played anything with me before. I wasn't able to pat his head, but that was just because he wouldn't stand still long enough for me to do it.

I went with Papa and helped bring back the dog's sticks, since they were our firewood, then realized how cold I was and went back to the tent. I hadn't seen Mr. Howell all day, and half wondered if we should check on him, maybe he skedaddled when no one was watching, like Elam did.

Mama stepped into the tent a short time later, dusted with snow, holding a steaming plate of fresh biscuits and the last of the bacon. The plate was smoking so much in the freezing tent you could barely see the food. Papa joined us and we had a cozy little supper, then played checkers until it was too dark to see the board.

Papa told me it was time for me to turn in, but I wanted to go out with the grownups who were standing around the fire. The snow was coming down good now, big flakes, and covering everything on the ground. As much as I had fretted about the Donner Party and getting stranded in the snow, now that it was finally snowing, I didn't have much of a thought about it. I had been in snow, even deep snow, every winter since I could remember. Maybe reading about it made it seem scary. Maybe the Donners didn't know how to take care of themselves like we did. I had learned a lot on our expedition, so maybe I thought we could handle anything, I don't know. And Mama was right, we really weren't *too* far from home.

I finally saw Mr. Howell. He had a ruler in his hand, was measuring the depth of the snow and trying to talk Papa into calling an end to the expedition before we were snowed-in. Why would anyone bring a ruler on an expedition?

All the men were drinking coffee, and I asked if I could have a half cup.

"Not tonight," said Papa. "Coffee's just for special occasions until you're older, okay? And you don't want to drink it at night, wouldn't be able to sleep a wink."

When I did turn in, I kept all my clothes on, just in case I had to run outside in a hurry. I thought it made sense to sleep in your clothes all the time anyway, because in the winter, putting on a cold dress in the morning wasn't much fun.

When Mama came in to lay down, she brought Jack, and they were both covered with snow. She dried him good before he buried himself under the blankets.

"Snow's really coming down, now," she said. "I'm sure it won't last long. You're not worried, are you?"

"No," I said, "I'm not worried. I like the snow. I know we won't get stranded."

That made Mama smile. "Well, I hope it doesn't snow *all* night, even if we don't get stranded. I think tonight's the full moon, too bad we can't see it."

I knew I wasn't going to sleep any time soon, even without coffee. I wasn't worried about getting stranded, but I *was* a bit anxious, because I was feeling my bear stronger than I had the whole expedition. Maybe he was in the woods closest to us and not by the traps at all. But if he was right by us, Jack and Fish would surely smell him. Can dogs smell through the snow? Maybe he wasn't anywhere near us after all, maybe I was just crazy.

"Knock, knock, anybody home?" Papa opened the tent flap and leaned in to give Mama and me goodnight kisses. He was sparkly white, had a lot of snow on his shoulders and hat, and his beard was wet and shiny from the snow that melted from his breath. Mama handed him a blanket to dry his whiskers before kissing us. "Snow's coming down good now. If you see a snowman out here in the morning, it may just be me."

"Papa!" I laughed.

"Or if the snowman's leaning to one side and looks grumpy, it's Bern. I've got first watch, so if you need anything just give a hoot."

"Hoot, hoot."

"Jack in here?" Papa held up his kerosene lamp and saw the blankets moving at our feet. "Jack, c'mon... Jack, out here, *now*."

"It's cold out there, Papa."

"I know it's cold out there, *I'm* out there. Jack!"

"Oh, let him stay," said Mama. "You know he'll run out if he hears anything."

"He's keeping our feet warm," I pleaded.

"What about *my* feet?"

"Men's feet don't get cold," said Mama.

"He's protecting us," I said.

"Uh-huh."

"Papa, can we make snow-people tomorrow?"

"I guess. Well, goodnight, my ladies." Papa gave us both kisses.

"Say goodnight to Jack, too," I said.

"No."

Papa left to keep watch. "Why don't men's feet get cold?" I asked Mama.

We were warm under the blankets, a little too warm with Jack under there. The tent had a pretty dancing glow from the fire nearby. I could see my breath, and blew harder and harder to see how much of the tent I could fill with it. I heard Mama softly snoring, then heard what sounded like a bear, but was only Mr. Bern snoring two tents over.

I pictured my bear getting snowed on, shivering in the cold. Would he smell the apples Papa threw into the woods? I pictured him stepping into a trap, surprising him at first, but not hurting too bad because of the rubber things. Hopefully it wouldn't hurt him. But if he could find the apples, he would have found them by now. Maybe he was even smarter than I thought, maybe he'd avoided all the traps and eaten all the apples. Maybe he'd been eating the apples all along, when the traps had been set up by the creek, and we'd just assumed that raccoons had been taking them.

I must have finally fallen asleep, because I woke up, needing to visit the outside. It was dark, but not as dark as when I had turned in, so maybe the full moon was finding it's way through the clouds. Climbing out of the many blankets I was buried under, I quietly put on my boots and coat, carefully stepped over Jack, and peeked outside the tent. It was lightly snowing, medium sized flakes, but there was a good four or five inches on the ground, at least. The light I was seeing wasn't from the full moon, but rather from the sun, which was working it's way up the backside of the mountain and wanting to break over the trees to start us on a new day.

After my 'visit' behind the big cedar tree, instead of going back into the tent, I walked over to the campfire, or what was supposed to be the campfire. It was down to glowing coals, with just a wisp of yellow flame. I placed a few small sticks onto the coals, the snow-wet wood hissing and smoking from the heat, then lay a medium-sized log on top of those. Near the fire-pit Mr. Howell sat in the wagon's seat, wrapped thick in blankets and covered with snow, sleeping on his watch. I wouldn't have known it was him if it weren't for his big Bowler hat perched on top of the blanket-bundle where his head most likely was. I *hoped* he was asleep and not frozen. I stepped closer, and yep, there were small clouds of breath pushing out through a hole in the blankets.

It was so quiet, I could hear my breath as it turned to mist in the cold air. And beautiful—snowflakes silently drifting down, the sun's faint glow from the east, throwing dim, purple-ish shadows from the trees onto the snowy meadow. I began walking into the clearing, looking straight up into the falling flakes. There was no sound except for the faint crunching of my boots on the light, powdery snow. I had the sensation I was an eagle, high in the air, flying through the snowflakes. I walked that way for a while, losing myself in the sky. When I returned to Earth, I looked around, and found myself near the middle of the meadow. The sun was shining a little more through the falling snow and the trees, the purples were lightening to a shade of lavender.

That would have been a good time to return to camp. I started to follow my footsteps back, when I looked toward the far edge of the clearing where the traps had been set. With it still being pretty dark, and with the falling snow, it was hard to even see the tree-line. But I thought I saw *something*. My heart started to race, then slowed down when I figured out that I was only looking at the bucket of apples near the traps. That would have been a *great* time to return to camp.

I hadn't planned on walking to the traps, I wasn't even planning on walking to them while I was doing it. I was *drawn* to them. That was going to be my story if I got in trouble for leaving camp by myself. Not a very good story, I worried. Mr. Howell would probably get yelled at too, he would have seen me leave if he wasn't sleeping on his watch. I didn't want Mr. Howell to get in trouble because of me, so I was going to check the apples and immediately walk back before anyone woke up and noticed me missing. I tramped *crunch, crunch* through the powdery snow, in a somewhat straight line, occasionally stepping around a sapling that stood in the way.

Standing in front of the bushel of apples, I looked at the red canvas flags marking the locations of the traps buried under the snow. *Flags to the left*, I thought, or was it *traps to the left?* Either way, I wasn't going any farther.

"Are you out there, Grizzly Bear?" I listened to the forest for an answer. So quiet. I could just hear a *whooosh* of wind coming through the trees. Maybe I had been wrong about my bear following me up the mountain.

Chapter Twenty-eight

I picked up a couple of apples from the snow covered bucket, frozen hard and very cold in my bare hands. I shook off some of the snow, wiped them on my coat, and tried to juggle. Starting with just two, tossing them up and catching them. Boy, were they cold, just like snowballs. I stuck the apples under my arms so I could blow into my hands to try and warm my fingers. I looked into the trees, it was very still and quiet. I picked up one more apple from the bucket and tried to juggle three.

Maybe because it was so cold, or maybe because I wasn't as good as I thought I was, I could not keep three apples in the air for even one try. They all fell and disappeared into their own holes in the snow. I juggled again and actually kept them all up for a couple throws before they all buried themselves again. I couldn't keep the apples going if my hands were frozen, and I couldn't keep my hands warm if I was always reaching into the snow to find dropped apples.

I wasn't sure I had heard anything until I heard it a second time. A low, breathy grunt. I slowly reached down and picked up the snow covered apples and tried juggling again. Wasn't much of a try, I was listening too hard. I heard it again, "hramph, hramph." I saw smokey clouds of breath, and knew it had to be my bear. I clicked my tongue, and he responded with his own clicks. I couldn't believe it, it had been so long!

He was hiding in the trees, behind where the traps were set. I stared at where the billowy steam was coming from and finally saw a dark outline of his furry head peeking out from behind the trunk of a big cedar.

We just stood and stared at each other, a growing fist in my stomach as I wondered what to do next. I started to have little second thoughts about capturing him which became *big* second thoughts. I decided if he could speak, he'd tell me he'd rather be free, dodging bullets and shivering hungry in the cold, than be taken off his mountain and put behind bars where he could never run again. Where people would stare and gawk at him, mean boys would probably throw things at him. And he hadn't done anything wrong, other than being born a grizzly bear. I had never felt so torn in my life. I didn't want to cry, but tears came to my eyes. I didn't know what I was supposed to do. The meadow was opening up to the sun, dawn was arriving, and the grownups would be awake any moment.

Not wanting to make a decision, I squatted down and picked up the snow-covered juggling apples and tried again. For some reason, even though I had tears in my eyes, I actually did okay with them. I only dropped them when I looked up to see if my bear was watching. He had moved a little away from the tree, stepping in between two of the traps. I could see into the trees where the snow wasn't as deep, and saw he had eaten every apple that Papa had thrown. He knew where the apples were and he knew where the traps were. Smart bear. I bet it was him all along that'd been taking the apples around the traps. The men thought it had been raccoons. I could see the familiar lolling of his head, and he playfully hopped a little on his front feet and clicked his jaws. He made a low whining sound like he wanted to run over, but was afraid to leave the cover of the trees. Would he be happy to see me if he knew I was out there to trap him?

I made clicking sounds back to him and threw him an apple. He cautiously moved out from the trees to find it under the snow, nervous to be out in the open, but he sure crunched that apple. He was still a little skinny-looking for a giant bear, but not as skinny and ragged looking as the last time I'd seen him. Maybe he had been catching deer and rabbits to eat, or maybe he had started to fatten up from all the apples we'd been leaving around the traps trying to catch him. He was doing okay, even with all the hunters and posses that had been chasing him.

He would rather be free. I would rather be free, too, if I were a bear. I had made a big mistake by helping Papa and Mr. Bern. But my mistake started when I kept looking for him and visiting him. Well, I didn't want to make the mistake of taking my bear off his mountain.

I wanted to walk back and tell them I was wrong about my bear being close, but then I was afraid he'd follow me out of the woods and either step into one of the traps, or be seen by Mr. Bern and Papa. Mr. Bern, I thought, would still shoot if he had the chance.

I scooped up some apples and threw them deep into the woods, as far away from the traps as I could throw. Maybe I could draw him away, but then what? He moved to the apples and quickly ate them, but then walked back toward me.

"Go away," I said through gritted teeth, "you have to go away."

"Ju-uune!" I heard my name being called. "June?... Ju-uune!" I turned around just as Fish and Jack flew past me in a powdery cloud. They were so quiet running through the snow, I didn't even hear them coming.

All that was so quiet a moment ago was now so loud. A *SNAP* shook me as one of the sprinting dogs triggered a trap, causing it to leap into the air, luckily missing. The horrible sound of two dogs and a grizzly bear exploding into a fight filled the quiet mountain.

"Jack! Fish!... NO!" I screamed. I stood trembling, unable to move. I saw the dogs running circles around my bear, lunging and snapping at him. *SNAP* went another trap, missing again. My bear roared, swatting and lunging at the dogs but they were too quick for him to catch. Fish ran in circles, yipping and taunting him. When my bear charged him, Jack would attack his back side, snapping his teeth and biting, then jumping away when my bear turned on him. It was the biggest, loudest fight I had ever heard or seen. It was worse than any animal fight I'd ever read about in any Jack London story, and I couldn't believe it was happening right in front of me. The dogs had my grizzly bear roaring, turning circles trying to get them. When he'd try to run and get away, both dogs would dive at his back side, viciously biting him, and he'd have to spin around to get them to stop. Fish would run his circle again, and the whole thing would start over.

Papa, without a coat or hat, sprinted across the field on a saddle-less Whiskey, knocking me over when he leaped off the horse to grab me. He picked me up with the arm that didn't have his big pistol pointed at the fight.

I looked back to see Mr. Bern coming fast on Willa, also without a saddle, and Mama holding on to him for dear life. Mr. Howell was on foot, just leaving the camp, running through the snow with the medicine stick.

"Take June back to the wagon!" Papa yelled.

Mr. Bern helped Mama off of Willa, she ran up and grabbed me, but stood and watched the struggle in the trees.

"Jack, no!" I screamed again, surprised Jack was attacking my bear. I thought they were friends.

Papa had his pistol and now Mr. Bern had his biggest rifle, both aimed at my bear. "Get her out of here!" Papa yelled.

Mama pulled me away and swung me high onto the bare back of Whiskey, then realized without a saddle and stirrups, there was no way for her to get up. I don't know how she did it before, but imagine she and Mr. Bern used the wagon as a step. She began to lead us away when we heard a third loud *snap*, this time followed by a roar.

The dogs had been crazy in their attack. It was horrible fight, what I could see of it through the big cloud of snow they were kicking up. My bear had made a run out of the woods toward us. For a second I thought he was going to be shot, but he saw the guns pointed at him and ran back to the woods, chased by the dogs. He had run right into a trap. *SNAP!*

"We got him!" yelled Papa.

Mr. Bern said, "Let's hit the other traps before the dogs get snapped. Doc, you got the stick? Doc!" Mr. Howell—still a minute away from us—was huffing like a train and unable to speak, but he had the stick.

My grizzly had stepped with his left rear leg into one of the traps, anchored to a tree with about eight feet of chain. He might have been more surprised than hurt by it, but I imagine it had to hurt, even for him. He let out a big roar, and tried to get away, but the chain stopped him. He tried pulling on it, his leg lifting into the air. The dogs were on him again, more vicious than ever. He lunged after them in a confused half-circle around the tree, bellowing and chomping his teeth, but the dogs were quick enough to stay out of his reach.

Whiskey was not liking *any* of the uproar taking place—not that I was either—and didn't want to wait on slowpoke Mama to lead him away. He was nickering angrily, jerking his head, and pulling Mama off of her feet. I was afraid he'd buck me, or take off running. I was holding onto his mane so tightly my knuckles were white. Mama managed to jerk Whiskey to a halt, then quickly pulled me off. He dashed back to camp just ahead of Willa, who wasn't sticking around, either. Instead of us following the horses, however, Mama pinned me to her side, and we watched.

Mr. Bern, jabbing in the snow with the butt of his rifle, struck a couple of traps, throwing snow, and leaping into the air with a loud, metal *chuk!* The traps were just as heavy, and almost as big as the dogs. They were very lucky they didn't get caught when they had triggered those two other traps. Would've chomped them in two.

"Is that all the traps?" said Mr. Bern. "I don't see no more flags."

Papa was able to grab Jack, and Fish heeled next to Mr. Bern. They moved the barking and growling dogs to one side of the bear to distract him while Mr. Howell was supposed to come up from behind and stick him. Mr. Howell only got so close before he stopped and wouldn't go any farther. Papa and Mr. Bern both were yelling at him to "Do it now!"

My bear had settled down some, with the dogs having been called off. He stood grunting and looking at the dogs, his back foot held by the trap. Mr. Howell started to move up behind him, my bear let out an angry roar, and Mr. Howell stopped again.

Papa yelled, "Now! Do it now!"

My bear sensed being snuck up on, and spun around. Mr. Howell, terribly frightened, dropped his stick in the snow, then backing up, put his foot into the only trap that was still alive and missing it's red flag.

"*AAAHHH!*" He made a worse sound than my bear did when *he* stepped into a trap.

The dogs were immediately back at the bear, snapping and barking. Papa ran to free Mr. Howell's leg, then tried to find the medicine stick under the snow. He found it just as a loud *yip* came from Fish, who had gotten too close and had been snatched up by his back, shaken like a doll, and thrown into the trees.

"*FISH!*" Mr. Bern raised his rifle to shoot as Papa ran to him with the stick.

"*No!*" I screamed. Mr. Bern shot into the air, scaring everyone.

"Give me that!" Mr. Bern snatched the stick from Papa. He marched straight up to my bear with that stick and stabbed him hard in the front of his neck. The bear lunged at Mr. Bern and belted him across the head, sending him right to the ground. I think I called out to warn him, but everything was happening so fast. My bear raised up and came down hard with all his weight on Mr. Bern's chest. I saw a lot of blood, wasn't sure where it was all coming from, but I was sure Mr. Bern was in terrible trouble. Papa raised his pistol and shot, hitting my bear in the side, making him jerk and jump back a step.

"*Papa, no!*" I cried. Mama had a tight hold on me and wasn't letting go. She began to pull me away when my bear dropped onto Mr. Bern with his teeth and claws both. Papa shot him again. "*Nooo!*" My bear jumped off of Mr. Bern after Papa's second shot. He turned and try to run, but was stopped again by the trap.

Papa dropped his pistol, ran to Mr. Bern and dragged him to safety as the bear lunged, just missing them. Jack jumped in to help distract him, but kept his distance, no longer trying to sneak in a bite. He'd seen what happened to Fish.

Frustrated and angry, my bear charged at Jack once more, and the chain broke in half.

"Papa!" I yelled, seeing the chain snap, but with all the noise from Jack, he must not have heard me, and might even have thought Mama and I were safe back at camp.

"Need you over here, Doc!" Papa called, unaware of the now un-chained bear not twenty feet away. My bear made a move to escape into the woods, but had trouble setting his back leg down that still had the trap clamped on it. He turned and glared at Papa

314

crouched over Mr. Bern. He had a different look in his eyes, one I hadn't seen before—a dark, scary look. My bear took a step forward, his ears pinned back on his head. He was going to attack Papa.

"Papa!" I yelled, the same time Mama yelled, "Patrick!" Papa looked up at us, then looked at the bear, who was making a popping sound with his jaw and crouching like Jack does when he's about to pounce something. I broke free of Mama as Papa stood up to defend himself from the inevitable charge. I rushed to his side and without thinking what I was doing, picked up his pistol, half buried in the snow, held it up with both hands, and pointed it at my grizzly bear.

Mama sprang up behind me. She reached around to the big pistol I was holding, but instead of grabbing it from me, she covered my hands with hers, pulled back the hammer and put her finger on the trigger, things my hands were too small to do.

We stood together, all facing the bear. Jack was barking, but the bear wasn't giving him a second look. His eyes shifted from Papa to me, went from fierce and wild, to hurt, and confused. Breathing heavy, bleeding, his back leg in the heavy trap, he stood staring at me, but didn't attack. I was softly crying, not wanting to shoot my bear if he came any closer, but ready to. He turned away, and with the trap still on his back leg, limped awkwardly into the trees, Jack on his heels, and slowly disappeared into the forest.

Papa was strangely calm when he asked, "Sonia, would you mind taking June to get Doc's bag?"

"What?" asked Mama, stunned at what just happened, what *could* have happened.

"Doc's medical bag? Would you mind taking June with you to get it?"

Mama un-cocked the pistol, eased it from my hands, and handed it to Papa.

"We'll hurry," she said, looking down at Mr. Bern. "Come on, June," and with her arm around my shoulder, steered me toward camp and started us running. I knew I was supposed to keep up with her, but as soon as she pulled ahead, I slowed down, then stopped. I watched Mama, who thought I was right behind her, fade into the falling snow like it was fog.

During all the fighting and shooting, the snow had begun to pick up, so that by the time my bear had hopped away, we had the makings of a real snowstorm. The wind blew in loud along the tops of the trees, dropping down into the clearing, swirling the big snowflakes above us, then releasing them to drift down to the ground. It would have been beautiful if we weren't in the middle of a tragedy. I couldn't see Mama, or the camp, or much of anything else that was farther than I could throw a rock. I couldn't see where my bear had hobbled off to, followed by Jack. I couldn't see Fish, poor Fish, who had gotten too close and was flung into the trees, no doubt killed. What I could see was Papa holding Mr. Bern, who lay motionless and bleeding. I saw Mr. Howell lying on his side, holding his leg and whimpering. The ground around us, which was perfectly white and smooth earlier that morning, like a sparkly sheet of brand new paper, was trampled and torn, with sprung bear traps sticking up, and a few red flags still standing. Blood streaks seemed to be connecting the flags like a dot-to-dot puzzle.

Papa looked a little overwhelmed by it all, cradling Mr. Bern with his left arm, his other hand pointing the pistol to the woods. I walked up to help, but froze when I saw how bad Mr. Bern was hurt. He was bleeding horribly from deep gashes on the left side of his head and neck, down his shoulder and arm, and across his chest. His coat and shirt had been nearly torn off, and Papa seemed to be trying to hold him together. I saw him move a little, so he was still alive, but he wasn't talking.

Papa yelled at Mr. Howell, "Get over here and help, now!"

"But my leg...it's broken," whimpered Mr. Howell. Papa gave him a fierce look and started to get up and drag him over.

"I'll help, Papa," I said. He was surprised to see me, and to see me without Mama.

"June, stay right here behind me. *Don't move.* Doc, get over here, *now!*"

"I can help," I said again, stepping right behind him, afraid to look any closer at Mr. Bern, but also wanting to see.

"I know, I know. I'll let you know in a minute, okay? Just *stay put.*"

I looked to the woods as Mr. Howell hopped over on his good leg. We heard loud grunting from the trees, my bear was still close.

"Here," Papa handed me his pistol, the barrel pointed toward the woods, hammer cocked and ready to fire. "Hold it with both hands. Move your finger to the trigger guard, *do not* touch the trigger unless you want to fire, okay?"

"Okay," I nervously said.

"Just keep it pointed at the woods," he told me. "Don't worry about hitting anything, the noise will scare him, okay? Keep it pointed *that way*."

"Okay." The big pistol seemed much heavier than it did just a few minutes earlier. I held it in both hands, but had trouble even lifting it. Papa saw the trouble I was having with it and gently took it out of my hands, releasing the hammer with his thumb.

"How 'bout if you see him coming back, you just let me know," Papa said, giving me a one-arm hug. He figured maybe I wasn't the best shooter of our little party, not with his big pistol, anyway.

I looked over Papa's shoulder and saw our veterinarian using torn pieces of Mr. Bern's shirt to wrap around his neck to stop the bleeding.

"No need to choke me, Doc," wheezed Mr. Bern, "I'm likely to...to die on my own."

"Hold still, Mr. Simms, please."

"How's...Fish?" asked Mr. Bern, but no one answered him.

Papa, who didn't even have a coat on, was taking his wool shirt off to lay on Mr. Bern, but the vet stopped him. "No, no, it's much better he stay cold. The cold will slow the blood loss." Mr. Howell, who had never shown any sign of actual medical know-how on any of our animals that I'd seen—much less on a person—now looked like a real doctor.

Mama came racing up on a now-saddled Whiskey, holding a big bundle with the vet's medical bag, some blankets, Papa's coat, and her scatter-gun. She dropped everything next to Mr. Bern and opened the bag for Mr. Howell. "June..." she angrily said. "You were supposed to stay with me."

"I'm sorry, Mama."

"Mrs. Allen, if you would," said the doctor, pulling a handful of metal instruments from the bag. "Keep pressure, right here."

While Mr. Howell and Mama were working, Papa tucked the pistol into his belt, picked up Mr. Bern's big rifle, checked that it was loaded, and started into the woods. "You stay here," he sternly told me. "You stay here with Mama." I nodded.

I didn't mean to break my promise to stay, my feet just started to walk. Mama was helping Mr. Howell and didn't notice me follow Papa.

My bear hadn't gone too far. I followed the bear's, Jack's, and Papa's tracks through a cluster of big trees that opened to a tiny clearing, right where we had shot one of the squirrels before. I saw Papa through the falling snow, standing still, rifle raised. My bear was sitting down, licking and mouthing the trap on his back leg. Jack stood looking at Papa, wagging his tail.

My bear looked up before getting wobbly and laying down in the snow. Jack walked over to him and sat down.

"We're over here!" Papa hollered back to Mama, who was calling my name. How did Papa know I had followed him? Mama ran up, blood all over her, even on her face, and her hair was big and wild. She looked like a crazy woman with a scatter-gun, and she wasn't happy with me.

Papa looked back toward us and even he was shocked by the crazy woman approaching. "I'm glad you're on our side," he said.

"Be quiet," huffed Mama.

Mama joined us, her shotgun raised, looking down at the huge bear lying on his side. His eyes were open, but glossy. He was moving them, trying to follow Jack as Jack sniffed his face. Jack looked back at us, then laid down against my bear. The snow was now coming down very heavy, was covering Jack and the grizzly bear. I guess was covering all of us, it was really coming down.

"Looks like Doc's sleeping stuff worked. What d'ya know," said Papa.

"Is he okay?" I asked.

"I think so," said Papa. "Appears so. He's breathing." Papa walked cautiously up to my bear, the big rifle pointing at his head, and with his boot nudged one of the bear's massive paws. He looked back at Mama and me. "Put the gun down, Mama," he told her. She had it aimed right at him and the bear. Papa kicked my bear's back leg a couple of times, with no response. "He's out."

"He's not dead?" I asked. "Didn't you shoot him?"

"Well," said Papa, who I think had forgotten that he shot him with the pistol. It was just a pistol, but it was a *big* pistol. "Not unless I hit something important, and I'm pretty sure the second shot missed." He set the rifle down, pulled out his pistol and knife. Pointing the pistol at the bear in case he woke up angry, Papa found where he had shot the bear in the side. With his knife, he poked around the wound, dug a little, picked out a bloody lead bullet and held it out for me and Mama to see. "Didn't even break a rib. These bears are something else."

"Now what?" asked Mama, lowering her gun.

Papa stood, and looked around the thick forest of trees surrounding us.

"Well," he said, "doubt we can get the wagon in here. We'll have to drag him, or sled him out to the wagon."

"Then what?" asked Mama.

"What do you mean?" asked Papa.

I tried to walk closer to my bear, but Mama grabbed my shoulder.

"Patrick," said Mama, "you're the only able bodied man left. Do you think you and I can get him onto the sled and then into the wagon? We're going to need the wagon to get Bern and Mr. Howell down the mountain. And there's going to be two feet of snow, maybe more, in another hour."

"How is he?" asked Papa.

"You saw him. He's lost a lot of blood. We stopped some of it, but he's torn up bad, and a bunch of his ribs appear to be broken. It's not good at all, we have to get him to town. And Doc's leg is broken."

Papa looked down at my bear. I could see his left hand squeezing the barrel of the rifle like he was trying to crush it. He looked at Mama, started to say something, then dropped his eyes to my bear again.

"I'm saying," said Mama, "I don't think we can get the bear down. Even if you and I were able to get him into the wagon, how long would that take us? And where would we put Bern? We need the wagon for Bern. We need to get him to town, *now*, for him to even have a chance. He's dying, Patrick."

"Maybe," said Papa. "Maybe...we could keep the bear tied to the sled, keep him sleeping."

"What if he wakes up?" asked Mama. "That little sled can't hold him, you saw how strong he is. And the horses are terrified of him, they'd never..."

"Okay!" snapped Papa.

"We can come back for him," said Mama quietly. "Trap him again. After the snow melts."

"Just let him go?" whispered Papa to himself.

Papa took a big long breath and looked all around. At Mama, at the big grizzly bear at his feet, at the trees all around us. He finally looked up at the sky and yelled, "Aaaghhh! ... After all this, after everything! And we have him, we have him, Sonia. We have him. Doc's medicine worked—which none of us thought it would—but it worked. The bear's *actually* asleep, ready for us to take him down."

"I know," said Mama.

"We have him..."

"I know," she repeated.

I quietly asked, "Is he okay?"

"Who?" asked Papa angrily.

"My bear," I mumbled.

I thought Papa was going to yell at me, but then his face softened, and he let out a deep breath. "I think so, Bug, I think he's okay." He motioned me over. Mama let go of my shoulder and I slowly walked over. My bear was lying still, the snow sticking to the tips of his thick fur.

"Why is he smoking?" I asked.

"Steam. Body heat. He really worked himself up," said Papa. I noticed that Papa had smoke coming off of him, too.

"What are we going to do?" I asked.

We all stood together, looking at the sleeping grizzly bear.

Mama and I stood back while Papa opened the trap's jaws. My bear popped his head up, giving us all a startle, then let out a big, long groan and laid back down.

"All right," said Papa, picking up the big bear trap. "Let's get Bern to town." He walked a couple of steps, then stopped. "You know...we won't have another chance at this."

"What's that?" asked Mama.

"We won't have another chance to trap him. Doc's going to talk," Papa said, looking at Mama and me. "Doc's going to talk. Elam, too, of course. Everyone's going to know there's a grizzly bear up here now, not just a rumor of one. The idiots that weren't looking for him before will surely come looking for him now. Maybe even the Fancy Posse, as June calls them. There won't be another chance for us."

"What if we tell everyone it wasn't a grizzly bear after all?" asked Mama.

"Doc's seen him," said Papa. "He knows the difference. And it doesn't matter, if Elam says we were after a grizzly, then folks are gonna believe what they hear."

"What if," said Mama, "we tell everyone that he died, that we killed the grizzly. But we couldn't bring him down because we needed the wagon for Bern."

"That's not bad," said Papa. "People may come up in the spring, looking for the bones to sell, but by then... Okay, here's our story. Doc's medicine didn't work, *did not* work, everyone will believe that. Umm...we followed the bear into the trees, I shot him a couple of times, he kept running, and ahh..."

"Mayor's Leap!" I shouted. "He fell off Mayor's Leap and died!"

"That's good," said Papa. "That's really good. Mayor's Leap is right over there through the trees. Okay...I shot him a couple of times," Papa held up Mr. Bern's big rifle, I covered my ears, and he fired it twice. Scared the britches off poor Jack, who didn't know Papa was going to do that, but my bear didn't flinch. "He kept running, ran straight off the cliff. Fell to his death. *Disappeared* into the canyon."

"Never to be seen again," I said, thinking it was just like a Jack London story.

"Never to be seen again," said Papa, looking at me. "Just like the mayor, huh?" A little smile showed on his face even though I knew he was unhappy about having to let the bear go, and about his friend Mr. Bern being hurt. "Okay, *this* goes over the cliff, in case anyone doubts our story." Papa picked up the big bear trap, and walked toward Mayor's Leap, which wasn't far at all.

While we waited for Papa to return, Mama let me walk up to my bear. If it weren't for his cloudy breaths I would have surely thought him dead.

"Is his leg okay?" I asked.

"I imagine," said Mama, who had her shotgun pointed at his head, just in case.

"How long will he sleep?" I asked.

"I don't know," said Mama. "Hopefully long enough for us to leave. He probably won't be in the best of moods when he wakes up."

Papa returned from throwing the trap over the cliff. "We ready?"

"I guess," I said sadly, looking down at my bear, wondering if it was the last time I would ever see him. Mama and Papa turned to walk back, I stood a second more, then crouched down and touched my bear's snow covered side. "Will he wake up, Papa?"

"Yeah, he'll wake up. He'll be fine," said Papa, a little nervous that I was touching my bear, but he let me.

I brushed the snow off of him best I could, then leaned over and laid on top of him, trying for a real bear hug. That brought Papa right behind me, grabbing the back of my collar, to yank me away if my bear woke up suddenly. "I hope you'll be okay," I told him. "I love you Grizzly Bear."

I felt Papa's hand give my collar a little tug. It was time to go. We had to get Mr. Bern down the mountain before the snow got too deep. I started to cry as I walked between Mama and Papa. I heard Mama sniffling a cry as she hugged me and kissed the top of my head. We heard a grunt, and looked back to see my bear raised up on an elbow, glazed eyes watching us go. He groaned and lay back down.

"I'm sorry I had to shoot him," Papa said.

"He was killing Mr. Bern, wasn't he?"

Chapter Twenty-nine

Returning to the meadow, the snow was falling with the biggest flakes I had ever seen. They were coming down like giant goose feathers being shaken from a torn pillow in the sky, covering everything.

"Stay here with June," Papa told Mama. "I'll check on Bern, then we can go hook up the team to the wagon and bring it over."

"How is he, Papa?" I asked when he returned and we hurried to the camp. "Is he dead?"

"No, June," said Papa, then picked me up and carried me to get me out of the deepening snow. He didn't say anything else about how Mr. Bern was, and I was afraid to ask.

While Papa hooked up the mule team, I helped Mama clean out the back of the wagon, leaving only blankets and what little food we had left. I rode with Papa in the wagon back to where the Misters were, with Mama following us on Whiskey.

Mr. Bern, when I finally saw him, looked more dead than anyone else I'd ever seen before. There was so much blood. He had strips of his shirt and a whole blanket wrapped around his neck and chest as bandages, and he wasn't moving. I didn't think there was any way he could be alive, and I started to cry. "Is he dead?" No one answered.

Mama and Papa carefully—though not easily—loaded Mr. Bern into the wagon, pulling him onto the padded quilt I laid out as a bed for him. Papa then helped Mr. Howell hop to the open tailgate, sat him down, then rolled up his pants to look at his broken leg. His right leg was red and purple, and swollen up like a cantaloupe between his ankle and knee, and hurt a lot worse after I accidentally knocked into it, running to retrieve a couple of the flag-sticks for a splint. "Sorry sorry, I'm sorry."

Mama made a splint for his leg, causing him to *yowl* a couple more times, but nothing like the pain I had caused him. I climbed into the wagon seat, wanting to get the heck off the mountain, and back home where only our chickens got hurt.

"I'm sorry I ran into your leg, Mr. Howell," I told him as he scooched himself into the bed of the wagon.

"I know," he said, but didn't say anything else, so I knew he hadn't forgiven me. Though sweating and wincing with pain, he checked Mr. Bern's bandages, piled blankets on top of him, and shielded his face from the falling snow until Mama and Papa could get the tarp in place.

"I thought he needed to stay cold," I said, looking down from the wagon seat, to no reply. Maybe Mr. Bern had bled all he was going to bleed.

"Miss June...?"

"*Mr. Bern?*"

"Miss June..."

"I'm here, Mr. Bern. I hear you."

"Miss June...I don't think your bear likes me."

A big smile came to my face, tears to my eyes. If Mr. Bern could still joke, maybe he'd be okay? "Well, I don't know that I'd like you either, if'n you'd stuck *me* with that big needle."

"Whoo...please, young'n...don't make me laugh...please."

"Are you okay?" I asked, not knowing what else to say.

"You...tell me. I got a dern vetra-narian tryin' to put me back together. Watch him close, Miss J. Don't let him give me nothin' that'll grow me a...a tail."

"I'll watch him." I smiled at Mr. Bern's joke, but looked to the vet, and he wasn't smiling. None of us smiled when Mr. Bern asked about Fish. Papa, who had started to tie the wagon tarp over the bed so we'd have cover from the snow, said, "I'll go."

"Did we get him?...the griz?" Mr. Bern asked, and the vet looked up questioningly at me, too.

"Uh..." I looked over at Mama, who was quickly changing out of her bloody dress and putting on a clean one, not worrying if any of the men saw her. She had heard Mr. Bern's question and nodded to me to tell him.

"Uh, no, we didn't get him," I said. "He was running, and Papa...um...he turned and ran at Papa, so Papa shot at him. He shot him, and...he turned and ran right off Mayor's Leap. Off the cliff. He disappeared. He's dead."

"Did the sleep mixture have any effect?" asked Mr. Howell.

"I don't know."

"Doc," said Papa, appearing out of the falling snow, "got room for one more patient?"

328

"He's alive?" asked Mr. Howell, moving a blanket to make room.

"Hurt bad, but somehow alive," said Papa. "Just like you, old man." He laid Fish delicately in the wagon beside Mr. Bern.

Fish, who did *not* look alive when Papa put him in the wagon, gave Mr. Bern's face a tiny lick before closing his eyes again. Mr. Bern didn't make a sound, but I saw his big shoulders shaking as he held his crying in, and worked his good arm around Fish to hold him close. Mr. Howell gave a quick look at Fish's wounds, shook his head, and wrapped him tight against his papa.

Mama rode ahead to saddle Russell and Willa, Papa climbed into the wagon seat next to me.

"Who's gonna ride them? Willa and Russell?" I asked.

"No one," said Papa, "but we don't have room to carry the saddles, and they'll help keep the horses a little warmer."

Our camp looked sad and cold. If it weren't for Mama throwing on Willa's saddle, it would have looked absolutely abandoned. Our tents were on their way to being buried, and the fire pit was all-but-covered, only the thinnest ribbon of smoke fighting it's way up through the falling snowflakes.

I helped Papa tie the horses to the back of the wagon while Mama ran to the tents, pulling out hats and gloves, and every blanket she could find.

"Mrs. Allen!" came Mr. Howell's voice from under the tarp. "Mrs. Allen! In my tent...the black saddlebag!" Mama ducked into the doctor's tent and came out shaking the bag, making a loud clinking sound.

"Mr. Howell, do you *really* need this?" she asked, pulling out a bottle of Elixir.

He stuck his head out from under the tarp, "Antiseptic, to clean Mr. Simms's wounds...and, honestly, to help with the pain." Mama nodded, handing him one bottle, and putting the bag under the tarp.

"Let's get outta here before we ain't gettin' outta here," said Papa. "You gonna ride Whiskey?" he asked Mama, who, after handing up my hat and gloves, was shortening Whiskey's stirrups to fit her little legs.

"Yes, at least for a while," she said.

"Wait!" I said, then jumped off the wagon. I ran to our tent, kicking up clumps of cold snow. Returning quickly as I could, Papa smiled and helped me back to the seat. I was holding my sword belt, my doll Sarah, and *White Fang*.

"Now are we ready?" he asked.

"Yes sir."

"School books?"

"I couldn't find those."

Papa hupped the mules, and the wagon slowly pulled through the snow behind Mama's lead. I looked around the mountain clearing, the meadow where we had trapped my bear. Where we had let him go after attacking Mr. Bern and Fish, both of whom may die. We trapped my bear with the toothless traps, and they worked. Mr. Howell's sleeping medicine worked. And my grizzly bear was still free.

It wasn't easy leaving my bear behind. He was skinny, hungry, and had followed me up the mountain into a big snow storm where we trapped, drugged, and shot him. Even though Papa assured me he would be okay when the medicine wore off, how could we know? We didn't see him get up. Nobody was sure the medicine would put him to sleep in the first place, and now that it had, how did we know he wasn't poisoned by it? Maybe Mr. Howell's sleeping stuff was really just poison. No one knew, but we didn't have the time to stay with him and make sure he was okay. If he was okay, I hoped he would forgive me one day.

* * * *

I don't think I'd ever seen so much snow as what was falling as we began our journey back down the mountain. Papa was doing an expert job of driving, though I could see he was anxious, feeling the urgency of getting his friend medical help, and beating the winter storm that was upon us. He looked frustrated at not being able to go faster, but, unable to see the holes and fallen tree limbs under the snow, was going as fast as he dared. We had nearly been launched from the seat a couple of times, effecting cries of great pain from Mr. Bern, and muttered curses from Mr. Howell. Mama was doing her best to search for obstacles, but unless Whiskey stepped in the hole or on the branch, they stayed hidden until a wagon wheel found them. I tucked Sarah into my coat so I would have both mittened-hands to hold me to the seat.

It wasn't long before Mama tethered Whiskey to the wagon and climbed under the tarp to help with the Misters. Papa fashioned one of the remaining torches into a kind of tent pole under the

331

middle of the tarp so it wouldn't be laying on everyone, and would hopefully keep the snow from piling on top. Jack and I got under there, too, to help, though I was immediately sorry I had offered. It was dark, Mr. Bern was moaning, Fish was whimpering, and Mama was cutting and tearing strips of blanket after throwing out an armful of bloody bandages.

"What can I do?" I asked, hoping Mama would say I should get back on the seat and help Papa spot obstacles, which I had already proven to be useless at.

"Just stay warm," she said.

It was only slightly warmer under the tarp, or maybe just not as bitterly cold. The wind and snow had little trouble finding ways to get in. I hugged Jack for warmth, and wished we were home by the fire.

Papa drove through snow drifts too deep for the wheels to touch the road, pulling the wagon over them like it was a sled. I could feel the snow scraping the bottom of the wagon, and watched closely a couple of floor-boards that were loose and in danger of coming apart.

The snow was getting deeper and deeper, and harder to get the wagon through, even without the drifts. Leaving Mr. Howell's Russell tethered behind, Papa hooked up Whiskey and Willa in front of the mules to help keep the wagon moving. The horses weren't used to pulling a wagon, and the mules didn't like having the horses lead, but Papa managed to keep us rolling. I couldn't help but think of the Donner Party, and that it really wasn't hard to get stranded. If we'd have waited another day to leave, there was no way the wagon could have traveled. We'd have been stranded for sure.

It was a long, miserable ride. The bottom of the wagon was ice-cold from sledding over the snow, there was no way to get warm. I squatted on my boots until my feet froze and my legs cramped, then tried sitting on a blanket wadded up like a ball. When Mama wasn't helping the Misters, she had me sit on her lap, her arms around me, a blanket around us both, but the cold still got to me. My fingers and toes were so painfully frozen, I wished they would go ahead and fall off. I didn't say too much about it to Mama, though. She knew I was cold. She was cold too, we all were. No matter what misery we were going through, though, it was nothing compared to Mr. Bern's suffering.

Mr. Howell didn't think Mr. Bern was going to live long enough to see the next morning. He whispered that to Mama, but I heard. While Mama helped change bandages, he tended Mr. Bern the whole time, Fish too, even though he was in a lot of pain himself from his broken leg. He shared with Mr. Bern his Elixir bottles, which after awhile Mr. Howell had to give it to him with a spoon. Mr. Howell admitted, after I asked him three times, that the medicine didn't really cure anything, but it was good at easing pain, which was what they were both needing. "And," he said, "it may help Mr. Simms sleep."

I was all for Mr. Bern sleeping. He was wet with burning fever, was tossing and babbling, talking like he was in a bad dream. I couldn't understand any of it, and it was scaring me. I was afraid he was dying right in front of us, but, after awhile—and I felt horrible thinking it—I just wanted him to stop.

333

✳ ✳ ✳ ✳

"Mama, I'm hungry," I said, not in a complaining way, but in a reminding way. We hadn't eaten all day.

"You're right, sweetie. We need to eat." She reached into the corner, under Mr. Howell's medical bag, and pulled out the apple pies. We had one whole one, and one half-one. Mama handed me the half-pie to give to Papa while she cut the whole one into pieces. I poked out through an opening in the tarp and couldn't believe how much snow was coming down. I didn't know how Papa even knew where the road was. He stayed between the trees when they were lining the road, but when we came to a clearing, it was only because he knew the mountain so well that we didn't end up lost or going off into a ravine

"Here, Papa...pie."

"Thanks, Bug," I thought I heard him say, though it was mostly lost in the wind. He was bundled with a blanket over his coat, an inch of snow covering most of him. He stopped the wagon long enough to shake the blanket, and to take the pie tin. "How is everyone?"

"Okay," I said

"Mr. Bern?" he asked.

"Not good. He's babbling, Papa."

"Yeah. How are you?"

"Cold. But okay. How far are we from the ridge?"

"Maybe two, three hours, if it doesn't get any worse. Just try to stay warm."

"Can we go home?"

"Bug, we've got to get Mr. Bern down, get him help. So...try to stay warm."

I was more afraid of Papa staying warm, which, there wasn't any way he *could* be warm. I was afraid he would freeze to death sitting out in the snow and wind in just his coat and a blanket. He had good gloves, but still. Mama was concerned too, but he wouldn't stop or let Mama drive the team. He said he'd be fine, and that the pie had warmed his insides. I don't think my piece of pie warmed me up any, but it did make me sleepy.

* * * *

I was shivering when Papa woke me, and I was getting snowed on.

"June...June, wake up, sweetie," he said behind a big cloud of breath.

"Where are we? Where's Mama?"

"She's on Whiskey. C'mon, let's get you home."

"We're home?"

Papa had his cold, gloved hands under my arms, lifted me from the wagon, and swung me up onto the front of Whiskey's saddle and into Mama's arms. My leg got caught on Mama's scatter-gun, fit into the saddle's rifle scabbard, and I almost fell, but Mama caught me. Papa handed me my hat, and the blanket I had been sleeping under. Mama wrapped it around me. It took me a moment to recognize the corner where our little road met the main road. We were back on Grizzly Ridge, in the middle of a blizzard. The wind was blowing right into my face, I covered my cheeks and peeked out through the mittens. Everything looked thick, soft and white. All white but for the trunks of the trees, and even those were largely caked with snow on at least one side. I pulled Sarah up through the collar of my coat, so she could see also.

"I still think we should stay together," said Mama, almost yelling to be heard over the blowing wind.

"There's not much light left. You and Bug need to get to the house. Get warm, get food, get out of the snow," said Papa, standing in it himself, up to his thighs.

"Then you come with us," said Mama. "Get Bern inside, then go for help."

"I've got to get him to town, both of them. I'll be home tomorrow."

"But Patrick, the storm..."

"Please don't argue," said Papa. He was shivering, his cheeks bright red, snow was crusted to his beard and mustache. "I need you to be safe."

He picked up Jack, who was stuck more than chest-deep in the snow after jumping out of the wagon. He swung him up onto my lap, saying he wouldn't be able to keep track of him in town. Jack had never ridden on the back of a horse that I know of, and didn't seem to like it much, but the snow was just too deep for him. He was stiff and shaking, but calmed down when I wrapped the blanket and my arms around him.

Mr. Howell sat up in the wagon where the tarp had been pulled away, I imagine to get a little fresh air. He looked awful. I couldn't see Mr. Bern or Fish, but I knew they couldn't have improved any since I had fallen asleep. Papa definitely needed to get them to town.

"You get going now," said Papa, squeezing Mama's leg and then mine. "Go to the McDougals if you need to, but don't worry about anything except warmth and food."

"Be careful, Patrick," said Mama, her voice breaking.

"I love you, Papa," I said.

"I love you. Now go...I'll see you tomorrow."

I didn't get to say goodbye to Mr. Bern or Mr. Howell before Papa re-tied the tarp and climbed to the wagon seat. With one last wave, he hupped the mules, still led by Willa, and continued the push down the covered mountain.

"Will he make it?" I asked Mama. She either didn't hear me, or didn't want to answer.

The little road to our house was unrecognizable. The cedars and pine trees were heavy with built-up powder, their branches hanging low. A lot of the smaller trees were bent right over the road. Some of them we rode under like in a tunnel. Some we could maneuver around, others we had to ride through— the sharp, frozen branches springing up like a snare, drenching us in icy powder. Whiskey did not like that one bit. We also got pelted with snow dropping from the tall trees. Even with the wind, I could hear the snow falling down through the branches, gathering speed and picking up weight as it knocked each succeeding branch, until a near wagon-full of tree-snow landed on top of us.

What little daylight remained was fading fast, but the trees finally opened up enough that through the swirling snow I could make out our house and barn, looking small and lonely. It was too dark to see if London and the longhorns were okay, or if they were even there. I was happy we made it out of the tunnel of branches and dumping snow, and into the more open area, but with the trees no longer an obstruction, the snow grew much deeper, all the way up to Whiskey's belly. He stopped. He had to have been very tired and cold, pulling a wagon all day in the storm, but we were so close to home. Mama gave him a few encouraging kicks, but only after a big boot in the ribs followed by a smack on his rear did he start moving again. Mama had to kick his sides over and over to keep him going.

Whiskey was having to lunge to make it through the deepest parts, and for us riders it was like he was trying to buck us off, and maybe he was, it would have stopped Mama's kicking him. Jack finally did get bucked off, or he jumped off, nearly taking Mama and me both with him, since I was holding onto him and Mama was holding onto me. He disappeared into the deep snow, leaving a dog shaped hole. For a second I had the thought that the snow was dozens of feet deep and that we had just lost Jack forever, or at least until Spring. Then Jack sprang out of the hole like he had frog's legs, disappearing into the snow again a couple feet away. He leaped and disappeared, leaped and disappeared the rest of the way to the house, getting there before we did.

It was dark, snowing hard, and the wind was howling. Mama stopped Whiskey close to the porch and got me to the door. Chica was sure surprised and happy to see us, but we didn't even say 'hi' to her as Mama opened the door with shaking-cold hands.

My feet were frozen and hurt so bad I couldn't stand. Mama sat me down in front of the fireplace, yanked the quilt off of the big bed, covered Jack and me with it, tried to make a fire, but was having trouble getting the wood to light. She remembered Whiskey still standing in the deepening snow. She looked a little frantic, deciding what all she had to do and in what order she had to do it. Jack and I, though both shivering, were safe. Whiskey needed to be safe too, and out of the blizzard. Mama lit a couple of lamps with shaking hands and fingers that didn't want to work, grabbed another quilt from under the bed, threw it over us, and ran back into the storm.

She tethered Whiskey inside the barn after seeing how long it would take to dig out the gate to the corral. After making a quick check on London and the longhorns, seeing that the McDougals had moved plenty of hay for them, Mama slowly made her way back to the house.

In the dark, snowing worse than ever, Mama fought her way through the waist-high powder. Her feet, hands, and cheeks were frozen numb, and if it weren't for the tracks that Whiskey had made, tracks that would be soon covered in the heavy and blowing snowstorm, she would have had a hard time even knowing where our house was.

I was getting worried. Mama had been gone a long time. The wind outside was howling like a train around our little house. I barely heard the stomp, stomping on the porch as Mama tried to knock off the snow that was holding to her clothes.

She swung open the door, and if I hadn't known it was Mama, I would have screamed at the monster standing there, a cloud of vapor blowing from its mouth. I don't know how much snow she had stuck to her before all the stomping, but she was still covered and caked in it. The flickering light on her face showed the strain and exhaustion of the longest and most trying day of our lives, to that point. As she closed the door behind her, shutting out the blizzard, the toil of that difficult day gave way to a look of surprise...

"June, you made a fire," she smiled, and sat down next me on the floor. She hugged me close, getting me wet with the snow melting between us, but I didn't mind. I didn't know she was trying not to cry until she spoke to me in sniffles. "How did you...get it started?"

"Just a little kerosene," I said.

She was shocked for a second, then, looking around for a kerosene can, figured out that I was teasing, and pulled me even closer, and cried out loud.

"Why are you crying, Mama?"

"I love you, Bug," was what she said.

We slept in front of the fireplace that night; blankets, quilts and pillows piled on the floor, Jack and Chica snugged up tight against us. The storm was whistling, howling and shaking the house. Piled-up snow would occasionally slide off the top roof and land on the porch roof, making a loud rumbling sound that Jack, and even Chica, barked at. It was pretty scary. Though we were both exhausted, we couldn't sleep, wishing Papa was with us, hoping Mr. Bern and Mr. Howell and Mr. Fish would all be okay. Two things we didn't talk about were whether the wagon with the men would get stranded in the storm before making it to town, and we didn't talk about my bear.

I, however, couldn't help but think about my grizzly, hoping that he, too, was okay. We had left him lying in the snow, injured and asleep. Though I was pretty sure Mr. Howell's sleep medicine had worn off, I feared he may be buried under three or four feet of snow. Waking up under four feet of snow would have to be pretty unpleasant.

The next morning, I was awakened by Chica, who was whining at the door, wanting to go out. Mama was still asleep, Jack too. I was wedged tightly between them and had to shimmy myself up out of the blankets. Still half asleep myself, I opened the door for Chica, who took two steps onto the snow covered porch, turned, and looked back at me. The wind was calm, but it was still snowing, and not just snowing, but piled high, higher than the floor of the porch. It was the most snow I had ever seen in my life, and it wasn't stopping.

"Mama, Mama wake up."

"Hmm?"

"Mama, I think we're stranded. Come look."

It was the most snow Mama had ever seen, too. We spent the morning shoveling and pushing the snow off of the porch and clearing the steps. Then inside, I swept and dusted while Mama made an inventory of our food. Luckily, we'd always been good about canning and preserving food for the winter, and even though Papa should have brought in a deer or two by then, we still had some meat, mostly jerked. And we had chickens. Mama killed two of them for eating, and while I was plucking them, she made up a little coop on the porch for six of our best egg layers. It was made of wood and wire, with a scrap piece of tin roofing for the top. It was comfy looking, and even though our chickens didn't lay as many eggs during the winter, we would still get a few fresh eggs per day without having to venture into the deep snow. "We should have brought chickens with us on the expedition," I said.

"Next expedition, we will," said Mama, and we both laughed a little. Was the first time we'd laughed about anything for two days.

We spent the day quietly plucking chickens for the pot, cooking beans, making bread, rolling tortillas, and bringing in wood to dry. We watched the snow get deeper and deeper, while keeping the porch and steps clear. I tried to read, but couldn't concentrate, and would walk to one window or another to look for Papa. We slept in the big bed that night, feeling very worried and alone.

* * * *

Jack heard him first, started barking and scratching at the window. I had just sat down with Mama to work on new curtains, not that we needed new curtains, but it was something to occupy our time.

"Papa..." I said, and scurried out onto the porch. I thought it was Papa, but then wasn't sure. The man was heavily clad in a big, long coat, the hat on his head was tied down with a scarf that was also wrapped around his face to keep out the cold. He was walking on top of the snow in big snow shoes, and was pulling a sled with a canvas covered bundle in the middle. Jack was growling and barking at the strange man, calling up Mama with her scatter-gun.

The man stopped, wearily lifting his head and pulling the scarf away from his face. "Papa!" I cried. Mama set her shotgun back inside the door and we both stepped into the snow, helping pull an exhausted Papa the last few feet to the steps and onto the porch.

Once inside, we worked quickly to get him out of his cold, snow-stiff clothes and boots, wrapped him in our thickest quilt and sat him in a chair in front of the fireplace. I climbed on his lap and wrapped my arms around him, wanting to warm him even more.

"June," said Mama, "your father might not want you in his lap right now."

Papa worked an arm out from the quilt and held me tight. "I just wish I had a bigger lap so both of you could sit."

Mama brought cups of hot tea for us all and a chair for herself and we huddled together.

"Almost didn't make it down the mountain," Papa told us. "Snow just kept getting deeper, the wagon was pushing the snow like a plow and the animals couldn't pull it, could barely walk in it themselves. I had to dig us out a couple of times, and just when I was thinking we weren't going to make it, and planned on turning into Bill Shad's place there, the snow wasn't as deep, the wheels found the road, and we pulled through."

"How's Bern?" Mama asked.

"Ahh...he's alive," Papa said grimly, "or he was when I left him this morning."

"Will he be okay?" I asked.

"I don't know, June. Got him and Howell into the doctor's office the other side of midnight. I don't know if he'll be okay. Doctor

Schwarz doesn't know either."

"What about Fish?" I asked.

"I have no idea," said Papa. "Howell sent for his assistant, who took Fish away. Haven't heard."

"Does Patty know Bern's been hurt?" asked Mama.

"I went and fetched her yesterday," said Papa. "Took her to him."

Papa sipped from the tea, his cheeks still bright red from the cold. He stretched his bare feet closer to the fire until they were so close I was expecting them to start smoking.

"Did you walk the whole way from town, Papa?"

"Oh, no, Bug," he tried to chuckle. "Brought Willa up as far as Old Man Jenkins's place, 'til the snow got too deep. She's nice and comfy in his barn. He loaned me his sled to bring the stuff I bought for us; food, new gloves, mittens, and snow shoes for everyone."

"Snow shoes?" I asked. "My size, too?"

"Your size, too," he said. "If you're not sick of the snow already, we can go snow-shoeing tomorrow." He laughed softly, then got real quiet, staring into the fire. Old Mr. Jenkins's house wasn't that far out of town, and Papa walked through miles of snow, up the mountain, pulling a heavy sled the whole way to get back to us. Mama leaned into Papa, and with me still on his lap, we wrapped our arms into one big hug. We were in the middle of the biggest snow our mountain had seen in years and years, but we were all safe, and warm, and we were together.

Chapter Thirty

W ell well, my my...look who's finally come to pay their respects to the nearly-got-hisself-killed," said a beaming Mr. Bern.

"Don't exaggerate," said Papa, stepping up to grip Mr. Bern's hand. "Doc Schwarz says it was only a few scratches."

"Whoo..." grimaced Mr. Bern, trying not to laugh, "Schwarz already used up the town's supply of thread sewin' me back together. You make me rip my stitches laughin' at jokes, I'm likely to jest fall apart. Say...is that the young Miss June Allen?"

It was two full weeks before the road was clear enough that we could make the trip to town to see Mr. Bern. We had heard news a week earlier about him from Sheriff Pettigrew, who was braving the road with a few deputized mountain men to check on folks and see if everyone was okay. He said Mr. Bern was alive and already telling grand stories of our adventure. He asked Papa if it was all true what Bern was saying, but Papa didn't know what Bern was saying, so he told the Sheriff, "We did have quite the adventure, but unfortunately, the bear's lost." I wanted to go to town that very day, but the road was still very deep and if it snowed again we might not be able to get back.

We finally made our trip into town. The snow was still too deep to safely take our wagon, so I rode with Papa on Willa and Mama rode Whiskey. Papa planned on leaving Willa at the livery stable for Mr. Bern if he was well enough to ride home. If so, we'd all pile on Whiskey for the ride back to our house.

Mr. Bern was recovering in his own room in the fancy new hotel, the *Golden Rose* it was named. The very hotel he more than once talked about setting aflame because it made our little town look like it wanted to be a city, and Mr. Bern hated cities. When Mr. Bern got well enough in the doctor's bed to talk, he quickly outgrew the small room. When he began telling stories about what had happened on our expedition, the owner of the Golden Rose proposed a nice big room that opened up with double doors onto the restaurant. He wanted Mr. Bern to tell his stories, wanted folks to come to the hotel to listen and to stay for dinner. He had an audience and could talk as much and as loud as he pleased. The piano player didn't like the arrangement, but everyone else seemed to.

He had an audience that day as well, and we had to squeeze our way through a little crowd that was gathered and blocking the entrance to his room.

"Is that the young Miss June Allen?" Mr. Bern saw me peeking excitedly around Papa. "Is that the world famous *Grizzly Girl?*"

The mention of 'Grizzly Girl' got the crowd, most of whom I didn't know, whispering and looking at me. I wasn't expecting that, and tried to hide between Mama and Papa.

"I say, young'n, come sit, come sit." Mr. Bern patted the bed next to him. "You folks, if you'd be so kind to let these'ns in, and give us a few moments." Mr. Bern's Patty shooed the people out and brought us in, closing the doors behind us, before giving each of us a hug.

I had been so excited about seeing Mr. Bern again, but now that we were in his room, and with all the attention given him, I felt shy. He had on a huge night shirt that covered most of the bandages wrapped around his chest and left arm, only the dressing to his neck was visible. His face was scabby and bruised, but he looked good. Fish was at the foot of the bed, bandages wrapped around his chest too. He looked a lot skinnier than I remembered, but he wagged his tail as I stepped to the bed.

"Oh, Miss June, it sure is good to see you again. You too, Miss Sonia," Mr. Bern told us, pulling me to his side with his good arm as he held his other hand out to hold Mama's. "I heard from our ol' vetra-narian how you two saved my life—standin' up to the bear on the mountain, then helpin' me all the way down. My, my, don't know how to thank you."

"No thanks are necessary, Mr. Simms," said Mama.

"Papa helped, too," I said.

"Yeah..." said Mr. Bern, "but I heard he took his sweet time drivin' the wagon back down." I looked up to Papa to make sure Mr. Bern was joking. "And not only that, Miss June, do you know that he dropped me right on my tuckus when he pulled me from the wagon? And then dragged me up the Doctor's steps like I wasn't no better than a sack o' flour. And the sheriff should be comin' by soon to take my statement about someone stealin' my horse."

"Old man," said Papa, "I should've left your hide up on the mountain, you know that?"

Mr. Bern laughed a big bear-like laugh, gritting at the pain it caused, "Ha haa!...owww, that hurts. You may not believe it, Allen, but you ain't the first one to tell me such a thing."

We visited the morning with Mr. Bern and Miss Patty, remembering the adventure we had, and happy that everyone made it down the mountain alive. We stuck to our story, even with Mr. Bern, that Papa shot my grizzly bear and he bolted off Mayor's Leap, never to be seen again.

"Knock, knock..." came a voice from the door. "Am I interrupting?" It was Mr. Howell! As he stepped into the room, I hopped from the bed and threw myself on him in a big hug. He was a little surprised, but to me, Mr. Howell was the one that saved Mr. Bern. Mr. Howell, out of all of us, was the most out of his element, and though he did complain a bit, he stayed with us. Mr. Bern was alive because of it. Fish, too.

"Hello, hello everybody," Mr. Howell said, shaking hands with Papa and getting a hug from Mama, too. "Just came to check on the patient." I first thought he meant Mr. Bern, but noticed Fish crawling to the far side of the bed, trying to hide. Fish didn't like getting poked by doctors either.

Mr. Howell hobbled over to Fish, using a cane Mr. Bern had given him. He had been visiting Mr. Bern and Fish nearly every day, sometimes twice a day. He had been telling folks stories as well of the Grizzly Expedition, but of course couldn't keep as large an audience as Bernard Simms.

We spent the afternoon together, until the hotel owner insisted we open the doors so the customers could hear the stories. Mama, Papa and I took a table and had a big supper 'on the house', listening and laughing at Mr. Bern the celebrity. It was a wonderful day.

The ride back home was wonderful, too. Mr. Bern insisted we keep Willa for awhile since he was still recovering and didn't want to pay the livery stable to keep her. He promised me he was joking about reporting Willa stolen, but I knew that already. We had to hurry to beat nightfall, after staying longer than we had planned. The hotel owner offered to give us a room for the night, but we had animals at home that needed us.

We did make a quick stop at the post office. We usually don't get much mail, but having been stranded on the mountain for weeks, Papa wanted to check. Mama and I were both excited when Papa handed us the new Sears catalog for 1910. Christmas was only a few weeks away, time for me to get my wish list written. While I looked at the catalog, Mama went through envelopes, looked at one closely, then handed it to Papa. The return address said *Selig Productions*, and came from Los Angeles. Papa opened the envelope and slowly unfolded a letter.

"What does it say?" asked Mama.

"Says," replied Papa, "he'd be very interested in a healthy California grizzly bear specimen. Says he'd be willing to pay up to one thousand dollars, depending."

"A thousand dollars?" asked Mama.

I looked up at Papa, trying to read the expression on his face. A thousand dollars was an awful lot of money.

He folded the paper, returned it to the envelope, and handed it back to Mama. "Too bad there's no more grizzlies in California, huh?"

Little flakes of snow began falling as we rode out of town, Papa's arms around me warm and snug. The town hardly ever sees a flake of snow, but there was still a foot on the ground and about to be more. Papa handed me Whiskey's reins as we headed up the Ridge, the snowflakes growing in size and the snow on the ground getting deeper. I started getting a little nervous, and wanted Papa to take over, but he told me, "Just keep it loose, Whiskey knows the way. Don't worry, we'll make it home fine."

I looked over at Mama riding Willa and she smiled, "*No mountain we can't tame*, isn't that what Mr. Bern likes to say?"

Not far from where I thought we should be coming to our little road, Papa pulled Whiskey to a stop. He stepped down then lifted me off. Squatting in the snow, he passed his hand over one of the many divots made by folks and horses on the road, which would all be covered up in another hour. "What is it, Papa?" I asked.

"Well, I'll be," he said.

"Patrick," said Mama, "What is it?"

"Here...both of you, look at this," said Papa. And though the sun had disappeared behind the trees, there was still enough light making it's way through the snowflakes to see the paw prints of an awfully big bear. It had to have been the paw prints of my grizzly, and it looked like he was heading to Elk Creek, to the little clearing where I first saw him. He was okay, and he was home.

About the Author

Olive Michael Markham lives on a ridge in the Northern California foothills with wife Diana, daughter Juhney, and dog Jack among the raccoons, skunks, bobcats, cougars, and black bears that are sometimes brown.

Grizzly Ridge is his first novel.

www.ingramcontent.com/pod-product-compliance
Lightning Source LLC
Chambersburg PA
CBHW020822180626
46814CB00001B/73